Fake

The Crimes of Han van Meegeren

A Novel

Thomas Thibeault

Ridgetop Press

www.ridgetoppress.org

Ridgetop Press
55 Diane Lane
Maggie Valley
North Carolina
USA
28751

The Library of Congress has catalogued Fake as follows:

ISBN: 692776230
ISBN: 9780692776230

Thibeault, Thomas.
  Fake/Thomas Thibeault

1 Art Crime - fiction.   2. World War II - fiction.
3. Holocaust - fiction   4. Espionage - fiction.

To

Roma and Lyuda

And All the Tribe

"Мы услышим ангелов, мы увидим все небо в
алмазах..."

Чехов

Chapter 1

Collaborators

He peeped through the grimy window, but the dirt on the pane blurred the figures in the street below. He heard the mobs pulsing around their prey. The cheering rattled the glass, and Joop's fingers rearranged the soot before his face, so he could get a clearer view of revenge.

The Germans had evacuated Holland, leaving behind their excess baggage and their women. They had hobbled east in retreat, with one hand grasping their weapons and the other clutching their loot. They abandoned their softer, useless spoils to the ravages of the liberated. Any woman who had been a German's wife, or lover, or friend, or maid was now just a Nazi-Whore, a moffenhoer. The slur was always contracted to a 'moffie" because it was easier to spit. Amsterdam rocked with the punishments of the moffie-maids. Some tried to run, others clawed red nails at the eyes of their tormentors. None could escape. Plump women were dragged from their hiding places and thrown into the streets, so their vengeful, jealous, and guilty neighbors could shave their heads in an orgy of public shame. After the "Starving Winter," any plump body was proof of collaboration.

Joop watched them chase a woman along the street. Skeletal fingers grabbed her luxuriant hair and tackled her to the ground. She swayed on torn knees and wiped the tears from her eyes and the blood from her nose, but the roiling mob pinned her to the cobblestones.

Joop's body had grown accustomed to the sounds of danger. His fists clenched at gunshots, and distant explosions pulled his shoulders and neck into a protective shrug. But the rumble of a mob made his throat strangle the rising bile. This noise was sickening. He sneered through the sooty glass.

Four years in the Resistance had given him a vital distrust of any group. He had confided only to Jan, "When two or three are gathered in my name, betrayal is sure to follow." When he read his own name on a stolen German death list, " Joop Piller - Terrorist - Jew," his faith in his fellows evaporated, but the disbelief kept him alive. He had battled the Germans, one contact at a time, because it was safer to follow an exposed back. The trusting were now dust. Before the war, he had been working in the garment trade and rose to manage a raincoat factory. The Occupation made him a freedom fighter. The Liberation turned him into a policeman. Now he was Lieutenant-Inspector Joop Piller, but there was too much to inspect.

Jan stood beside him, impatient to view the spectacle. He raised the window and the mob's growl invaded the room. Curses shouted above the laughter, and Joop wanted to shut his ears to the sickening howl.

"They have another one,"Jan said.

"There will be more," Joop sighed.

Joop turned and watched Jan finger a large Webley .45 pistol.

"I've told you before, you don't need that."

"Oh please," Jan whined. "I never get to play with a real gun."

"You don't go armed to the teeth to make a simple arrest."

Jan slid the gun into his pants pocket. "But I'm not armed to the teeth. Just to the balls."

Joop smiled at Jan's bulging crotch. "You'll scare the women."

"Oh. They don't have to be afraid of me."

Jan pulled the pistol from his pocket and sighed as he reverently set it on Joop's desk. "Just once," he pleaded, "I'd like to feel like a real policeman."

Joop twisted his mouth into a wry question. "You have the address?"

"Keizersgracht, 321."

"Sure you can remember the number?"

"Of course I can. Kass Grate," Jan joked. "Number three... What was the rest?"

Jan was the willing butt of Joop's wit. Bemused racketeers and smug collaborators dismissed his simpleton's grin at their peril. Jan Flushing really did look like the village idiot, but his appearance disguised his greatest talent, playing dumb. The cells of Weteringschans Prison were filled with the captive audiences of the Jan and Joop comedy routine.

"Let's get this over with," Joop commanded, and they rattled down the marble stairs to the front door.

They left the Office of Collaboration Investigation and turned away from the islands of riot swirling along the banks of the Amstel. They marched through the Bloemenmarkt, and Jan's nostrils flared. A few pitiful women squatted over pails of drooping stems, but it was just enough to remind Jan that they still had some flowers, even if Amsterdam was blooming in happy violence. They stopped to look down a side street and watch a gang of happy avengers posing for the camera with their moffie. Men with faces of ecstatic fun mugged for the photographer, while others shouted into the lens. The woman was lifting a hand to smooth her missing hair, and her fingers seemed confused by the unfamiliar scalp. "The Germans took the flowers, but they left their stink," Joop said and he spat onto the cobblestones.

They marched quickly along the canal away from the raucous amusement. Joop's clenched jaw pulled at his ears, but the rowdy cloud of laughter and screams could not be denied. The noise softened as their stride lengthened, but they were soon over the bridge and relaxed into a shambling stroll down Keizersgracht.

The buildings stood in ordered files, and Joop's eyes followed the line of stairs, each leading up to the landings at the front doors. Jan mouthed the numbers like a bored schoolboy, and when Joop halted, he declaimed, "Hey Presto. Three... Two... and One." Jan followed Joop up the stairs. They stood on the landing, hearing the racket flooding over the canal. "Show Time," and Joop thumped the door with three echoing knocks.

There was no answer. They stood slightly embarrassed, as curses from over the water bounced off the silent walls. "Maybe he's not at home," Jan whispered. Before Joop could turn away, the door glided open to reveal a middle aged man with a pencil mustache twitching between his gleaming eyes and wry smile.

"Han van Meegeren?" Joop demanded.

"Yes," the man sneered. "Who else?"

"Han van Meegeren, I arrest you on a charge of treason."

Van Meegeren spread apart his hands, pathetically offering his wrists to the handcuffs, and Joop caught the mischievous glint below the raised eyebrow. The dapper little man threw the door wide and crooked his finger in invitation. "Why so formal, Joop? We have time for a drink." Van Meegeren's back disappeared into the house. Joop and Jan stood, exchanging befuddled glances.

"Well. He did invite us in," Jan said.

"Oh. Why not?" Joop shrugged and stepped over the threshold.

Their heels clattered over the marble floor, and van Meegeren approached them offering glasses. They stood clutching the unfamiliar ridges of cut crystal in tight fists. Their host splashed cognac into their glasses and gently assured them, "This will take the bite off the morning." He gently touched the rims of their glasses with the base his own and set a tingle like a morning bell trembling between them. He raised his glass, "To the future, whatever it might be," and streams of color sparkled through his fingers.

Jan slugged back his glass and coughed. Joop took a gentle sip and examined the room. Rectangles of framed faces looked at them from every wall. Jan slid his worn boot sole over the marble floor, and it felt like skating when he was a child. There was a slight chill in this strange place that was some sort of reception room.

Rumors of fabulous wealth had bubbled through their preliminary investigation. Jan had heard all the gossip of van Meegeren's house, but after one look at the satin covered walls, he could believe every one of the envious whispers. He had pestered Joop about the house for days, but all he would say was, "You'll see it all when we pay him a visit." The house smelled of money.

Joop calmly lifted the glass to his lips and asked, "You have made arrangements?"

"My lawyer will meet us there."

"Please don't waste his time. I am merely the investigator. He will have to deal with the Prosecutor, but that will only be possible after you are formally charged."

"When can I have that appointment?"

"That will happen as soon as we arrive at the police station."

Van Meegeren emptied his glass with a sigh. "Thank you for getting it over so quickly."

"There is no need for cruel delays."

"Most kind of you," van Meegeren beamed. "But that is what I have come to expect."

Van Meegeren set his empty glass on a low table. "How thoughtless of me. I will just be a moment."

He turned to leave the room, and Jan jumped to bar his exit through a door into another room. Van Meegeren cocked an eye to Joop. "I assure you, gentlemen, I am too much of a coward to kill myself."

"Let him go," Joop ordered, and Jan stood to one side.

"So. You trust me?" van Meegeren teased.

"If you are too cowardly for suicide," Joop joked, "you're too lazy to run away."

"Ah. You know me so well."

Joop greeted such aplomb with an admiring laugh, and saw that Jan was quite captivated by their prisoner.

They had just enough time to set their empty glasses on a table beside a statue of a stag, when their host returned. Van Meegeren stretched forth his open palms. "Do excuse me. I forgot these," and offered Jan and Joop two tin boxes. Jan carefully read the advertising for "MacDonald's Gold Standard Virginia." It was a box of foreign cigarettes, and the wrapper proclaimed they were, "Like a High Grade English Cigarette."

It had been many years since either Joop or Jan had beheld such treasures. Joop looked for the source of such generosity in van Meegeren's eyes, but found only an impish glint. Of course, the man was charming, and it worked. But there was also consideration in his offering, an assurance that all would be right again, as it used to be. Joop held the tin firm in his sweating fingers. He could feel the whispered promises nestling in the fifty little tubes.

"Shall we go, gentlemen?" their host suggested.

Jan and Joop led him to the door, but he stopped them to examine a rack of hats lining both sides of a Venetian mirror. He took his time selecting just the right shade of gray felt on a fedora to match his suit. Joop waited for his prisoner to compose the line of eyebrow, ear lobe, and hat brim. When the angle revealed a tuft of distinguished gray clipped delicately behind his left ear and hid the thin patch on the right, van Meegeren picked up his matching gloves and malacca cane. Assured that the mirror reflected the man he wanted everybody to see, he stepped to the door and waited. Jan opened it, and van Meegeren made his exit onto the landing.

He looked up at the four ranks of the windows of his house. Jan watched him gently mold the calf-skin gloves to his fingers and hook the crook of the cane over his forearm. Jan had a fleeting image of the man standing on a scaffold and speculated, "Even if he were waiting for the noose, he would do it in style."

Van Meegeren rummaged in his pocket and offered Joop his house key. Joop turned the lock and heard five tumblers seal the house. He offered van Meegeren the key, but the man smiled and assured Joop, "You will need it more than I will."

"I think you will be back here," Joop calmly assured him.

"I presume they will feed me in prison, but I would not wish my cat to starve."

Joop pocketed the key with a laugh that assured his prisoner the pet would not be inconvenienced.

They heard the voices drawing nearer. Three women dragged their moffie along the pavement below them. Dirty claws clung to the arms of their victim. Joop lowered his eyes, and the woman's twisted foot filled his vision. They drove the screaming woman before them and her head jerked back when her shattered foot touched the cobblestones. Shrieks of red mist splattered her tormentors. One eye was an agonized slit, but the other glowered defiance up to the landing. Joop's eyes bored into the crimson semi-circle of her jaw where an iron shod heel had pulped her mouth. The crown of her head was shorn and hash-marked by a blunt razor. Blood writhed down her neck and over the fist clutching at her torn clothing. She had almost been scalped. The little procession staggered past the landing, and Joop growled his disgust, "Now every patriot is a barber."

"What a pity," Van Meegeren sighed. "She had such a beautiful mouth."

Joop, Jan, and van Meegeren walked down the steps and strode along the canal. If anyone cared to look their way, they would only see a trio of gentlemen out for their morning walk.

Chapter 2

Cat

They marched away from the prison on weary legs. Their day had been full of enough excitement to fuel their labors, but now they had to force their feet to retrace their steps. Joop waited for Jan to bid him a cheery, "'til the morrow," and they parted their ways at the Keizersgracht canal. When the clicking of Jan's heels faded into the gloom of the Bloemenmarkt, he sauntered down the street.

Joop trudged up the stairs and stood rigid before the door to van Meegeren's house. The key felt greasy in his fingers as he swung open the door. The street lamp pulsed just enough to spread a dim carpet through the door frame, but the light was so weak it could not seep into the dark room within. Joop had every right to be there, but he felt like an intruder. He banished his jitters and stepped over the threshold.

He pulled a flashlight from his pocket and played its wan beam over the reception room. The framed portraits crowded the wall, but he ignored their glowering faces.

Joop and Jan had stayed with van Meegeren until the jailer turned the key. The magistrate had decreed, "The prisoner will be held without bond in Weteringschans Prison until the Office of the Procurator assigned a preliminary hearing." Van Meegeren had stood quietly holding his impatience, wishing the judge would hurry, so he could have a cigarette. Joop and Jan had to accept his grateful thanks for their care and were surprised to see his joy when he was led into a private cell. Jan winced at the annoying whine when van Meegeren had begged Joop,

"Please, the cat." Joop nodded, and they left the prison for his last chore of the day.

The house was chilly, which was a normal for these unheated nights. Padding through the private world of the richest man in Holland was completely absurd. Feeding a felon's cat was a good excuse to see the criminal's lair. His previous interviews had given him a rough idea of the house, but he had only been familiar with the ground floor. He knew he was not alone.

Years of hiding had trained him to be still and know that you are being watched. He could sense the other presence, but heard nothing. He felt the trembling nudge against his trouser leg and heard the faint thrum. The flashlight caught two unblinking obliques in its circle, and the cat sat gazing up as if to say, "A new one." The black face disappeared, so Joop waited for the instructing meow in the distance and then followed the sound into a small kitchen.

The cat sat expectantly beside a door to a tall cabinet built into the wall between a sink and a stove. The door trembled expectantly beneath the cats's caressing flanks, telling Joop where he would find its food. The cabinet was much deeper than he had expected, and when he splayed the light into its depths, cans packed the shelves from floor to ceiling. "Open Sesame," he laughed to himself and looked at metal containers hammered into every imaginable shape.

There were hundreds of squares, circles, huge rectangles, and some canisters were metal bowls. He could just make out the contents inscribed in many languages. There was French paté and German eintopf. From the cows head on the strange rhomboid, he gleaned "Fray Bentos." He grabbed one can from shoulder height and hefted it in his free hand. This was enough meat to feed an entire family for a week. Such luxuries would never be printed on a ration card.

The insistent meowling up his knee reminded him of his mission, and he grabbed a small can. He placed the flashlight on the table and sat the can in its beam. He squinted into the cone of light until the delicious word "Spam" danced before his eyes. He found a butcher's knife and gouged the top of the can until the pungent aroma of meat filled the room. He almost passed out from the long forgotten scent, and his fingers pulled the soft contents through the jagged lid. He sat on the floor alternately feeding the cat and licking his fingers.

He had never tasted such meat. There was no need to chew for the paste dripped over his tongue and slid down his throat. He could feel his stomach rebel at this new invasion, but clenched his belly to soothe this feast. The cat thought all this was so normal. The servant had changed, but the meal was the same. Joop felt the animal's joy along with the rough tongue exploring his hand. He took another lick of the paste and decided to share a second can with his dinner guest. In a drawer he found a simple can opener that folded its sharp tooth into a flat handle. He pierced a neat circle around the lid of the second can. This was some sort of meat with vegetables in a thick sauce. Whatever the thing was, it was a joy to chew the potato and pick strings of the meat from between his teeth. The cat chose the gravy, but soon padded away to calmly clean its nose with moistened paws.

The skirts of his raincoat spread into a dirty ruffle beneath him, but Joop stared into the can's filmy throat. After the Starving Winter, this was too much.

Five years ago, the Germans had come in like lambs. They left like lions. The Dutch had suffered more from liberation than from invasion, but the last winter was the worst. Joop could recall the meagre winter's meals by counting the holes he had hammered into his belt to hold up his pants. His shoulders reminded him of an child's coathanger, straining to hold its burden of wet wool. Only the whistling terror of falling bombs had relieved the constant hunger. The rumble of distant gunfire was no more threatening than a summer shower, but the rattle of a truck engine barked the hope that soon the bastards would be gone. A house pet became rarer than a fat girl. He confessed to the cat, "You are so lucky. Your friends ended up in the stew-pot," but he knew he was talking to himself. 'Normal' was feeding a cat, and not having to wonder when the cat would feed you.

Joop pulled himself up through his memories and followed the cat back to the reception room. The drapes were pulled tight, so one lamp would not betray him to nosey neighbors. He fumbled his fingers up the stem of a lamp until he felt a chain, pulled it, and the room flickered like a movie theater. The electricity was cut off at ten every evening, so he would have half an hour to enjoy the quiet. Beside the lamp stood an upholstered Queen Anne chair and its cushion was as enticing as the meat cans. Joop nestled into its cozy cuddle and pulled the newspaper from his raincoat pocket. He smiled at the headline, "Traitor van Meegeren Arrested," and wondered how his prisoner could be so nonchalant.

Joop's investigation started with four pages of blank paper inscribed with the questions: "Who?", "What?", "Where?", and "When?" Joop had filled in every scrap of fact he could discover or Jan could beat out of a witness.

Between them, the four pages had become a thick dossier, testifying to an audacious crime and proving van Meegeren the criminal.

Joop always compared the newspaper reports to his file, because sometimes when the reporter filled in the blanks with his imagination, Joop would see a possibility which had escaped him. So, he studied the soggy print, searching between the reported facts for anything he might have missed. The reporters could hardly get the "who" wrong, for "Han van Meegeren is the well-known artist from the provinces who has become infamous for his lavish lifestyle." True. Everybody knew that.

The "what" was that "the traitor sold Holland's heritage to the enemy." Also true, for it was impossible to deny that van Meegeren had sold Vermeer's *The Supper at Emmaus* to no less a celebrity than Hermann Goering.

The Americans had discovered the painting in Goering's personal train, so it was obvious who was the last owner. When the Vermeer was returned to Holland, Joop set himself the task of discovering who had sold the painting to Goering. It did not matter to Joop whether the seller was a monster or a saint in other parts of his life; the seller was a thief. Jan and Joop had waded through an avalanche of shipping labels, receipts, bills of lading, insurance policies, and the memories of terrified collaborators, until Joop connected the dots from Goering back to van Meegeren.

The "when" was as clear as the dates on all the documents in the charge sheet. "Where" was every place the painting had rested or changed hands along the route. Joop's report was a net of facts trapping van Meegeren's treasonous guilt. All that was left was to present the evidence, convict the accused, and cart him off to the hangman. Joop's eyes landed on the newspaper's date, 29 May, 1945, and he marveled that the whole investigation from discovery to arrest had taken less than a month.

He sat reading the columns declaring how, "van Meegeren, motivated only by greed, had betrayed his country for money." The reporter waxed vitriolic that "this traitor was not satisfied with thirty pieces of silver but demanded 300,000 guilder." Joop laughed aloud, "The press is in its counting house, counting out his money," for he knew from the bank accounts that the sums were in the millions. For once, the facts far surpassed the fictions of the journalists. The rest of the reports just repeated the same story, but one was kind enough to offer his readers a potted life of Johannes Vermeer, the genius of Delft. Joop found this paragraph of biography peculiarly enlightening. The writer claimed that Vermeer was a recluse, but Joop had read somewhere that Vermeer was also involved with the artists' guild of his town. The stay-at-home, civic minded painter appealed to Joop.

The lamp flickered, and announced the prelude to the black-out. The authorities would cut the supply to all homes and businesses to keep the lamps burning in the hospitals. He pocketed his paper and picked up the flashlight before asking the cat, "Want some more?" He followed the twitching tail back to the kitchen and stabbed another can. He found a saucer and emptied the whole can into the dish, for he did not know when he would be back.

The door to the cupboard beckoned, and he stood gazing at the bulging shelves. Hand over hand, like a swimmer nearing the shore, he filled all his pockets. The cans were heavy, but he distributed the load evenly. He stretched forth his hand to the packets of cigarettes and stuffed as many as he could into his pockets, hoping the thin material would not burst. The light went out, and he stood laughing at himself. "I must look like a kangaroo." For a moment, he knew why Vermeer worked at home. The strain of leaving this beautiful comfort was daunting. He petted the cat's head to assure the creature that he would be back, but the animal was lost in the thrill of Joop's touch.

Joop waddled to the front door, opened it to look for any watchers, and disappeared into the welcoming night.

Chapter 3

Porridge and Spiced Jam

Jan's heels echoed over the cobbles of the Bloemenmarkt. He slowed his pace when he neared the Westerkerk, hoping not to wake the old ghosts snoring through the emptiness.

He stopped to gaze at the church's stepped roof. His eyes sailed up the tower to the moon peeking around the spire. Somewhere in that massive wall, Rembrandt was buried.

Jan's father had taken him to the church and had told him how the famous painter's first wife ruled him even after she had died. "She left instructions in her will that if he ever married again, her money would be given to support his many bastards." Young Jan had run his hand along the wall, almost feeling for the old rascal's bones. "Saskia didn't mind his girlfriends, as long as he didn't marry any of them," his father had explained. They had laughed together at the first Mrs. Rembrandt's cleverness and her determination to be the only Mrs. Rembrandt. "Daddy could play, but mummy would pay." That was their first visit to the Westerkerk and the first adult joke Jan's father had shared with him. But tonight the laughter left a very long echo.

His father had also given him "the numbers." When rage filled Little Jan's heart and pumped the tears to his eyes, Father would take him for a walk. He made Jan count "one" every time his left foot hit the ground, and by five hundred, they were marching in time together. Father had said, "When you can't laugh, you can still walk."

The church's tower rose defiant above the huddled roofs, and Jan hoped there were many more trysts than betrayals huddling in its shadow. He trudged from the cobblestones to the gravel path leading to the bridge, and the curious moon peered over the glowering roofs.

He had decided to return to the house, to make another pilgrimage, hoping for relief. He stepped off the bridge, turned right into Prinsengracht, and stared along the line of lamp posts feebly glowing before him. There was just enough power for each lamp to cast a trembling circle to the ground.

Jan counted his paces from post to post, "Two times three is six," and stopped in the next apron of light. "Divided by two equals three." The repetition of numbers silenced his steps and slowed his pulse. All through the Resistance, the counting had mastered his fears. He could not tell of all the times he had added, subtracted, multiplied, and divided the terrors within. Such arithmetic could map a long night march. If he rested for one hundred counts every time he reached four thousand steps, he could walk all night.

The hundred paces from the bridge to that house was the longest march. He kept delaying this visit, even this night. The number of the house still haunted him.

He stood before Number 263.

It was nothing special. The usual three stories piled up when Rembrandt was playing with his girls. Each house had added an annex at the back connected by a hallway, so what you saw at the front was really the side of a building that had grown and sprouted more rooms over three hundred years.

The window filled with blank night. He had never seen a light flicker and he wondered if the house had been empty all these months. There were so many places where evil had touched lives, but this one groaned the loudest.

It had only been a few months, just last August. Joop had told him the raid would be in the morning. He had whispered the address into Jan's ear and then ran off to warn another Resistance man. Jan figured that there was no hurry and fell asleep. There was no bed because he had spent the last six months hunched in a chair with his pistol. Morning jerked him from his mottled dreams, and he ran to the address.

The truck's gently idling engine told him he was too late. He turned the corner just in time to see the people herded from the house to the back of the truck. A frightened smile circled a young girl's face. Jan saw the German place a reassuring hand on her shoulder, but he also felt the terror seeping through the exhaust fumes.

Eight people sat on the benches lining both sides of the truck. The canvas opening framed their faces. The truck moved forward, and the German teetered on the tailgate for a moment. One of the people grabbed his arm so he wouldn't fall out. He lurched forward to stand guard and steadied himself with one hand on the canvas cover's frame. The truck moved as slowly as a milk cart plodding its morning rounds. The tranquility, the very ordinariness of the arrest, was terrifying. The girl's face looked directly at Jan from the back of the truck as it turned the corner. It was all over in two minutes.

Joop had berated Jan for his stupidity. They had received the warning of the Gestapo *aktion* for the next morning, so it was vital that the people be moved in the night. The roundup netted eight Jews. Joop had become very quiet, but the shame raged inside Jan. Although Joop never mentioned 263 again, Jan saw that girl's face smiling at him every night in his slumbering chair.

He tried to wring some comfort from his grandmother's proverb, "He who has spilled his porridge cannot scoop it up again." She had been right, of course. "What's done is done and cannot be undone," but you have to live with the guilt just the same. There was no old woman's saying on just how to do that. There was no advice on how to forget that an exhausted night's sleep had cost so many lives. It would be easier if he had been just too late to see that girl. The very gentleness of her face accused him of his dereliction. That smile was gouged into his memory, as if it were a razor slash.

He knew how her journey would end. Sometimes he envied her.

His feet could not move. His ankles hurt from the day's determined walking, but something other than fatigue now held him. He could smell jam. Not the weak red slurry they sold in the Jordaan, but the heady aroma of strawberries boiling in sugar. He could almost feel the wooden spoon stabbing through the crimson lava in Granny's pot, waiting for the moment it would congeal for the winter. She would let his finger wipe the spoon, but the heat almost burned him. The sweetness would cure all his childish hurts. Her jam was like Father's game of counting the steps. One time, a fly had landed on the jam, frantically fluttering to pull a foot from the sweet trap. He had felt so sorry for that insignificant insect that he released it with a finger and beamed at Granny when the little thing finally flew away.

Jan breathed deeply and the scent of spice beckoned him closer. He shook his head to cast the flavors from his mind and turned to walk away. He lurched back through the necklace of straining lampposts, counting with his chilly breath, "Two times three is six." He stopped in the next apron of light but could not purge the taste of cloves from his nostrils. "Divided by two equals three."

Chapter 4

Dossier

Jan was as impatient as he was annoyed. "Why do we have to do this all over again?"

Joop heard the exasperated sighs; it was a sure sign Jan was about to make a costly mistake. Jan threw the papers at the desk, and Joop calmly gathered the sheets back into a neat pile. "To be sure," he said.

"Sure of what?" Jan threw up his arms in the air. "He's guilty. Van Meegeren's getting justice." He twisted his head, stuck out his tongue, and pulled an imaginary rope behind his neck. "Case closed."

Joop pulled a complete drawer out of a filing cabinet and hoisted it onto the desk like a drayman delivering a beer keg. "Only the judge can say that." Jan watched Joop pull fists of documents from the drawer. Jan knew he would have to give in again. Ignoring him was one of Joop's little tricks. Joop simply continued what he was doing and the only choice he offered was to either join in or shut up and keep out of the way. Jan sat in a pout watching Joop sort through the papers, and he remembered how they had attacked those Germans in Hilversum. Jan had sweated behind a fence, cocking his Sten gun, but Joop stood in the street calmly loading his pistol. Just like then, Jan joined Joop, with a little whining.

"So why do we have to do it again now?"

"So the judge can believe the evidence and hold him for trial," Joop slowly explained.

"He doesn't need us for that," Jan protested.

"But he does need us to keep track of all this," Joop swung his arm over the papers. "One mistake and the case falls apart. Then what do we do?"

Jan could not evade the logic of the question, for he had no answer. It was just like this new job. Two months ago, they were the center of a Resistance group fighting with the Allies. Joop had spent years hiding Jews and smuggling downed Allied pilots through the lines, so he knew every rathole in and out of Amsterdam. A Dutch unit in the Canadian Army was grateful for his services, so they were the first liberators to speed into Amsterdam.

Jan hadn't known why he and Joop were racing into the city, but Joop was quick to commandeer a building. They had jumped out of the half-track with all guns ready to blaze and stormed the offices of Goudstikker and Company. Jan would have killed anyone in the way, German or Dutch, if they had not all scattered. When Jan asked, "What are we doing here?" Joop simply informed him, "This was the headquarters of Alois Miedl." Jan's face was a grimace of question marks, until Joop assured him, "Now it is the Capital Flight Control Bureau, and we work for the Ministry of Finance." Jan dropped his jaw into feigned understanding and said, "Oh, yeah. Okay."

Jan rose out of the chair and stretched himself into a submissive yawn. "One more time. Then can we go home?"

"One more time." Joop picked up a thick file, and Jan followed him with sleepy steps to the long table they had set up. Jan resigned himself to two more hours of Joop placing every sheet of paper on the table in chronological order.

"First: the picture." Joop placed a glossy print of Vermeer's *Christ and the Woman Taken in Adultery* at the extreme left of the table. "The prosecutor will have the real painting on an easel when he opens his case."

"Do we have to haul it from the bank?"

"We will escort the painting. The bank cops will carry it."

Jan was relieved he didn't have to lug the infernal thing around town or guard it.

They heard muffled steps groaning up the marble staircase, and an old man appeared in the open double doors clutching more papers. "Ah, Bobo," Joop hailed the old fellow, "You're just in time."

"Lucky for you, I always am," Bobo shot back.

Bobo shuffled toward the table, and his nose snorted at one of the document cases, breathing in the aroma of the dossier. "That paper has never seen a tree," Bobo exclaimed, as if he were nosing a fine vintage. "Here's your rogues' gallery." Bobo offered Joop a stack of large, newly developed photographs.

"These will make it all the easier for the prosecutor," Joop said.

"Van den Broek is prosecuting, right?" Bobo asked.

"Yes. He was very eager to take the case."

"He is eager for any ass he can kiss. He loves the taste and the smell of anything sitting on a judge's bench. I should have made larger prints for that idiot."

Jan and Joop chuckled at Bobo's contempt for anything associated with the law. Joop held out his hand, "The Americans," and Jan offered him a photograph.

Next to the photograph of the Vermeer painting, Jan placed the image of two American officers, a man and a woman, holding up the Vermeer. "Wait a minute," Bobo interrupted, and he started sorting through the pile of photos. "I made captions to go with each print." He picked out one piece of stiff cardboard and placed it under the photograph proclaiming that the above was "Major Harold V. Anderson (101 St Airborne Division) and Lieutenant Evelyn Tucker (American Red Cross)."

"Very nice, Bobo. This will make everything clear."

"A congenital idiot can see that the same painting is in both photos, but van den Broek will need a little help." Bobo pulled out another sign bearing the inscription, "17 May, 1945."

Jan held the dossier open and fed papers to Joop as he called for them. "The Anderson report comes next." Joop placed five sheets of closely typed lists under the photo and the date. "When the prosecutor reads this aloud, the court will hear of the discovery of the painting in Altausee, Germany."

"You mean this Anderson found the whole thing?" Bobo asked.

"Goering's loot was in an abandoned train in a tunnel near Hitler's residence in Berchtesgaden. The report was signed by the Major Harry Anderson in that photo."

Then this will help you, too." Bobo placed a portrait of Hermann Goering on the table. Under it, he placed a sign, "Fat Bastard." Jan picked it up, "We won't need that."

"Pity," Bobo sighed.

"Since Anderson is the American holding the picture and this is his official report from the Monuments, Fine Art, and Archives operations of the American Army," Joop reviewed, "we don't need to have Goering make a personal appearance in court."

"Wouldn't he like a holiday?" Jan added.

"He could take home some tulips as souvenirs," Bobo said.

"We've eaten all the tulips." Joop explained. "The Americans have him in a jail, along with his wife, his children's nurse, the curator of his art collection, and his cook."

"Good. He won't starve."

"We can get hold of him any time we want." Bobo placed a cardboard placard under the report, "19 May, 1945."

"Now. The newspapers," Joop commanded.

Jan thumbed through sheets of tattered newsprint, their headlines running from New York, to London, to Australia.

"We wouldn't even be here without these," Joop sighed.

Indeed, without Major Anderson's publicity stunt, van Meegeren and Joop could still be passing each other in the street. Joop would be oblivious. Anderson had found Goering's hoard of looted art and immediately organized an art exhibition for his soldiers, right in Hitler's country retreat. He had also invited reporters to this "viewing in the clouds," and the sensation of art worth millions of dollars had appeared on breakfast tables around the world.

"He was pretty cagey," Jan admired.

"You mean Goering?" Bobo asked.

"No. This Anderson."

"He is a paratrooper," Joop explained, "but he is also an art expert."

"These Americans are amazing," Bobo added, "they even have professors falling out of the sky."

Joop nodded his approval as they gazed into the beaming faces of soldiers surrounding the Vermeer, all supplied by Reuters News Agency.

Besides Anderson's savvy, Joop was impressed with Anderson's thoroughness. His report listed all the people he had interviewed, including Goering's wife and nurse. The two women were fighting over the paintings when he found them. The wife was screaming, "These paintings are my property." Anderson dropped into the middle of the cat fight and sensed there was something else between the nurse and the wife.

"I don't care," he had demanded, and the nurse stomped from the room. She came back with a length of stove-pipe and fished out the rolled up Vermeer. Anderson immediately knew what it was and confiscated it from the Field Marshal's bickering wife and girlfriend.

Joop had seen the news releases along with everybody else in Holland, but he also saw a coup that would put his little unit on the map. He contacted the Americans, and they were very happy to send him a copy of Anderson's report. When Anderson recorded that "one Alois Miedl had sold the painting to Goering," Joop smelled victory. He had been keeping a large file of racketeers in everything from potatoes to Rembrandts and had been searching out the Dutchmen who had grown fat collaborating with the Germans while the rest of the country starved.

Alois Miedl's name peppered the files like mold. Joop did not have to threaten anyone. One glance at the prisoner's own signature on a bill of sale was enough to open the floodgates of memory. A simple interview in a collaborator's cell and he was blaming Miedl for everything.

They thought that if Joop had one document, he had them all, and sieved their brains for anything Joop wanted. They all presented Miedl himself as another victim of the Germans because, after all, "his wife is a Jew." Joop resisted the temptation to smash in their faces. But enough of what they said was true.

Joop had spent the Occupation hiding in plain sight, as Joop-the-Jew covered his tracks in the Resistance under the mantle of a simple milkman. He protected himself from his friends by finding out just enough about them to blackmail them into patriotism. If they betrayed him to the Germans, they would implicate themselves. There was also the threat of silencing informers. He had dirt on many functionaries in the Dutch Civil Service and used his threats of exposure to hide Jews and protect the undesirable elements.

All of Joop's prisoners claimed that Miedl had been forced to trade diamonds, property, art, and money under threat of his wife being sent to a concentration camp. Joop's face remained stone, but his perseverance paid off. One little sheet of paper proved that van Meegeren had sold the Vermeer to Miedl, and a letter to Goering proclaimed their guilt. One of Miedl's henchmen whined, "You see. I was just the go-between. It was van Meegeren who stole the painting. I was just the salesman." Joop also had the bank records proving that the salesman's commission was fifteen percent of the transaction worth 1,600,000 guilders. Joop placed the bank statements beside the record of the interrogations and put Bobo's date card at the top, "22 May, 1945."

The last photograph was of van Meegeren. The man's face was pleasant with just the hint of a supercilious smirk lifting the corners of a nostril. It looked like he was pulling up his lip with his nose.

At the first interview with the suspect, Joop had stared long into that face and hit him with the question, "So, how did you come to sell a Vermeer?" Van Meegeren knew the game was up, but sat waving his cigarette between two fingers raised as if he were a priest giving his blessing.

Joop's ear caught the tone of complete assurance, but he knew this was the hallmark of the habitual liar.

Van Meegeren rose and casually said, "Who can trust a thief such as Alois Miedl?" Joop watched Van Meegeren's hand. It was so steady the cigarette ash curled before it dropped to the ashtray.

"Who, indeed?" Joop had left the house with a slow and deliberate stride.

With all the papers lined up in parade order along the table, the case was as simple as van Meegeren's guilt was obvious. There was a clear line of documented connections from the photograph of the Vermeer to the receipt of Miedl, and from the letters of Goering to the face of van Meegeren. The rest of the files was just insurance.

They stood before the table, each silently admiring his contribution to their work. Tomorrow's hearing would be a mere formality: present the evidence and then wait for the trial and its inevitable judgement. "It's so simple," Jan sighed. "Tomorrow's the last time we'll have to lay all this out."

"Yes," Joop grunted.

"And you assembled it so quickly," Bobo said.

That was the worry tickling Joop. He scanned the table from left to right along their make-shift calendar. "It's been just over two weeks."

"It's amazing."

"We can thank our Civil Service for keeping such complete records," Joop said

"Even if they did it for the Germans."

"Otherwise, we would never have known of van Meegeren's treason," Bobo sneered.

Joop, Jan, and Bobo stood gazing at their handiwork, but each pair of eyes clouded with doubt. It was all so very simple.

Chapter 5

Court

Joop and Jan walked determinedly up the steps of the Central Municipal Criminal Court. The porter greeted them with an open door and beaming smile. Joop's lips returned the greeting, but his eyes refused the conspiratorial wink. The porter ignored Jan's silly grin.

They walked along the corridors, and Joop clutched their fat dossier. When they arrived at the main courtroom, they swung open the doors to an excited hubbub. They stood looking for their places, and Prosecutor van den Broek scurried towards them, his body twitching with barely restrained anger. "You were supposed to be here an hour ago," he accused.

"Breakfast was delayed," Joop answered.

"Where are the documents?"

Joop offered the heavy file. Van den Broek grabbed it from Joop's hand and stomped to the prosecutor's table between the dock and the judge's bench.

"He's in a bad mood," Jan said.

"He always is," Joop smiled. "Leaves everything to the last minute."

Even though this was only a preliminary court appearance, the case had attracted an unusually large crowd. Joop knew the proceedings would be as tedious as the process was simple. The judge would read the charge, the prosecutor would present evidence, the defendant would plead "Guilty" or "Innocent," and the judge would decide whether or not there would be a full trial. It would be finished by lunchtime.

Joop saw a reporter lounging on a bench with notebook and pencil poised for anything that would interest his readers. Joop and Jan walked down the aisle between the islands of excited gossips. Some had come seeking confirmation that the defendant really was as rich as the rumors claimed. Others just wanted to gloat.

Jan saw *The Woman Taken in Adultery* sitting high on an easel beside the judge's bench. He knew it immediately from Bobo's photographs and the pictures in the newspapers, but the thing itself was a surprise. He expected something special, but the ordinary rectangle looking down at him was a boring disappointment.

Joop focused on van Meegeren sitting casually in the dock. Van Meegeren waved and smiled at Joop. "I saved you the second-best seat in the house," and gestured to the bench reserved for witnesses.

"Ah," retorted Joop, "always the gentleman."

They passed beneath van Meegeren's charming face. Jan was amused by van den Broek's frantic reshuffling of papers. "Didn't we put them all in order when we packed the file?" he asked.

"Of course we did," Joop assured him. "Don't worry. He'll make a complete mess of it."

Van den Broek's display of preoccupied eagerness was interrupted when the bailiff called out, "All rise for His Honor, Judge Samuel Voss." The courtroom echoed with respectful shuffling as they all rose to greet the judge. Voss's eyes surveyed van Meegeren in the dock, who stood at casual attention and ostentatiously examined his finger nails. The judge paused to read the charge sheet and to rearrange his robes as he sat down. The room relaxed into the simple, and hopefully not too long, formality of the reading of the charges.

Judge Voss called out, "Is Han van Meegeren present?"

The accused rose to affirm his presence, "Yes, I am, Your Honor."

"Are you Henricus Antonius van Meegeren?"

"Yes, I am, Your Honor. But my friends call me Han."

Voss's scowl quickly silenced the audience's laughter. He returned his gaze to the papers on his desk, and without looking up, asked, "Do you reside at Keizersgracht, 321, in the city of Amsterdam?"

"That is my usual residence, Your Honor, but I am presently not at home."

"Where do you now reside?"

"Weteringschans Prison, Cell Number 472... It's a bit chilly."

Giggles rippled around the courtroom. Voss clasped his fingers together, as if in prayer, and his smile challenged van Meegeren's bluff. "The Court will have a plumber inspect the heaters in your cell. That should make your stay a bit more comfortable."

The judge's eyes briefly acknowledged the polite insolence, and he read aloud from the charge sheet. "Henricus Antonius van Meegeren, you are charged with the crime of high treason. How do you plead?"

"Not guilty," was the confident reply.

Voss turned to the prosecution desk. "No doubt, Prosecutor van den Broek will remind us all of the gravity of the charge."

Van den Broek stood and bowed to the judge. Jan noticed Voss ignore the display of fulsome deference. The judge restored the atmosphere of formal distance when he ordered, "The Prosecution will offer its evidence why the accused, who has denied the charge, should be tried in this court for the crime of high treason."

Van den Broek waved a fistful of the papers Jan and Joop had collected and shouted at the judge, "This man is a traitor to our country," and he pointed the forefinger of his free hand at van Meegeren. The bald statement was followed by a torrent of words that rose and fell through octaves of invective, sneering accusation, and patriotic outrage.

Van Meegeren sat with his elbow resting on the rail of the dock and his hand propping up his chin. Joop nodded to van Meegeren and confided to Jan, "I think he's enjoying the show."

"He's doing better just sitting there than The Babbling Broek," Jan whispered.

Joop sat back and waited for the prosecutor to finish his performance. He saw that van den Broek had the bit between his teeth, but thought, "Even a real bit wouldn't make him stop talking." The judge was impervious to the prosecutor's antics and sat patiently waiting for van den Broek to stop waving his arms in the air, screaming at the prisoner, and ignoring the impatient amusement of the audience.

All faces rose in anticipation when Voss cut van den Broek short. "Thank you, Esteemed Public Prosecutor." Van den Broek, looked confused that the judge had so summarily closed the curtain on the first act. His assistant tugged at his coattails for him to sit down and, hopefully, keep quiet.

Voss looked to the witness bench and called Joop forward. Joop rose and stood before the judge's bench, ready with his answers. "You are Lieutenant Inspector Joseph Piller?" Voss asked.

"Yes, Your Honor."

"Do you reside at Jordaanweg, Number 928?"

"Yes, Your Honor."

"Please state your occupation."

"I am the Inspector of the Capital Flight Control Bureau of the Office of Collaboration Investigation."

"An impressive and lengthy title," the judge added. Voss politely commanded, "Please explain your duties."

"I investigate cases of collaboration with the enemy. In particular, my function is to seek money which the enemy stole from the people of Holland during the Occupation of our country."

Voss was relieved to be dealing with facts, but he prodded Joop to lighten the proceedings. "You are not concerned with the public displays of vengeance which have become such a notable feature of our common streets and public places?"

"No, Your Honor. We have bigger fish to fry. We look for large transfers of capital out of the country and seek the Dutch people who assisted the enemy in their major thefts."

"So, in this financial game of Hide-and-Seek you are investigating major crimes, not petty thefts?"

"That is correct."

"You are under the direct authority of the National Board of the Treasury?"

"The Capital Flight Control Bureau is a department of the Ministry of the Treasury."

"So it was in the course of your investigations for the Treasury that you discovered the activities of this man, Miedl?"

"Yes, Your Honor."

"Please explain further, but in a more factual, less general manner than the Prosecutor."

"Alois Miedl is a banker from Bavaria. He started a bank in Amsterdam in 1933. Upon the invasion, he became the banker to the enemy. Almost all of the major transactions of the Occupation were administered by Miedl directly or through his offices."

"And just what do the activities of this Miedl have to do with the accused?"

"I discovered that a famous painting had passed through Miedl's hands. The painting is called *Christ and the Woman Taken in Adultery*, and it is attributed to Johannes Vermeer. Miedl bought it for 1.65 million guilders."

The audience sat up at the price of the betrayal, eager for the crux of the matter. Joop raised his voice to continue, "and then sold it to Goering."

The judge allowed the audience to finish chattering and asked, "How did you make the connection between Goering, the buyer, and van Meegeren, the seller?"

"By interviewing various middlemen, I realized that this work must have come from the artist Han van Meegeren."

"The court shall receive your evidence. Was this painting the only one sold?" the judge prodded.

"It was the only one purchased by Goering. I discovered that a total of six paintings by Johannes Vermeer had appeared on the market since 1937 and suspected a connection to the accused. I then went to van Meegeren for an explanation."

The judge savored the silence as Joop finished his presentation. Voss calmly sucked the nib of his pen and made entries in his notebook. He could sense every eye aimed at him and every ear hanging on his words. The stillness of the room made Joop feel a shudder run over his shoulders. The judge heightened everyone's attention when he pointed his pen to the dock. "I think we should now turn to the accused for his explanation."

Van Meegeren rose dutifully and promised to answer the judge truthfully.

"Did you sell this painting, *Christ and the Woman Taken in Adultery*, to Feldmarschall Goering?"

The room squirmed in anticipation of the admission of guilt. Joop and Jan sat waiting for their work to blossom into a confession.

"I sold it to Miedl. He sold it to Goering," van Meegeren asserted.

"So, you are the source of this business transaction, as demonstrated by the letters, bills of sale, and receipts offered by the prosecution?"

"Yes, that is correct," van Meegeren admitted cheerfully.

"How can you claim to be innocent of the charge of high treason when you have sold our national heritage to those who robbed us?"

"It is not treason. It was just business."

The rows of hate-filled faces spat frowns at the dock.

"If you sold a Vermeer as a mere business deal, you profited from the pillage of one of Holland's greatest artists. Is that not correct?" Voss demanded.

"That would be correct."

"Then how can you deny the charge?"

"Quite simply. The painting in this court is not the work of Johannes Vermeer of Delft."

Van Meegeren swung his head from the judge to van den Broek and paused to let the gasps fill the courtroom.

"How do you have the audacity to say such a thing?" Voss demanded.

Van den Broek cast a confident sneer at van Meegeren, and the judge's pen stood poised to record the answer. Van Meegeren released the barest smile from his lips. His eyes twinkled with long-awaited glee, and his voice echoed over their stunned heads.

"Because I painted it."

Chapter 6

Potato Eaters

Joop watched the wrinkles on Bobo's face flow into a mischievous grin. They sat around the rickety kitchen table, and Bobo savored every detail of the courtroom shocker. Jan recounted the prosecutor's shock: "I thought the Babbling Broek was going to shit his pants." Bobo threw back his head to cast derisive laughter to the ceiling.

"You should have been there," Joop commiserated.

"I wish I could have. But this is even better," Bobo confessed, wiping his eyes with a damp handkerchief.

Joop turned to see Liese poking a knife under the pot of almost boiling water. She was teasing the last heat out of the Miracle Stove, a make-do monstrosity in every kitchen. The stove was nothing more than a cylinder of metal pipe with a wire grid. If Liese fed enough twigs into its ravenous mouth and tended it for an hour, she could coax the water into a lazy bubbling. "It needs more attention than a baby," Liese grumbled. The stove was more dangerous than a child, for it could set the room aflame quicker than you could feed a baby.

Jan quipped, "It's a Miracle Stove because it's a miracle it hasn't killed us all."

She pulled the lid off the pot and turned her head away from the steamy cloud. Joop felt the almost forgotten pride of being a good provider. It had been many months since he could bring such delicacies home to his wife. When he returned from his first raid on van Meegeren's larder, he looked like an obese clown. He had piled the cans on their table, and Liese had slumped into the chair, nearly fainting from the abundance. Dozens of gaudy labels assaulted her eyes in as many unknown languages. She had picked up one of the cans, and her eyebrows steepled into the unspoken question.

"We'll find out what it is when we open it," Joop said.

Liese laughed and told him, "We'll have a party." The morning's court fiasco was the perfect excuse to feed Jan and Bobo.

The two rooms of this hovel were her enemies, but she refused to capitulate to their squalor. She could not clean the floor for the thirsty boards drank the water, leaving only glistening stains. When Liese shifted her weight from foot to foot, the wood creaked beneath her and coughed a rancid stench. The more she breathed the city's soot, the more she cursed this slum and longed to return to Emst. It was a quiet village only thirty kilometers from Amsterdam, but it may as well have been on the moon.

Bobo looked around the kitchen and swelled with pride as he recalled how they had found this place. Jan had wandered through a tunnel between high buildings and stumbled upon a two roomed house in a deserted yard. As the houses had grown up over the centuries, they turned their backs on the secluded yard. The old cottage in the middle of the quadrant of streets had been forgotten. Jan and Bobo surveyed the whole area and discovered five entrances connecting the yard to the surrounding streets. They had established eight look-out posts through the warren of galleries and empty rooms. On their first reconnaissance, Jan had found a wooden board, and when they swatted away the dirt, they saw it was an old store sign featuring a new moon. Bobo laughed at the irony of moonlight over their heads and christened the cottage the Crescent Moon Cafe. It was the perfect safe-house.

"Tell me again what the judge said," Bobo begged.

"'The prisoner is remanded for further investigation,'" Jan pronounced. "But it took him a while to get the words out."

Bobo regained his mirth and blew his nose into the worn handkerchief. Liese smiled into his dancing eyes and decided she would have to clean his clothes, as soon as there was enough gas to give her a tub of boiling water. She would leave Joop to deal with the dirt on Bobo's body.

"But what did his face say?" Bobo asked.

"Complete shock," Joop said.

"But he smiled at van Meegeren as much as to say, 'You Cheeky Monkey,'" Jan added.

"That Judge Voss is a real foxy one," Bobo proclaimed.

The light spluttered across their faces, and Jan picked up the oil lamp to trim its wick. They waited for the light to return and heard Jan curse, "Damn these old lamps." Bobo struck a match and touched the flame to the wick. They all blinked at the sudden vanquishing of the darkness.

Joop turned down the wick, adjusted the glass globe, and put the lamp beside the sink. Liese nodded her thanks, for if the lamp burst, she could douse the burning shards with the pot water. There had been many fires in the past winter because people were no longer used to oil lamps. On her daily rounds to find anything to eat, she had noticed people with soot curling around their nostrils and knew they had slept with the lamp burning the whole night. "It's a wonder they're still breathing," she had sighed to herself.

Joop looked into Bobo's bleary eyes. "Lucky for us, Voss isn't the only fox." Bobo smiled shyly at the compliment. Joop remembered the day, three years ago, when the old man had so terrified him.

Jan had stood on the street with the Sten gun cradled in his elbow under his raincoat. Joop gulped a deep breath before he opened the glass door advertising "Lermolieff - Photography - Paper Goods - Artists' Supplies." The store was empty, but a gruff looking man about fifty years old scurried from the back room to the counter to demand, "Yes?"

Joop pulled a small card from his left pocket and placed it on the counter. He watched the old fellow examine the card. When the man saw it was an identity card with the letter "J" stamped across it, he stared an unblinking challenge. Joop gathered his smile and explained, "This has been spoiled, can you fix it?"

"The Jude stamp cannot be removed," the man said. "All such cards will have to be replaced."

"Can you do the work?"

"I can do anything with paper."

He glowered straight into Joop's twitching eyes and growled through his uncombed white beard. "I can even convert Jews into goyim."

The joke eased Joop's nerves, but not his suspicions. The man asked, "How many do you want?"

"500."

"The Gestapo pays two and a half guilders for one Jew. What will you pay?"

"I pay in tobacco."

"Come back tomorrow for your uncircumcised cards."

The next day was a repeat performance, but Jan's thumb fingered the cocking handle of the Sten gun. Joop's ears twitched at every scrape, but he held both his hands clenched in his raincoat pockets. The man looked up and assured him, "I think you will find that these haven't been ruined."

He offered Joop a box of freshly printed German Identity Cards. There was no large letter "J." Joop pulled his hand from his left pocket and gently placed two pounds of high quality pipe tobacco on the table. The man sniffed the contents and scowled approval. Joop asked him, "Are you Russian, Mr. Lermolieff?"

"Swiss. But you know we are all mongrels. Half Italian, half French, and 100% Son-of-a-Bitch."

Joop put the box in his pocket, and the man placed a sheet of paper on the counter. "What's this?" Joop demanded.

"It's the order for 500 identity cards from the State Office of Records and Documentation." Joop gazed into a perfectly printed requisition order from the German Government of Occupation and realized that the man had created the document himself. If the Gestapo paid him a visit, the receipt would prove his naive innocence. "An official receipt always satisfies their curiosity." The added touch was the letterhead bearing the insignia of the Dutch Civil Service.

"You sign at the bottom," and offered Joop a pen. Joop's right hand grasped the pen, but he froze. This simple gesture could be him signing his own death warrant. He slowly pushed the nib over the paper to steady his nerves.

The man cast a professional eye down the receipt to the signature. "Thank you, Herr Schmidt." The man smiled at Joop's discomfort. "Now you can hold the pistol in your pocket."

He stretched forth his hand. "You can call me Bobo... Herr Schmidt."

Bobo felt the gratitude and the relief jump from Joop's fingers. "Come back soon. I am a very heavy smoker."

The next three years had seen frequent exchanges of tobacco for blank identity cards, official requisitions, travel permits, passports, and anything else Joop needed to hide his Jews, his compatriots, and the downed Allied pilots he was smuggling back to their commands. Bobo had even made a set of German Army passes that allowed Joop and Jan to travel between cities dressed as simple soldiers carrying orders from higher commands. Jan loved posing as Nazi while he was hiding their victims.

When Joop ran out of tobacco, Bobo demanded to be paid in blank paper. Joop found him the highest quality they could steal.

*   *   *   *

Liese fished the potatoes out of the pot with a spoon and filled four bowls with misty nourishment. Later, she could make a soup or wash little Sarah's face with the potato water. She had fed their child an hour ago and lulled her to sleep under their coats in the other room. The promise of real chocolate in the morning gave Sarah dreams as sweet as the taste she could barely remember.

Liese placed each bowl on the table, sat, and asked, "Do we start the Mystery Menu now or later?" Joop set the tall, rectangular can in the center of the table and took the knife from Liese's hand.

Bobo turned to his host. "Wait. I want a souvenir."

He gently teased at the corner of the wrapper with a horny thumb-nail. He tickled the paper seam and slid his thumb down the can as neatly as if he were skinning a fish. The paper label collapsed into his palm.

Bobo squinted through the dim glow of the oil lamp and waved the label before his face so he could translate. "It says, 'Product of Uruguay.'"

"Where's that?" Jan asked.

"It's in South America. Somewhere near Argentina," Liese added.

"What is a Fray Bentos?" Jan enquired.

"It's corned beef," Bobo explained. "Completely kosher."

"Kosher is only good for Passover, these days," Jan quipped.

Something greater than hunger silenced their banter. The can stood defiant amid its escort of waiting bowls. Its four naked sides reflected their faces through the beams scattered over the table from the lamp and the Miracle Stove. They sat gazing at their lives through the opalescent mirrors on the can. Bobo looked into the face of an old man and wondered how long he would have left. He glanced at Joop and Liese and listened to Sarah's muffled snores. "They are such heroes," he confessed to himself. "They even raised their child when they didn't know if any day would be their last." The hope that he had cast aside to survive came welling up to his eyes, so he hid behind his own sly reflection.

Jan winked at the smile staring back at him, but it did not hide the sadness in his eyes. The metal mirror demanded that Liese look at herself, and she rubbed the dirt from her rippled forehead. The last five years had tattooed her brow. She vowed to find soap enough for them all.

Joop gouged open the can, and Liese scooped the beef over the hot potatoes. Their winter meals had been swallowed with the desperation of uncertainty. Eating had provided the most meager fuel. But now the grease dripping over their potatoes said they had survived. The rivers of golden fat flowing round the white mounds offered them the simple pleasure of tasting what they ate. Slowly, they all listened to the meat gently whispering, "You are alive."

Everybody breathed a sigh, and Jan joked, "I can just smell the gauchos riding their horses."

"They can probably smell us," Liese retorted.

"Still, beef is beef," Bobo said. "I like it rare, but not quite as rare as it has been lately."

There were at least another eight pounds of meat waiting for them. The very fact that it would be waiting for them was proof that they had a future.

"It's like when the planes came," Liese said.

"I didn't believe such a thing was even possible," Bobo confessed, as he put down his spoon.

A month ago, they were all starving. The Germans had blasted open the dykes, so the sea would flood the fields. They said it was to defend against paratroopers, but everybody knew it was really to punish the Dutch. Then the Germans destroyed the bridges and mined the canals. Dutch railroad workers went on strike, thinking the Germans and their own Dutch Nazis would give up. The Germans simply brought in their own railroad workers and proclaimed, "Any Dutchman on a train or near the tracks will be shot as a saboteur." Nothing could grow and nothing could move. Holland stayed at home and starved.

Nevertheless, the Resistance got messages through to London, and somebody came up with the hare-brained idea of bombing Holland with food. Beyond anybody's belief, it worked. In the last two weeks of the war, almost four thousand American and British bombers dropped thousands of tons of food. The British made their mission almost biblical, calling this food from the skies "Operation Manna." The Americans were more humorous. Their mercy flights were dubbed "Operation Chowhound." The Dutch just called it "Life."

"I saw it with my own eyes at Schipol Airport," Bobo confessed.

"We saw them fly over us at Emst," Joop said.

"One of them was so close to the ground," Liese remembered, "we thought it was going to hit the church's steeple."

"We heard on the radio," Jan said.

"A leaflet dropped into the street," Bobo said.

British planes flew over Holland, scattering leaflets telling people to "gather in an orderly fashion" at such a place, on such a date, at such a time, "to receive supplies of emergency food." This was too good to be true, but Bobo trudged out to the airport, expecting nothing so he would not be disappointed. As he had expected, thousands of Amsterdammers milled around looking to the sky. Nothing came. They waited a whole day and through the night, and still there was no sign of the planes. They had started to wander dejected back to the city when the faint thrumming tickled their ears. The throbbing crescendo of four engines hit the back of Bobo's head. He turned and looked up into the face of a man waving back at him from the glass bubble in front of the plane. Bobo's amazed eyes watched the plane's belly open and disgorge an oblique stream of crates, boxes, and burlap bundles from the sky. The plane gently waggled its wings from side-to-side, and Bobo raised his arm to the hand bidding him adieu from the tail-gunner's little window. There wasn't time for Bobo to lower his arm when the next plane roared towards him.

"I brought Sarah out to wave to them," Liese added with pride.

When he saw Bobo fiddling with his empty pipe, Joop opened one of the cigarette tins. "These will help." He offered two tubes. Bobo skinned off the paper, filled his bowl, and lit a cloud of Virginia shag into the room.

"Can we invite Herr Shee to dinner?" Jan asked.

Liese laughed and brought out the bar of Hershey's chocolate she had promised Sarah. She cut neatly along each of the fat rectangles and saved two pieces for their child's breakfast. Each adult held one piece in patient fingers.

"What will happen with van Meegeren?" Liese asked.

The men laughed and guffawed in syncopated mischief. "Nobody really knows," Joop said.

"He's certainly not guilty of treason," Bobo proclaimed.

"How so?" Liese asked. "Didn't he sell the picture?"

"He did, but he didn't sell a Vermeer."

"How can you be so sure?" Joop demanded.

"First of all, van Meegeren said so. Believe his word or don't. But it's obvious from the newspaper."

"You mean the photo of the Americans with the picture?" Liese asked.

"Exactly."

"But the newspaper told us it was a Vermeer," Jan replied.

They turned their faces to Bobo, and his lips flowed into a sardonic smirk. "The paper is wrong."

"And you can tell just from the photo that the painting isn't a Vermeer?" Jan sneered.

"Of course."

"How?" Jan challenged.

"The painting in the photo is ugly."

"That's it. It's ugly." Jan sneered.

"That's it."

Bobo blew his annoyance into a smoke stream over their heads. "I'm sick of hearing about that vile little man. I'll show you later. Let's just enjoy this wonderful 'Product of USA.'"

"What does it say?" Liese prodded.

"Ingredients: Sugar, chocolate, nonfat dry milk," Bobo intoned.

They listened to Bobo, as if this were the litany of their hopes, captivated by his every declamation of the material of a chocolate bar. "Cocoa butter. Vanillin. Artificial flavoring... and Vitamin B1."

"What is the B1?" Liese asked with genuine curiosity.

"B1. That is thiamine," Bobo said.

"What's that?" She continued.

"It's one of the things you need for energy."

Bobo did not tell them what a lack of thiamine would do. It was too frightening, for they saw the effects of thiamine deficiency every day. The weight loss and its attack on the nervous system. The women hobbling to the empty markets on swollen feet. Children pointing boney fingers from hands they could not stop shaking. Without thiamine, they could drop dead marching to the irregular heartbeats. No. It was better not to know a problem they couldn't fix.

What he would never confess was the prosaic diagnosis of Korsakoff's Syndrome. He knew all about this terror of thiamine deficiency. Korsakoff himself had revealed its poisonous secrets. "The lucky ones who survive the heart attack must wait for the dementia." Bobo counted his years, and fifty-five was too soon for the bleak ending of not even knowing who you were. The shaking had started four months ago. Each tremor down his fingers told him these were the first signs of madness. The knowledge that he had started on the spiral of the disease was eating his mind with cannibal fear.

The worst would be not being able to tell the difference between what was real and what you invented. He had tried to laugh himself into courage by joking to himself, "At least you won't be able to remember how crazy you are," but he could not believe the joke. He would become confused. He'd seen people who thought they were Napoleon simply because they couldn't remember that they were really Jan Kaisse and that they lived in Deventer.

Bank notes couldn't buy thiamine when there was none to be bought. Bobo grasped the chocolate, hoping it would keep reality from melting through his fingers. "Hm." He grunted to Liese. "Make sure Sarah gets as much of this as she can take." He lovingly placed the rectangle onto his tongue.

Chapter 7

Through a Glass Darkly

Joop walked up the stairs and heard shouts escaping from the office. He opened the door to see Jan reorganizing the papers scattered over the table and restraining himself before van den Broek's rage. Joop picked up a handful of documents from the floor, calmly placed them on the table, and asked, "How can we be of assistance?"

Van den Broek stopped his rant to turn on Joop. "This is completely unacceptable!"

"What is?" Joop asked pleasantly.

"Van Meegeren is laughing at us all."

"Hardly all of us," Joop said. "We gave you all the documents."

"And they were useless."

"Only to you."

"This is all your doing!" van den Broek accused.

"May I remind you that we are merely the Inspecting Officers," Joop explained. "You are the Prosecuting Attorney."

"Are you trying to make a fool of me?"

"Certainly not," Joop admitted. "I have too much respect for your mother's handiwork."

Jan leered into van den Broek's purple face and hoped for a further fit of even worse temper.

"I suggest you address your complaints to Judge Voss," Joop added. "He is the expert in the law."

"This is not the end of the matter," van den Broek threatened.

Van den Broek looked past their grinning faces to see Bobo framed in the doorway. Van den Broek's fluttering hands cleared a path, and he blustered down the stairs, mumbling revenge at every step.

Bobo walked up to Joop and Jan. "It seems our eminent prosecutor enjoys a good joke." He offered them a flat leather folder of documents.

"Another present?" Joop asked.

"A lesson," Bobo corrected.

Bobo placed the portfolio on the table and opened the cover to reveal photographs of paintings. His gentle fingers spread the sheets before them, allowing the images to flicker past their eyes. "These are all Vermeer's paintings," He said. "The real ones." He stood back and opened his hand in invitation. "Choose one."

Jan riffled the pages until his attention was caught by a woman in a blue smock reading a letter.

"Ah. So you like the girls," Bobo complimented. "Now, you pick one."

He offered the collection to Joop, and his eyebrows danced into a sly question. Bobo appreciated that Joop took his time and examined each page in turn, hunting for a connection. Joop stopped before a landscape, his face beaming with familiarity. "Is that Delft?"

"You remember." Bobo pointed to a house on the left of the image, and Joop nodded. "That's where we collected the paper."

They recalled the little house they robbed of four rolls of newsprint, which their comrades transformed into twelve thousand printings of "Free Holland."

"That was a tight job," Joop recalled.

Bobo's fingernail rested on the house's roof, guiding Joop to understanding. "And that is what it looked like almost three hundred years ago, when Vermeer painted it."

Jan craned his neck to get a fuller view, and Joop's memory hovered between their terrifying raid and the peaceful, distant past. Bobo could see the regret and the envy flicker through Joop's gaze. "These pictures are so very clear," Joop said. "How did you get them?"

"I took these photographs myself. It was almost ten years ago. There was an exhibition of Vermeer, and the Rijksmuseum wanted extra photos for their catalogue. I got part of the job, but I saved the negatives." Jan turned his admiration from the photos to the photographer. "So what's the lesson?"

"First you each pick a favorite," Bobo teased.

Joop cast aside his longings for a happier time and continued to turn the photographs until his eyes rested on one image. They looked over a plump girl standing behind a table and pouring something from a jug.

"Ah. Excellent," Bobo exuded. *The Milkmaid.*

Bobo traced the girl's outline from her shoulders to her left arm cradling the pottery jug. "It's so nice to see a woman with some meat on her."

"She's a real handful," Jan admired.

Bobo separated *The Milkmaid* from the collection. He let their eyes linger over her until the image was printed on their minds. Joop's attention was drawn to Bobo taking a new print from the bottom of the pile. Bobo positioned the rectangle beside Vermeer's *Milkmaid*. Joop caught the chemical perfume rising from the new photo, and Jan instantly recognized *The Adulteress.*

"This is what we saw in the court," Jan said, "the Vermeer."

"But I have told you that is exactly what it is not," Bobo corrected.

Joop waited for more, but Bobo's silence captured their full attention.

"So, what is it?" Joop asked.

"This is van Meegeren's masterpiece," Bobo pronounced.

"You are very sure."

"I should be," Bobo said. "I have eyes."

Jan grimaced in suspicion, but he followed Bobo's finger leading them back to *The Milkmaid*. Bobo saw Joop's eyes squint at the photo. He could feel Joop's frustration. "What am I looking for?"

"What about the girl?" Bobo slyly suggested.

"She looks really warm and comfortable," Jan said.

"Which would you prefer? Have her in the kitchen or the bedroom?" Bobo pressed.

"I'm up for both," Jan eagerly blurted.

Bobo waited for their attention to follow his lead. Their eyes shuffled between the two photos, weaving impressions as hazy as their knowledge. "What do you see?" he demanded, and Joop listed the objects, "A table. Bread on the table."

"What is the girl doing?"

"She's pouring milk out of a jug," Jan added.

"What about her eyes?" Bobo asked. "Are they open?"

"I think so," Joop said.

"They're looking down at the milk," Jan observed.

Bobo judged the moment to push them. "Now look at van Meegeren's fake. What about the girl's eyes?"

"They're also looking down."

"But she's not pouring milk," Bobo explained. "She doesn't want to look at Jesus. Is he looking at her?"

"No. His eyes are closed."

"What about the shadows over his eyes?"

"They're dark."

"Now look back at *The Milkmaid*. Are her eyes dark like in *The Adulteress*?"

"No."

Jan scratched his forehead, as if trying to tickle a meaning into it. Joop was ready, eager for Bobo's understanding. Joop was enjoying the game. They turned to Bobo with one eye each on the table.

"Vermeer was a master of light," Bobo almost whispered. "He took his time to get everything just right. Van Meegeren was doing a rush job. The adulteress and Jesus have the same eyes with the same boring circles. He could have painted these faces with the same brush you'd use on a wall."

The pictures would not release Jan's attention. The fake was ugly, and it wasn't logical. Bobo's finger led him to a new understanding that frightened as much as it intrigued. The joy he felt was as strange as it was new.

"Now look at Jesus' hand," Bobo ordered. "Does he have a thumb?"

The question brought Jan's attention back to the van Meegeren painting and with a surprise that was as sudden as it was delightful he answered, "He has a finger where a thumb should be."

"This Jesus isn't even human," Jan quipped.

Bobo raised his chin to Joop. "Now trace your finger along the thumb." Joop obeyed, and Jan said, "They don't match."

"Precisely. Vermeer's milkmaid has real thumbs, so she can hold the jug steady."

"If she had the same thumbs as in the van Meegeren fraud, what would happen?" Bobo quizzed

"She couldn't hold the jug," Joop offered.

"It would fall out of her hands," Jan concluded.

Bobo could not hold back his indignation as he continued to condemn the glaring flaws of *The Adulteress.* Jan and Joop listened to every detail and saw the whole truth of Bobo's destruction of van Meegeren's painting.

Bobo pointed to a building behind Christ in the background of *The Adulteress,* and his face formed into a smirk.

"You could see such walls on the Riviera, but never in Jerusalem. Jesus never went to Monte Carlo. The whole thing looks like he is telling her, 'I told you not to play roulette.'"

Bobo pulled a magnifying glass out of his coat pocket and offered it to Joop. He grabbed the handle as if it were a knife. "Look closely at the bread on the table in *The Milkmaid.*"

Joop bent over the picture and wiped the dirt from the lens and searched the ridges of the loaf.

"What is she doing?" Bobo commanded.

Jan watched Joop puzzle out the answer. He squinted through the brightened disk, searching for clues. "Now we're really playing Sherlock Holmes," he remarked as he explored Vermeer's little girl. He jerked up his hands in frustration and protested, "I know nothing about this." Bobo turned his kindly face to his students and assured them, "The more you know, the less you see."

Joop's determined fist held the magnifying glass away from his eyes, and the objects in the photo exploded into an elliptical shower before his face. He followed the light streaming from the window over the girl and could feel its warmth. There was something shimmering on the wall beside her, but he could not make out what it was. Her forehead glowed as if she had been sweating, and the moisture mirrored the milk flowing from the jug she held. Her arm wriggled around the rim of the glass, and the blue of her skirt flooded his vision.

He pushed the glass further from his face, and the table wobbled before his eyes, inviting him to stop and ponder. The basket on the table wobbled into a sharper focus, and he saw the gleaming points on pieces of broken bread. The loaf had been torn into rough pieces and piled beside the dish. The girl stood with the jug poised over the dish, but the curve of the bread caught his attention. The varied clusters of light along the ragged edges reminded him of Liese in the kitchen at Emst. He had watched her do this simple thing so many times, and it was just another reminder of how much he loved her. The milkmaid and his wife flashed through his mind, vanquishing the centuries between them, and he sighed to Bobo.

"She's making bread pudding."

"Exactly."

Jan aimed his eyes at the photo and swooned, "I love bread pudding." For a moment they all savored the thoughts of sweet treats from their childhoods, and the painting resurrected the taste of crusty sugar ground between their baby teeth.

Bobo stood with them in the enjoyment Vermeer so generously offered. He knew you could like or hate a picture immediately, but it took time to love it. The girl in the photo had saved his sanity over a winter when she had filled his mind when there was nothing to fill his stomach. He had shared many a candle with her, and the delights of her offering milk and bread let him hope there would be pudding waiting for him. She told him there would be an end to silent kitchens. He had listened to her quietness, turned away from the empty cupboards, and ignored the clatter of disappointed cockroaches.

He pointed an accusing finger at *The Adulteress*. "You will never get bread pudding from this Jesus." Jan and Joop understood the difference. Vermeer invited them to enjoyment. Van Meegeren's picture offered only cold indifference. Bobo was showing them how Vermeer held out hope to hungry souls, but van Meegeren only demanded that they worship the figure without a proper thumb. Joop laughed his gratitude to Bobo. "You can't fake bread pudding."

Chapter 8

Feathers in the Wind

Last night's bread pudding lingered still on Jan's lips. He knew something strange was happening to his senses, but he wished to ignore these curious but frightening sensations. The first shock was when he had smelled the spices on his last visit to the house. The city was empty of anything other than the barest necessities, so it was impossible to sense the exotic aromas of the East in a gutter. He tried to deny that it had ever happened and consoled himself with the belief that it was some sort of temporary hallucination. But a few days later he heard a broken sewer pipe singing a lullaby. He convinced himself that he would just have to surrender to this new peculiarity. The world was getting stranger, so it was completely normal that he was feeling and hearing these new mysteries. He licked his tongue under his upper lip and accepted the little thrill of tasting sweetness from a picture.

Joop had told him to take another look at the ransacked headquarters of the Dutch Nazi Party, so the morning was a bit of a holiday. He walked into the forsaken courtyard and smiled to remember how the previous tenants had all run away as if their asses were on fire. The broken windows assured him that this wreck posed no threat, for it could offer nothing unexpected or dangerous. It was light work, he chuckled to himself.

What had once been a place of terror now beckoned him with one splintered door hanging from a bent hinge, and slumping into a pool of shattered glass. The corridors were slippery with dirt and the stench of mold assaulted his nostrils. He mounted the stairs, and the wind wandered through gutted chambers and sighed across gaping transoms. There was nothing to retrieve, but he wandered through the building, as if he were a tourist admiring ancient ruins. He would not go to the cellars. Too much pain lurked in corners, and he feared he would hear the bygone screams.

On the second floor, he froze at the sound of rustling from a far room. Whoever was there, could not be on business. There was nothing left to steal, so he concluded that someone was seeking shelter. He crept down the hall, hugging the wall, his steps too soft to press an alarming creak from a floorboard. He glided up to the doorway and placed himself beside the empty frame. He deftly stepped into the room and confronted emptiness.

He stood for a moment wondering if the intruder was hiding behind the door and then realized there was no door. The wind was sighing through a smashed window and blowing a torn curtain in and out of the gaping casement. Jan chuckled to think it was a battle stained flag and laughed aloud because there was nobody to rally round the soiled cloth. The material ballooned into a grubby gossamer dome and then collapsed exhausted onto the floor.

Mold spoors pitted the flapping wall paper that swayed with the curtain every time a breeze invaded the room. The stink crept up the walls from stagnant puddles, and Jan sneezed at the squalor.

The mobs had taken anything they imagined worth stealing. Even the desks that shuddered under the heads of the interrogated left only a trail of splinters to the corridor. Two legs of a broken chair cringed in a corner, and Jan was careful not to step on them.

The sound that tensed his muscles and pumped his aggression was nothing more than the wind blowing discarded pages over gritty linoleum. The room breathed again, and the curtain hem pushed a sheet of paper towards him. He picked it up and deciphered "Accounts Payable" in German. It was nothing. Too insignificant to be looted or even noticed.

The page had been torn from an accounts book. He saw one of the cardboard covers lying where it had been tossed over a pile of discarded papers. The pages had been torn in two. Jan imagined that somebody had vented their hatred on the book because they could not get their fingers round the throat of the accountant who had used it.

He picked up some of ripped shreds and clutched them like a fistful of dead leaves. The neat rows of numbers and letters stood in perfectly executed lines. They were all small sums, a few guilders and even one line boasting that ten cents had been paid to "Marthe" for a "pencil, 2HB, new." The entry amused him and he thought, "I wonder how much they paid for an old pencil, also 2HB?" There was no accounting for such meticulous care, but the precise handwriting was testimony to the writer's pride. Jan laughed at this calligraphy of petty cash.

The room breathed again, as if its lungs were rotten bellows, and the papers circled him in drunken spirals. Crumpled pages clung to his legs, and he picked at them like lint. Someone had tried to rip through all the sheets. Some papers were more gouged than torn through, so Jan supposed that the vandal's strength wasn't as strong as his rage. He found the other cover and picked up both boards in each hand. He swept the papers into a pile, as if using a dustpan and broom. He did not know why he was doing this, except that he did not wish to return to Joop empty handed. Soon he had a collected the scattered fragments into a neat little sugarloaf of tattered paper. He bundled everything together and pressed the two linen covered boards together. He chuckled to think that his collection looked like a huge sandwich and laughed ruefully that this was a pretty dish to set before a king.

The curtain billowed once again, and he saw the girl's face framed in the truck's canopy. Her lips parted in a smile more terrifying that any scream, and Jan smelled the truck's pungent smoke. The engine drummed inside his forehead and he caught himself stepping towards the fleeting vehicle. The exhaust fumes stopped him and a cloud faded her hair. The smoke curled around her, so only her head remained. Then her eyes sank into her forehead and silently vanished, but her lips and teeth remained, wide and open with innocent invitation.

He shuddered the vision away and turned to march down the corridor. His bundle of lacerated pages was little to show for a morning's work, but Joop would say that it was better than nothing. There would be no condemnation of a wild goose chase, for Joop could always tease something from the most useless of remains.

He walked heavily down the stairs to the courtyard where he turned to confront the watching windows. The curtain plunged out of the haunted room, and Jan thought the building was sticking out its tongue. He wrapped the skirts of his raincoat over his shredded treasure. The morning would be wasted, if it all blew away like feathers in the wind.

Chapter 9

Throw Down the Gauntlet

Joop, Jan, and Bobo walked towards the Court House, their heels clicking determination. The porter's face was a bored mask as he held the door open. Their footfalls echoed ahead of them along the corridor to Judge Voss's chambers.

His wry smile greeted them, and his open hand offered them seats. The four chairs placed before his desk told Jan that the Judge had expected all of them. Voss sat first, with a relaxed slouch that was his invitation to set aside formalities. Bobo sat rigid, recording every gesture, but Joop's eagerness perched him on the edge of his seat. The door opened, and an attendant placed a tray of cups and a steaming pot on Voss's desk. "We will have coffee to lubricate our discussion," Voss assured them. He poured the brown wonder and offered each a cup.

The previous evening, Joop had called them all to the kitchen of the Crescent Moon Cafe. Over the tea and chocolate, they debated what would happen now that their star prisoner was admitting his guilt to the wrong crime. Liese had laughed the loudest at van Meegeren's confession, "He's quite the card." They shared her respect for the man's audacity but the admission was still shocking. They felt a little embarrassed when Bobo revealed to them the obviousness of the fake. "But what to do now?" Bobo asked, and the rest of the evening and much of the night was spent discussing the case.

Joop had received the note stating that Judge Voss "would very much appreciate your thoughts on this matter." The polite words did not disguise the seriousness of this summons to the court. Voss's invitation included "your assistants" but left the number vague. They could not appear in Voss's private chambers the next morning with nothing, so they talked through the hours, grasping at thoughts as slippery as eels. "This is giving me a headache," Liese had complained, and Bobo assured her, "That's just what van Meegeren wants." The conversation bounced from "Guilty" to "Innocent" to "Traitor" to "Trickster" to "Forger" to "Fraud," and the words stretched their understanding on the horns of each dilemma. Just before she fell asleep, Liese came up with the solution. Joop kept the night-vigil beside her and Sarah. At sunrise, he roused the others.

Bobo looked through the fumes rising from his cup, studying Voss's face.

"Well, hasn't he turned this into a strange game?" Voss sighed.

"I must admit," Joop confessed, "I was completely shocked."

"We all were," Jan added.

"None more than the Prosecutor," Voss chuckled. "Despite his outrageous merriment, van Meegeren has challenged the court. This we can neither ignore nor dismiss. What do you think, Inspector?"

Jan shuffled in his seat, nervous to talk so openly to a judge, but Joop jumped at the invitation. "The problem is simple. He has been charged with high treason and pleaded 'Not Guilty,' but -"

"All the evidence you have presented of his guilt is now proof of his innocence," Voss interrupted.

"Yes, that's the problem."

"So, you are telling me that everything you have against him will exonerate him of the charge."

"Precisely."

"So, this van Meegeren has completely turned the tables on the entire justice system of Holland by claiming that he sold a fake painting to a Nazi."

"His confession in open court is an explicit challenge," Bobo said.

"But he hid the truth until he was under oath." Joop explained.

"That same oath is his protection," Voss mused.

"Now, the oath and the court are working in his favor," Joop concluded.

Bobo coughed over his cup, and Voss smiled towards him. "Don't we know each other?"

Joop placed his cup and saucer on the table. "Please forgive me. May I present to Your Honor, Mr. Jan Lermolieff."

Bobo raised his cup to Voss. "We have been acquainted professionally."

"And what is your profession, now?"

"Mr. Lermolieff is our photographer," Joop was quick to add, "and consultant to the Capital Flight Control Bureau."

"Hm," grunted Voss. "Every rogues' gallery needs a photographer."

Voss tried to place Bobo's face in the parade that passed before his bench over the last five years, but there was only the vaguest memory of some purloined ration cards. For a moment he thought he was getting old and losing his memory, but he comforted himself with the thought that there had been so many such cases, nobody could be expected to remember them all.

He turned to Joop, "We have identified the problem. Can you offer a solution?"

"I believe the solution begins with the acceptance of the facts."

"Which fact?" Voss demanded with an edge of impatience. "There are so many of them."

"The fact that all the evidence proving he is a traitor is useless before his claim that he himself painted the picture which he so readily admits selling to Goering."

Voss slowly sipped his coffee to sharpen his point.

"So it is the picture that is the problem," Voss said.

"Yes," Joop eagerly agreed. "He will have to prove that he painted the picture."

"How is this possible?"

"Have him create another Vermeer."

Voss scowled at the suggestion and hinted they were grasping at straws. Bobo read the disappointment in Voss's face and waited patiently for the judge to grasp the significance of Joop's offer.

"You are suggesting that the Criminal Court of the Netherlands commission a fake?"

"Yes."

"What will this prove?"

"That he is a forger. A good enough forger to fool the experts, or at least fool a German."

Bobo saw the fog clear from Voss's eyes, and they all smiled at the judge's laughter. Voss savored the simple truth that Van Meegeren's defense against treason was that he was merely guilty of counterfeiting. Convict him of selling a fake painting, and he is simply a clever rogue.

"So, if he can paint another Vermeer, he is a forger," Voss said.

"But if he can not," Joop capped the argument, "he is a traitor."

Voss giggled like a schoolboy invited to a prank and confided to them, "Forgers pay fines. Traitors swing from ropes. The defendant has every reason to paint at his best." Voss's laughter soothed their anxieties.

"What a brilliant idea," Voss complimented them. "Did you dream this up together?"

"Actually," Joop admitted, "it was my wife who thought of it."

Voss was impressed with a man who would give the credit to his wife. He admired Piller's refusal to claim his wife's idea as his own. "If your wife pulls us out of this herring barrel, she is smarter than our lawyers."

"That's not difficult," Bobo interjected.

"What is difficult is to find a simple solution to a complex problem. I suggest that you keep listening to your wife."

"I always do," Joop proudly stated.

Voss turned, cocked his eyebrows at Joop, and swung his head over them all, pausing to command their full attention.

"There will be practical problems," Voss said. "How will you solve them?"

"The only problem will be guarding the painting as well as the painter."

"What do you propose?"

"We set up his studio in our offices. The room will be guarded around the clock, and van Meegeren will only be allowed into the studio to actually paint."

"What if he tries to switch the painting for a another one?" Voss probed.

"The investigatory commission will state that the painting will be on canvas ten feet wide by eight feet tall and that it will be nailed to the easel in the studio."

"Why are the dimensions so precise?"

"A canvas of such a size cannot be taken out through the doors or through the windows, and it will be impossible to roll up."

"How will you determine if he is not bringing in another painting rolled up?"

Joop was quick to allay such concerns. "There will be guards and observers in the room at all times when he is at work."

Bobo lifted his cup again to Voss. "I will take a photograph of his work at the end of each painting session."

"That way we will have a complete record of everything he has done," Joop said. "The photographs will be the court record that he is the actual artist."

"I see," Voss commented with growing respect. "You will control everything and everybody who comes and goes to and from that room?" Voss asked.

"Yes."

"So, if he tricks anyone, he will have to trick you."

"He can't."

"Why not?"

"My wife won't let him."

Voss sat contemplating the simple beauty of their scheme. He was always suspicious of anything too complicated. People came to him all the time with fantastic, complex plans that would benefit only those who offered the plans. Worse still, were those who brought him a problem with a solution that would enrich only themselves. The three of them were not asking him for money or pleading clemency for some worthy relative. The test was simple and the monitoring was little different from guarding a prison cell.

He could see they were digging for the truth, but their shovel had no handle. If what van Meegeren claimed was true, there were certainly more victims than that tasteless monster Goering. It was unlikely that *The Woman Taken in Adultery* was van Meegeren's first and only forgery. The painting was just the only one they had caught. His other victims would be right here in Holland. Van Meegeren's dupes would have the money to buy Vermeers. They would be desperate to hide their very expensive fakes and their folly in being fooled. Voss's eyes scanned his guests and he realized they were completely ignorant of the people who could afford a masterpiece. They could not appreciate the retribution that would fall upon their heads for revealing the gullibility of wealthy connoisseurs. Such people could crush the three little nobodies sitting before him.

"Let me ask you again: Can you guarantee that he will be continually watched whenever he is in your office?"

"Yes." Joop said, and Voss was impressed with the man's firmness.

"Of course, you realize that, if you fail, you will trade places with van Meegeren."

"We know." Joop stated.

Voss was sure they had no idea what they were getting into. Liberation was a catastrophe; they just didn't realize it yet. Five years ago the Germans came in like lambs, but they left as the wild beasts they truly were. The liberating armies were bad enough, but at least they could be controlled. Into the soggy vacuum of their evacuation streamed every type of power grabber imaginable. It wasn't just a matter of the local mobs. Voss told himself, "Our own people are our greatest threat."

Voss was well aware of the political maneuvers behind the speeches. The Dutch generals wanted martial law to maintain order. They welcomed the rising tide of desperate crimes, which they claimed they alone could control. The Government-in-Exile had returned, convinced they were the rightful rulers and that only they could restore Holland's sullied glory. They had spent the war in London squabbling amongst themselves and had brought their petty hatreds home to roost in a land destroyed. The Trade Unions, the Bankers, the Resistance, all staked their claim to the future, but none offered a commonsense plan to resurrect a people trodden into their flooded land.

Nothing could grow until the dykes were repaired, but the water could not be pumped back into the sea until enough coal could be dug to generate the electricity to run the pumps. One problem depended on the answer to ten other problems, and each of those remedies gave birth to a hundred more problems. Voss had despaired of grasping this simple arithmetic of survival. He had read economic reports that predicted only doom. He had ruefully sung the old nursery rhyme, "For want of a nail, the shoe was lost, For want of a shoe, the horse was lame."

Meanwhile, the rest of the world was tending to their own problems. The Canadians had been so shocked by the hunger and the desperation of the Dutch that every Canadian soldier had given a week's pay to keep alive the people they had freed. But the meat-bombing had ended. The British already expected gratitude. The Americans were too busy chasing Nazis in Germany to bother about the Dutch.

Queen Wilhelmina would be returning to her country, but her ministers considered her a Communist. Some of them hinted that the Royal Family was in the pay of the Soviet Secret Service. In any case, most of the people could care for nothing beyond their daily needs. They were just too exhausted to think of tomorrow and would follow anyone who could fill their bellies. The Ministers, and the Queen, and the Generals, and the Liberators would all wave the Orange Flag like a magician's cape, claiming they could conjure a country out of the terrors of the Occupation and the chaos of the Liberation.

Voss stared at his guests over his steepled fingers and silently examined their faces. This test would help prove whether at least some of the Dutch still had the mettle to maintain the rule of law, distinguish mirages from reality, and find justice. These three determined men were focused on this one case, but van Meegeren could have them riding a see-saw, just as he had pulled the wool over the eyes of those who had bought his paintings. Voss looked deeply into their eyes, but they neither blinked nor flinched at his gaze.

For twenty-four years, Voss had seen every type of face pass before his bench. There had been murderers with the angelic smiles of playful infants and pimps he would have passed in the street as kindly grandfathers. Joop Piller was clearly their leader, but just bringing the other two to his office showed that Piller trusted them. They all had been in the Resistance. They all had chosen to stay and fight the monsters with whatever weapons they could make or steal.

Voss had even read a very confidential British report complaining that Piller was insubordinate. Piller could not have received a higher recommendation, for Voss believed that defiance was a sign of good character. Besides, the eyes of the old one flashed intelligence, and the younger one looked like he was hiding something behind his silly grin. Their simple words and firm demeanors appealed to his trust. These three faces revealed determination, passion, and wisdom. They were worth the risk.

And so he ordered, "Bring van Meegeren to my court tomorrow."

Chapter 10

Fiat Lux

Sarah wailed as Liese screamed, "Turn it off!" Joop stood on tip-toe and groped for the cord dangling from the ceiling. The bulb burned his palms.

It had been a very good day. Jan had scrounged a laundry basket full of light bulbs just when the Amsterdam City Council announced that electricity would be restored to all areas of the city. The lights could be switched on between 7:00 and 10:00 that very evening. Jan thought the numbers a good omen because the civilian time of seven o'clock was so different from the military time of nineteen hundred hours the Germans used in all their orders.

They had picked through the basket, gently shaking each bulb to their inquisitive ears until they found five globes which did not rattle disappointment. Joop had screwed the most promising orb into the light socket hanging from a twisted wire snaking from the ceiling. Joop had proudly pulled the little chain and blinded them all. The pain bore through their tight lids and invaded their skulls until he yanked back the darkness. Jan struck a match to guide him to the oil lamp near the sink, where he lit the wick and raised the lamp, so Joop could inspect their tormentor. Joop grabbed the cord to peer at the bulb, trying to decipher the faint numbers. When he blew his breath over the glass, they appeared. "One thousand watts!" he proclaimed. They would have to be more careful with the remaining four bulbs.

Jan picked a bulb from the basket and mimicked Joop blowing at the little globe. His breath clouded over the arch and dripped a white frosting over the fragile dome. He watched the numbers swim up through the filmy gauze and offered the treasure to Joop. "30 watts." Joop gently held the lightbulb pronged between his fingers and thumb, rose onto the chair, and listened to the squeaking grooves spiral up the socket. When he dare not apply any more pressure, he grasped the chain and proclaimed, "Let there be light, but not so much of it." The bulb shimmered faintly, as if unfamiliar with the current dancing over its filament, but soon settled into a snoring glow.

Joop felt a fatherly pride in the new lightbulb and admitted to Jan, "Well, that's better than the stupid oil lamp." They giggled at the glass monster beside the sink. "But we'll keep it just in case." Joop placed it carefully in the basket of broken lightbulbs. Jan told him, "That's right. We never know when somebody is going to steal the electricity."

The end of May pulsed with promises from the City Council. The electricity ration was one of the few they did not break. There had been high-level meetings on how to generate enough electricity to power both the lamps on the streets and those in people's homes. The experts had calculated that it would take six months to have the power at full capacity, so the Amsterdam Board of Public Amenities composed lists of "the most essential requirements for sustaining civil order." Nobody knew what amenities were being offered, for this was another of the new committees that had sprung up like weeds over garbage. There was a chance that something would actually be accomplished.

The unfamiliar names on the leaflets had assured them, "The first priority will be the communal kitchens." This made some sense to Jan because they would have to heat whatever they could eat. He had looked down the list from "schools," wondering if the children would have any lessons, to "hospitals," knowing they were all called "dead houses," to "residential sections," which meant, "wherever we sleep under our coats, if we haven't sold them already." He looked up to the light, and his satisfaction struggled through his cynicism. "Well. Now we can see how dirty we are."

Joop and Liese cast approving laughs at Jan, but Liese assured him, "If we have a light, soon we will have some hot water. Then I will take the brush to you."

They stood looking at the lightbulb, naked without a shade, and basked in its feeble warmth. The constant search for food along Amsterdam's canals and alleys had worn her out. She wanted to go home to Emst, to the relief of just two roads meeting in the village. She had come to the city so they could be a family again. Liese turned her head to a scuttling sound and saw a cockroach retreat under the sink. They had disappeared during the winter and had not bothered either her or Sarah during the month they had been huddled in these decrepit rooms.

Her eyes followed the cockroach to a new understanding. There was now something for the insect to eat, even if it were just a crumb. In past times, she would have dispatched it with a stomp of her foot, but now she merely wished it luck on its travels. That very morning she had seen a cat sunning its loose belly on a fence. Liese stopped and blew the creature a little kiss. It slowly blinked at her over alert eyes devoid of anxiety. It did not leap away from fear of becoming a "roof rabbit" hunted by desperate neighbors. She could see the bare patches of fur clinging to the boney hips, but the cat was more concerned with preening its tail. It was another sign of mangy hope.

Jan sorted the old bulbs around the rejected oil lamp in the basket. "What should we do with the leftovers?"

"Put them in the shed," Joop said.

"Right," Jan answered. "We never know when somebody will come looking for broken lightbulbs."

Joop nodded at the allusion to the Germans confiscating wires, sockets, and bulbs from Dutch houses after proclaiming, "Dutch People: This is your chance to contribute to the war effort in more practical ways." The proclamation made no mention of the threat that those who did not contribute willingly would be shot. Joop remembered how they had arrested a Dutch Nazi and Jan telling the tardy runaway, "Give me back my bicycle, and my underpants."

"I'll put these in the back," Jan said, and hoisted the basket through the door to the yard. Liese took Sarah's hand. "Come. Let's play outside." She led Joop and Sarah out of the house and down the tunnel to the street. They watched Sarah swing girlish circles around each of the lampposts, the only toys left to any of the children. Liese watched Sarah disappear into a squealing game with four other children and basked in the evening calm.

She asked Joop about his day's work. His tales enthralled her, and she was proud that he was her husband. They had discovered boxes of documents. She was not surprised to hear that many people she had seen in the newspapers had been collaborators. "It's not just our own Dutch Nazis," Joop told her, but she grimaced to hear, "They forced almost everybody to help them. Some were eager, but most were forced." Liese had guessed that the informers and collaborators went from the highest to the lowest, and she had lost the habit of trust. The investigation of Miedl's dealings revealed many Dutch streams flowing into that river of dirty gold. The papers piling up in his office were just the proof of what he had long suspected. "You can't imagine just how much money there is."

"You mean all the rich getting richer?"

"Not all of the fat ones. A few of them were also in the Resistance, but we couldn't even breathe their names. No. No matter if they're bankers or rag pickers."

Joop recalled his last visit to his old factory, only two weeks ago. They had traveled to Deventer to arrest five black marketeers, so he decided to see what was left of the textile business. Jan kept the truck running and his pistol cocked while Joop walked into the main building. The only thing left was the manager sitting on one chair with one cup of weak tea. Joop scanned the emptiness. The vast hall where the looms had once deafened him echoed to his own footsteps. The doors to the warehouse that once bulged with bolts of bright cloth now gaped into forsaken darkness. The manager's quizzical gaze glimmered faint recognition, and he sighed, "They took everything long ago." But the manager had nowhere else to go. This barren chamber whispered the simple truth Joop had been desperate to deny. His whole working life was now rusting in some bombed-out ruin in Germany. He could not return because there was nothing left.

"But they didn't take you," he said to the indifferent manager. Joop had turned on his heel and marched proudly back to his waiting prisoners and into his new future.

"Yes, it was a good day, topped off by 30 watts. One lightbulb and I feel like a millionaire," Liese said.

"I am the rich one," Joop replied.

Jan held the basket and pushed his thighs the few steps to the shed leaning up against the house wall. At one time the shed had been some sort of workshop. Jan speculated that they had repaired cars here, for there was a hook on a chain hung from a beam and threaded through a tackle block. "They probably used that to lift out the engines." But then he realized that it was impossible to drive a car into the yard. The house was a brick island in a sandy moat. Bobo had named their refuge well because only a sliver of moonlight ever pierced the battlements of the roofs surrounding them. He put the basket on the earthen floor and breathed in years of musty neglect.

He looked down into the basket and saw one of the bulbs light up. This was stranger than singing sewer pipes. He watched to see what would happen. The light spread from bulb to bulb, and soon the basket blossomed into a blinding wicker ball. "Lightbulbs don't light on their own," he silently screamed. He speculated that, "Maybe there is something in the bulb which keeps the electricity," but he knew the bulbs were dead. They had heard the rattling of the broken glass. He was afraid of the marvel and joked to himself, "Well. Now you can carry out the sunlight in a basket," but the laughter didn't lessen his curiosity or calm his fear.

The brightness swept over him like a insistent wave, and he bent closer to the basket. He waved his hand along the side of the basket and watched the shadows romp and frolic over the floor. The beams left little footprints in the dust and his grandmother's Old Dutch word *schampen* flashed in his mind. The lights were scampering around him, but his mind could not believe that they were not really there. He stretched his hand to the side of the basket and felt the heat bathe his palm in friendly whispers.

Chapter 11

The Eel By the Tail

Judge Voss smiled at Joop, but his lips lapsed into a smirk when he turned his attention to van Meegeren.

"Well," he said, and he took a deep breath. "You may be curious about why I have summoned you."

"I have my suspicions," van Meegeren hissed.

Voss ignored the bored sigh. "You have insinuated a most interesting twist into the proceedings."

"The truth is always interesting, Your Honor," van Meegeren shot back.

Voss leered at van Meegeren through a contemptuous scowl. "Especially to a fraud who makes a fortune producing lies."

Voss was not letting van Meegeren off the hook, and Joop enjoyed every twist. He watched the judge's eyes following the burnished glimmer of the paneling circling his chambers. Joop felt the tension straining through the silence and knew Voss was hiding much more than he was saying. Joop valued tight lips, for there was survival in such stillness. The years of hiding in plain sight had taught him to walk softly and carry a sharp knife. Voss understood this, and his tongue was as sharp as his words were double edged.

"Inspector Piller has supplied us with the facts, so we need not review your dealings with Goering."

Van Meegeren relaxed just enough to assert, "I never met Goering."

"No doubt," Voss agreed. "I am sure you were never personally acquainted with any of your dupes."

"I cannot be held accountable for the minions of the art market."

"And so I have heard from some of the inmates of your present residence."

"They are different."

"I will grant you that," Voss said with a kind edge to his compliment. "They just sold everything within their grasp to the Germans, irrespective of who owned it."

"Are you to condemn every businessman in the country?" van Meegeren audaciously suggested.

"Only those who traded with the enemy."

"There was no choice."

"Of course there was no choice," Voss stated. "When such huge sums are involved, who in their right mind would choose not to become rich by trading with murderers? Yes, you are quite right. Those people had no choice."

"There are many more people guilty of collaboration."

"And you all had no choice," Voss sneered. "You were forced at gunpoint to create fake masterpieces for the Master Race."

Voss sat back and crossed his legs, his hands resting on his lap. Joop looked into Voss's eyes, and the black tunnels frightened him. Voss leaned forward and offered his open palm. "I must admit that I admire the wonderful symmetry of a counterfeiter dealing with thieves." Van Meegeren's toothy smile graciously acknowledged the compliment, but his lips pressed into a worried line when Voss said, "I draw the line at dealing with murderers."

Van Meegeren grasped the arms of the chair, summoning the courage to face his judgment. It was the first sign of a break in his composure. Joop sat rigid as Voss's grim silence vanquished van Meegeren's insolence.

Voss raised his chin as if to sniff the air. "You claim that you are the creator of *Christ and the Woman Taken in Adultery.*"

"That is correct," van Meegeren admitted in a shaky whisper.

"You are in no doubt that you are the author of this painting?"

"None whatsoever."

Voss ran his forefinger along the bridge of his nose. "In that case, I have a commission for you."

"A commission?"

"Yes."

Van Meegeren straightened his back and rose his chin to answer. "My work is very expensive."

"I appreciate that you are the most successful artist in the world, at the moment," Voss conceded. "But do you know how I will pay?"

"I presume that the funds will come from the Treasury."

"I will pay you in rope," Voss said quietly.

"Rope?"

"Yes. As the matter now stands, some of your associates have agreed to assist the Prosecutor."

Voss waited for the implications to seep into van Meegeren's consciousness. When he thought that he had inflamed van Meegeren's imagination, he started to enjoy his little anecdote.

"When your former clients left our country," Voss recalled, "they took their most experienced executioners with them. We are left with just our native incompetents. We Dutch are not so experienced at the other end of a noose. The fellows at Weteringshans try their best, but really, they are amateurs. Last week, it took them three attempts to hang one of our very own Nazis. The first time the rope broke. Then it was too long, and he just plopped down on his haunches below the gallows. So they hauled him back up. But this time it was too short, so it took about half an hour for them to strangle him. It really was funny. We must institute courses in this trade at the Technical College."

Joop watched van Meegeren's eyes search Voss's face for a glimmer of compassion. The judge glared stone, and Joop hoped he would never have to appeal for mercy. Van Meegeren tried to hide the gasps Voss's vision inspired, but his trembling chin betrayed his fear.

"I see you don't much care for such currency," Voss observed. "I hang traitors." Voss's voice echoed from the wooden walls. "Forgers, however, merely go to jail. You will prove that you are a highly accomplished forger."

"How do you expect me to do that?" van Meegeren begged.

"You will paint another picture in the style of Vermeer. We will supply you with the materials you require. The better the picture, the looser the noose."

Van Meegeren swung his head to Joop for assurance that this offer was genuine. Joop returned a bemused shrug.

Voss added, "I will not pay you in the rope you deserve. You will be paid in, shall we call them, futures. You will serve your future in prison, provided that your success at the canvas will keep you from the scaffold."

Voss nodded to Joop, and he took his cue. "It's all rather simple. Paint the picture and you live. Screw it up and you die."

Van Meegeren could feel the tremors in his arm subside. He dredged up just enough gall to tell Voss, "If I am to paint, I need my hands."

"What's wrong with them?" the Judge demanded.

"It is very cold in my cell."

Voss showered pity on him with a staccato of laughter. "I have already dealt with that problem. I am releasing you from the Weteringshans."

"I can go home?" van Meegeren burst forth in relief.

"To your new home," Voss qualified. "You will be given better accommodation at the Offices of the Flight Control Bureau. There you will work and live under the supervision of Inspector Piller and his staff."

Joop joined in Voss's merriment. "I'm your new landlord." He added to himself, "And I'll keep taking care of your cat."

Voss was becoming impatient with the prospect of negotiating the details. He had said all that was needed for the time being, so he rushed through his closing statements to clear his office.

"Inspector Piller will explain the particulars to you. For the present, we have finished with the business of the law, and I am sick of your oily little face. May I express my sincere desire that you accomplish this task without deliberate delay, and let me also assure you that I loathe the very sight of you. Get out."

Joop rose and guided a stunned van Meegeren to the door.

"That went well," van Meegeren sighed.

Joop cast his eyes under quizzical brows, and van Meegeren assured him, "I get a better room."

Chapter 12

Studio

Joop and Van Meegeren walked along the Herengracht to the offices of the Flight Control Bureau. The guards followed at a respectful distance. Van Meegeren accompanied Joop up the stone steps and waited for him to open the front door. Joop stood his ground, waiting for the guards to catch up. Van Meegeren shook his head and pushed the handle forward.

They stepped into the foyer, and van Meegeren gazed up the marble staircase and swiveled his head up the wall and over the ceiling. He slowly paced a circle, looking into the rooms leading off the foyer. He noted clerks busily examining boxes and listened to the drone of muted conversations. Jan was unloading documents from crates, but stopped his labors when he saw Joop. Men wearing the uniforms of six countries walked between the halls clutching documents. The whole of the ground floor was as lively as a railroad station. Joop stood waiting for van Meegeren to recognize the location.

"This is Goudstikker's Gallery," van Meegeren declaimed in astonishment.

"It used to be," Joop said.

Van Meegeren looked into the large hall to his left. He admired the carved plaster arches.

"How did you acquire such splendid premises?" he asked.

"With a machine gun," Joop said.

Van Meegeren gazed farther into the room, recalling the exhibitions of happier times. Where once stood Rembrandts on easels enticing the envy of the wealthy, columns of boxes now spilled paper from their bulging mouths. Men in rolled sleeves hunched over long tables or huddled in animated little clutches over packs of index cards. Paper dust hung in the air, swirling around van Meegeren's memories. "The Queen once came to visit. It must have been ten years ago."

Joop let the old times percolate and listened to van Meegeren's memories of departed patrons, figures now swallowed in night and fog. "I knew Jacques Goudstikker when he was just starting out," van Meegeren reminisced. "He was very smart. His father made the business, but Jacques turned it into an international sensation." Van Meegeren shook his head at Joop. "You should have seen his client list. Von Rath, van Hadeln, Proehl, and the best of them all, van Beuningen."

Joop recognized the names from old newspapers and his office files He knew they were the wealthiest men of prewar Holland. With each name dropped, Joop saw van Meegeren's eyebrows rise higher, as if he were tallying bank accounts.

Jan passed them and mounted the stairs. Joop turned to inform van Meegeren, "We work here now."

The words jolted Van Meegeren back to the present, but he casually asked, "Whatever happened to Goudstikker?"

"He escaped in 1940. Just ahead of the Germans."

"I'm glad he made it out."

"He got on a boat headed to England," Joop continued, "but he fell through an open cargo hatch and broke his neck."

"What about Desi?"

"Who?" Joop asked.

"His wife. The beautiful one."

"She survived."

"And the collection?"

"Miedl got hold of it," Joop exclaimed.

"Ah. So that's how you have these offices."

"The guns helped. And that's why we have you. I will show you your new accommodation. I need not remind you that the same guns continue to guard this building."

Joop turned to ascend the staircase, and he slowed his pace so van Meegeren could follow him. Van Meegeren could hear a distant tapping at the top of the stairs. The hammering grew louder with each step, and van Meegeren's smile melted to the rhythm of the blows. They stood facing smaller rooms on the second floor.

Joop curled his lip in wry amusement as he watched van Meegeren grit his teeth to the thumping coming from the room before them. He opened the door, and they saw Bobo in his shirt-sleeves and waistcoat raise a hammer over his head.

Van Meegeren turned to Joop. "For a moment, I thought Voss had changed his mind."

Joop was quick to reassure his prisoner. "Oh, he'll stick to the agreement." He waited for the color to bloom back into van Meegeren's cheeks. "You just have to fulfill your part of the bargain."

Bobo nodded to Joop but ignored van Meegeren. Joop turned to the right and led van Meegeren to another door. He flung it open and gestured for van Meegeren to follow. "The carpentry won't disturb you in here." The solitary camp bed, chair, and folding card table blared out the room's sparse function. "These are your new quarters."

Jan entered with an armful of bedclothes. He threw a clean sheet over the thin mattress, smoothed out the wrinkles, and folded the corners into triangles. He smiled up to van Meegeren. "Just like in the best hotels. I'm making your bed, so you can lie in it." Van Meegeren turned abruptly to Joop. "What if I wish to go for a walk and take the night air?"

"You can leave at any time, but the guard will shoot you."

"What if I want to do a little light reading?"

"I'll get you a lamp," Jan was quick to add. "Now that we have a little electricity."

Joop looked at van Meegeren opening his cigarette case. The authorities at Weteringschans strictly controlled such indulgences. Joop left van Meegeren lighting his cigarette and went to find an ashtray. He made a mental note that he would have to devise an escape route in case their guest set fire to the building.

Joop walked back to the central room and saw Bobo standing back from a rectangle of wooden slats. Joop admired his handiwork. "What about the size?" he asked.

"I measured the door and the frame won't fit through it."

Joop stretched his arm along the top rail and gauged the distance from his middle finger to the center of his chest. "It's three meters by four meters." He looked back at the door opening onto the gallery.

"Twice the dimensions of the door - two by one and a half meters," Bobo added.

Joop ran his fingers along the sanded wood. "Is it possible that he could get it out?" Bobo picked up the planed rectangle, and Joop followed him across the room to an ornate easel placed near a window. "I'll screw it to this. We told Voss we'd nail it, but screws will do. I found this in the basement."

The base of the easel was too heavy for Joop to lift. It would anchor the frame to the floor.

Bobo's finger beckoned Joop back to the table. He pulled at a roll of canvas, and the dust filled their noses. "I had this in the shop. These days, nobody wants the finest Irish linen."

Joop felt the tiny ridges of the material tickle his fingers. "Is there any way he can switch the canvas on the frame? The guards won't hear him screwing like they would hear him nailing."

Bobo grinned and pulled his wallet from his pocket. He opened it to reveal four postage stamps. "These were issued many years ago." They looked down at the young face of Queen Wilhelmina beaming in her coronation robes. Bobo carefully detached one stamp. He bent the little rectangle, licked it, and pressed it into the back of the canvas. "When I attach the canvas to the frame, the stamp will be trapped between the material and the wood." Joop swiveled his eyes between the table and the waiting frame. Again, Bobo had devised the simplest solution to a complex problem, and Joop admired the man's ingenuity. "If he removes the canvas, he'll tear the stamps." Joop kicked the easel. "He can't get it out and he can't stick another in."

Joop saw Jan pass the door. He picked up an old saucer and left Bobo to his work. He entered van Meegeren's room just in time to catch the falling ash. He would instruct the guards to remain just outside van Meegeren's room and always have a water bucket close by.

Van Meegeren raised his chin to Joop, who invited him to view his new studio. Van Meegeren cocked a disinterested eye, and Jan followed them both back to Bobo's work bench. The stamp was already hidden in place.

Van Meegeren fingered the canvas between his thumb and forefinger and sighed, "This will have to do." Bobo's face was rigid, but Jan laughed aloud, "Beggars can't be choosers."

Van Meegeren turned his lips to Joop but kept his eyes on the easel and the frame. "As I have mentioned, I'll need my own brushes and paints," he exclaimed.

"As we have promised, we will supply you with all the materials you need to fulfill your commission. They will arrive shortly."

Van Meegeren objected, "I mix my own paints. They are superior to those offered by trade." He sneered at Bobo, and Joop caught a whiff of suspicion. "May I retire to my new quarters?" van Meegeren asked.

"For tonight," Joop responded.

"You are not sending me back to that hovel of a prison," van Meegeren whined.

"Much better. We're sending you to the Lying-In Hospital."

"I'm in perfect health," van Meegeren protested.

"That's what Judge Voss wants to know."

"But why?"

"The Department of Justice," Joop explained, "demands that you will spend a day or two with the doctors, under guard."

"This is ridiculous."

"Call it insurance," Joop retorted.

"Against what? I can hardly escape."

"They want to have a Certificate of Health, just in case you die in prison."

Van Meegeren snorted derisive laughter, and Joop enjoyed his prisoner's merry contempt.

Chapter 13

Cobwebs in the Sun

Jan hoisted yet another box of papers onto the table. The crate coughed a dust cloud, and he leaned back to dodge the inevitable sneezing fit. He watched the stinking little particles spiral in the beams of light from the window and cursed this endless torrent of papers. Joop had assigned him to "Receiving" which was their joke for the truckloads of documents, bulging with long-forgotten information. When they had enough evidence for an arrest, they called their deliveries to Weteringschans Prison "Shipping."

Two months ago, Joop had appeared at the office with three distinguished and very frightened gentlemen. Somewhere, he had found an economist, a banker, and an art dealer and offered them positions as Investigators of the Flight Control Bureau. The extra ration cards would soothe their fears and insure their loyalty to the Bureau. Their first task was to recruit two of their associates because the volume of work was too much for even such an accomplished band. Within days, Joop was explaining their tasks to nine skeptical, curious, and hungry experts. "You are to search through the documents we will give you in order to discover the major criminals of the Occupation," he commanded. His commission was greeted with a Babel of unanswerable questions, cringing complaints, and assured vows that what he wanted was impossible. Joop calmly considered each of their objections and reminded them, "You all know the old proverb that the big fish eats the little fish. We are doing the opposite. We will find the little fish and use them to catch the big fish." They feigned knowing acceptance of Joop's homespun wisdom, and just when they were on the verge of consenting to join the Bureau, he casually said, "Who knows? Some of you may find your own names in these mountains of paper." They rushed to sign their contracts, and Joop smiled at the dedication they brought to their work.

Soon the large salon was a buzz of activity. Three sets of tables formed an open square before the windows and each department of the Bureau scrabbled through the piles Jan brought to them. In the other salon across the foyer, Jan ordered the random shipments into three sections marked "Industry," "Commerce," and "Culture." When each pile threatened to topple, Jan gave it to the appropriate team of experts. They would do the fine sieving. Jan's only function was to feed them the first crop.

He looked over his table and listened to the silence flooding from the other salon. When they were quiet, they were working hard. Jan had noticed that, after about the first hour, their conversations started to bubble across the foyer into his gallery. That was the signal that someone had stumbled across something which he thought was important. Gradually, the conversations became more heated, and even though Jan could not hear the words, he knew that the experts were starting the morning fight over their discoveries. When he heard the insults fly, he listened more carefully. He imagined they were like a windmill that first turned in lazy rotations and then revolved into a squeaking wail. Their bickering mounted to a reeling and steady throb until they were all shouting at each other, and the windmill spun like a propeller. That was when Jan knew they were pumping something clear from the inky sludge that surrounded them. The rumble always built to a crescendo of disagreements until it finally erupted into a verbal boxing match. Jan was sure they wouldn't actually resort to fisticuffs, but there were times when he had to break up a squabble that threatened to become a not-so-polite brawl. The morning's silence was to be enjoyed, so he leaned back with his hands entwined behind his head.

He heard the front door swish open and almost muffle Joop's footsteps. He looked up to fire a welcoming smile. Joop nodded to the experts' room and asked, "How goes the game?" Jan cocked his head to the foyer, "They's just dribbling the ball and I'm listening to the sun." Joop was used to Jan's strange little sayings, but sometimes wondered if he was going out of his mind. Lately, he had caught himself excusing Jan's weird words and admitting that "he is still a boy in many ways. I won't worry about it."

Joop walked to the window and played with the shutters. When they were closed, the louvres could be adjusted to control the flow of sunlight. Jan had placed his tables in a line so he could sit with his back to the windows and let the slatted frames heat his shoulders and illuminate his work. He had often found Jan just staring at the sunny strands that engulfed him. "What's the next job, Boss?" Jan asked. Joop wriggled his lips into a compliment. "Your promotion," he announced.

"What promotion?"

"Congratulations. You are now Lieutenant First Class Johannes Peter Flushing," Joop pronounced.

"My Oh My. The honor of it all. I don't deserve this elevation."

"Of course you don't, but it's better for the work for you to be Lieutenant Flushing than Jan Met de Pet."

Jan caught the drift of the slang, for "Jan in the hat" was just the usual slur for a common working man.

Joop nodded to the other room. "You see the way they disregard de Groot. He's only a sergeant." Jan immediately saw the purpose of his new rank. Joop turned his face full towards Jan's laughing eyes. "They will listen to a lieutenant."

"So," Jan enthused, " Do I get a badge or stripes on my overalls?"

"You get better than a badge, Lieutenant."

"What could be better than a uniform to impress the girls?"

Joop leaned closer and chuckled a whisper. "You get their obedience."

Jan liked his new position. The experts tended to treat him as if her were their delivery boy. His situation had not improved since the arrival of the advisers in uniforms from the Allied Military Commission. Short of wearing a coat dripping with golden crowns, the title of Lieutenant Flushing would make his life a bit easier.

"You have that cat and cream look to you," Jan said.

"The cream is a name. Rienstra."

"I've seen that name before."

"I'm sure you have," Joop assured. "It's the name on quite a few deeds of property owned by one Henricus Antonius van Meegeren."

"What sort of property?" Jan quizzed.

"Houses, mainly," Joop explained. "Everything from a country mansion to a row of workers cottages. There are farm houses, tenements. There's even a brothel or two."

"How did you find that?"

"You gave a dossier to Commerce and one of the bankers remembered the address. They fought it out until I had a list of addresses and contracts all signed by this Rienstra character."

"So we get to work?"

"Tomorrow is soon enough. We'll let him cook another night and then chat with him in the morning."

"You have his address?"

"Yes," Joop answered slyly. "Weteringschans. Cell 237."

"I can remember that."

Joop turned to leave, but a strange piece of paper caught his attention. He looked at the puzzle of a torn page. Jan had fitted the parts together by lining up lines and numbers. The pieces looked like cracked earth curling in the sun. "What's this?" he quizzed.

"Just a little game to pass the time," Jan responded. "Because we have so little to do."

"We'll have enough to do tomorrow at Weteringschans."

Joop nodded and turned to shuffle up the stairs to their prisoner's quarters.

Jan returned to his reverie. He could not care less about Rienstra, or van Meegeren, van den Broek or any of the others, for he was fed up with their antics. The experts and the prisoners all took themselves so seriously, and he was fed up with the lot of them. They could all fall off the face of the earth, as long as they left Joop and Liese, and himself and Bobo alone. There was now so much to live for and so little time to waste on these high up people and their baubles. Take away their toys and they cried like babies.

He listened to a scratching noise and concentrated to see if it were coming from inside or outside his head. Lately, he could sometimes not tell the difference. He leaned forward, propped his elbows on the table, and covered his ears with his hands. He opened and closed his fingers, until he was sure that there was no sound when he clasped his palms tightly to the side of his head. Now that he knew that it was coming from beyond his imagination, he searched for whatever was buzzing so plaintively. A sniff of the new dust brought his attention to the window shutters.

He searched along the louvres following the noise until it grew to a roar in his head. A cockroach was struggling to escape from a spider's web. It was a large creature, and Jan marveled at the length of the antennas thrusting from its skull. The more it pushed against the net, the greater was its exhaustion. Jan watched it pause, gasping for air and seeking the last threads of its strength. He pulled at the web and the cockroach fell to the window sill. For a moment, Jan thought it was already dead, but then it scurried over the ledge and down the wall to disappear somewhere in the corner.

Jan was filled with joy that he had helped the insect to live. He looked for the spider, but it was either gone to better hunting grounds or already dead. All that remained was the tapestry of webs ranging up the steps of the shutter. He pulled more of the silver loops into his hand and held them up to the light. They were fascinating. So many tiny little connections and worked with such cunning artistry.

He stood gazing at the waiting box of clutter and it shimmered like the web clinging to his fingers. There would be answers somewhere in all this mess. He knew that their searches would not be useless and recalled the old saying "nothing can hide when the sun shines."

Chapter 14

Bath

Joop couldn't keep up with Sarah. She was skipping along the sidewalk, dragging Liese behind her. Since the moment her mother told her, "We will go swimming today," Sarah had hopped with persistent demands to go now. Her mother hadn't even wiped her face with the wash cloth.

They sauntered along the Rembrandtsplein, and Liese could smell the little islands of people chatting on the sidewalks. The simple pleasure of a father, mother, and child enjoying the day brought smiles to some of the grimy faces they passed. She reined in Sarah and held Joop's hand and their eyes wrapped their child in a caressing net.

Joop led them to a strange crossroads. They turned off the main street and they squinted through back-alley shadows. "You're sure it's working?" Liese asked.

"Very sure," he said confidently. "It would be too sad if Sarah went home dry."

He guided them along the Heiligeweg and around and over mounds of newly dug earth spilling from the sidewalk. Amsterdam's checkerboard of streets and hidden paths frightened Liese. The two roads of Emst were a comfort, but in the last month, she had forced herself to learn just enough of the city's byways to get to the Jordaan and rush home with whatever food she could haggle out of the black marketeers. Amsterdam would always be a forest hiding wolves.

Sarah escaped Liese's clutch and scampered up one pile of dirt to look at a man digging a hole below her. He stood in water up to his knees and attacked the hole with his shovel. Sarah was fascinated when the shovel bit into the earth and the hole filled with more water. The man just kept digging, ignoring the rising filth from a broken pipe. Joop saw old bones in the hole and took Sarah's hand, in case the man was digging up something that would hurt her.

Liese was happy to follow because the Heiligeweg was so quiet. Joop led them to a building surrounded by large pipes. They were deafened by a huge generator standing on four wheels and filling the street. Liese's eyes followed a tangle of cables from the machine to an old fire engine. Hoses snaked from the fire engine and into the windows that opened at street level. The thunder of a large crowd crashed through the open doors. They walked into steamy clouds of joy bubbling from hundreds of screaming children.

They walked down a corridor and through open swinging doors to a swimming pool so packed it looked like a fish stall in the market. Liese's nostrils bulged with the chlorine clouds enveloping them. A woman came up to them clutching a pencil and offering them a paper tag on a long string. "Tie all the clothes together and put you child's name and address on this."

"Why?" Liese demanded with maternal suspicion.

"They will have to be deloused and we don't want the children wearing the wrong clothes."

Liese had difficulty undressing Sarah's wriggling body. As soon as she was naked, Sarah squirmed out of Liese's grip and plunged into the water. She immediately started to fan water into the eyes of the nearest little boy, who parried her liquid thrusts with his own swinging launch of a wave, a curving scimitar of chemical fun.

Joop left Liese to gossip with the women and watched Sarah cavort in the basin. The hoses from the street were gathered together at each end of the swimming pool, and he noticed soldiers walking in and out of cubicles which lined one wall. One of the men was bending over a hose with a wrench. He looked up and walked over to Joop with an open palm and a curving grin. "It's you. The Dutchman."

"There are plenty of Dutchmen here."

"You no remember. I remember," the man said.

Joop was suspicious of anybody with a memory for his face, but the maple leaf embroidered on the man's sleeve jogged his memory and eased his apprehension. Liese walked over to Joop but kept a wary eye on the pool. The man in front of Joop wore brown pants gathered tight over black boots. He wore a green shirt soaked with sweat and pool water. She strained her ears to find the meaning in English clouded by the man's thick French accent. "Hilversum," the man said. Joop shrugged his shoulders, but the man was persistent. "I am Boudreau." He stabbed his thumb at the insignia on his shoulder, and Liese could barely make out the letters "Régiment de la Chaudière" through the steam.

Boudreau was all grins and smiles as he grasped Joop's hand. "You are called what?" Joop looked embarrassed but kept pumping the hand, "My name is Joop. Joop Piller." Boudreau finally released his grip. "Eh voyons, Joop le Pilier. And this is the Madame Pilier?"

Liese smiled, and Boudreau raised his hands to his eyebrows. "Eh bien," he gasped, and Liese thought he was going to hug her. She looked over to the pool and said, "Our daughter would like to meet you, but the water is too exciting."

"The water is very good for des enfants."

For a moment, Liese saw the seriousness invade the man's face, but his eyes beamed respect to Joop. "Your husband. He is real hero."

The memory now flooded up, and Joop wanted to throw the man into the water. He could not stop Boudreau's torrent of words without creating a scene. "We had really bad job. Three months past. Hilversum."

Joop gritted his palms for what was to come. Liese stood open-mouthed. "We all very scared. Bullets everywhere." Liese was glad their daughter was beyond range of Bourdeau's voice. "Joop he walk into that street like he walking to a bus." She got just enough to know that her husband had put himself in mortal danger just a few weeks ago. Boudreau turned his full face to Joop and spread his arms around Joop's shoulders. "Joop le Pilier. Boudreau is now alive this day because of you."

Joop waited for the embrace to spring open. He dared not look at Liese. "Thank you, Monsieur. Boudreau. I am glad you are OK. We have to take care of our daughter."

Joop slunk a few steps along the pool to guard Sarah, who was attempting to drown a little boy. Boudreau gazed into Liese's face and saw the shock floating above her smile.

Three months ago, that was the time when Joop and Jan had run into the house in Emst. They had bundled her and Sarah into a truck and drove through the night to Amsterdam. The truck was filled with soldiers in British uniforms. Some spoke French and some others spoke Dutch, but through a babble of English and shouts and laughs. They raced into the city, and Joop rushed them through one building to the back-house. Jan stayed with them. Joop kissed them and disappeared into the maze of alleys. Jan hid them in a little house and told them, "Everything will be good."

Now she knew why there had been such a frantic rush. The day her husband saved Boudreau's life was the same day he had rushed her and Sarah to Amsterdam. She looked kindly on Boudreau and accepted the man's admiration. His few words had revealed that her worst fears had been as true as her most vivid nightmares. But Boudreau's hands and shrugs told her that fixing the hoses was the most dangerous thing they would have to face today.

Her face glowed with more than bath steam and her cheeks moistened with relief. She walked to the edge of the pool, and just like Boudreau, knew her family was alive this day because of Joop.

Chapter 15

Pentimento

Van Meegeren paced semi-circles around the studio. Joop had read aloud the commission from Judge Voss, and van Meegeren breathed relief at the command that "the subject of the painting is to be the Christ Child Discovered in the Temple."

Van Meegeren stood before the easel, as if paying it a compliment. Joop and Bobo watched their prisoner step back to stand in the light reflected from the huge white canvas. He struck a thoughtful pose, and stroked his chin in concentration. Joop and Bobo waited for his judgement. Van Meegeren ran his hand over the canvas screwed to its easel and rubbed the dust between his fingers and his thumb.

"What did you use for a ground?" he asked.

"Gesso," Bobo replied.

"The composition?"

"Rabbit skin glue, chalk, and white."

"The proportions?"

"One and a half ounces of glue to a pint of water. I stroked in the chalk and white pigment."

"I can see that," van Meegeren admitted. "How very thoughtful of you."

Van Meegeren ran his forefinger along the edges of the canvas. He tugged at one corner and drummed his fingers on the stretched cloth, and the frame trilled to his beat. When he pressed his palms to the material, it surrendered to his loving touch. "You cooked it?"

"Yes. I used an electric heater to shrink it to the stretcher."

"But you didn't sand it with pumice." van Meegeren observed.

"No. I left that for you. Each artists has his own preference."

"That is most thoughtful of you."

Van Meegeren turned to bathe them both in his most grateful smile. "I could not have done better myself." The compliment crept into Joop and Bobo.

It had taken Bobo two days to prepare the canvas for painting. He had mixed the glue and water, but took care to add the powdered chalk and ground gypsum a little at a time. He laughed at himself to think he was mixing pancake batter with a wooden spoon. When the mixture felt like strained applesauce, he added just enough lead to make his bowl of home-made gesso brilliant white.

He had taken extra care brushing on the first layer of the ground, so that every space between the fibers of the linen would be filled evenly. He had placed the electric heater before the easel, and stood guard against any scorching. The heater glowed like a votive candle in an empty church.

When the canvas was dry to his touch, he repeated his work with all the brush strokes in the opposite direction, so that no paint could seep through and lurk in the threads of the canvas. His vigil continued until each wet island shrank into the gleaming white surface. He could almost see the cloth pull itself onto the wooden grid, but he waited patiently for the heat to finish its magic. The prepared canvas stood stood before him, thirsty for pigment and oil.

Van Meegeren cocked an eyebrow to Joop. "Your man did an excellent job. This ground is perfect."

Bobo stood to the side, distractedly filling his pipe. He could not resist feeling pride in van Meegeren's recognition of his work. Joop watched van Meegeren raise his hand to his mouth and saw the tip of his tongue probe the ends of his fingers. Van Meegeren swiveled his head towards Bobo. "You used lead white."

"As Vermeer would have."

"Where did you get lead white?" van Meegeren asked and then sneered, "From a tube?"

Bobo took his time lighting his pipe and defiantly blew smoke between them. "I melted an old pipe from a toilet."

Van Meegeren was getting neither information nor advantage from their word jousting, so he stepped to the table to inspect the meagre offering of materials. He sneered at the few brushes, their heads blooming out of an old water jug. He drew forth one brush, made a great display of inspecting the ferrule, snorted at the splayed hairs, and snapped the handle between his fingers. "I can't use these," and cast the broken brush over the table.

He picked up a stick of charcoal and rolled it between his thumb and forefinger until it crumbled. A gray dust collected in his palm. "I need some string."

"I know where I can find a rope," Jan offered.

"Something less coarse. Packing twine will do."

Joop nodded, and Jan walked out of the studio and down the stairs. Bobo watched van Meegeren place his hands on his hips to strike a contemplative pose. He smoothed his mustache with his thumb, and Bobo thought van Meegeren was looking younger when the charcoal dusted the stubble on his chin. "You seem to have some training in art," van Meegeren commented to Bobo.

"I sell supplies to painters and sculptors."

"Do you paint?"

"No," Bobo admitted. "I can't draw anything but monkey faces."

"Ah," van Meegeren laughed as he turned to Bobo. "Then you would have made an excellent portraitist for our Dutch lords and their ugly wives."

Joop and Bobo shared the merriment and the studio filled with expectation. They heard feet clattering up the stairs and turned to see Jan juggling a ball of string from hand to hand. "Our friends downstairs have more than enough of this." He threw the ball to van Meegeren and they watched him pull out ten feet of string, like a draper measuring out ribbon. He clutched the stick of charcoal in his left hand and drew the string through his fist with his right. Black dust swirled from his fingers as he coated the string with the charcoal. He offered the end to Bobo, who held it firmly at the bottom left corner of the canvas. Van Meegeren was pleased Bobo knew what to do and pulled the string taut to the opposite corner. He stood at the right of the frame but his arms were too short to reach the center of the diagonal. "Will you do the honors?" he asked Joop.

Bobo saw the confusion and told Joop to, "Pull back the string from the middle and let it go." Joop obeyed and felt like a rather stupid Cupid playing with a bow too big for him. He released his finger, and the string slammed onto the canvas. Bobo stood up to place his end of the string at the top of the frame, and van Meegeren knelt at the opposite corner. "Again," he commended, and Joop took another shot at the canvas.

The string went slack between them and they stood before two perfectly placed black diagonals etched into the white ground. "Good," van Meegeren exclaimed, and put his nose close to the canvas.

"What's he doing?" Joop asked.

"He's lining out the canvas for his composition."

"Just like that?"

"Now he has divided it into four triangles to center the composition. He will use them to paint the picture," Bobo explained.

Joop peered at the heads of the four triangles meeting in the center of the canvas. He had never seen any artist work, and except for *Christ and the Woman Taken in Adultery*, had seldom seen an actual oil painting. Jan's eyes spread out from the center to the bases of the triangles, reminding him of a Maltese cross. Bobo knew that the finished painting would have four basic elements and the criss-crossed lines fed his curiosity to see how van Meegeren would fill the voids.

Van Meegeren lit a cigarette, crossed his arms, and seemed to be looking at something in the top triangle. He turned to Joop and commanded, "Come here." Joop stood beside him and van Meegeren positioned Joop so that his back was even with the left edge of the frame. He gazed long into Joop's left eye, until Joop started to feel ridiculous. Van Meegeren's right arm jerked towards the canvas and sliced an elliptical slash into the upper triangle. "That will do," he said, and Joop stood back to see what would happen next.

Van Meegeren's arm curved like a fencer parrying a foil, and a perfect black oval appeared on the canvas. He drew two more semi-circles within the oval. He glanced back at Joop and then placed a black circle in the middle of the oval. He licked his thumb and smeared charcoal above and below the curving lines. Joop was almost frightened as he saw his own left eye staring back at him from the canvas.

Van Meegeren placed the thumb of his left hand over the pupil and spread his fourth finger to the left. He carefully rolled aside his finger tip and thrust a point of charcoal into the swirling fingerprint. He stood back, judging the distance between the two centers, and called to Jan, "Now for you."

Jan took his position where Joop had stood, and van Meegeren captured his right eye in a few strokes of the charcoal. They all stared at the two eyes on the canvas, but Bobo's brows arched in suspicion. He wondered why Jan's right eye did not quite match with Joop's left eye. There had been much bravado in van Meegeren's first attack, but it made Bobo question if their maestro was not a little deficient in draughtsmanship. "Maybe he also paints monkeys," he thought to himself.

Van Meegeren turned to study Bobo's face and lunged at the canvas. Below the eyes, he scratched vertical lines into the gesso very similar to Bobo's nose. Bobo immediately realized how he was working.

"What's he doing?" Joop asked.

Bobo breathed a conspiratorial whisper over his pipestem. "He is making the pentimento."

"Isn't that something in an olive?" Jan asked.

"The what?" Joop prodded.

"The pentimento," Bobo continued. "It's the drawing underneath the paint. Sometimes it's what you can see below the surface of the paint when it takes a long time to dry."

Joop felt a little stupid because he had thought a painter would be using the brushes. Now he understood that there had to be a drawing to use as an outline and told himself, "It's just like Sarah's coloring book, without the crayons." Joop also realized that in a few strokes, van Meegeren had copied their eyes and Bobo's nose. He had captured his jailers with his magic.

Van Meegeren tossed the charcoal onto the table and wiped his palms together as if dismissing his work. "I will make you famous, my friends."

Joop, Jan, and Bobo stood uncertainly before the beginnings of the painting. Van Meegeren lit a cigarette and savored their admiration of his talent. He judged them "Not so bad," and waited for them to break the spell of the canvas. Jan shuffled from foot to foot.

"Well," he breathed. "That's enough work for one day."

He turned to leave, but Joop commanded, "We haven't finished."

Van Meegeren obeyed Joop's pointing finger and stood beside the canvas. Bobo picked up the camera from the table and did not have to look down when he turned the aperture ring. "Judge Voss wants a photograph of you and the painting at the end of each session."

Van Meegeren straightened his tie and brushed back his hair. Bobo crouched to capture the scene and saw van Meegeren in the viewfinder, raising his arms to the canvas in offering and smirking into the lens. The flash bounced off the white canvas and they all winced at the unexpected glare. Bobo's thumb pressed the flash release and the bulb sailed from the camera towards van Meegeren. He mimed dodging a bullet, and Bobo laughed. "Photography is my art."

Van Meegeren joined in their laughter and casually proclaimed, "I will need some supplies."

"Judge Voss ordered that we would supply you with everything you need," Joop reassured him.

"Excellent," van Meegeren blew through his smoke. "I'll need three or four cartons of cigarettes to begin with and some spirits."

"Turpentine or linseed oil?" Bobo asked.

"Gin. I like *Geneva*, it has more of a bite."

Her turned to walk into his sleeping quarters, and Bobo heard him collapse into the bed.

Chapter 16

Princess

Joop walked up the stairs to van Meegeren's front door, fumbling in his pocket for the key and the note. Van Meegeren had insisted that he scrawl a "little message introducing my friend Joop Piller" on a piece of torn wrapping paper. Joop had laughed at how easily his prisoner had turned him into a messenger boy, but the cupboard of canned delicacies beckoned.

He stood on the landing and looked at a car parked on the street. It was pre-war, like everything else that could move, but it was clean enough for him to see the red paint through the road dirt. He joked to himself, "Maybe even cars have their own pentimento?" The strange car made him pause long enough to knock on the door and clutch the key like a blade.

There was no answer, but he could sense someone on the other side. He turned his left shoulder to the door, gently inserted the key, and pulled back his right leg. The door creaked. Joop swung his body and kicked it open. A woman jumped back and ran away, screaming, "Police!" Joop stepped over the threshold, ready to lunge. He ran into the living room and caught her arm. "I am the police."

The woman cowered in his grip, and Joop demanded, "Who are you?"

"I am Mrs. van Meegeren."

Joop's face drenched her with his scowl, and he waited for her panic to melt into submission before releasing her.

"What do you want?" she asked.

Joop drew the brown note from his pocket and slowly offered it to her between two pointed fingers. She did not know what to do, so Joop waited and allowed her curiosity to dredge up enough courage to grasp the note. He judged her age by the slash of white roots pushing through the dyed brown tresses. His eyes lingered just long enough over the matronly bulge of her stomach to increase her discomfort. The clothes were well-made and clean. He lowered his eyes to the shoes which were definitely not made for walking the lines of black-marketeers. He snapped his eyes back to her face and casually stated, "Your former husband sends his regards."

She stared back her contempt, but Joop knew she was startled by his knowledge that she was divorced. Clearly, he had information from van Meegeren, but he left her ignorant of just how much he knew.

Joop watched her regain her composure. "Get his necessities," Joop ordered. She turned to lead him into the kitchen. She opened the cupboard, grabbed the necks of two bottles, and stood defiantly before the intruder. Her red varnished nails reminded Joop of talons. He pointed to the table, and she thumped the the bottles down in grudging obedience.

She grabbed a handful of cigarette packages and petulantly threw them beside the bottles. "I trust these will be sufficient," she said. "I expect you to deliver whatever you do not steal."

Joop ignored the insult and the defiance of her stance. He would not bow to the lady of the house. Joop had seen enough of the cruelty of the weaker sex and never underestimated its viciousness. He stood rigid, waiting for her surrender.

"He has been moved to more suitable quarters," Joop informed her. He pointed his fingers at her face and moved them away from the cupboard door. "His former cell can house his former wife."

She stepped aside, and Joop helped himself to the shelves of bottles and tobacco.

He slid four bottles of gin into his raincoat pockets and completely ignored her. She seethed with barely contained outrage and crossed her arms in a petulant sulk.

He gathered twenty metal containers of cigarettes and expected her to make some comment about the police robbing her. When his pockets could hold no more, he turned to her and ordered, "He will need more when these are finished."

She walked away as if dismissing a rude servant and stood in the living room. His eyes followed her retreat, studying the back of her head. The thinning hair had been carefully teased to hide the shining scalp. The bald patch testified to the years that her lipstick denied. He walked into the living room, where she started her demands. "If you are a policeman, you can dispose of that."

Joop had no idea what she was talking about. She pointed to a corner, and he could just make out something black under a chair. "It has already ruined the furniture," she accused.

Joop saw the eyes blink at him and recognized his dinner guest from his previous visit.

"That chair is Louis XVI," she intoned, confident he would not comprehend. "It is very expensive." She stressed the furniture's cost with an effusive wave of her hand from a loose wrist.

Joop could see the claw gouges down the leg. "I am not a carpenter," he admitted.

"You're a policeman, are you not?" She demanded. "Shoot it."

Joop blinked back at the cat and wondered if it understood the pronouncement of its own execution. He paced slowly to the corner, lowered his hand, and made little kissing sounds. He wanted to laugh at himself for not understanding a word of cat language, but he enjoyed the woman's rising anger. Joop prolonged the conversation, until he sensed that the cat recognized him. The cat offered its arched back, and Joop stroked the boney ridges below the fur. He picked up the cat and let it nestle under his coat. He turned to leave and casually informed her, "Make sure the supplies are well stocked when I return."

He walked out of the door and cuddled the cat down the steps. He heard the door slam shut behind him and confided to the cat, "It's a good thing they married each other. Can you imagine four people that miserable?" The cat purred agreement and buried its nose deeper inside Joop's coat sleeve.

He walked along the canal, his pockets jingling to the rhythm of his feet. The other pedestrians cast curious glances at the strange man talking into his armpit. The day was clear and he breathed the crispness of late spring. The trees had all been decapitated for fuel over the winter, and he hoped a summer would give them a few stunted branches. It would take decades for the streets to cool under their shade, but he knew there would eventually be leafy reflections dancing in the shimmering canal water. He imagined Sarah riding a bicycle to a school that did not teach her about all the sorrows of her first years but filled her with hope for all the years she had yet to greet. These scarred trunks would grow with her, and when she was old enough, some man would kiss her lovingly under the hopeful boughs.

He told the cat, "You must be good, for you are going to meet a very special little friend." He explained that the girl would not be like the woman in the house. There would be kindness and good things to eat. He stroked a paw and the claws relaxed. "You don't need a knife where you are going, so let's get rid of any stupid ideas about scratching the hand that feeds you."

He continued his lecture through an alley, but when he walked into the main street, a man walked up to him. He had heard the bottles and wanted to trade. "How much the bottle?" he asked gruffly, and pried open his pocket to reveal six inches of stale, dry tobacco. Joop was well aware of the exchange rate of ten cigarettes for one cigar, but didn't want to disappoint the man who looked like he was about to cry.

"Sorry Friend. I don't smoke and I haven't change for a stogie."

"One bottle, please."

The man eyed the bulge under Joop's coat and new hope sprung into his face. "What else you have?"

Joop pulled back his lapel, and the cat glowered at the interloper. The disappointment filled the man's face, but Joop saw it fight with the disgust. "Two panatelas or three ounces of Cavendish," Joop demanded. The man walked away, desperate for a drink, and Joop called after him, "OK. The cigar and two ounces." He laughed down to the cat, "See. You're hardly worth a good smoke."

He chuckled, "You're no roof-rabbit," and trod home through familiar alleys. He explained as if to a smart child, "You see, it was the right decision to bring Liese and Sarah here. Emst was in the direct path of the Canadians clearing out the last of the monsters."

Joop turned into the street towards their home and paused at the entrance. He no longer had to linger at the tunnel, his back sensing for anybody following him. He whispered silent thanks to Jan and Bobo for finding this refuge that "even the born Amsterdammers don't know about." He let the cat peep out from under his coat to watch the sunlight turn to cool shadow. He shuffled the few paces through the tunnel and froze before the cottage. Smoke was billowing out of the window. He ran to the door, and Liese's apron blew steam and squealing smiles towards him.

"Look," she commanded, and dragged him by the hand into the kitchen.

Bobo was sitting in his undershirt, looking bemused, and Sarah was standing at the table stirring a bowl of some pungent concoction. Liese opened her arms to present Joop with two pots bubbling on the stove. "We have gas," she proclaimed, as if they had won the lottery.

Joop slumped into a chair. "And I have presents."

He unloaded his trove and the bottles rattled onto the table. Decks of cigarettes rose up around the bottles. Bobo took his one ration, "For later."

"They are for van Meegeren," Joop explained, but added, "Well, most of them."

Sarah rested her face in her hands with her elbows on the table, and expectantly stared at her father's coat. If there were presents for the grown-ups, there must be something for her. Liese joined in the wait, until Joop could not longer restrain himself. He unbuttoned his coat and held the lapel between trembling fingers. "And this is for you." He pulled back the lapel, and Sarah squealed delight into the cat's face.

Bobo shook his head in mock reprimand and smiled at the child's joy. She thrust forward a hand to pet the animal, but Liese caught it. Joop told her to, "Wait. She'll come to you." They sat until the cat felt safe enough to test the table with a paw and an inquisitive nose. It jumped onto the table and looked back at Joop. He told Sarah to, "put out your hand, very gently." She commanded her impatience to be still, and the cat's nose examined her finger. Joop nodded once, and Sarah delicately raised her hand and the cat ribbed its head into her palm.

After a few strokes, Joop picked it up and carried it into the other room. He placed it on the coat lying on the thin mattress and instructed Sarah, "Sit down, quietly. Don't make any quick movements." She plumped herself onto the coat out of paw range, and the cat raised one crooked foreleg, unsure of this new place. "Just watch and let it come to you. Then you can make friends." He left her to her vigil, but made sure he could see her through the gaping doorway.

Liese looked at him. "That's lovely."

"So is this," Joop replied and waved his hand around the kitchen. "How did you get all this?"

He looked into the pot on the stove and a gooey paste assaulted his nose. "Whatever it is."

"Your friend from the bath."

"Who?"

"The Boo man."

"Boudreau?"

"Yes. Him."

Joop grimaced at the pot. "We're not that hungry. Besides he's too big for this pot."

Bobo laughed at the hint of having a friend for supper, and Liese explained their good fortune.

She and Sarah had been walking the line of marketeers. She had haggled a bread loaf and a pat of butter for only three cigarettes when a man shouted to them from across the street. As he ran towards them, she recognized Bourdreau. His deluged them in English and French, but the man's face and his arms showed only happiness at seeing them.

"He is so like a Frenchman," Liese exclaimed.

"He is French," Joop said.

"Arms waving all the time, and he hugs me like a bear."

"He is a very happy man."

"And very generous too. He gave the vultures coins and now we have a chicken."

She presented another pot crammed with fleshy chunks which really did smell of fresh poultry. "And vegetables. Real ones. Cabbage and carrots."

"This is wonderful," Joop complimented, and he and Bobo beamed at Liese standing with the trophy pot, as proud as a hostess serving honored guests.

Joop pointed to the other pot bubbling over the heat. "But what about this? Whatever this is."

"Amazing," She crowed. "We came home and there was gas."

She picked up a large box and thumped it onto the table. "He gave us this."

Joop cast a confused stare at the gaudy cardboard rectangle.

"It's called 'Boraxo'," Liese said. "He says it is soap in a powder."

Joop shook the box and it rattled like sand in a bucket. "What does it do?"

"You simply pour it into hot water and it can clean anything."

Bobo looked up from the table. "Just wait."

"There's more?" he asked in disbelief.

"Yes. Isn't it wonderful? There is a night just for men at the bath."

Joop looked to Bobo for support. "You better do as she says," was the resigned advice. "She's already skinned my shirt." Joop looked into the pot and confirmed Bobo's confession.

"Boudreau explained it all. You two will go and have the clothing deloused with something called DDT. You will have a good scrubbing, and when you come back, you will have two shirts."

Joop and Bobo shrugged to each other in happy capitulation.

They heard the purring from the other room play a counterpoint to the bubbling pot. Joop stood and passed his hand over Liese's shoulder as he walked to the door. He rested his head on the frame and gazed at Sarah enticing the cat.

"What does it eat?" she asked.

"Tonight she will eat chicken with us all," Joop assured her.

The cat blinked at Joop and turned tail to have Sarah stroke its head. She held her hand open and the cat reared up to stroke her palm with its chin. It launched into a moist purring when Sarah royally declared, "I name thee, 'Princess.'"

Chapter 17

Atlas

Joop shuffled across Dam Square and glanced up at the statue of Atlas rising from the roof of the Royal Palace. The Government had summoned Amsterdam's chief civil servants to an emergency meeting, but Joop was in no hurry for their company. The Queen had not been in residence for at least ten years, and the Occupation had scattered her courtiers. He hated the building, for it was the lair of the compliant and the guilty. He dallied long enough to have the pigeons swoop curiously around him and calm his anger.

A porter held open the main door and told Joop to go to Room 401. Joop followed the room numbers through the maze of corridors, until he faced two glass-fronted doors. The right door swung wildly open at his push to reveal a throng of happy men. The meeting did not warrant one of the palace's more formal salons. Two hundred of the city's most essential bureaucrats scraped their chairs over the dirty parquetry floor and gawked at the ornate decorations, impressive enough to inspire envy, but not so sumptuous as to capture their interest. Cigars, cigarettes, and pipes spewed a cloud that hung over the congregation.

Joop stood in the aisle between the clusters of chairs. He squinted through the smoke to see the ceiling and walls covered in murals. His eyes sailed from picture to picture and he felt as if he were driving through fog. The clouds wafted apart, and he saw scenes depicting Holland's historic rebellion against the Spanish and its continuing war against the sea. People from long ago attacked cannons with daggers. On the opposing wall, shovel wielding peasants raised dykes and built windmills. Joop wondered if the heroes of the rebellion were the fathers of the dyke builders.

He turned around to leave, but a large picture on the wall over the doors stopped him. Between the top of the doors and the ceiling was a big map worked in swelling plaster. The closer he approached the door, the clearer he could see it was a map of old Holland. When he stepped back a few paces, the map formed itself into the shape of a lion squatting on his hind legs and resting a sword on its shoulder. Two rows of medallions containing views of cities flanked the map, but when he walked away, the circles became the lion's eyes and the towns merged with the animal's fur. Joop was intrigued by the trick and paced back and forth to repeat the illusion of a map becoming a lion. He recognized Amsterdam, Rotterdam, and Delft, but the pictures only brought to mind things he was trying to forget. He stepped to the side of the doors and stood beneath the lion's claws.

Laughter erupted from the islands of chairs, and the atmosphere was more fitting to a reunion than a crisis. The doors swung open, and van den Broek ushered a procession of dignitaries into the chamber. They strode down the aisle to the podium, and the room rose in respectful expectation. Joop cocked his ear, and listened to van den Broek revel in his role of master of ceremonies. "Gentlemen. Please be seated," he invited, and the chairs scuffled so they could all see the podium and the dignitaries could see them.

The door groaned beside him, and a young man entered just far enough to take in the whole room. Joop recognized him. He was the journalist who had been so bored during van Meegeren's court appearance. The man nodded once to

Joop, slid past him, fished a pencil and notebook out of his satchel, and leaned against the wall. He was too close for Joop's comfort, who wondered what the man was doing here. A gavel cracked onto the podium, and their chins rose together to see Van den Broek raise his arm and sweep his open hand to an elderly man in a Canadian uniform.

"It is my great pleasure," van den Broek announced, "to introduce Major General Galloway. The Canadian Army of Liberation has kindly offered General Galloway's outstanding expertise to help us with the most immediate problems. Without further fanfare, may I extend to our distinguished comrade our most heartfelt thanks."

Van den Broek started to clap, and the room rose to a thunderous ovation. Van den Broek was the last man clapping, as he stepped from the podium. Galloway waited for the shuffling to subside, and his tone matched the seriousness of his message.

"Thank you for your accolade," he acknowledged, "which I receive on behalf of the soldiers of the Third Canadian Army and I thank you all for the enthusiastic welcome you have extended to our troops."

The civil servants beamed their gratitude at the General's gracious compliment, but Joop saw the journalist's pencil capture each word. He heard Galloway speak of the "deceptive quality of the Liberation," and the journalist paused his scratchings, his pencil poised in annoyed expectation of nothing new.

"The ecstatic crowds," Galloway explained, "which welcomed our soldiers led us to believe that the reports of starvation were greatly and purposely exaggerated." The journalist inclined his head, and Joop was drawn by the General's words. "I must confess that when we received news of the urgency of the food situation, we thought that the reports were grossly inflated in order to influence military decisions. The sea of flags which greeted our columns only confirmed our suspicions that the rumors of mass starvation, and they were only rumors at that time, were simply unbelievable."

The journalist swiveled his head to look directly into Joop's eyes and winked. A friendly glance in a courtroom a few weeks ago did not merit an appeal to such intimacy. There was confidence in the gesture, and Joop wondered how this man knew him. He a raised an ironic eyebrow, and the journalist shot back a disgusted shrug. Joop wanted to know more, but Galloway's report caught his attention.

Van den Broek was sitting impatiently for Galloway to finish, but the General was taking his time. He would not allow them the excuse for misunderstanding his message. "The deception was due to our ignorance. Men and women who are slowly dying of starvation in their beds cannot walk gaily about the streets waving flags and kissing soldiers."

The journalist leaned over and breathed to Joop, "That's just what we told them six months ago." Joop nodded agreement, and they turned sharpened ears to Galloway.

"It is an empty country, inhabited by a hungry and, in the towns, a semi-starved population."

Joop knew that Galloway was telling the truth, a truth he shared with the journalist.

"The existing food supplies are practically nil. In March, the daily ration was 525 calories per day, per person. In April, the ration was reduced to 400 calories. We calculate that this is also the nutritional ration available to the inmates of the camps recently liberated in Germany."

The journalist clenched his teeth, for he knew that their country had been one vast concentration camp. He was livid that their reports to London had been ignored.

"Even with the emergency airdrops, a day's ration consists of a very small cup of "ersatz" soup, an even smaller piece of an unappetizing and sticky substance called bread, and a wafer of beetroot."

The journalist whispered to Joop, "He forgot the tulip bulbs."

"That's because his audience hasn't had to eat flowers," and Joop could not disguise his sardonic smirk. Galloway's statistics snapped them back to attention.

"It is hardly surprising that the large proportion of the population who were unable to buy on the black market have lost, on average, forty-five pounds in weight."

Joop was trying to place the journalist's face beyond Voss's court, but the image hid behind bad memories. The man knew something, and that worried Joop. Galloway's voice cut through the maze of Joop's memory.

"I wish to read from yesterday's report from the Royal Canadian Medical Corps. 'Out of a hundred people taken at random in the streets, and these are people who are seen walking about every day and does not include those who are so weak that they remain indoors, fifteen percent showed signs of malnutrition, fifty percent were definitely undernourished and thirty-five percent were more or less normal.'"

Joop sneered that it took a foreigner speaking English to tell the Dutch government what he had known all winter. He had survived, but only because he knew how to get the food that kept the network alive and active. Through a hundred ruses, he had fought the barbarians, but the fight had also fed him and his family.

"It is of interest to note," Galloway added, "that there are five times as many males suffering from starvation as females."

Joop decided that he would follow the journalist's unspoken invitation and nodded agreement. Whoever this man was, he knew very personally what Galloway was saying. Maybe he had hoarded slices of bread and slivers of sausage for a wife, or a mother, or a sister. The thought pulled Joop closer to the man.

The journalist cast frigid scorn over the hall, nodded to Joop, and left. Joop stood between the beckoning door and Galloway's voice and quickly followed the unknown acquaintance.

In the corridor, the man fished a dry cigarette from his satchel and lit it, careful to keep the tobacco dust within the tube. "So, Joop Piller, you're now a civil servant."

"How do you know me?"

The man walked down the corridor, towing Joop along. Joop kept pace with the man, and he insisted, "You haven't answered my question."

"And you have so many of them. We met when you delivered those rolls."

"I'm not a baker's delivery boy."

"The rolls donated from Delft."

Joop recalled the raid, when Bobo and Jan jumped into the truck, giggling like schoolboys. The prank could have ended in a spray of gunfire, but they got five huge rolls of newsprint to the Hague and into the hands of the underground press. Over the next few months, the raid became routine, so the journalist's face was lost in the crowd of frightened and grateful smiles.

"We got over fifty thousand copies out of that paper. I never had a chance to thank you."

Joop accepted the offered hand, trying to shake more information out of his admirer. "I still don't know who you are."

"I am Jan Spierdijk," the man admitted, "but you may know me as 'Orange Blossom.'"

"You wrote those stories in the newspaper?"

"Yes."

"Then it is I who should be thanking you."

They stood sharing their connections, and the answers drowned Joop's suspicions.

"Let's get some air," Spierdijk almost ordered, and they marched ostentatiously through the palace, just to annoy the occupants with the echoes of their clattering heels.

They stood in the square. Spierdijk coaxed a few more puffs from the cigarette that flared like a fuse, and opened his fingers. The wind carried away the glowing ember, and Joop's eyes followed its rise to see the clouds hiding Atlas's burden on the roof.

Spierdijk turned and seemed to be staring at the corner of the palace. Joop left him to whatever was crawling through his mind. Patience had been a difficult lesson, but Joop had mastered it.

Three months ago, Spierdijk had stood on this same spot. He had rushed to Amsterdam's center along with hundreds of other people to celebrate the Liberation. The cheering deafened him, but he saw a column of Canadian troops enter the square. He turned to see a line of worried Germans pushing their way through the dancing throng from the opposite side of the square. Spierdijk froze at the sight of the two lines weaving through the throng to the inevitable eruption when they met. The Germans and the Canadians passed him without even seeing each other. He breathed deeply and shouted himself hoarse for the next two hours. He was recording his impressions, when the shots rang out.

Seven Germans crowded the balcony of a building beside the palace and started firing a machinegun into the crowd. Spierdijk threw himself on the cobblestones, but saw the women clutching their children and running out of the square on bare feet. When he looked back, the square was littered with women's shoes. The Germans had done this in the very last hours of the war. It was then he knew that he would walk into the future on bleeding feet.

"You think Galloway will do anything?" Joop asked.

"He's foreign enough to actually accomplish something. He is completely ignorant of his audience."

Joop nodded agreement. "That might be a good thing."

"As long as he's here," Spierdijk qualified, "he might keep them from making money out of the misery he is trying to relieve."

"Let's hope he stays for a while."

Joop knew there was more than shared grumbling to this meeting, so he motioned to a bench facing the river. Inviting this new man to a "good sit" was one way of opening his tongue.

"I saw you at the court," Joop aid.

"That was a pleasant surprise. Van Meegeren timed it perfectly."

"We have him in custody. We'll get to the bottom of his little games."

Spierdijk fumbled with his satchel, as if deciding to release whatever it hid. Joop saw the gesture and let him settle into whatever it was he was up to.

"So, you're not a fan of our famous artist," Joop commented.

"I have to admit he's good at what he does."

"You mean he's a good painter?" Joop prodded.

"I mean the man could feed us horse turds and we'd thank him for the tasty figs."

Joop laughed at the pleasantries and waited for Spierdijk to open his mind.

"You know they are as bad as the Germans."

"Who?" Joop asked.

"Our illustrious and so respected civil servants."

"The ones we've just left?"

"And the rest of them."

The bitterness oozed through Spierdijk's words like rancid grease, but there was also the hint of a challenge. There was no denying that the Dutch who could not escape had worked for the Germans, but there must have been thousands of them.

"What can we do?" Joop shrugged.

"You are now working to bring the collaborators to justice."

"I am working to find the money that was stolen from us."

"Money can be returned. What about the lives that were stolen?" Spierdijk demanded.

"There will be trials. The guilty will be brought to justice," Joop assured him.

"By their own accomplices?"

"You're talking about van Meegeren?"

"No."

Spierdijk petted the satchel, but hesitated with his fingers on the clasp. Joop looked ahead, willing him to open it. He could sense Spierdijk's need to confide after years of battling with mistrust, for Joop had shared his life of well-honed suspicion. "Show me," Joop ordered.

Spierdijk's fist clutched the satchel, but then he suddenly pressed the clasp and drew back the flap. Joop leaned his body closer to see the paper half peeking out of the worn leather. It was clearly a map, but he waited for Spierdijk to enlighten him.

"Do you recognize anything?" he asked as he passed the folded paper to Joop.

"It's Amsterdam."

"Look closer."

Joop squinted at the Amstel river running through the center of the fold before his nose. Spierdijk offered the map and commanded, "Open it."

Joop peeled back the next fold to reveal the east side of the river. He looked up and gazed over the map at the same streets which the map represented. His eyes narrowed to the empty houses over the river, as if conjuring the departed and the forgotten. He raised and lowered his face between the paper and the distant scene, until the map merged with the view.

"What is it?" Spierdijk demanded as if testing Joop.

"It's the Jewish Quarter."

Black dots filled the spaces between the river and the square on the map. They peppered the entire area across the Waterlooplein.

"Now you will tell me what these black spots mean," Joop demanded.

"Each little dot represents ten Jews. The letters and numbers are a key to lists of addresses. This map tells you how many Jews lived in each section of the city."

"Who else has seen this?"

"I showed it to the Canadians."

"What did they say?" Joop asked.

"They asked what a razzia was, so I explained how the Germans used this map to round up the Jews."

"They understood?"

Spierdijk's face was struggling with the truth. "They seemed to understand a razzia as herding cattle. You know, like cowboys."

"How could they understand?" Joop said. "Their cowboys are in the movies. Ours round up people on the streets."

"Unfold it, please." Spierdijk said.

Joop obeyed, slowly, until the map lay fully open across his knees. He read the date, "May 1941." The title proclaimed, "Prepared by the Bureau of Statistics for Greater Amsterdam." The legends, titles, and dates were in Dutch.

"The map is the proof that our own civil servants led the lambs to the slaughter," Spierdijk said.

"When you touch this," Joop sighed, "you don't need long explanations."

"Now you see?"

"As clear as the day."

They looked at the cloud enveloping the palace and rolling over the river.

"Clearer," Spierdijk whispered.

Joop nodded his sad agreement. Spierdijk's fingers rummaged in his satchel for another tube of dry comfort, hoping that his last cigarette would bring an exhausted silence. Joop turned away to see the palace behind them. The feet of Atlas clung to the building's roof, and Joop hoped the statue would not falter under the weight of a world turned upside-down.

Chapter 18

Gallery

Bobo stood before the canvas resting his hands on his hips. The black diagonals still shot from the four corners to the center. The unfocused eyes still stared over the twisted line of the nose. He scowled at the two smudges of chrome yellow van Meegeren had daubed around the eyes, the sum of two days' work. The rest of the canvas was as virgin as when Bobo had first prepared the ground. Bobo jammed his thumb into the bowl of his cold pipe and grunted, "Looks like he's been pissing in snow."

He twisted his thumb over the ridges lining the sides of the bowl, feeling the dottle of dank tobacco. He squinted and noticed a spray of black dots below the eyes. They looked like the footprints of a drunken spider, staggering down the canvas. He blew his contempt through his pipe, and the ashes splattered his thumb and forefinger. He turned his back upon the master's work and examined the table littered with splayed brushes, crumpled rags, clean mixing bowls, and a pristine palette. He picked up a small case from the table and caressed the worn grain of the leather.

The little wallet always gave him a sense of wonder, for the thing was a miracle. His thumb snapped open the clasp at the back, and he smiled down at the name "Kardon" engraved in the white metal. He pulled back the lens clasp and gently removed the cover, as if he were helping an old and too soon feeble friend out of his coat. His thumb nudged the inscribed ring around the lens, as he sucked on his pipe stem. He didn't have to look at the numbers to know the focal settings, but just holding the camera brought back the day two years ago, when Joop appeared with this amazing comrade.

The bell over the shop door had clanged its annoyance, so Bobo knew it was Joop. A particularly proud smile was plastered over Joop's face when he placed the camera into Bobo's hands with a peremptory "Here." Bobo had examined his own image distorted through the exquisite lens, and with one turn of his palm, it separated from the body. His thumb touched a catch, and the bottom of the camera fell into his palm. The film reservoir was cleverly designed to spring open with one hand. "Where did you get this?" he demanded gruffly.

"There was a delivery."

That was all Bobo needed to know. Joop and Jan had spent an anxious night out on the polder, their ears straining for the sound of the engine coming in low. Bobo could imagine them spread out, aiming their flashlights at the rumbling clouds and waiting for the parachute to mushroom. They would have rushed the field and dragged away the container by its silken shroud before the thrum of the airplane's engine faded on the trip back to England.

The Germans had confiscated every camera in Holland, so they could take their own holiday pictures in the East. A German Leica was now rarer "than an honest woman in a brothel." The camera Joop gave him was an improved American copy of a Leica, so Bobo had joked that it was "our Yankee whore." Joop told him to file off the words "Made in the USA," but Bobo lovingly fingered the name "Kardon" and said, "Why? Just having this is a death sentence. We may as well be good advertising while they shoot us." So the camera kept its blaring name as pristine as the day it left the factory in Brooklyn. For two years, the Kardon had been his weapon of choice, but now it was returned to civilian service.

Bobo turned back to the besmirched canvas and held the camera away from his body. He did a little dance, until he was sure he could capture the entire scene. He locked his stance and held his breath, until he heard the assuringly muted click of the shutter. He picked up a pencil and inscribed in his notebook, "Expos. No. 2." He was adding the date when he heard Joop's footsteps behind him.

"So, you are keeping up your record of our artist?" Joop insinuated.

"Not much to record."

Joop scowled at the canvas and turned to the clutter of the painting table. "This is all he's done?"

"Aside from a couple packs of cigarettes and some gin."

"Have you been watching him?"

"Mainly he just sits before the canvas, making a great show of artistic concentration."

"We'll have to light a fire under him."

"Do it outside. This place will explode."

The room full of paints, chemicals, and alcohol had worried Joop, but his guest's cavalier manner of dropping lit butts into ashtrays was his chief concern. He had impressed upon Sergeant de Groot to be attentive to the risks, but there was always the possibility that van Meegeren could end it all with a match. Joop decided to indulge van Meegeren's disgusting habits, but he insisted on the vigilance of the guards. He had coached de Groot to act as the prisoner's room servant and carefully cultivated van Meegeren's delusion of being an honored guest. The prisoner's belief that he was in charge obscured the fact that Joop was in control.

They heard footsteps rising behind them to the accompaniment of a metallic scraping and turned to see de Groot stirring a saucepan of boiling coffee with a fork. De Groot nodded from the balcony, and when Joop asked, "Where did you get that?" he jerked his chin to van Meegeren's bedroom. He didn't wait for Joop's permission to strain the fluid through the fork's tongues into van Meegeren's cup.

Bobo rolled down his shirtsleeves, donned his coat, and clasped the camera into its case.

"You deal with them, unless you're also room service," Bobo chuckled to Joop.

"Where are you going?"

"It's a good day to play the tourist."

He slung the camera case over his shoulder as he walked down the stairs and through the noisy researchers to the street. The door crashed shut behind him, and Bobo welcomed the slight hum of the murky day. He looked over the canal and turned up his collar. The late morning fog had not yet cleared, so this was no day for pictures. Everything would come out too moody, and he had had enough of that.

The cobblestones were slippery, but this only increased his pleasure as he had to step carefully and look at the moist patterns below his feet. He stepped from stone to stone around the little pools that had flooded the holes left by the cobbles ripped from the pavement. Walking home was now a delightful game, for there was no reason to hurry. He wondered if these same stones held their memories of Willi's running feet fleeing from the fire.

Such an odd duck was Willi. Most homos hid their sin, but Willi's love for men had neither shame nor pride. It was nothing special to him, and Bobo had learned that there was so much more about the man to admire than to condemn.

Years before, he had joked to Willi that the Occupation had brought so many good looking men to Holland. Willi had laughed and confessed, "Why do you think the Germans invaded? They wanted some new acquaintances." Bobo heard the contempt bubble through Willi's laughter.

Willi and his artistic friends had issued proclamations when they realized that the deportations of the Jews were just murder in disguise. They called themselves "The Free Artists" and organized secret exhibitions and clandestine concerts inspiring their audiences to a feeble courage. They painted murals on the walls where their comrades had been shot. One of their best tricks was to pose as begging street musicians, so they could spy on the movements of the Gestapo. A coin tossed at the feet of a corner violinist would clink in the coffers of defiance. They challenged their countrymen to rise against the deportation orders and appealed in the name of human dignity to hide, shelter, and feed the Jews. Their insistent demands on the Dutch conscience were met with the whispered offers of trembling volunteers.

When the Kardon had dropped from the heavens, Bobo had shared the wonder with Willi and he immediately knew what to do. The camera would be their silent witness long after their voices were strangled. They practiced for days, passing the camera to each other on the run, so that Willie could take a picture, toss the camera to Bobo, and run away. Outraged victims would chase after the sprightly young man and ignore the old fellow shuffling past them. They became as adept at taking snapshots in public, as if they were prosperous pick-pockets plying their trade through Dam Square. Willi even had the gall to lure a

German officer into a public toilet, where Bobo lurked with the Kardon to capture shaky images of their pleasures. They calculated that one such photo was the ransom of ten Dutch lives. "There has always been a most profitable return on blackmail," Willi had boasted, and Bobo chuckled venomously.

Willi passed the Kardon to Jack van Heel, who taught himself to take pictures around corners. From a second story apartment on Albrecht Durerstraat, Jack caught the whole scene of a razzia with one stretch of his arm through the open window. It was no more than three seconds, but there was urgency in Jack's speed because the flat belonged to his uncle. Bobo had developed the film before the Jews were packed off to Westerbork, but too late to stop their train to the East. Willi had consoled him with the assurance that, "At least someone will know what has been done."

Bobo shrugged his shoulders deeper into his collar and his eyes followed the eddies in the canal water. They gurgled around the bridge supports and their spirals seemed to be dragged behind a solitary boat. A man leaned against the tiller at a lazy angle and spit over the side. Bobo watched the graceful white arc dive into the water. It seemed that the river was spreading its waves in welcome.

He stopped to look at the Municipal Registry and waited for his memories catch up to him. The building had been repaired, but the bricks above the windows still held their scorch marks. Bobo smiled to think that the windows reminded him of women with too much languid eye shadow over lashes dripping with mascara. They almost winked at him, for Bobo was proud of his small part in Willi's triumph.

He had helped Willi and his gang produce more than eighty thousand false identity papers, so it was nothing out of the ordinary when Joop made his first frightened order for his own counterfeit cards. The Germans got wind of the false papers and started comparing the cards with the master rolls of personal statistics in Amsterdam's Municipal Registry. In the midst of the panic, Willi's answer was simple, blow up the building. Bobo had heard the explosion from three blocks away and poked his head outside the shop door to see a fire truck race past. He had followed the crowd to the blazing windows, and with the light bathing his face, bellowed his joy above the roaring furnace. Bobo looked up to a red storm blowing paper flares over their heads. In one glorious flash, Willi had saved thousands.

A week later, Willi was betrayed and arrested. The Germans were fastidious about the law, so they gave him a lawyer and a trial before shooting him. Willi had carefully instructed his lawyer how to play his part in the farce. It helped the man to cope with the trial. In return for such kindness, the lawyer had promised to pass on Willi's last message, "Tell the world that homos are no less courageous than other people."

Willi and his comrades disappeared into the night and fog. The Gestapo were the masters of silence, so nobody knew of Willi's fate. Much later, Bobo caught faint glimmers of gossip of the executions. They had been shot on the dunes past Bloemendaal, and Bobo hoped a friendly hand had gripped Willi's last look at the waves.

Bobo turned away from the Registry and quickened his steps along the pavement. He breathed in the canal fog and blew his memories away from his pain. He could feel a slight clicking in his knees and lurched forward until he was able to amble at a more comfortable gait. He dismissed the pain as just old age creeping towards him and wove his way through the crowds back to his shop.

The bell swayed once to his familiar touch on the door, but the dust attacked his nose. For a moment he looked over the barren counter and turned to the display window, opaque to the world outside. He took off his coat and rolled up his sleeves with a more determined air than when he awoke in the morning. He had reached his limit. He could mumble "Enough," but complaining never did much good.

From the back room where he slept, he retrieved a broom, and attacked the cobwebs connecting the lights on the ceiling. Even if they didn't work, he would clean the shades so the bulbs would not ignite the dirt at their next lighting. He swung the broom at a winter's neglect and cut swathes through the crumpled papers littering the floor. Soon he had to open the front door just to breathe without sneezing.

He leaned the broom beside the door and pinched a few strands of tobacco into his pipe. He stepped onto the raised platform which was the display area of the storefront window. The condensation dripped down the glass. It was so typical of a cloudy noon-day in Amsterdam. The windows could never gather enough heat, so they would only clear when the west winds blew the clouds over the river and onto the Ijsselmeer.

He flared a match at the bowl and blew the smoke at the window. A dry island formed on the glass and a moist runnel flowed to the bottom sill. He sucked in another puff and a second circle appeared on the glass. Soon the water was running from island to island down the window, and Bobo could see the shapes of people walking on the sidewalk. They trundled through the mist, ignoring the window because there was really nothing to buy.

He turned, stepped painfully down onto the floor and shuffled through the litter to the back room. His hands rummaged in an old box full of large envelopes. Each held a fistful of photos and he searched through them looking for one he knew so well and had hidden so carefully. Lurking in a pile of posing sports teams, he found the portrait of a young man dressed in a smart suit with a clean shirt and a crisp collar. He placed the photo on the counter and gazed at it just long enough to make his decision. In a drawer he found the remnants of a bottle of India ink and a broad-nibbed pen. Slowly he etched the letters onto the bottom of the photo until he was assured that anybody looking through the shop window could read his calligraphy, "Willem Johan Cornelis Arondeus, July 1, 1943."

He dragged an easel to the platform where once his goods drew curious eyes, and placed Willi's photo on the easel. He puffed the bowl into a weak ember and stood in the door. The rhythm of the street was a relief after the silence of the shop, so Bobo leaned against the door frame watching the parade from where-to-where he did not care. He watched to see if anybody noticed the solitary picture of a man smiling back at them.

Chapter 19

Tunnel

Jan thumped down the corridor, carrying a bucket, and slopping water in step with his feet.

Liese looked at the water flooding towards her and sighed, "This floor needs a good soaking."

The tunnel between the yard and the street had not been cleaned for years. Liese was determined to attack its filth with a fistful of rags, a box of lye soap from Boudreau's carton of smelly delights, and a tired old brush. Jan had dropped by to see how Sarah and the Princess were doing, so Liese commandeered him for the scrubbing.

They had started at the end of the corridor closest to the yard and were determined to work their way to the entrance to the street. They could push the rancid water before them to the gutter so it would not ebb back to their yard. Liese knelt in the soapy puddle, her arm carving a figure-eight through the muck with the brush. Her nose confirmed her suspicion that the hallway had been used as a public toilet, and she vowed not to rest until they poured the last bucket into the street.

Jan placed the pail beside her with a soggy thump, and Liese rested on her haunches to look up to him. "Who started it? The Old One or the Young One?"

"The Old One," Jan explained with a boyish grin.

"Just like that, she attacked her?"

"No. They eased into it. They were pestering van Meegeren for money."

"Poor man," Liese commiserated with a giggle, "he can't even escape his women in prison."

"You'd think that was one of the good things about being in jail, but iron bars can not hold Mrs. van Meegeren."

"I thought you said they were divorced?"

"They are, but they're like an old couple. You know, the kind that hate each other so much they keep coming back for more."

Liese nodded knowingly and cocked her head into a question. "And the new one?"

"She's not that new," Jan added. "The Old One is all gray-brown hair and bulges. She has legs like a chicken. The Young One, he calls her Kootje, she has legs like a piano. Strong too. She could pull a plough."

"They were fighting over money?" Liese asked.

"The Old One wanted money for a closet. Can you believe it?"

"She needs a larder?"

"No," Jan guffawed. "For her shoes. She needs a special room their big house for all her shoes. You know how much she wants?"

"I have no idea what such a thing would cost."

"Over one thousand guilders."

Liese stopped in mid scrub, and the brush dripped in her hand. "For that, she could buy a whole house," she speculated.

"That's just for the carpenter and the wood," Jan added.

Liese shook her head, and her eyes shot a challenge at Jan's tale. "And this wood costs a thousand guilders?"

"Not just any old wood," he assured her. "She demands that everything in this special room be made of cedar wood."

"Why that wood?" Liese asked. "She's not doing it herself."

"Maybe her feet smell," Jan laughed.

Liese rose and picked up the box of Borax. Jan watched her sprinkle the powder ahead of them onto the floor and stood ready with his bucket.

"So they just started hammering away. Just like that?" Liese asked.

Jan cast the water upon the curling linoleum, and they watched the powder dissolve into a spreading pool of foam.

"Not immediately," he said. "They were both pestering Han for the money."

"Han?"

"That's what de Groot and the guards call him now."

"That's very neighborly."

"Not so his women," Jan explained. "He shrugged his shoulders and was about to say something when the Old One got so mad she threw a can of turpentine at him."

"Was he hurt?"

"He ducked," Jan added, "but the the canvas looks like an old diaper."

"It's so childish."

"They're a bit like that, but you can't spank them."

"I'd take this brush to them," Liese admitted.

"You'd have to separate them first. They went at each other like mating cats."

"The man and his wife?"

"The old wife and the new girl."

"That's bad trouble," Liese said.

"They were clawing and scratching." Jan was eager for the punch-line. "The Young One pulled a fistful of greasy hair out of the Old One. The Old One bit the Young One, and then they were going for the throat, rolling around on the floor."

"What was van Meegeren doing?"

"He lit a cigarette."

"He didn't stop them?"

"De Groot grabbed the Old One and dragged her down the stairs. I held onto the Young One, until she stopped cursing."

"That's when you found out she could pull a plough," Liese added with a sly smile.

"She's very... healthy."

They chortled at the antics of the van Meegeren menagerie and their laughter lightened their work. They were half-way down the tunnel, following the retreating brown tide toward the street, but the most stubborn stains were still ahead of them.

"It all sounds like something out of those cinema magazines," Liese suggested.

"I suppose they're our very own Hollywood, right here in Holland."

"I can't see Clarke Gable letting a woman throw shit at him," Liese pronounced.

"Maybe that's the way we do it," Jan thought aloud. "It was really funny. Han just shrugged it all off as if it happened every day."

"Hm," Liese speculated. "Probably does."

Liese sloshed water and Borax over a plateau of old dirt and waited for the liquid to soften the mound. She nudged it with the blunt end of her brush and grains of crumbling earth collapsed onto the floor. "Did she expect him to give her the money right away?" she asked.

"You wouldn't believe all the money that's out there."

She looked up eager for more, "Joop says he is very rich." Jan ground his boot into the mud to loosen it for her. "Not just rich. Clever."

He waited for Liese's ears to perk up with curiosity, and explained. "He told everybody he'd won the French Lottery and then bought houses all over Amsterdam."

"Houses?"

"All sorts of them." Jan added. "We have been following all the papers. Leases, contracts, even rent books, and there are as many as one hundred and fifty properties he's got his money in. Doesn't matter if it's a palace or a row of slums. They pay rents, so it's all very legal.

"But even his money won't last with all that?"

"That's just it," Jan said and she caught the disbelief in his voice. "When people asked about his money, he told them he won the lottery a second time."

"And they believed him?" Liese gasped.

"Yes. He was paying all their bills and invited them to fancy parties, so they were all very happy to believe anything he told them."

"I guess when you want the presents, you have to believe in Santa Claus," Liese reflected.

"He was a very good Santa," Jan complimented. "Lots of people sat on his knee."

Liese leaned over the the sodden ripples and pushed the brush forward a few more inches. She attacked a foul smelling blotch, but she hadn't the strength to dislodge whatever was encrusted before her. A pattern of green and grey swirls emerged through the water, so she knew she had scrubbed down to the design of the linoleum.

She tilted her head to examine the stubborn splodge and hoped it was dried chewing gum. If she had a scraper, she could lift the scab from the flooring and sweep it away, but any such handy tool was lying useless in the kitchen in Emst. She bathed the blot in chemical bubbles and left it to soak. Jan offered to find a broom, and she was glad to send him on his errand, so she could think over what he had told her.

She shook her head at the thought of such people who had everything, but were fighting over nothing. All that money, just to make shelves for her shoes. Liese had thought of finding a few seeds to grow in a can on the window, but that would be too permanent for this place. She wanted to be gone from the back alley rooms well before anything could flower.

These rooms had been good for them. She was proud that Joop had spent so much care in finding a safe place where they could hide and from which they could easily escape any razzia that fell upon them. There were so many ways out through the surrounding buildings that she felt the comfort of a furry animal, secure in its burrow. The two rooms and the sagging shed had served them well, but it was time to leave the city. She had grown to hate the pressure of so many people. They would go home, but they would not bring danger with them. She hoped they would leave before the weeds sprouted in the yard.

She laughed to think how glad she was that they were not rich. Their lives were solid and bound together by their few necessities. Van Meegeren and his women would never be happy if they had all the money in the world. One thousand guilders. If she and Joop had such wealth, they would not fight over a cupboard, no matter how fancy. No. There would be new clothes to replace the tatters they now wore. Simple furniture to sit around a new radio would be enough for them. But most of the money would be hidden, waiting for a day when there was no work and little hope. But these big people, they could not be happy in a palace. Maybe they really were like the people in the moving pictures. Maybe such people needed paintings and big parties with food that would hardly last an hour but would cost a week's rent.

Liese could not understand such riches and was thankful that she could not. "If that's what they do with the money, let them keep it," she mused. She remembered a joke she heard in Emst, "God does not think very highly of money. Just look at the people he gives it to." Everybody in the the village who could still laugh had howled at the jest, but Liese mulled over the thought that there was a type of happiness which could not be bought.

She scraped away at the floor and composed a list of her joys. Joop and Sarah were at the top. Without them, there would be neither laughter nor the comforts of loving and being loved. "Yes," she thought, "That's all." But other things loitered in her memory, waiting their place in her list. Walking the canal with Sarah and smelling the rushes peeping out of the water, was not something they could have here. The city smelled of a winter's unwashed bodies, and every breeze blew more worries into each head.

She gazed long at the little bubbles skating over the floor and giggled at the little blue domes. "It's like the whole floor wants to blow soap through a pipe." She remembered Joop pulling his ears forward to make Sarah laugh in the bath. He made sounds like a monkey and blew the suds through his fingers to wash her face. That was something more for her list. It did not cost a cent, but such memories would light them through their lives.

Her knees ached and the red blotches on her legs protested the chemical assault. The grimy water drenched her skirt, and she thought how nice it would be to have a new house dress with a linen apron. Something strong, so she could keep clean while doing the housework. She slumped back for a moment joking to herself, "Good thing I don't ask for much."

Jan clattered down the corridor and proudly presented an old broom he had found in the shed. It was really a bundle of twigs wrapped around a stick with old twine, but it was still strong. He pushed the broom into the mire and soon the blunt points of the twigs cut a cleaner channel through the mire. Pieces of moldy earth crumbled before him, and Liese scoured a yellow scab from the floor. She felt the bile rise in her throat when she saw hairs tangled in the bristles of her brush. Jan felt her disgust and commanded, "I'll sweep the rest."

She was glad to stand at the opening to the street and breathe deeply. Jan cast another pail of water and swung the broom, as if he were scything through weeds. Slowly he approached her, and she could see little stones and flakes of dull amber in the wake of his broom. He swept past her and pushed the noxious tide into the gutter. He stood resting on his broom on the sidewalk, and they watched the stream disappear into a drain hole.

"You've done so much," she praised. "Thank you."

"At least it smells better."

They gazed along the corridor, and when they could see sunlight blinking back at them, shared their satisfaction of work well done. The walls awaited their efforts, but for now, they could walk home without trailing too much dirt behind them. She looked at the steps connecting the corridor with the sidewalk and said, "One more bucket and I can finish the stoop."

She watched him march down the corridor, the walls echoing the jaunty beat of his heels. "It will take a few more cleanings, but we'll get it done," she called after him, but he had already disappeared into the distant light.

Three steps mounted from the pavement to her feet at the corridor's floor. Liese knelt and rubbed her thumb through the slimy film until she could see the steps were tiled with a blue glaze. Jan returned with the bucket, and she scooped up enough clean water with her brush to douse the bricks. With each scrubbing, she made a little cascade that seeped from step to step to the gutter. Liese grinned to see the brightness of the tiles return.

She rung out the last of the old rags and polished the bricks until her own face smiled back at her. White puffs danced behind her reflection, and she turned to look at the patch of lighter blue above the roofs. It was good to sit on the steps and look up. The clouds blew to the east and they left an azure trail behind them. In an hour or two, they would be over Emst, but now she had another entry for her list. Clouds.

Silent and happy just to float. Now was their time to have hopes that were longer than a day. For years, they had found only the shortest joys because they never knew if they would have another day. Now, all that was finished. It would take some effort for all of them to catch this new hope. The clouds told her that there would be a happiness that would fill their long tomorrows.

Chapter 20

Ducking and Diving

Joop smiled to see the artist actually working. Van Meegeren gripped a wide brush and pushed a slurry of brown and yellow over the top of the canvas. He plastered over the dripping stains where his wife's temper had befouled the eyes and nose. The swishing of the bristles alternated with the scraping of the palette knife to fill the studio and Joop relaxed under van Meegeren's heavy breathing. Sometimes the master's breath stank like a rotten fireplace bellows, but today there was only the wheezing of productive work. Joop's curiosity concentrated on van Meegeren's thrusting as he watched the colors seep into the canvas.

"What's that going to be?" he asked.

"It's going to be nothing, other than burnt sienna and a little chrome yellow," van Meegeren pronounced, "but people will think it is a wall."

Van Meegeren grabbed a broad-headed brush that reminded Joop of a chisel, and dabbed it into the yellow on his palette. He smelled the brush before teasing the colors into a mellow depth. The outline of a window appeared before Joop's eyes. Van Meegeren's sharp plunges pulled shapes out of the muddy paint. Joop followed van Meegeren's hand filling the spaces between the lines criss-crossing the canvas. The brown puddles swirled into a murky cloud, leaving a brilliant white emptiness around the eyes and nose. It all happened so quickly.

Joop looked down at de Groot, sitting guard on his chair, armed with another cup of tea. De Groot whispered,

"It's like watching a magician." Van Meegeren let out a satisfied sigh, and they looked up to watch him drag his brush over a bar of soap. He worked the soap into the bristles and pressed the paint out with his thumb and forefinger. Van Meegeren thoughtfully swirled the brush in a beaker of water, preoccupied with his next attack on the voids before him. Joop quietly left the studio, careful not to break the concentration.

He stood on the landing, savoring the calm between the creation behind him and the hum of shuffling papers below him. The Flight Control Bureau had grown to fill the two drawing rooms on the first floor. It was now a factory processing the mountain of documents that were the memory of the Occupation.

The Ministry of Finance had set up their own investigation. The Ministry was actually a few old cabinet ministers who had been waiting in England and reminding anyone who would listen that they were the Netherlands Government in Exile. When they returned, they grasped collaboration by the throats and the newspaper headlines. They had planned to set up offices in the old Goudstikker Gallery but hadn't counted on Joop's audacity. They could not control someone who had the cheek to just commandeer their own offices on the very day of liberation. Joop had waved his commission from the Irene Brigade in their faces and told the bureaucrats that they could use the bottom rooms of the building, and then placed Jan at the foot of the stairs, casually fingering a Sten gun. The researchers of the Ministry never crossed the line and Joop's old network were now working closely with the minions of the government, when they were not eyeing daggers at one another.

Joop quickly realized that the Ministry's eagerness to find Goudstikker's hoard of paintings might have something to do with the fact that Goudstikker was very conveniently dead and his widow was out of Dutch jurisdiction. The Ministry of Finance had carte blanche to look into anything, without fear of exposure. Finding collaborators was the perfect hiding place for a collaborator.

The appearance of van der Vegen was a minor glitch, but they were soon calling each other by their first names. Giles van der Vegen was charged by the Ministry with compiling a list of names of the most heinous collaborators, and Joop was commanded to work closely with this representative of the Ministry. Van de Vegen praised Joop's service in the Resistance, assuring him that it was an honor to work with such a hero. Joop graciously accepted the compliments to grease the palms of this man who was so willing to be a friend. Such admirers were to be cast beyond the circle of enemies, for Joop did not believe that you keep your friends close and your enemies closer. Enemies were best viewed over open gunsights. Giles was relieved to have Joop on his side and never questioned that he did ten times more for Joop than Joop did for him. Joop knew that Giles would spread butter over any crust Joop threw his way. The friendship was most beneficial.

"Good Morning, Giles. I see you are busy bright and early."

"Ah, Joop. There is so much work," van der Vegen sighed.

"Yes. It will take years to get to the bottom of this."

"If ever."

"In the meantime, we all have work to do."

The hairs on Joop's ears bristled. People joked about the "flaps on the side of his head," but such twitching carried a warning. Something in van der Vegen's voice was perturbing. The man would kiss any ass for advantage or protection, but Joop was offering neither today. Something else was triggering this camaraderie, but it was just out of Joop's grasp.

He walked into the main room to see Jan rifling through another crate of documents. "What's all this?" he asked.

"Dutch Nazi Party Offices. Some of their account books. There must be a ton of it."

"Where's the rest of the ton?"

"Someone in the Justice Department got there first," Jan said. "They were throwing bundles into a truck."

"Any idea what they have?"

"I don't even know what we have," Jan confessed.

Joop pulled out a sheaf of accounts. "It's all a jumble."

"They were pretty messy when they went into the HQ."

For a moment Joop pondered why the investigators of the Department of Justice did not take more care with what could be their main evidence to present before a judge. Joop sensed that this mess of papers was somehow connected with van der Vegen's fawning.

"Friendly Giles must think we have something valuable," Joop said.

Joop picked up a bent ledger book. It was stained and the pages had dried. They crackled when he opened it. "Looks like someone turned a hose on this," he speculated to Jan. He tossed the book back onto the pile. Jan glowered at the pile and said, "We have something they want. Whatever it is."

"You keep digging through this," Joop ordered, and Jan caught the edge in his voice. Joop turned and walked away from Jan's pile, his heels echoing on the marble. He pushed open the door and strode down the steps to the street.

He pulled down his collar to let out some of his annoyance. The hairs on his neck twitched, so he kept a steady pace with his fists in his raincoat pockets. Whatever was behind him was getting closer, and just when he was about to twist back into an attack, the voice cut through his coiled violence. "It's only a few kilometers." Joop turned to see Dirk Kragt's amused face, just as it looked two years ago.

"You're a very easy man to find these days," Dirk admonished.

"Been in town long?" Joop quipped.

"Just long enough to want to leave."

"Let's go home. Liese will be thrilled to see you."

"How is the Little One?"

"Not so little now. She tells me what to do," Joop said.

"Smart girl. She must take after her mother."

They walked in step along the canal. Dirk always just appeared and they took up wherever they had left off at their last meeting. Joop joked to himself that if they were talking about ice cream and Dirk vanished for ten years, his first words would be, "I like vanilla best."

Joop laughed to himself as he always did, whenever he accepted the plain truth that the most reliable man in the Resistance was Captain Dirk Kragt, a British espionage agent. He gulped the air and enjoyed his time with one of the few people he completely trusted. After all the hints and suggestions of the morning at work, it was a relief to ask a direct question, knowing that he would get an equally straight answer. "Just what are you doing here?" Joop demanded with mock authority.

"I'm getting demobbed."

"So soon?"

"Seems they don't need any more spies now that the war is over."

Joop joked that the government would have plenty of use for Dirk's skills.

"I see you have a job, Lieutenant Piller."

"Yes. I'm quite respectable."

"Pay anything?"

"We're getting fistfuls of ration coupons, until they can find money for a regular salary."

"So, you're rich."

"Keeps the wolf from the door."

"Even better when the wolf is living upstairs."

Joop enjoyed Dirk's banter and their laughter spiraled between them like soaring and diving birds. Dirk seemed to know where they were going, and Joop just accepted that Dirk knew much more than he ever let on.

They had been comrades for two years, ever since the day Dirk Kragt knocked on their door in Emst, as casual as if he were selling lottery tickets. Nobody would have guessed that Kragt was running escape routes for downed Allied airmen. Nobody, except Joop. The local gossips spread the tale that Kragt was an *Englandvarter*, who had escaped across the North Sea to continue the fight. When he first appeared at their door, all Liese said was, "Can I have your parachute? I want to make some stockings." Dirk collapsed into a bundle of laughs, confident that Joop's woman was as cheeky as he had hoped. She gave him some tea and they gulped down pots and plotted the destruction of the Third Reich.

"Does Liese know I'm here?" Dirk asked.

"Nobody knows where you are."

"That's the way I like it."

Joop stopped at the opening to their home and waited for Dirk to realize he had stopped. Dirk retraced three unthinking steps and followed Joop through the tunnel and into the yard. He looked at the tiny house and shed, scanned the surrounding walls and roofs, and said, "Good choice." Dirk had always been impressed with Joop's ability to see possible danger and to find the greatest safety with the fewest risks. They stepped through the door into the kitchen, and Liese flew at Dirk throwing her arms around his tight shoulders. She spluttered accusations about disappearing and chastised him with the towel she was using to dry the dishes.

"I sent word through Jan just after the Liberation," Dirk said.

"All we got was, 'Dirk's alive,'" Joop grumbled.

"That was enough," Liese assured him.

Sarah heard the commotion and rushed out to charge at Uncle Dirk. She squawked her usual demand, "What did you bring me?" Liese refused to chastise the child because they all wondered the same thing. Dirk never appeared empty handed. He sat on a chair and commanded, "Close your eyes and put out your hands." Sarah obeyed with one hand and a squint just tight enough to convince the grown-ups that she was not peeking. "I said 'hands' and close those eyes," Dirk insisted. He let Sarah's anticipation grow until she bounced in frustration. She felt something big rest over her hands and forearms, but waited for the release. Dirk whispered, "Open your eyes," and she danced around the kitchen waving a coloring book over her head.

Joop and Liese reminded her, "Now what do you say?" and Sarah showered Dirk with thanks and kisses. He dodged the child's attentions and told her, "You have to save the kisses until you get all the presents." He drew a small bag from his raincoat pocket and gently placed it in her shaking hand. When she opened the bag, Joop was touched that Dirk would get the coloring book but also remember to find the colored pencils so essential to the gift. If there were no pencils, the book would been a cruel disappointment. The colors and the lines captivated Sarah, and in the silence of complete absorption, she was lost in the wonderment of blue rabbits and pink horses. Liese turned to Dirk. "So what are you doing in the big village?"

"Well, I had these presents and couldn't think of anybody I'd rather give them to," Dirk confessed and pulled a white silk scarf from his pocket.

"So, you think a present is going to forgive you for not letting us know if you were alive or dead?"

"Yes."

They immediately recognized the strip of white they had hung from the clothes line in Emst, the warning sign that Dirk was to stay away until it disappeared. Liese poured water from the protesting sink tap and Dirk exclaimed, "So, the water is finally working."

"A month ago. Now we actually have gas."

She placed the pot on the stove ring, struck a match, and watched the blue halo flare around the water pot.

"Tea?"

"Yes," he answered eagerly. "I can't stand what they're calling coffee in the Jordaan."

Joop drew two more chairs to the table and Liese scalded tea leaves in the pot. She set three cups before them and waited for the brew to steep.

Dirk inhaled the fumes, as if gulping draughts from distant hills, and they waited for him to part with whatever was troubling him. "I need your help."

"Can I drive?" Liese begged.

"Not that type of help," Dirk joked. "I need your memories."

"You're too young for dementia," Joop jibed.

"I have to make a report on our activities for the British."

"Why the rush?"

"They won't give me a ticket to Canada, if I don't give them the report."

"So what's the problem?" Liese asked.

"I need to get some facts. You know, the right kind of facts."

"Right." Joop agreed. "The facts that make them look good."

"There's no fooling you."

"Especially when we're all fooling together," Liese said.

They spent the evening laughing at the adventures that could have killed them. Raiding German warehouses for supplies was so mundane, they didn't mention it in the list Dirk was creating in his notepad.

"They are more interested in the soldiers we got out of Arnhem."

"Why not the pilots we smuggled through the lines?" Joop asked with suspicious curiosity.

"I guess they already know about them. They have been asking me about the high ranking officers."

"But we took almost two hundred through the German lines," Liese said.

"That's the soldiers, the ones who escaped."

"The first night," Joop remembered. "We took about forty of them to the rendezvous point."

"We got them through from house to house," Liese recalled, "but I can't remember the houses."

"The places aren't important. I just have to put in the numbers of the rescued."

"Only six the next night."

Who was that guy in the car?" Dirk asked.

"He was so frightened," Liese recalled.

"He still got back." Joop added. "Strange name, even for a Britisher."

"That was General Hackett," Dirk said.

"I remember him," Liese added.

"How can we forget a man forcing himself to not scream when he was holding the stitches keeping his guts in." Joop said, unable to conceal his admiration.

"We all thought he was dead, at least twice," Liese said.

"We called him Resurrection Johnny," Dirk remembered.

"Because he just kept dying and rising again," Joop said.

Dirk scratched some more notes into his pad, and looked up to Joop. "That's when you came with the car."

"It was really comfortable," Liese said

"Yes, it was," Joop smiled. "I'd forgotten."

One by one, the three of them added each memory of the nights they had rescued so many paratroopers from the shambles that was the battle of Arnhem.

"Who was that other guy in the car?" Dirk asked.

"He was pretty scared too," Liese said.

After another sip of his cold tea, Joop blurted. "Warrack."

"That's the one, I think he was a colonel." Dirk scribbled.

"The other had a name that sounded German. It was two names put together."

"Lipman," nodded Joop.

"Kessel," added Liese.

"Lipman-Kessel," Dirk wrote. "Let's call him a captain. They can fix it."

"If he's still alive."

"They're very good at keeping track when you're dead," Dirk said. "Not so much when you're still breathing."

"Without us, there would be a lot less breathing." Liese crowed.

Dirk tossed his pad and pencil onto the table. "And there would be many more still breathing if they had believed us."

"That's the hardest part."

"So senseless," Liese almost wept.

They let Dirk's anger bubble to the brim, for they sensed he needed to talk about his reluctant part in the catastrophe. "We told the British that half the agents they sent into Holland were working for the Germans."

"When did you know?" Liese asked.

"At the training camp in England. There were two Dutch. Oh they were so enthusiastic, so patriotic. They made me suspicious, but there was nothing I could do about a feeling."

Dirk looked at Joop, as if to confess something they already knew. "I noticed there were more Dutch than Belgians, as if they were trying to replace losses. If so many were being captured, they had to be working for the Germans. The British just kept sending more agents. I think they filled up the Gestapo quotas better than the Gestapo could do."

"We told them the Germans had moved two whole divisions of tanks into Arnhem and what did they do?" Joop's face was stone.

"Dropped an army out of the planes," Dirk accused, "right unto the tops of those German tanks."

"They wouldn't listen to reason."

"Worse."

"What worse than that?" Liese asked.

"We sent them the map coordinates," Dirk explained, "and one of their photographing planes flew over Arnhem. They had the pictures before their eyes, and they still sent in their paratroops. They jumped into certain death."

"What's worse than not listening to reason?" Dirk stared at Liese. "Ignoring proof."

They sat mourning the loss of so many people sacrificed to the arrogance that is deaf to anything it doesn't want to hear. Joop and Liese had ferried hundreds of British soldiers and Allied pilots through the German lines to safety, trusting only to what was before their eyes. After Arnhem, they guided the damned and the forgotten over the rivers of eastern Holland to friends who would take them home. They were proud of their accomplishments, but wise enough to remain silent. They sensed there was more to this visit than just Dirk's report. They knew it was useless to force the man to talk, so they waited for him to speak in his own time and in his own way.

Dirk stood up with a screech of the chair and stepped to the door of the sleeping room. He leaned against the jamb watching Sarah carve colors into her book. "You like it?" he asked, slightly nervous, as if hoping for another hug. Sarah held the book over her head and commanded, "Look!" He stepped to the pile of warm coats in which she nestled and examined her composition of a bear cub. "What's that?" he asked, pointing to the mass of green she had drawn behind the bear. "That's the trees," she proudly explained. She told him a story about the little bear who got lost and then scraped the pencil point through the trees to a rough rectangle. "And what's that?" he coaxed. Sarah's pencil wandered through the woods to the distant house. "That's home," she said, as if indulging a rather stupid grown-up. Dirk held back his tears and returned to the table with a determined step.

"I can't give you a photo," he admitted, "But I can warn you." He paused until he felt the old trust rising through his heartbeats. "Don't be as stupid as the British."

"The war is over," Joop said.

"The same people will be fighting the peace."

"What are you talking about?" Joop demanded with an edge of exasperation.

"Those same fools who wouldn't listen to us are the same fools who now lead us."

"Fools are everywhere," Joop said.

"These ones are dangerous," Liese said.

They both looked at her because she only used this word for people they should never trust.

"So who are they?" Joop asked.

"You should be asking, 'who are they fighting?'" Dirk advised.

"So?"

"You," Dirk pronounced.

Liese shuddered to hear Dirk say aloud what she had been keeping to herself for so long. She had pieced together questions that led to more questions from all the tales Joop brought home from work. She would not press him, for she would not burden him with even more uncertainty. She had kept her worries to herself, until she felt like a pot forgotten on the stove. She was so grateful when Dirk finally hit Joop with the truth they all knew but feared to speak.

"Joop, you are a great pain in the ass," Dirk complimented.

"That's why I love him," Liese said.

"Before, you were hunting Nazis. Now, you are hunting their friends."

"That's my job," Joop stated.

"Hunting their Dutch friends," Dirk emphasized.

"Collaborators are now the enemy," Joop insisted.

"And you have become the enemy of some of the worst of the collaborators."

Dirk knew that Joop was evading the truth. He would have to be blunt.

"They don't mind a few hangings and shaving the women in the street," Dirk explained. "But the money, their money."

"That's it," Liese said.

"The ones you seek all have friends in high places."

Joop nodded his acceptance. It was a sign for Dirk to continue without fear of hurt. "You sniff too close along the trail and the foxes will turn and attack."

"We survived the Nazis."

"Through our own cunning," Dirk was quick to add. "Remember, you kept us all alive with one piece of paper."

"It was so funny," Liese laughed aloud. "They came for Joop and I showed them the paper and screamed them out of the house. Joop was in the back-house the whole time."

"That was then," Dirk proclaimed.

They sat drinking in the care from each other's eyes. Dirk would talk of cunning and guile, but Liese knew there was something deeper than the game. There was the trust they had accepted and she knew that was all that had lighted them through the terrors of the last two years.

"Now the papers you are seeking will hang the same people who betrayed us," Dirk said slowly.

"So what are we supposed to do?" Liese asked.

"Don't be stupid. Don't be like the British. Believe me. Watch yourself."

"And you?" Joop asked.

"I'm going to Canada, for now. They say Norway is very bright this time of year."

Liese laughed at Dirk making such a long detour to get to a place he thought would be better. It was so like him. He would work out a complicated route that only he could follow. He would lead them all on this chase and the very deviousness of the path confused everybody but himself. It was a long way to Norway, but it was Dirk's way. Liese watched him rummage in his coat pocket, until he pulled out some papers.

"I almost forgot," he said with mock shyness.

He gave them something that looked like a ticket. There was a picture of a naked man running with wings on his feet and his head, carrying a torch. Liese read, "Admit One" aloud, and Dirk explained.

"Our Liberators want to entertain us tomorrow evening."

Joop thumbed through five of the little strips of paper and their laughter cackled to the sky when he told them, "You are all invited to the movies."

Chapter 21

Orpheus

Sarah swung high and threw her feet in the air. She loved it when she could hold onto Mummy and Daddy's hands and swing between them. Joop and Liese savored her squeals of delight and lifted Sarah higher every time she commanded them to, "Do it again!" The crowds on the pavement parted before them, clearing a path for the man and woman and their laughing little monkey.

Sarah's constant curiosity exhausted Liese, but as usual, Joop seemed to have enough strength for everything the day required and the bold demands of their child. Every night he would come home to Sarah's shrieks and play with her until Liese called them for supper. But then they would walk the dusty path around the Crescent Moon where they knew they could always find her and let Sarah exhaust herself with a game of Hide-and-Seek. He called their evening ritual "Turning Off Sarah" and always let her run until she fell into their arms. Joop would carry her into the sleeping room and settle her under the coats. The day was only complete when she would surrender to sleep half-way through her bedtime story. He knew she would finish the tale in her dreams.

But this evening was special. Joop and Liese dangled Sarah as they shuffled along the impatient line to the gleaming portals of the Orpheus theater. Dirk's gift would be Sarah's first motion picture. The lights in the lobby entranced Sarah, and she stood like a votive before the columns of glowing bulbs rising over her head. Joop turned to Bobo and Jan and nodded his admiration for the spectacle of lights. "Our Liberators certainly know how to fix things," he said. Bobo smiled agreement and added, "It's taken two invasions to clean up this place."

The Orpheus was the largest theater in Amsterdam, so the Canadian authorities used it as bait to discover the health of the city. What better way to collect information than by offering free tickets to a movie. But the theaters were wrecked, and the only films were discarded reels of German propaganda. So, General Galloway simply commandeered the Orpheus and found two companies of the Royal Canadian Engineers full of carpenters, house painters, plasterers, glaziers, one very bad-tempered architect, and an overly-fussy interior designer. General Galloway strode onto the stage of the Orpheus, and in his most fatherly voice praised "this extraordinary collection of talent." The soldiers blasted cat-calls, whistles, and laughter at him when he commanded them to "make this shit-hole fit for the public." In ten days, they restored the Orpheus, and the Dutch marveled at the transformation of the notorious flea-pit.

The Royal Canadian Signal Corps installed three movie projectors in the balcony, and the Royal Canadian Dragoons herded five enormous generators into the back stage dressing rooms. When there was enough dependable electricity for reliable lighting, the Royal Canadian Electrical and Mechanical Engineers scaled the walls with assault ladders, and loud speakers blossomed throughout the auditorium. Two hundred volunteers from the Royal Winnipeg Rifles armed to the teeth with rags and cans of Brasso attacked every piece of metal until the foyer and the auditorium gleamed gold. The Royal Twenty-Second Regiment watched all this furious rubbing and dubbed them *Les Aladdins.* They serenaded the entire workforce with the

March of the Seven Dwarves in French. The theatre erupted in whistles at the chorus of "Heigh-ho, Heigh-ho, On rentre du boulot. Pas plus du vin que de beurre au cul, Heigh-ho, Heigh-ho." The Royal Canadian Army Service Corps had driven all the materials for the renovation from the Hague, and when the Royal Canadian Ordnance Corps judged everything safe, the Engineers patched up the bullet holes in the silver screen. Bobo had taken a special interest in this resurrection of something that had always been dead, and Jan had joked that "everything in Canada must be royal." Bobo reminded him that there were a few more Royals in Canada because that's where the Princesses of the Royal Dutch House of Orange had been evacuated.

When they flooded through the theatre doors, it was no surprise when members of the Royal Canadian Army Medical Corps gave every person a handful of vitamins. As they were milling about the lobby someone spoke to them in Dutch wearing a uniform with the badges of the Royal Canadian Red Cross, and told everybody to "please turn over your tickets and fill in the information requested." Soldiers passed out pencils and everybody used everybody else's back as a writing desk. Joop answered the questions about the number of people in your household and gave the normal weekly rations as their number of meals per week. When the tickets were presented, there was enough information about a slice of the city's healthy population for graphs and predictions to be composed by demographers of the Royal Canadian Corps of Logistics.

Bobo led Sarah by the hand around the lobby, focusing her attention on the pretty lights. She drank in every new sensation, and the more she fed on Bobo's enthusiasm, the more curious she became. She touched the glass holding the poster for the movie and demanded, "Who's he?" Bobo asked her, "Which he?" and she blurted back, "The fat one." Bobo smiled to think she had first been drawn to the well-fed part of the duo. "That's Oliver," he revealed. "And the skinny one?" Bobo felt Sarah's sympathy for the skinny man bubble through her question. "His name is Stan." The strange names satisfied her for a few seconds, but her hand waved over the poster and she shrugged the question to Uncle Bobo. "Way Out West," he read, and she soon turned to look for her mother. Bobo threaded his way through the crowd, and Joop's head nodded them to the ushers opening the doors to the auditorium. They found seats in the center aisle, and the loudspeakers oozed the soft smoothness of a Glenn Miller record.

Sarah watched a man in a long coat and a bow tie walk to the center of the stage. She soon ignored him to look at all the lines of colors running up the walls and across the ceiling. This was the biggest place she had ever seen. It made even a church look small, but Momma had only taken her once to that place where there were so many people of Emst all together. That little church place was not happy, but this place was so big and so happy that Sarah could not stop shaking her legs. The man was saying something, but he was not as interesting as the colors and the music.

Joop and Liese paid close attention to the maitre d' and applauded when he thanked the members of the Liberating Army for having the kindness to restore to us some of the joy which had been robbed from us. Bobo felt stirrings of gratitude for the soldiers who had done such a thing. A movie was far down the list of necessities, well below food, shelter, clothing, and safety. For a moment he fought back the moisture in his eyes and hid his appreciation behind the thought, "Well, it's good for Little Sarah."

Jan was only slightly less excited than Sarah and was glad when ten more people appeared on the stage. The compere explained that "this evening's presentation of 'Way Out West' will be in English," but continued to introduce "our very talented actors who will speak the dialogue in Dutch." Soldiers walked down the aisles passing out little cards listing the cast of characters and the names of the actors who would translate the roles from Hollywood to Holland. Everybody understood that the program card could be exchanged for two extra ration coupons. All they had to do was place their names and addresses on the back of the cast list to receive the extra ration as they left the theatre. Dinner and a movie were reversed; if you went to the show today, you could have dinner tomorrow.

The lights dimmed and Sarah stood up to leave. Liese settled her on her lap and explained that "the lights go out so we can see the moving pictures." Sarah followed her mother's fingers to the stage and a huge chicken looked back at her. Wide-eyed and open-mouthed, Sarah could see every feather of its ruffling neck. The chicken was as big as a house and when it made its big chicken noise, it was like happy thunder rolling through the sky. The chicken flew away and soldiers walked in front of her. She knew they were soldiers because they all wore funny hats and drove those cars that were huge monsters with long beaks. They made noises like the chicken, but that was not the happy thunder. The soldiers all made way for an old lady. The lady was fat and she had an animal wrapped around her neck. Sarah remembered the picture from her coloring book and knew the animal was a fox. It must have been the fat lady's pet because it was sleeping around her neck, just like Princess slept holding Sarah's face. Everybody stood up when the fat lady talked to them and then the grown-ups all started singing together. She looked to Uncle Bobo and wondered why he wasn't singing along with everybody else. The fat lady disappeared and Sarah saw a lion roaring at her through a big circle. The lion was so scary that she hid her face in Liese's neck. Joop patted Sarah's head until she mustered the courage to look back. The lion had gone away and something that looked like a big book stared back at her. The pages of the book turned, full of words and she heard Bobo mumble, "Ah. Hal Roach."

Jan read aloud, "Laurel and Hardy" and the whole audience burst into applause. Sarah could see people walking to a big building. It was a strange place. It looked like a barn but it was full of light coming from every window. She had seen the barns in Emst, but they never had lights because the lights would keep the cows awake at night. A man in a tall hat walked along the street and into the barn place. She slid out of Liese's embrace and stood between her parents, her attention dragged to the people dancing in front of her.

The whole audience sighed when the camera pulled them through the doors of Mickey Finn's Saloon and into the throng of reveling cowboys. Hundreds of people were singing along with the scantily clad girls in the saloon. The bartender was throwing foaming glasses of beer along a polished bar as if it were a bowling alley, and the cowboys deftly caught each glass without spilling a drop. Joop heard someone behind him yell, "Two more steins here, please," and the giggles snaked along three rows of seats. Bobo smiled to think there was just enough joy left in this audience to share a sardonic laugh.

The crowd settled down to watch the saloon captivated by Lola Marcel asking every man in the joint, "Will you be my Lovey Dovey, My Little Honey Man?" Liese chuckled when Jan eagerly agreed, "I certainly will." Bobo caught the joke and wondered whether Jan was more interested in being Lola's man or eating her ham. After the first number was followed by the obligatory barroom brawl, Joop became interested in the problem Stan and Ollie were facing.

They had some sort of paper they were supposed to deliver to a poor woman in a place called Brushwood Gulch. Joop followed Stan and Ollie through a trail of prat-falls, dunkings in horse troughs, and faces splattered with cream pies until they could restore the rights to some property to the rightful owner. Joop found himself delighted by their foolishness. Stan started to sing something which annoyed Ollie, but Joop could not make out the words, even when the actors sang in Dutch. He was trying to understand what was happening on the screen, but everything sounded like a hail storm in two languages. He could not help laughing when Ollie tried to stop the singing by taking a mallet to Stan's head. The more he hit Stan over the head, the higher he would sing, until Ollie hammered the tune out of Stan's skull from basso profundo to a ridiculous contralto.

The more farcical the action, the more Joop appreciated the seriousness of their situation. They had to maneuver their way through false loves, friends who were as dangerous as they were unscrupulous, and situations they clearly did not understand. They were somehow innocent in a world as brimming with malice as the foaming beer glasses sliding down the barroom counter.

He found himself looking through the movie to his own situation, grasping Liese's hand and stroking Sarah's hair. The laughter swirled around him, but he did not resent the distraction, for he could see in the merriment of the comedy his own ridiculous situation. Ollie and Stan were ignorant of all the machinations, but they weathered each storm together. Joop understood Ollie's embarrassment when he said, "A lot of weather we've been having lately." Joop chortled at the obviousness of the statement and said to Liese, "Of course there is a lot of weather; there always is a lot of weather." Liese laughed along with him, not knowing what he was talking about, but happy to humor him. It was good for him to talk out loud like this. "That's as silly as saying 'we've been having a lot of air, lately.'" Liese was content to let his sleeping thoughts lie, until they woke up and explained themselves.

Joop's mind swam through the movie and his problems, and it seemed to him that the two were linked, but he couldn't figure out how. These two actors playing the fool made him think they had all been fools for acting as they did. Laurel and Hardy risked so much because they knew so little. They happily stumbled through their adventures, too stupid to know the dangers. Jan and Bobo, Joop and Liese had known the dangers from the very beginning. The corpses would not all rise up when the movie ended. But there was something else seeping into him. He felt Sarah's breath staining his shirt and he sighed in rhythm with his sleeping child. She was a good sleeper, and he knew he would have to carry her home.

Joop felt a strange warmth for the comedians as he watched Stan and Ollie stagger through the last song of the film. Oliver disappeared into the final hole in the stream they were crossing, but Joop knew it was not the end. Somehow, Ollie would rise dripping from the water and kick Stan's ass into tomorrow for leaving him in the water yesterday.

The lights shuddered from a dim glow to an assured glare and everybody rose to stretch their way to the exits. Joop folded Sarah over his shoulder and held Liese's hand, waiting for the row to clear so they could get to the aisle. Jan and Bobo shuffled behind them, the movie whirling in their imaginations. Jan could repeat every joke and added each of Oliver's quips to his hoard of witticisms, even if he didn't understand them. Bobo was glad to once again feel the artistry of a film, not caring if such entertainment was considered beneath the dignity of higher minds. He had followed the movements of the duo through the choreography of their adventures and loved every crazy twist and insane pirouette of the story.

When they walked into the street, the evening air was sharp with lively cold. A thousand bodies wrapped up in overcoats filled with laughter had generated enough joy to heat the town.

Joop and Liese slowed to keep Sarah balanced in her slumbers, and Bobo and Jan followed to take their turns in carrying the child home. Sarah squirmed in her father's arms and Joop leaned his ear closer to hear her sigh, "the foxy is so pretty."

Chapter 22

Rabbits and Weasels

Joop stood outside the studio, listening to van Meegeren finishing his morning toilette. The Master was taking his time, carefully scraping the years from his stubbled chin. Joop understood the man's vanity and his need to present his best and most youthful face. He looked down the marble cascade of the stairs and watched Jan and Bobo herding chairs across the foyer into the large salon. Joop heard the legs scrape over the floor and Jan loudly accusing a chair of attacking his knee. Bobo laughed and offered to kiss it all better. Joop felt anxious about this morning, but he was confident that their little ruse would work. Liese had again come up with the idea.

Laurel and Hardy's antics had troubled Joop, until he had talked it all out with Liese. "They did a good thing, helping that woman in the cowboy town."

"Yes," she smiled back at him, "It's so nice to see two fools become heroes."

She sensed that the movie had made him think about their own situation. She teased at whatever was vexing him, coaxing his troubles out of his tangled frustrations. "They had a big problem to solve, just like us," he admitted.

Liese knew that van Meegeren was the problem and just why he was their problem. The Flight Control Bureau was their only source of income, even if they were paid with increasingly worthless ration cards. Like so many other tendrils of the government, the Bureau had appeared in the midst of the chaos. She guessed that Joop had created the job at gunpoint. Chasing collaborators was good work, but it would come to an end when there were no more collaborators to hunt. Van Meegeren had become their star prisoner, but without him, the ration cards would evaporate. In the Resistance, Joop and Liese had become accustomed to living or dying by their own decisions. Now that peace had broken out, van Meegeren controlled their choices. They had few facts about the man and his activities. What little security they now had hung on the thin thread of van Meegeren's lies. Getting to the truth was never more vital.

Liese sensed his growing anger and patted Joop's hand. He felt her warmth and the reassurance that she wanted him to speak. He sucked in the dusty air and exhaled, "What are we doing here?"

"I don't really know any more," Liese confessed with a restrained sigh.

"Could it be all one big mistake?" Joop asked what she had been thinking for some time. "A joke and we're the ones they're laughing at?"

"Maybe," she shrugged.

She waited for their breathing to settle into a more comforting rhythm. "All I know is that we're not laughing at each other, but our artist certainly is."

Joop looked a little embarrassed, when Liese cut through the nonsense to the core of whatever they were doing. She calmly asked, "Just what does he do all day?"

"He paints," Joop explained. "But mostly it's just gin and cigarettes, when he's not talking."

"But he talks to you?"

"All the time," Joop sighed, "but we never get down to the facts."

"Just you. His confessor."

Liese listened carefully as Joop told her that van Meegeren's favorite, indeed only topic of conversation, was himself. "When I leave, De Groote and the guards are his audience," Joop added, "but he talks to anybody who will listen."

She knew Joop was bored with van Meegeren's endless accounts of his adventures. Joop confided his weakness. "I feel like I'm drowning in his nonsense."

They tried every way of untangling van Meegeren's net, but every thread lead to another, tighter knot. She leaned back to gaze at the first stars of the evening sky. Jan was entertained by van Meegeren's glamour, but Jan would follow wherever Joop led. De Groot was van Meegeren's biggest fan and was now more of a servant than his guard. "Looks like he has them dangling on his hook," Liese observed. She found comfort in the fact that Bobo clearly detested him. Liese brought him back to the practicalities, "If half of his tales were true, he should have been dead long ago." Joop smiled at her and sighed, "Somewhere in all that chatter," he admitted, "there must be the truth."

She was glad that he could let his anger blossom before it poisoned him. He sensed he was being hoodwinked, but he needed proof. "So," Liese continued, "the problem is not finding the truth, but sifting through all his lies." Joop eagerly agreed and felt better when Liese pronounced, "You could grow tulips in all his wild tales."

"Yes," Joop chortled, "and he would sell you the bouquet."

They sat watching the sky darken into dotted brilliance. The evening calm soothed their weary search for answers hidden behind more questions. "It all goes round-and-round," Joop said in exasperation. "But where it comes out," Liese sang, "the weasel knows." Joop laughed at the children's song they had known all their lives and which they now sang to Sarah. They had seen many a poacher in Emst put a weasel down a rabbit hole and then wait for the rabbits to pop out of the ground. "He's like a rabbit warren. You never know what will jump out of the burrow," Liese said.

Joop's eyebrows erupted into double question marks, and Liese laughed to tell him, "We already have the weasel. Now how can we have the rabbits ferret out the truth from the weasel?" She had turned the hunt on its head, so now it made sense. Joop laughed aloud and praised her plan, "Now we have the rabbits hunt the weasel."

Bobo, Jan, Liese, and Joop spent three evenings arguing over pots of tea how best to trap van Meegeren. Bobo's simmering hostility finally burst. "Getting the truth out of that bastard is like peeling a rotten onion. After a while, your fingers stink." Bobo blew an indignant cloud from his pipe, and they laughed when his temper spewed embers over the table.

Liese insisted that they should encourage van Meegeren to talk. Bobo countered that this would just bore even more people. "True," Liese answered, "but he is bound to let something slip and then you can catch him."

Bobo concentrated on the accuracy of Liese's shot. "So," he said, "We get him to talk, let him lie, and he reveals himself to be a fraud, a liar, and a traitor." Bobo's admiration of Liese's plan sent him into a fit of laughter. They waited for him to dry his eyes when he finally said, "Since he likes an audience, give him the best he will ever have. Invite the newspapers to hear his story, directly from the horse's mouth."

They had no idea how to organize such a meeting, so they invited Jan Spierdijk to join their little plot. He brought a small cake, and after another evening of sweet tea and sour laughter, they knew exactly what to do. Spierdijk looked into Bobo's furrowed brows and explained, "A press conference is just work for these fellows." Spierdijk's own experiences in the Resistance had honed his instincts. Hope only lived within narrow horizons. Now they had to look to the future, and the view could be terrifying.

The Bureau was their leaky lifeboat in all this squalor. "But look how things are getting better," he told them. They waited for his proof and nodded their thanks when he said, "We have some sugar for our tea." Bobo pulled his cold pipe from his lips, "and a guest who brings cake." They all felt just enough confidence to clear their minds. Spierdijk wrapped them all in his kindly gaze and said, "There's another important aspect to this."

Bobo had an inkling of what Spierdijk was getting at. "The Bureau is a very temporary affair," Spierdijk stated. They all nodded in begrudging agreement, but Bobo was relieved to know that Spierdijk was leading them to the reality they were trying to ignore. "I have a salary, as long as the newspaper sells," Spierdijk explained, "but this Bureau is very shaky." Liese breathed deeply, for she feared to think of what would happen to them without the ration cards. "This release of information to the press may be just what you need." Jan was confused, and Joop wanted Spierdijk to make it clear to them all. "This Bureau of yours could disappear tomorrow." He waited until he sensed their anxiety was ready to receive his equally vague promise. "But it could become a permanent department of the Ministry of Finance." His vision of a settled life lured them into hope, so he assured them, "There is no such thing as bad publicity."

Joop smelled a jet sprayed from a cologne bottle and turned back to van Meegeren's boudoir. "You look very charming," Joop complimented as van Meegeren slid his arm into his coat sleeve. "Of course," he said and inquired if the guests had arrived. "I'll call you down when they do," Joop left van Meegeren to finish the details of his costume.

He heard the front door swing open and descended the stairs to meet Spierdijk entering the foyer. Spierdijk had made the rounds of the journalists' haunts, promising his colleagues an amusing story, "If you just happen to be anywhere near the old Goudstikker Gallery at 9:00 AM tomorrow." Joop glanced at the doors over Spierdijk's shoulder and asked, "Do you think they'll all come?" Spierdijk shot back a smirk, "Oh they'll come. This will fill many pages." They walked into the salon and Joop was pleased to see half the chairs were already occupied in a semi-circle before the large conference table.

Spierdijk's casual suggestion had snowballed from ear-to-ear until half the journalists in Amsterdam were champing in anticipation for a major announcement in the van Meegeren case. Spierdijk sensed Joop's nervousness, "Tell them the basic facts. Keep it simple for the people stupid enough to read their rags." When the last of the seats was filled, Spierdijk led Joop to the front and tapped his pen against the table, until they were all as attentive as if they were at an auction.

"Good Morning, Gentlemen," he said, "and thank you for being so prompt. I would like to present Captain Joseph Piller, Head of the Flight Control Bureau of the Ministry of

Finance. We have some developments to report in the case of the collaborator van Meegeren."

A voice from the back intoned, "When will he be hanged?" and the rest sniggered at his eagerness for the gallows. Spierdijk was quick to assure them, "You will all be invited to be official witnesses of the execution." He let the laughter fade and added, "if there is to be an execution." They all started scribbling with one eye on their pads and the other on Joop. Spierdijk slowly informed them of "new and startling developments, due to Captain Piller's careful investigation of this major case of collaboration." Joop noticed that Spierdijk was just repeating the same information in different words, but also saw that he had the audience hanging on his lips. "Captain Piller would like to introduce you personally to the accused, so that you can judge the facts he will reveal." Joop knew this was his cue to retrieve van Meegeren and excused himself.

The journalists' chatter blossomed as his steps faded up the stairs. Questions coated in guffaws burst behind him. Spierdijk caught some of the inquiries and parried them with a shrug, but others he deflected by claiming, "van Meegeren will clarify that point." He evaded every subtle hint and direct question and stoked their impatience into a frenzy that flared when they heard two pairs of footsteps descending towards them.

Van Meegeren entered first, and Joop was surprised when they all stood up. They waited for van Meegeren to be seated at the center of the table before squatting onto their chairs in attentive curiosity. Joop stood for the formal introduction, and Spierdijk wondered how they would react. He nodded to Bobo standing rigid behind the audience.

Van Meegeren slowly uncurled himself from his chair and rose to his full height. His suit was fresh from this morning's ironing and his shirt gleamed as white as Liese could make it. The loose bowtie added to his Bohemian air and contrasted with the white silk scarf draped casually around his neck.

"Gentlemen, I thank you from the bottom of my heart, that you have taken the time from your busy days to hear my story," van Meegeren almost whispered. "It is my honor to discuss with you today some of the rumors concerning my behavior, rumors which have been circulated with so much malice and so little understanding." They all leaned forward with pens and pencils poised before open notepads. Van Meegeren raised his chin and aimed his voice above their heads, "Please, allow me to assure you, I am no collaborator."

One indignant journalist demanded to know how he could have the gall to say such a thing when "you were caught red-handed with the Vermeer, the very painting you sold to Goering."

"Red is not a color on my palette," van Meegeren confessed with a hint of surprise, "so it would never be on my hands." He jested as if talking kindly to a dull child and joined in the giggles of his listeners. Joop felt the heat rise through their hubbub.

"Gentlemen, I have a confession to make." His impish smile jumped from face-to-face and he waited just long enough for his silence to kindle their greed for more. He heard a slight wriggling of impatience and slowly lifted his chin.

"I painted Goering's Vermeer."

Joop and Spierdijk had waited with expectation for the punchline. They had expected an explosion of ridicule and laughter, but only heard the silence that followed the collective gasp. One journalist demanded to know how such a connoisseur as Goering could be taken in by an obscure Dutch artist. "Very simply, My Dear Friend," and van Meegeren fired a full salvo of smirks at the questioner, "that German connoisseur knows nothing about art... and less about our Dutch masters."

The laughter finally exploded. He had lacquered his jibe with smooth logic and it was an invitation for them to ridicule their persecutors. The chairs wiggled in the sheer delight of van Meegeren's pulling the wool over Goering's eyes and they heartily agreed that van Meegeren's trick only proved what they had thought all along. Goering was a fraud. Their admiration for van Meegeren fooling the fool and defrauding the fraud mounted with their eagerness to hear more. Joop saw how skillfully van Meegeren had used their hatred of the Germans to convince them he was telling the whole unvarnished truth. Another voice shot over their heads to van Meegeren. "Of course, you did it for the money."

Van Meegeren lifted his nose and cast a narrowed eye at the questioner. He shook his head in kindly indulgence with a mere suggestion of condescension. "The price was not in money, but in paintings," van Meegeren explained.

"So you exchanged your fake Vermeer for another painting," the voice continued. "Goering just gave you his junk for your fake."

"But what glorious junk it is," van Meegeren recalled, his voice trembling with wonder. The journalists leaned towards him eager for his next pearl. "I sold him a fake," van Meegeren raised his hand and whispered, "to save the heritage of Holland."

The pens blotched his words into their notebooks, and Spierdijk could hear the crack of a pencil point. Van Meegeren leaned back in his chair and gazed at the ceiling, as if recalling a fond dalliance but with the reticence of a true gentleman who would never reveal the intimate details they so craved. "An exchange was arranged," he teased. "Goering would get his "Vermeer" and we would keep our Rembrandts, our Vermeers, our Frans Halls." The names were spewed over eager ears, straining at each revelation. "I must confess that along with preserving Holland's artistic patrimony, our true genius and our gift to civilization, we have also kept our honor, as Dutchmen."

Joop could see the moisture rise in their eyes, but he heard the emotion wobble van Meegeren's voice, "I gave him a lie to save the truth."

The scribbling fell silent, and taut fingers clutched the notebooks. "I dedicated my talent to our cause." All eyes rose as he stood before them. For a moment, he rested with on one hand on the table, as if needing to support such a weight of feeling. He then stretched himself and threw back his shoulders. Every eye lifted to his face and every ear tuned to his final declamation. "I am no traitor. I am a patriot."

Joop and Spierdijk sat stunned by the bare-faced lies. He had completely turned the tables. It was as if the reporters were carrying him on their shoulders away from the lynching they had so anticipated. There was not a flicker of a suggestion of falsehood on van Meegeren's face. He could have convinced Arabs they needed a better desert and have them pleading to buy his superior sand.

The story was so good that it took many more questions for someone to ask for proof. Van Meegeren rose to the occasion and announced. "Gentlemen, the proof you seek awaits you above." One journalist looked up as if seeking favors from Heaven. Van Meegeren turned towards the foyer and invited them to a private viewing. "If you will follow me, we will show you."

Bobo and Joop stood aside to let van Meegeren lead his procession to the upper floor. Bobo's chin hung loose in his fury and his eyes darted incredulity. Spierdijk took a deep breath, as he and Joop mounted the staircase.

The journalists huddled together before the canvas, drinking in van Meegeren's lecture.

"Gentlemen, what you see before you is the beginning of a painting. Captain Piller can offer you photographic proof that this work came from these hands." The journalists all gazed at the gnarled fingers van Meegeren thrust before them. "These are the instruments of creation." He slowly pulled his hands to his chest, begging for their patience. He turned to face the canvas, and raised one arm, as if beckoning them to the feast.

Confused eyes peered into the brown blotches before them, but van Meegeren explained, "What you see before you are the walls of Jerusalem." His finger traced the outline of the muddy rectangles at the top of the canvas, until they saw the battlements of the Temple of Solomon. "And in the background," his fingers splayed over the splotches of yellow, and the hills of the Holy Land appeared before their eyes.

He let them drink their fill of the paint, until their minds conjured every little story book catechism they had been given as little boys. "This is the beginning of my latest masterpiece. The subject is Christ in the Temple Confounding the Doctors."

"In the areas where you see no paint," he intoned, and they gazed into the white voids scattered before them, "there will be the Holy Doctors." His forefinger gently touched five brilliant white spots about the size of his hand. They strained their eyes to fill the emptiness and their eagerness oozed over their doubts, Van Meegeren cupped his hands in the center of the canvas, as if holding the face of a beloved friend. "Here you will see the Christ Child teaching the Elders."

Their excitement flared with the knowledge that "this painting is at the command of the High Court of Holland." Every amazed head nodded in agreement. "I have been accused of high treason. My defense is that I myself painted the Vermeer which I sold to Goering. The court has commanded that I create another painting in the style of Goering's Vermeer."

The journalists gulped at the task before him. He stoked their desire and delayed the final statement, until they begged him for more. He swept his arm over the table holding his paints, brushes, and jars of oils. "I will use these to create another Vermeer equal in quality and subject matter to my work which Goering so prized." He rubbed his palms together before them, as if mustering the courage to share his last trial with these his trusted friends. "If I can paint this picture, I will prove that I am a forger." He waited for their laughter to echo and assured them, "I will be found guilty of tricking our oppressors and saving our treasures."

Joop, Bobo, and Spierdijk stood framed in the doorway fascinated by the performance. Van Meegeren raised his hand above his head to exclaim, "If I fail, I will suffer the penalty deserved by every traitor."

Bobo was breathing heavily as they watched van Meegeren pick up a brush and raise it slowly before the journalists' faces. "This is all that stands between me and death." He opened his fingers, and every eye followed the fall of the brush as it tumbled to the table. They trembled at the twist of such an extraordinary tale and were already composing tomorrow's headlines.

Spierdijk and Joop turned from the doorway. Joop was the first to break their disgusted silence. "They believed everything." Spierdijk shook his head and, exclaimed, "If he served them sandwiches of green cheese from the moon, they would say, 'How tasty!'"

The press conference they had so trusted to get to the truth was a shambles. The journalists were happy to have van Meegeren as their host, never realizing that now they were his hostages.

Bobo leaned his heaving shoulders over the edge of the balustrade and spewed rueful laughter down the stairs until his howls echoed through the foyer. He turned to Joop and Spierdijk, scratched the top of his head and said, "This is a fine mess, Ollie."

Chapter 23

The Morning News

The bell bothered Bobo. He was wading through the muddle of many years of family photos, but the bell called him to an annoyed but welcome break from his labors. He stepped from the back room into the shop to see an old lady waiting in an impatient huff before the counter.

"Can I be of assistance, Madam?" he said with a slightly perturbed edge.

"Do you sell photographs?" she demanded.

"Yes. I also take photographs. What would you like?"

Bobo's eyes followed her direction as she raised her arm and flung her index finger over her shoulder to the window. "That one," she said, and Bobo could see her jaws clench tighter than her perturbed pouting.

"Of course, Madam," he said. "It will be an honor."

Her eyes blinked at the softness that had curled through his words. "I can have a copy ready for you tomorrow at any time which will be convenient." She nodded coldly and demanded, "How much?"

Bobo breathed in the anxiety behind her frigid stance and knew she would be insulted by his offer of a free copy. "One guilder," he said as casually as he could.

The woman opened her purse and fished out a single coin which she pressed onto the counter with a sharp snap. "Shall I have the photograph mounted for you?" Bobo offered.

"That will not be necessary," she informed him. The woman looked Bobo hard in the eyes and abruptly turned on her heal, clanging the bell as she shut the door behind her.

Bobo stood leaning on the counter and gazed through the window, watching the woman disappear into the traffic. She did not stop to look at Willie's photo. Nothing in her movements revealed any connection between herself and the face smiling from the window. Bobo thought of the film over her old eyes and thought he saw a resemblance between the image and the reality of the woman's rheumy gaze. He shrugged off his speculations and growled to himself, "It's none of my business."

He looked at the coin which reminded him that this was his business. He picked it up and it was still warm from the woman's grasp. When he looked closely, Queen Wilhelmina's profile shimmered in the golden glow. She was much younger than the stout matron in the newsreels. "Pre-war," he said and wondered why the woman was so willing to part with a valuable coin. He shook his head to cast aside his musings and tossed the guilder into an empty drawer. He now had bigger worries, such as finding enough chemicals to make the copy he had promised, and for which she had already paid.

If he were to deliver her print, he first had to find his equipment. Two years of dust could be blown away easier than the remembrances of all that time. When Joop first clanged through the shop door, he had not expected to live long enough to ever again need his bottles and jugs. He found three rusty developing trays and part of him greeted them as old friends, but there was a still small voice in his head that wished them dead. After a half hour of grumbling to the metal pans that laughed at his antics, he told them, "All you need is a good cleaning."

He placed them in the sink and attacked the rust stains and dirt with rags and cleanser. When he could see his own face in the burnished metal rectangles, he rinsed away the froth, and placed them beside the sink to dry. He watched the moisture evaporate and the years dissolve. When they were dry enough to move, he laid them side-by-side on his work table, and in the dimness of his hovel, they looked like a canal bridge. He stood staring at their challenge and soon went in search of a box of abandoned chemicals.

Under a cardboard carton spilling old prints through its torn sides, he retrieved three bottles of developer, fixer, and his own chemical concoction of a stop bath. The bottles were mainly full and he remembered that the last time they were opened was for a family portrait. They had never come for their prints and the negative was somewhere in the cascades of celluloid leaves scattered throughout the darkroom. The bottles stood guard beside each of the trays, and he wondered if they were as out of practice as he was. He shook away the thought and told them, "It's just like riding a bicycle."

He had to convince himself that the bicycle still worked, so he poured some water into the the tray on the far left. He let the negative slip from his fingers into the chemical bath and waited just long enough for the gelatin on the film to swell and make it hungry for the developer.

Bobo had always mixed his own developing fluids, and it gave him a feeling of competent superiority over the other merchants of images. When they called the developer "metol," he would correct them with a patronizing grin and teach them the proper terminology of monomethyl aminophenol hemsulfate. The words slid off Bobo's tongue like an indecent suggestion, and people complained of his snobbish airs. They never quite realized that their aversion to him was surpassed only by his contempt for them. His corrections kept the competition at a safe distance. He had often told himself, "Odd thing. These same chemicals could be recombined to make an explosive." Today was no time for word games with idiots. The coin in the counter drawer called him to higher duties.

He grabbed a pair of wooden tongs, fished the negative from the first bath and gently swam it in the solution of the middle tray. The acetic acid would stop the action of the developer and reveal the latent image. He crooned to the tray, "Ah my little, darling particles of silver, you are looking most fetching this evening." His breath clouded before his lips, an assurance that the room was cool enough for the alchemy of darkness and silver halide. "I see you are teasing me," he confessed to the tray. "Now let the bath ooze into every one of your lovely pores. Show me what you have." Bobo squinted at the vague outline in negative of Willie's face. "You have such an endearing smile," he complimented. "But you are also a very dirty fellow and need to wash yourself."

He thrust the tongs under the negative and deftly flipped it into the final tray to fix the image. In the past, he had sung as the fixer washed out the last of the silver halide and made the image as sharp as diamond-cut crystal, "You are my sunshine, my only sunshine." He counted to ten and continued his serenade to the unseen, "You make me happy, when skies are gray." He paused through the count of another decade and finished, "Please take all the ammonium thiosulfate away."

He fished the dripping image out of the bath and clasped it to the little close-line above the tray. He waited with the patience of growing certainty for the little cascade of clear water to settle into a slow and trembling drip.

When he saw Willie's head upside down and in reverse negative, he knew the final print would be clear for as many years as the old woman cared to gaze upon it. He sat back and indulged himself in a satisfied smile, knowing that he could still produce a very fine portrait.

The outraged bell invaded his reverie, and he knew it was Joop. He heard another pair of boots thump into the shop and pulled back the curtain between the darkroom and the counter.

"What kept you?" he demanded of Joop and Spierdijk.

Spierdijk pulled rolled newspapers from under his coat, as if he were drawing a revolver, and threw them on the counter. "How could we have been so stupid?" he groaned.

"It seems we're not alone," Bobo jibed from under his glasses raised to his forehead.

Joop watched Spierdijk pace through his frustration. "It was a completely reasonable idea," he almost whispered. Bobo smirked at them both. "Unfortunately, the audience was completely stupid."

"Not just them. The readers. This is a disaster," Spierdijk growled.

"Just what the bastard wants."

"And we organized the whole thing for him," Joop confessed.

Their anger danced with their shame and filled the the shop, but Bobo smiled beyond them at the people passing by the window. He separated the newspapers and spread them over the counter. Van Meegeren's face smirked up at Bobo below the headline, "He Paints For His Life." Bobo picked up the sheet and dangled it before them between his thumb and forefinger. "Isn't he photogenic," he complimented, and Joop giggled like a child. Spierdijk had yet to vent his spleen, so Bobo was happy to goad his temper. "I am sure he will fill many a reporter's glass," he said and watched his words stoke Spierdijk's ire. Bobo let the paper flutter to the counter and licked the stale ink from his thumb.

The next edition featured the same photograph, but proclaimed, "Our Hero Forger." Bobo's eyes compared the two photographs and saw the blurring around the edges of van Meegeren's head. "They've copied this image from the first newspaper," he observed. Spierdijk calmed slightly as his attention was driven to van Meegeren's face. The third newspaper shared the same photo with the first two, and the image was even more blurry. "This looks like a copy of a copy of the first photograph," Spierdijk said with growing interest. "They probably have only one picture of him and have to repeat it," Bobo said. "How fitting for a fraud," Spierdijk lamented.

They stood with their balled fists resting on the counter, glaring at the beige sheets before them. Joop saw Van Meegeren as cocky as ever, for he had become accustomed to the eyes glittering over the twisted smile. Spierdijk could only summon contempt for the arrogant lips pursed in condescension. Bobo was studying the area behind the head. The background in the first picture was clear and distinct, etched through the lens and resurrected in the developing baths with considerable skill. The third picture was the same as the first, but it could have been taken anywhere. Van Meegeren's face was in half profile, framed in a cloud of chemical smudges. The head was circled by a hazy gray halo. When Bobo's eyes bounced through the sequence of pictures, the coy jester was transformed into the artistic saint. The unspoken message was what worried Bobo. He knew that pictures were worth thousands of words, but so many of those words were lies. "The bigger problem is on this side of the newspaper."

Joop was confused, and Spierdijk wanted to hear more. "How so?"

"Seeing is believing," Bobo pronounced, "but believing is an art."

Joop looked carefully at the pictures and understood that the real danger was not just in what van Meegeren was saying, but in what his listeners were hearing. "What do you think?" He asked Spierdijk.

"After yesterday's performance, I have lost what little faith I had in my colleagues," he confessed.

"They are no different than their readers," Bobo lamented.

The newspapers were all the evidence they needed. Bobo was right, and Joop capped their understanding, "Bullshit baffles brains."

"That should be the headline," Spierdijk laughed.

They stood thoughtfully around the witches' brew van Meegeren had concocted for them. Joop was the least surprised that van Meegeren had turned the tables, so he was the most angry that he had been taken in. "I should have known better," he sighed.

Spierdijk could follow a news report as if playing chess with his readers. For three years, he had written the truth, and every article could have been his execution warrant. All that time, he had earned his living offering the Germans classes in conversational French and English. None of his students had made the connection between their innocuous teacher helping them to preen their pick-up lines and the Dutch Resistance newspapers. They were much more interested in fishing for fräuleins than reading the news of the conquered. He had survived because of his pupils' laziness. Now he feared his neighbors' gullibility. "I don't know what we can do," he confessed in disgust.

"We have some time," Joop assured him.

"Yes," Bobo said. "He is taking his time with his latest masterpiece."

"Well I don't," Spierdijk told them.

Joop furrowed his brows at Spierdijk. "Why the hurry?"

"I have to go to Berlin. The newspaper is sending me to report on the new government of the victors."

"Oh good," Joop said with exaggerated relief. "For a minute I thought you had a dose."

They laughed together at the standing joke in the Resistance that their more cowardly comrades had contracted syphilis from the Germans. There was always a warning behind the laughter. Spierdijk shook their hands and offered them the best luck they could find. "I'll be back in a few weeks."

The doorbell rattled at his exit, and Joop looked sheepishly to Bobo.

Chapter 24

Snakes and Ladders

Joop was enjoying the quiet of the studio. Only the determined swishing of the knife punctuated the stillness.

Van Meegeren was awake and at work on the canvas. He had taken to rising early to get as much accomplished as he could before the daily invasion of hopeful admirers. Some came to bask in his celebrity, but Joop and Bobo noticed others who were seeding his friendship to reap future rewards. Everybody wanted something, and Joop was struck by van Meegeren's talent to give all his guests exactly what they wanted, after he had convinced them that they needed whatever he had to offer.

Van Meegeren was scraping oil and pigment over a large piece of marble with a palette knife. "This is just how Vermeer would have mixed his paint," he said over his shoulder. The knife swirled through the moist ridges and reminded Joop of Liese icing a cake. The scraping stopped abruptly. Joop's silence puzzled van Meegeren, so he turned to see Joop standing with his legs apart and his hands in his pockets, contemplating the canvas. He liked Joop's questions and enjoyed instructing him in the basics of art. After all the years of working alone, van Meegeren delighted in having such an inquisitive and appreciative pupil, even though Joop's education would never amount to anything. He wiped his fingers on a rag, lit a cigarette, and stood beside Joop. "It's certainly coming along nicely," he said and blew a cloud away from Joop.

Joop's eyes moved from the corners to the center of the canvas. Van Meegeren had been painting from the edges, so the middle of the canvas was blank. Joop could see where the perspective lines crossed and how van Meegeren was using them to build his composition. "I thought you started from the middle and then worked out when you painted a picture," Joop said. Van Meegeren smiled, "That is for students. A real painter knows better."

Joop ran his gaze along two thick, brown lines van Meegeren had gouged at the bottom of the canvas. With his finger, he traced the outline gently falling from the left border and ending in the delicate curve of a scroll. "That looks like an old-fashioned chair," Joop offered. "You are correct," van Meegeren praised. Van Meegeren pointed to the horizontal line on the right of the canvas that balanced the descending thrust on the left. "And what is this?" he asked. Joop did not hesitate. "Another chair." Van Meegeren clapped his approval and cast a confident smile over Joop. "Perfect. It's two chairs facing each other."

Joop returned van Meegeren's grin, for he was enjoying the game. "And what will be on those chairs?" van Meegeren inquired. "People sitting," Joop shot back.

Van Meegeren stepped to the table to retrieve a stick of charcoal. He quickly drew a figure sitting in the chair with its elbow resting on the arm. Joop watched van Meegeren slash a black line from the arm of the chair to the outline of a face. Van Meegeren ground some charcoal between his thumb and forefinger and the line became indistinct. Under his thumb, van Meegeren teased the black stoke into smudges and a forearm and hand emerged from the murky gray cloud. Van Meegeren's hand whipped charcoal circles onto the canvas and a face appeared before Joop's amazed eyes. Van Meegeren clutched Joop's coat sleeve and pulled him back to the table. He thrust his chin to the canvas, commanding Joop to look back.

Where there had been white nothingness, now sat a man with his chin in his palm and his index finger stretched up his cheek. It took van Meegeren only a few minutes to create the head cupped in the hand and the elbow resting on the arm of the chair. The profile captivated Joop. He looked deeply into the single eye in the shadow of the nose and was filled with wonder. It really was a face, and Joop had to acknowledge his respect for the talent that could turn dirt into such simple beauty. He could feel both the tension and the comfort of the man sitting in the chair. "That's amazing," Joop sighed. "Yes," van Meegeren agreed confidently, and took a congratulatory puff of his cigarette.

After he drew the figure of the sitter, the white blotches made more sense to Joop. The empty spaces in the middle and on the right would contain two more figures. The voids were waiting, and Joop understood that the finished painting would be a triangle of people. He was eager for their appearance. "Who are they?" he asked. Van Meegeren was happy to explain. "In the chair on the left, sits one of the learned men of the Temple," van Meegeren stated, with affected boredom. "He will be balanced by one of his colleagues on the right," he casually commented. Joop's imagination filled in the blanks, and in his mind, he could see two men sitting and looking towards the center of the canvas.

"Who will be in the middle?" he asked. "Jesus, of course," van Meegeren answered with surprise. The question puzzled van Meegeren, until he remembered that Joop was a Jew. He would not be familiar with the story of Christ in the Temple. He savored the irony and took a perverse pleasure in explaining to a Jew that a Jewish child was lecturing two Jewish doctors on the Jewish law. Joop caught the condescension in van Meegeren's voice and rankled at the tale that was just like the jokes which all started with, "Two Jews walked into a bar."

Van Meegeren leaned closer to the painting, examining some detail only he could see. There had been so much uncertainty, so much left unsaid, that Joop was tempted to rip through the canvas in the vain hope of releasing a nest of answers. The more he pondered its meaning, the more the painting bred confusion in Joop's mind. He knew it was useless talking to the painting. His respect for the artist only increased his contempt for the man. But when he asked van Meegeren about his technique, he was eager to boast. Then, the answers were clear and proven by the facts of the painting. Maybe van Meegeren was just vain enough to reveal the secrets of his alchemy of lies. Joop decided on one last gamble. "How did you do it?" he asked, never taking his eyes off the canvas. Van Meegeren took a step back to stand beside Joop, as if sharing a distant vista from a high mountain.

Joop glanced sideways to see van Meegeren studying the center of the canvas. He raised his wedge of charcoal and placed a dot below the nose and eyes. Joop watched him draw an oblong and surround it with hashmarks. Van Meegeren whispered to Joop out of the side of his mouth, "With the right shading, this could be the hindquarters of a baboon." Joop forced a childish giggle to keep van Meegeren's attention.

Van Meegeren scraped the hairy circle with the heel of his right hand. Joop dared not move for fear of breaking the spell. Van Meegeren drew parallel lines across the smudge and his finger formed them into pouting lips. He shaded in the nose and then gouged dark eyelids under heavy brows. Van Meegeren moistened the tip of his little finger and jabbed it into the eye sockets, until they became squat barrels bounded by the heavy lids. He took a step back and studied the inverted triangle of the eyes and the mouth and then lunged his charcoal at the eyes. He rotated the tip of charcoal into the eyeballs. A face appeared and stared straight at Joop.

They stood looking at the face. It was realistic enough to be recognized as a young face, but Joop could not decide if the face belonged to a man or a woman. Van Meegeren chortled. "A few lines more and the monkey's ass becomes the face of Christ." The face reminded Joop of advertisements for cosmetics. He had seen the same coy face touting lipstick from posters on ruined walls and selling mascara in the blowing pages of magazines thrown into the gutter. The face filled him with revulsion.

Joop felt the pride oozing from van Meegeren and knew he had to let the current flow to the answers. "It's magical," Joop complimented, with only half-feigned admiration. "It is art," van Meegeren corrected. Joop continued in deepening respect, "It is more than magical. It is breathtaking." Van Meegeren lit another cigarette and sucked in Joop's approval. When he was sure that van Meegeren was relaxed enough to lower his guard, he asked, "But how did you do it?" Van Meegeren's brows compressed in mild annoyance, "I just showed you how I do it." Joop stepped over the line of his own fears. "Please forgive me. I meant, how did you turn such wonders into a Vermeer?"

Van Meegeren blew laughter and fingered the charcoal stick. With the cigarette dangling from his lips, he drew a rectangle below the mouth. He looked at Joop with such pride that Joop felt pulled into his smirk. Van Meegeren printed a capital 'G' in the rectangle and added the number ten. "What's that?" he asked with exaggerated simplicity.

"A price tag," Joop replied.

"How much?" van Meegeren suggested.

"Ten guilders," Joop answered.

Van Meegeren drew two more zeros on the tag. "Now how much?" Joop was determined to submit to the lesson. "A thousand." Van Meegeren chuckled in a crescendo of contempt, as he added more circles to the rectangle. "Now?" Joop shook his head from side to side and exclaimed, "One million." Van Meegeren clasped his hands behind his neck, threw back his head and laughed with such abandon that his cigarette fell from his lips and somersaulted to the floor. "And that's how you turn a van Meegeren into a Vermeer."

Joop picked up the burning cigarette and crushed it into the bulging ashtray. Van Meegeren slumped into his armchair and crossed his legs. Joop looked dumbfounded, and van Meegeren enjoyed his discomfort. "You can't just hike up the price and convince people your work is Vermeer's," Joop protested. Van Meegeren held a cigarette poised for Joop to light it. Joop knew he was close to an answer, but felt as if he were stepping over slippery stones to cross a filthy stream. He picked up the lighter and kept his hand from shaking in rage. Van Meegeren spewed forth a cloud. "Ah Joop. You are so naive, but how could you be otherwise."

Joop held back his bile and stood respectfully before the master. "How so?" he asked. Van Meegeren looked him over with studied judgement. "You are not used to such fine things, now are you?" Joop nodded and waited. Van Meegeren's eyes examined the canvas. "Your class of people don't have pictures hanging in every room." Joop sighed in regret. "That is true," Joop confessed. "Only photographs, sometimes in a frame." Van Meegeren cast a pitying glance over Joop. "We simply cannot afford one million guilders worth of wall paper." Van Meegeren howled and praised. "That's good. Out of the mouths of babes."

They looked at the painting, and Joop asked with a hint of avarice, "But why is this so expensive?" Van Meegeren smelled money and was eager to share his shrewdness. "What would you do with an old painting?" he challenged. Joop posed upright in the quandary and said, "I simply don't know." Van Meegeren prodded him, "Say you found an old painting and you needed money. Money for your house or your family. What then would you do?" Joop shot back. "Sell it."

Confident that Joop had taken the bait, van Meegeren revealed his method. "Very good. But where can you find a buyer?" He asked.

"I'd go to an art store," Joop replied.

"And they would cheat you."

"I would find the best art dealer," Joop objected.

"You have no idea where to go, so you take it to Duveen because he's the only art gallery you have ever heard of. One of Duveen's assistants quickly escorts you to the door and very politely tells you to take your piece of shit elsewhere."

"So I can't sell the picture," Joop concluded.

"That's where you are wrong," van Meegeren proclaimed. "There is always a market for paintings, if you have the right certificate."

"Paintings have certificates?" Joop asked, the surprise clear on his face.

"And a painting with a certificate is a passport to riches," van Meegeren confided.

Joop kept shaking his head and with each nod, van Meegeren warmed to his subject.

"Step One. You take the painting to an appraiser, and he also tells you it is a piece of shit. So, you start making the rounds of the experts. You go to Italy, and for a few hundred lire, the expert congratulates you on being the proud owner of an exquisite example of the school of Rembrandt."

"Just like that?"

"Ah," van Meegeren intoned, "Step Two." He waited for Joop to bend in anticipation and revealed, "Then you take the painting and the Italian's scrap of paper to a Frenchman, for of course, you need a second and more trustworthy opinion. The Frenchman's vanity is assuaged because he doesn't think much of the Italian. He pockets a couple of thousand francs and focus pocus, your school of Rembrandt turd has become an authentic Rembrandt, certified as genuine from the master's own hand."

Van Meegeren paused for Joop's curiosity to catch up with his exposition. "The Frenchman suggests that you take it to the Louvre, for they are always looking for bona fide originals for their Dutch Gallery in the Salle Richelieu."

"So the French buy the picture," Joop continued, "and you make a fortune."

"That's what the fools do," van Meegeren objected. "Such idiots are happy to have one hundred thousand francs. But here's the final twist."

"I keep the painting and it becomes even more expensive," Joop exclaimed.

"And the market crashes and all that remains is the original piece of shit," van Meegeren chuckled. He waited until he thought Joop would burst and finished.

"Step Three. You refuse the French offer and take it to Berlin."

"Why Berlin?" Joop asked. "Why not London or some other rich place, like New York?"

"Because of Step Four," van Meegeren whispered after glancing to the door. "You do your homework." he leaned back, as if recounting one of his amorous adventures. "The Berlin expert hates Italians in general and the French appraiser in particular because the dirty Frenchman fucked his wife. The German seethes, but being a true gentleman, waits for his revenge. He sees the painting and reads the Frenchman's signature on the certificate. The painting is his vengeance. He will snatch this Rembrandt right out from under the nose of the bastard who cuckolded him. The newspapers are full of the German's triumph in discovering an unknown Rembrandt and he is famous as the only art expert in the whole world who has the connoisseurship to know that he is looking at a masterpiece."

"So, the Berlin guy buys the painting," Joop said.

"Even such a shyster can't afford your Rembrandt."

"So who gets the painting?"

"Step Five. And this is where the real money appears. Such a priceless treasure belongs in Germany, where people can appreciate it."

"So you sell the painting to the Germans," Joop said.

"You very graciously allow the Germans to buy it," van Meegeren corrected.

Joop saw the whole process laid bare before him. Van Meegeren didn't just copy a painting. He created the whole process of making the money. Joop felt a twisted admiration for the trickster below his loathing of the cheat. He stood looking down at van Meegeren, eager for more. Van Meegeren could not refuse such an admiring audience. "It's all greed," he smiled up to Joop. "All greed, and avarice and making them want something nobody else has.

Even you could afford ten guilders for a picture, but only very special people can spend one million guilders."

"What makes them so special?" Joop asked.

"The one million guilders," van Meegeren replied.

Joop stared at the price tag that seemed to be floating in the center of the canvas. Joop could see through it all in the waiting whiteness of the canvas. The victims were so willing to be duped that they would pay for the pleasure of owning the paintings. Van Meegeren was merely the foundation of something much bigger than them all. He could not do all this by remaining in the shadows. There were others involved. The zeros in the price tag danced before his eyes and each added to his hatred of Han van Meegeren.

"You deserve a drink," Joop said, and he went to the table and filled a glass full of gin. He raised the glass in salute before offering it to van Meegeren. The shaky hand reached out, and when the stained fingers circled the glass, Joop saw the dark arches under the nails. Crows had such talons. "You are very kind," van Meegeren confessed. "I won't forget you, Joop." Joop placed the gin bottle on the arm of van Meegeren's chair. "It is a privilege to hear you speak, Sir," he shared. "It is a real education." Van Meegeren smiled his thanks, and Joop took his leave, claiming his other pressing duties.

Joop walked down the stairs and out of the building, desperate for air. He leaned over the balustrade of the canal and breathed deeply. He must have inhaled ten of van Meegeren's cigarettes during his lesson, but he could cough them away. When the cold air restored him, he pulled his notebook and pencil from his coat pocket. With each frosty breath, he wrote down every detail of van Meegeren's unwitting confession. Now that he knew the pattern, he could look for van Meegeren's accomplices. The facts ordered themselves into little boxes marching up the paper, and Joop thought they looked like a workman's ladder. He would wait for the snakes to start climbing the ladder.

Chapter 25

Thieves' Honor

"You keep me in this stinking cage and you expect me to help you? Idiot."

"You will identify this document, Stuyvesande," Joop calmly ordered.

"It's van Stuyvesande."

"Do excuse me for not using your formal title Prisoner Number 66347... van Stuyvesande," Joop apologized with little formality and less respect.

Jan sat facing the prisoner, balancing a thick dossier on his knees. Joop lounged in the chair beside Jan. Van Stuyvesande squirmed impatiently in the third chair. The cell was devoid of any other furniture. Joop and Jan had joked about their game of musical chairs that always played a cracked tune.

"I'm not telling you anything until you get me out of this shithole," van Stuyvesande declaimed.

"You will leave when we are satisfied with your answers," Joop assured him.

The interview room at Weteringschans Prison was as cramped as it was hot. The Warden had cackled when Joop asked for a large broom closet where he could interrogate prisoners. The Warden gave him the key to what had been an old coal bunker with one barred window ten feet above the floor. Heating pipes ran along one wall, so Jan called this chamber the sweat shaft. The longer they sought answers, the more the prisoner felt the walls were closing in on him. Joop did not have to tell van Stuyvesande that he was in a tight spot. The stagnant air hissed the fact that he was caught between van Meegeren's defense and Miedl's millions.

Joop took a letter from Jan's dossier and offered it to his prisoner. Van Stuyvesande snatched it from Joop's grasp and insolently crossed his legs. Joop wanted to kick the chair out from under him, but the information was more pressing than his desire to relieve his own fury. He nodded to Jan, and they rose and stood by the door just out of hearing.

The page shivered in Van Stuyvesande's fingers, as if it were a prescription for a mercury flush. He could hear them murmuring near the door, but most of the words collapsed before they reached his ears. Van Stuyvesande watched Piller pointing to the bundle of papers the big one held. Piller was nodding his head and grunting "Uhm" and the big one replied, "Yes." He would watch Piller. He could make a deal with the boss better than the lackey.

Van Stuyvesande scratched thoughtfully at the raw patch on his neck. Peeling the skin gave some relief from the incessant itching. The guards wouldn't even let him wash, so his collar was a salt encrusted garrote. His shirt sleeves had grown white tide marks under his arms, and he thought he must stink worse than one of van Meegeren's whores. The big one was showing Piller something in the dossier. Piller stroked his chin, and the big one mumbled something about Kamp Vught.

Van Stuyvesande uncrossed his legs and held the letter tight. The prison guards took great pleasure in recounting tales of the collaborators awaiting their trials at Vught. The letter he held could have him transferred from Weteringschans Prison to the Internment Camp for Collaborators at Vught. The guards at that camp were freed prisoners. They knew all the tricks and had old scores to settle. He had done business with some of them, and that was reason enough to cut his throat. The Vught guards carried rifles when they made the prisoners exercise. Sitting in solitary at Weteringschans was preferable to getting shot while doing push-ups.

Piller' sneering chuckle snapped van Stuyvesande from his gloomy speculations. He heard the word "transfer" and the big one scribbled in the dossier. Van Stuyvesande closed his fist on the letter, and his eyes sought out Joop's face. Joop ignored him and pointed at the sheets. He glared imploringly at Joop, but their soft voices ignored him.

"I typed it," he whispered.

Joop continued his consultation, and Jan scribbled studiously in the dossier.

"I typed it, " van Stuyvesande moaned.

Joop slowly turned towards the prisoner's chair. "Then you may be able to help us with the curious wording."

Joop calmly took his seat before van Stuyvesande, pulled up his trouser crease, and crossed his legs, waiting.

"Goering insisted on this letter," van Stuyvesande confessed with a sigh.

"Goering himself wanted this?"

"He wanted everything to be legal," van Stuyvesande recalled.

Even after all these years, Joop was still surprised by the German fascination for order. They could kill their millions, but they needed an account to justify their crimes. He swallowed his indignation and commanded van Stuyvesande. "Read the last part just above van Meegeren's signature."

"'I will reveal the owner of the painting within two years of the date of purchase,'" van Stuyvesande mumbled.

Joop looked over to Jan, who nodded as he wrote. "I still don't understand," Joop admitted.

"I had to get a letter from van Meegeren," van Stuyvesande explained.

"Why did you do this?"

"Miedl was pressuring me and van Meegeren was stalling, so I went to his house with a typewriter, wrote this letter, and made him sign it."

"That was in his house on Keizersgracht?"

"Yes," van Stuyvesande explained. "He was living in that town mansion."

Joop pictured the room where he had first met van Meegeren and wondered what the cat had thought of the typewriter and its strange tappings.

"And this letter with its vague promise of two years was what Goering demanded?" Joop asked suspiciously.

"If anything went wrong, they could blame van Meegeren," van Stuyvesande said.

"So," Joop agreed, "you suspected van Meegeren."

"Miedl said without a letter, Goering wouldn't pay up."

"It was just business as normal," Joop agreed.

"Normal," van Stuyvesande snorted. "The painting was worth a million and a half guilders." He paused to shake his head and confessed. "Even Nazis have insurance policies."

Joop and Jan clenched their teeth at the proof of the painting's price. Van Stuyvesande had so casually confirmed all the rumors of unbelievable wealth. They could not imagine what they could buy with so much money.

"Why did you have the painting in the first place?"

Van Stuyvesande threw back his head and sucked the stale air. "Van Meegeren brought me this Vermeer. He told me it belonged to an old lady from a distinguished Dutch family. She was living in Italy and was having a hard time making ends meet."

"So, you wanted to help an old widow?"

Van Stuyvesande jumped at the excuse. "Yes, that was it."

Joop whispered to Jan and more notes filled the dossier.

"Who was this woman?"

"He wouldn't tell me."

"Why?"

"He said it all had to be kept quiet. He didn't want to embarrass her by revealing she had lost her fortune."

"And you believed this?" Joop accused.

"I trusted him."

"As did so many."

Joop gauged the growing frustration in van Stuyvesande's face. He let it percolate and then pressed him with the facts. "And so you became the middleman between van Meegeren and Miedl."

"He knew I could deal with Miedl."

"Your business dealings with Miedl were quite extensive," Joop agreed.

Van Stuyvesande blanched, and Jan smirked over his pages. Joop spread his hand and counted the facts from finger to finger. "He goes to you. You go to Miedl. And Miedl goes to Goering."

"Yes. That's what happened."

"I forgot to tell you," Joop casually added, "Miedl is in Madrid."

"What?"

"Yes," Joop calmly stated as if recounting something everybody already knew. "He simply packed his car with loot and cash and drove to Spain. He's living in the Ritz Carlton. Rented a whole floor for himself and his family."

Van Stuyvesande raised his fist to smash it down onto the arm of the chair, but there was no arm. He felt so foolish all he could do was punch empty space and scream "The Bastard."

Joop's knew his relaxed manner was infuriating and he waited to see the shame of betrayal flood over van Stuyvesande. He laughed to himself that this high and mighty maggot now looked like a beet, the same beets that were the last barrier against creeping starvation. Now this grumbling thief was about to cry because his friends had absconded with his money. It would have been funny, if they were not all so utterly despicable. Joop glanced at Jan and his face was blank.

Van Stuyvesande wanted to smash his fists against the wall, so Joop leaned forward and commiserated. "I really do feel sorry for you." Anxiety rippled over Van Stuyvesande's slack lips and silently begged for Joop's sympathy. Joop knew all too well the terrors of such uncertainty and was alert to dispense just enough comfort to keep him talking. "If I were in your position, I'd be more careful who I trusted."

Van Stuyvesande grasped at the kindness in Joop's voice. The big one was terrifying. He would not think twice about pulling off van Stuyvesande's head. He said nothing. At least Piller was talking. The big one just scribbled. The papers now looked like traps baited with his own words. He tried to remember all he had said, but it was useless.

Joop watched the sweat well over van Stuyvesande's eyes and wondered if he were crying. Van Stuyvesande decided they would keep him here until he drowned in his own piss.

"It was all van Meegeren," van Stuyvesande cried.

"You mean the property deals?" Joop prodded.

"No. Just the paintings."

Van Stuyvesande brushed his brow and whimpered. "I was such a fool. I was only trying to help an old lady." His moist eyes begged for compassion. "It was van Meegeren all along. How could I have trusted that drunken, dissolute bastard?" Joop nodded once, and waited. "He's insane," van Stuyvesande whined. "The syphilis has driven him crazy."

Joop watched the tiny blue lines wriggle through the crimson motley of van Stuyvesande's nose. Beads of desperation pooled on his forehead and dribbled down his cheeks.

"I just wanted to help," van Stuyvesande whimpered. "I am the victim here." He appealed to Joop. "Why are you blaming me?"

Jan clenched his teeth and carved dark circles into the page before him. Van Stuyvesande's emotions were spinning through ever more violent convolutions. He jumped from snarling rage to simpering self-pity. The twists of anger and turns through selfish sorrow made Jan dizzy. He was tumbling through his tantrums of wounded temper and weeping regret. Jan wanted him to hit the ground hard.

"But your name appears on some of the deeds to his property," Joop continued.

"It's not his property."

"But you sold him houses."

"I did, but they are no longer his," van Stuyvesande revealed.

"Who owns them?"

"His wife."

Jan poked Joop's shoulder, and they nodded agreement to some unknown understanding.

"Explain," Joop commanded.

"They are divorced. He gave her all his houses in their settlement."

"So you deal with her, with what's her name?"

"Joanna."

Van Stuyvesande grew confident in his answers and hoped this was something to trade. "Let me clarify."

"Please do."

"He had so much money, he had to hide it, so he bought up vacant properties and then rented them out. The rents are his income and he pays the taxes on them, so no one would find all the rest of the money."

"But there are bank records."

"In Miedl's bank," van Stuyvesande corrected. "Nobody has those accounts."

Joop removed papers from Jan's folder. "You mean these documents?"

Van Stuyvesande looked at the single page of van Meegeren's bank statement. If they had this, they had more. There was no way of telling what they had or if his name was on any of the transactions.

"Most of these properties are residential," Joop observed.

"There are too many for me to remember."

Joop examined van Stuyvesande's bland expression. He knew exactly why the houses were empty and why they were bought and sold. Ghosts can not pay rent.

Van Stuyvesande heard the chair creak under the big one. Joop did not follow his eyes when Jan's voice cut through the maze of lies and stillborn truths.

"Prinsengracht... Number... 263," Jan slowly spat.

"What?"

"Prinsengracht."

"I don't know what you're talking about," van Stuyvesande evaded.

"Number… 263."

Jan's eyes held van Stuyvesande in a vice. Joop waited for van Stuyvesande to break contact, and stood to shower the prisoner with disgust. "We have people who can help you remember." He turned imploring lips to Joop but could not speak. Joop waited and then told him. "Tomorrow, three men will visit you."

Van Stuyvesande could imagine what tools they would bring to their work. Jan breathed deeply to restrain his fists, but Joop relieved van Stuyvesande's cringing terror.

"They are bankers," Joop said. "They will present you with the rest of van Meegeren's accounts and you will inform them of all the people mentioned in those dealings.

Joop opened the door to let the cooling draft clear the chamber. He could not resist informing van Stuyvesande, "You make more money in a week than I do in five years."

He could feel the resentment in Joop's words; it matched the hatred in the big one's eyes. "I will speak with your colleagues," he surrendered.

Joop called for the guards and ordered them to return the prisoner to his cell.

They walked out of Weteringschans's main gate and gulped the night air. Joop smiled to Jan and asked, "I suppose you took full notes of the interrogation?" Jan laughed as he did every time Joop made the same joke, and proudly displayed the pages he had covered with drawings of windmills.

Chapter 26

The Blue Cloak

Jan heard the swish of the opening door and raised his head from his littered table. The quadruple tapping of heels on marble drummed up a pleasant grin that pulled him to the entrance to the foyer. His eyes stalked the swaying seams bulging over Kootje's calves as they disappeared up the staircase. Old Mrs. van Meegeren's feet strained to keep pace, until they reached the upper gallery.

He didn't notice Joop sidle up to him, but nodded in anticipation when Joop declared, "They're back." Jan's eyes narrowed as he added, "They hunt in pairs." Joop's mouth twisted in annoyance. "I'd better make sure they're not smashing up the place," and his shoulders squared in preparation for the inevitable scene their appearance always provoked. Jan placed a comforting hand on his shoulder, "You're a brave man." Joop chortled as he walked away, and Jan assured him, "Call me, if you need a hand." He smiled at Jan's eager offer as he ascended the stairs and said to himself, "You can have the Young One. De Groot can take care of the Beast." Jan laughed at the nickname de Groot had bestowed upon the former Mrs. Joanna van Meegeren and recalled that de Groot made himself very scarce whenever the Beast's whine screeched through the building. Joop could not tell which was worse, the old woman's arrogance or the young girl's bubbling emotions. He cast aside his apprehensions, for he was too busy to deal with their duet of bad temper and stupidity, and resigned himself to protecting his prisoner from the attentions of his women.

He was as surprised as he was relieved to feel the calm in the studio. They had placed two large picnic baskets on the table, and van Meegeren grinned his approval as he lined up the gin bottles. They were soon joined by cartons of cigarettes, and Kootje beamed when he thanked her for her thoughtfulness. Joop felt the Beast swallowing the insult, and braced himself.

Van Meegeren pulled brushes and small glass vials from the second basket and examined each with a most professional eye. He picked up a long stick, and Joop wondered why it had a ball stuck on one end. Van Meegeren raised the stick before his ex-wife's face and growled, "This?" She pulled back her head and hissed at him, "It was the only one in the house." Van Meegeren waved the stick before her nose and accused, "How do you expect me to work with this?" He threw the stick onto the table. Its ball bounced once and swung the wooden handle over the palette, paints, and brushes, until it clanged against one of the gin bottles. Joop was shocked to see the Beast bite her tongue. Kootje quickly opened a bottle and filled a glass. She offered the drink as if soothing a child with colic, and she soon had van Meegeren gurgling in disgruntled resignation.

The Beast turned to Joop. "Look what you have done to him. He is skin and bone." Joop was in no mood to suffer her temper. "The court has granted you permission to visit the prisoner," he pronounced. She stiffened and glowered at him. Joop waited for her face to rouge in indignation. Just when her ire was about to blossom into a fit, he ordered, "on condition that you do not disturb his work." She felt the determination in his stance and deliberated if her defiance was worth the fun of the fight. Joop stared her down, and when she slowly closed her eyes and swept her head dismissively aside, Joop knew this morning would be bearable.

Van Meegeren examined a basket and picked out a small container that reminded Joop of the glass jars of cold cream at an old cosmetics counter. "What's this?" van Meegeren demanded. The Beast dug her red talons into her palms. "That's all there is," she whined. Van Meegeren sucked his breath through clenched teeth and unscrewed the lid. He dipped his finger into the jar, and Joop heard a fingernail burrow through sand to scrape the glass bottom. When van Meegeren pulled out his finger, it glistened with a whitish blue coating up to the first joint. Joop wondered if the jar contained shattered glass. Van Meegeren raised the finger to his former wife's nose. "I can't use this." Mrs. van Meegeren thrust her hands to her hips and her face froze into an aggressive pout. "There is no more," she shouted and parried his accusation with a dismissive wave of her hand. Joop watched van Meegeren's stubbly chin quiver for a moment, until he bared his teeth. "In the studio. There's a whole bag of it. At least a kilo." He fired a salvo of contempt into her face. "On the top shelf. It's even marked, 'lapus lazuli.'"

He stood firm before her, and neither would budge. Kootje padded up to the Beast and quietly bleated for calm. Joop felt a little sorry for her, but caught himself before his sympathy trapped his better judgement. Kootje pleadingly tugged her aside, and Joop was glad to stay beyond the range of their whispering. Their angry twittering roused neither his concern nor his curiosity. Whatever was happening was between them, he refused to be dragged into their bizarre menage. Kootje guided the Beast to the door, assuring her, "I know where it is. Wait for me and I will show you."

Van Meegeren raised his open palms and lifted his eyes to the ceiling, before letting them fall on Joop, insinuating that gentlemen had to make allowances for the ladies. Joop shrugged his response and wondered what this anarchic trio was up to. Kootje returned and told van Meegeren that she would take Joanna home and return with the right jar. "I hope you don't need it today," she said as sweetly as she could. "That's not the point," van Meegeren objected. "Lapis is very expensive. It shouldn't be wasted. She knows that. She's just trying to vex me." Kootje crooned back at him, "Well then, we just won't let her."

Van Meegeren collapsed into a the chair, sniffed himself into a sulk, and whimpered, "It is cold in here." Kootje smiled at him and thrust her hand into the basket. "I thought it would be," she said, and withdrew a blue blanket. She shook out the folds and carefully spread the material around his shoulders. She wrapped her arms around him, and he trembled with exaggerated and largely imaginary chills. Joop was happy to be excluded from such intimacy. Van Meegeren's eyes beamed his thanks to Kootje, and she began her preparations to leave. She turned her back to van Meegeren and faced Joop. He watched her balance her weight on her toes with her heels just off the floor and twist one foot into profile. He could not tell whom she was asking, "Are my seams straight?" Van Meegeren answered after a long, lingering pause, "As they always are." She giggled herself into a swaying saunter to the door, and blew farewell kisses over her shoulder. "I'll be back with the lapis," she blurted, and her heels clattered down the stairs.

Van Meegeren gazed sadly at the empty door. "You are a very lucky man, Joop."

"How so?"

"You will never be able to afford such women."

Joop strangled his laughter and agreed, "Yes. Very lucky."

Van Meegeren sighed and pulled the blue blanket tighter around his throat. "She can behave herself when she wants something," van Meegeren assured Joop.

"She was very kind to remember the blanket," Joop observed.

"No, not Kootje. My wife," van Meegeren corrected. "The trick is to keep her wanting."

Joop wondered which of his women van Meegeren meant, until he grumbled to Joop. "They are never satisfied, you know." Joop steadied himself for another barrage of amusing anecdotes. "You give them a house, and they want furniture. If it is not new clothes, it's shoes. Now that she has the shoes, she's pestering me for a new closet for all the shoes. There's no end to it." Joop commiserated with a sigh and let van Meegeren float on his memories.

"I remember one glorious dinner party, oh years ago. Joanna served the hors d'oeuvres wearing nothing but black high-heels and an exquisite silver necklace from Faberge." He paused to let his wife of younger days rise in Joop's imagination. "Poor Joanna. If she tried that today, she would just be an embarrassment." Joop waited for van Meegeren's memories to pass, but he wondered how many regrets the man held close to his resentment. "Now she thinks the roof is tiled with custard pies," van Meegeren grunted.

"At least, there's Kootje," Joop reminded him.

"Ah. Kootje is magnificent," van Meegeren praised, "but she will never have the poise Joanna had," he added. "You could serve Kootje naked on a wheelbarrow full of pêches à la Melba and you'd still be looking for the apple in her mouth." Joop forced a knowing smile, so van Meegeren could feel he was sharing confidences with another man of the world. Van Meegeren stretched himself out of the chair, and Joop followed him back to the table.

Joop watched him lean forward and shake his head in disappointment. "Never send a woman to do a man's job." He glared at the basket of brushes. "These are useless for this canvas and she knows it." Joop had to ask, "What is useless? The paint?" Van Meegeren chuckled. His hand wriggled from under the blanket and grasped the stick. "This," he said. "Oh, the ball stick," Joop replied. Van Meegeren's throat bellowed a grainy chortle. "A ball stick," he wheezed. He passed the stick to Joop, and his hand disappeared under the blanket.

Joop examined the wooden rod, and when he felt the ball at its end, he realized that it was made of worn leather packed with some softer material. "This is something to paint a ceiling?" he asked. The hand reappeared and van Meegeren took it from Joop. "No," he said. "It is a maulstick." He saw that Joop was no more enlightened. "Here," he turned to the canvas. "I'll show you."

Van Meegeren picked up a brush with his right hand and his left firmly held the handle of the maulstick. He stretched forth his arms and the blanket fluttered to the floor. "You can't put your hand on the paint when it is wet," he said, and rested the bulbous end of the stick on the frame to the right. He raised and lowered his left hand so that the stick advanced and retreated from the canvas. Joop saw it swing like a loose door on one hinge and nodded his understanding. Van Meegeren pressed the edge of his right hand onto the center of the stick, and the point of the brush stood poised above the canvas, secure in his firm fingers. "The stick supports the hand while I paint." Van Meegeren pushed the end of the maulstick and the brush turned through a gentle arc. Joop watched a segment of a circle appear over the eyes of the central figure.

Van Meegeren turned to the table and dipped the point of his brush into a vermillion paste. He held the brush between his teeth, and Joop thought he looked like a hungry pirate. Van Meegeren selected a slightly bigger brush and charged it with a daub of something brown. He turned and looked at the center of the composition for just a few seconds and then raised the maulstick, as if saluting before a duel. The leather ball sat firmly on the frame and van Meegeren moved the stick to draw the brush closer to the canvas. His hands were perfectly steady and he gently manipulated the stick, so that just the brush's loose hairs marked the whiteness below it. Joop watched van Meegeren's hands waltz with brush and stick until delicate brown lines filled the empty spaces. He threw the brush onto the table and then turned back, snatching the small brush from between his teeth. Tiny red dots pebbled the brown lines, reminding Joop of insect bites on a sun-tanned arm.

Van Meegeren stepped back and selected a different brush with dry, tired hairs, and rested his hand on the maul. The brush just touched the red spots, and Joop could feel the quivering pressure of van Meegeren's finger almost kissing the canvas. Van Meegeren breathed strongly through distended nostrils for five minutes, and Joop could not pull his eyes away from the crimson framing the face. The wet paint reflected Van Meegeren's approving gaze.

Joop now saw a cascade of glistening brunette hair tumble from the top of the head and weave around the figure's eyes. Now that it had hair, the face became even younger than its bald outline and sweeter than any boy Joop had ever seen. The hair was so sensual he wanted to wrap its strands around his fingers and breathe the musky scent. For a moment, Joop thought he smelled spices, but it was the painting convincing him of its own reality. Again, he was astounded by the man's talent.

"And that's how you use a maulstick," van Meegeren crowed.

Joop could not understand why van Meegeren had complained so ardently. "What's wrong with the stick?" he asked. "Not big enough," van Meegeren said in disgust and threw it onto the work table.

Joop had learned that van Meegeren was composing from the edges to the center. Now it became clear why the stick had to be very long, so that he could paint comfortably in the center. The short stick just didn't reach far enough. One cough, and van Meegeren would drop the maulstick and ruin the painting. He tried to be helpful. "Would it be possible to do this with a broom stick?" Van Meegeren looked at Joop as if he had just crawled out of the woodwork, but his brows fluttered as he pondered the offer. "You know," he admitted, "that's really not a bad idea." Joop was pleased that he could help. "We could cut the stick to the length you need and then wrap the end with a sock and some tape," Joop thought aloud. Van Meegeren may have been a genius in devising new ways of making new paint look and act like ancient pigments, but he had always been too rich to have to improvise. Materials were to be bought from stores or commissioned from skilled craftsmen. He never needed to fabricate his own tools. He looked at Joop with quiet approval. "Yes," he exclaimed, "the very thing. A made-to-measure maulstick will suit me just fine."

Van Meegeren's yawn broke Joop's concentration. He heard the splashing of gin in a glass, the prelude to the morning nap. When he turned around, van Meegeren had already burrowed into the chair and was wrapping himself in the blanket. Joop paused until he felt van Meegeren was comfortable and asked, "What is lapus lazuli?" Van Meegeren took a moment to decide that the question was genuine, and raised his nose to the table. "Pick up that jar. The one my wife brought."

Joop retrieved the glass jar and waited. "Open it," van Meegeren ordered, never taking his eyes off the canvas. Joop twisted the lid from the container and looked into its shimmering hollow. Grains the size of fine sand glittered in the tunnel of glass. Brilliant sparkles of blue dazzled his eyes, as if a light had been turned on in a dark room. The blue mingled with   gold and white granules. "It is a very hard and precious stone," van Meegeren said. "And is very expensive, more expensive than gold," van Meegeren sighed as he sipped his gin. "Even rarer than gold," he continued. He waited and judged Joop's silence to be patient attention. After another taste of the gin, he explained, "Vermeer used it to achieve his magnificent coloration on robes and other garments."

"So you get the blue color from this stone?" Joop asked. Van Meegeren laughed and could not resist instructing his only pupil. "It is sometimes called ultramarine because it comes from across the sea." Joop nodded enthusiastically, for he really did enjoy his art lessons. Van Meegeren warmed to his subject and told Joop how he first ground the stone in a mortar with a pestle, until it was as fine as refined flour. "Now comes the really difficult part," he bragged. "I mix the stone dust with wax, resin, and olive oil to make a paste. Then I strain it through a fine silk stocking, really pushing hard with the fingers, so the paste oozes through the cloth."

When he was assured of Joop's complete attention, he revealed his secret method. "I do this three times, strain as hard as I can, and only then is the lapus ready for the brush." Joop understood how to work with textiles and easily followed the explanation. Van Meegeren put aside his condescension and shared, "but you must be very, very careful to keep the mixture inside the cloth so only the purest lapus arrives at the canvas."

Joop looked back into the jar and asked, "How much paint can you get from this?" Van Meegeren gargled back half his glass and grimaced. "One, maybe two, good brush strokes." Joop understood how this palmful of pigment was insufficient for such a large painting. "You teach me something new every day," Joop said, and van Meegeren felt the genuineness of his appreciation. When he was convinced that Joop was sincere, he warmed to his thanks. Van Meegeren waved the glass dismissively. "You are actually a very good pupil," he complimented.

At the second yawn, Joop mentioned that other duties awaited him in the rooms below and took his leave. Van Meegeren raised his glass in a farewell salute, and his eager lips moistened around the crystal rim.

Joop stood on the landing before the stairs, fingering through the pages of his notebook. He shuffled to a clean page and pencilled in, "maulstick," "lapus lazuli," and "ultramarine," and stopped. The remaining white in the page told him that he had no idea what he had just witnessed. He had received his lesson, but learned nothing. The Beast, Kootje, van Meegeren; their world was more distant than the mines across the sea that held the brilliant color. He knew they were a bundle of broken trusts and exciting betrayals, but the van Meegeren ménage left him as frustrated as he was confused. It was like listening to Dirk's finger tapping out Morse messages on his transmitter. He could see Dirk's finger jiggle the key and hear the crazy clicking, but it may as well have been in Chinese. He could never understand what was being said and had to trust his life to Dirk's mastery of the code. He decided to discuss it with Bobo.

He smelled the fumes of linseed oil and turpentine and reminded himself to winkle de Groot out of his hiding place and have him guard the ashtray before van Meegeren awoke to his next cigarette. He snapped shut his notebook and quietly walked down the stairs, for he wanted to leave van Meegeren to the comfort of his woolen cocoon. He ignored the fretful snores escaping from under the blue cloak.

Chapter 27

Steps

Jan bent over to the lift the crate. Every morning he was greeted by boxes of waste paper which the experts dumped in the foyer. When the first boxes appeared, van der Vegan had graciously instructed Jan to "keep anything you want." Jan had smiled vacantly and clenched his teeth at the man's smug generosity. Jan's first job of the day was to take out the trash. The duty was one of the little jobs he hated, and they were starting to multiply.

When the experts were finished rummaging through the documents, they stuffed them into any spare container. Van der Vegan had instructed them to "leave the garbage for Flushing." Jan resented being their rubbish boy, but kept his mouth shut because Joop wanted to find out what they were up to. Jan carried the box to his table in the opposite salon and it reminded him of a rotten cabbage. They rarely culled information of any value, but Jan performed the motions of flipping through the cast offs. He plowed through the tangled papers with a desultory hand, but it was the usual bundle of nothing. He pushed a few sheets aside but stopped abruptly when a cover of gray cloth rubbed his fingers.

He tugged the board from the muddle, and it confirmed his suspicion. It was a notebook. The cover was made of the same material as the disemboweled account book he had salvaged from that windy room. It smelled of the same damp mold, slippery as a fish. His fingers skimmed the cover, as if he were reading braille, He placed it on the table and retrieved the tattered shreds and their broken cover. "Yes," he thought, "exactly the same." He surmised that Nazi bureaucrats must have used the same books to record all their petty cash transactions.

He cracked open the new book, and his eyes cascaded down the neat ranks of a ledger. The first page offered him the thrilling adventures of Trude, who had bought twenty cents worth of milk "for office use." Each line listed the number and quality of "writing sticks," the absorbency of a "blotter - fifty cents," the colors and prices of various "inks - one guilder." The sums were collected and the prices combined to a thrilling finalé of "total" for each page.

He turned the page and the accounts jumped from cents to guilders. Jan wondered if they had been eating the pencils. There were entries for more paper, and he smiled at the expenditures for "underwear - male one guilder - female - two guilders and fifteen cents." He chuckled out loud as he imagined German soldiers goose-stepping in frilly French panties and their women clad from neck to ankle in one-piece suits of "flannel - winter" complete with the ass flap at the back.

The morning fights had yet to start, so he casually thumbed through the ledger, as if it were a magazine, minus the gossip and the pictures. He wondered who would need a "stapler - two guilders," but scanned down the lines to "health salts - one guilder" and "privy paper - best quality - seventy-six cents." Clearly, someone was having digestive problems on June 10, 1944.

It was then he noticed that the ledger listed the date at the top of each grouping of payments. If he followed the entries, the book became a diary of the all the people working at that office. He was soon engrossed in the tale of the daily routine at the "Ministry of Occupation - Office of Race Purity."

The more he looked, the more the ledger revealed. Most of the listings were for office supplies and all the little extras people purloined from budgets and wheedled out of indulgent supervisors. Jan wondered just why "Marthe" was being compensated for "wine - one bottle - two guilders." Maybe they had some sort of party, a celebration that required a toast, like a birthday or a promotion.

Jan's thumb lazily flipped pages, and the dates sped across his vision as if he were watching a passing train. June tumbled into July and the month slouched through the dog days of high summer. He tried to think of what he had been doing while Marthe was emptying her wine bottle. July was when they raided that warehouse in Delft for those rolls of newsprint.

Bobo had been shaking hard, but was perfectly still when they were stopped at the control. Joop had said they were taking their father to the hospital and the Germans waved them through without checking the truck. When they were out of hearing, Bobo laughed so hard they thought they would really have to find a doctor. Between his fits, he gulped fresh breath and shouted, "I haven't had so much fun in years." He had suggested that on the return trip they should lay him down under a sheet in the back of the truck and say they had been just a little too late at the hospital. Joop thought it was a good plan, but knew a different road around the checkpoint, so it was better not to risk two meetings with the same Germans on the same trip. Jan could now laugh at a night of terror and remember it as an adventure.

He turned the next page of the lever and found that July was a slow month. Either there were no more parties or Marthe had sobered up, for the wine bottles disappeared from the accounts. Jan concluded that they didn't have much to celebrate. In the second week of July, he started to note addresses. There were house numbers neatly scribed beside payments. They were mostly in Amsterdam. Then in the third week, the entries became more expensive. Instead of "ink - bottle - one - sixty-eight cents" there appeared just a number "2" in ornate curves followed by "80." His curiosity led him to a "5" balanced next to "200." The end of July was a boom with "Deventer - 440." He wondered what was happening at "Deventer - 440" to be worth four hundred and forty guilders.

Jan let his memory march in time with the accounts. "Deventer - 440" coincided with the trip to Apeldoorn. That was where he'd first met Dirk and all the big jobs started. They were able to get downed pilots through the German lines and smuggle them back to the British. Dirk liked the Americans, mainly because they were so willing to jump into the fight. Some even wanted to stay in Holland and kill more Germans. Joop had been very worried when two of them insisted on staying to "help the Resistance," but Dirk convinced them that they were doing a much better job dropping bombs on German tanks. Dirk had a real way with words.

As his eyes slipped through the expensive days of July, Jan started reading names, beside addresses, numbers, and amounts. All the names on each line were different, but they were all Dutch. Somebody named Simons received eighty guilders, but there was also a back payment of two guilders and fifty cents. Jan shook his head in wonder at the paymaster's diligence. This accountant even recorded such a small sum down to the cents.

The two and a half guilders scraped at Jan's memory. He lay the ledger on the table trying to recall when he had heard of such a sum, but the memory was slippery.

Somehow it was mixed up with a pencil, and he again wondered if he was losing his mind. What with hearing colors and seeing sounds, who could know what was going on in his head. He certainly didn't. The torn sheet from his visit to the house of mournful wind danced over his vision, and he searched for the torn papers he had saved. On the back of the fragment was the number one drawn as if it were a platform board at a railroad station. Beside it stood "two guilders and fifty cents." The ripped fragment was older than the bound sheet in front of him, but there was some sort of connection just beyond his grasp. He copied "one - two guilders and fifty cents" into his notebook and told it, "You're not running away this time."

He returned to the ledger, searching for any pattern to the payments. He did not know what drove him to the names and the numbers. They were glowing darkly on the creamy paper, and he felt like a little boy entranced by his first fireworks. The numbers burst into incandescent questions and flared their brief lives between the black lines. Each explosion illuminated the addresses and Jan sat waiting for their climax. He started to divide the amounts by the solitary numbers until they revealed that the payments were all multiplications of forty guilders each. There was a brief pause when his mind clouded over with confusion, but the next line was too bold to ignore. "One hundred and twenty guilders" were paid to "Ans van Dijk" for "three" on "July 26." The address was in Zaandam. What was so valuable in a backwater like Zaandam that this van Dijk should receive such money?

Jan copied "forty" onto his notebook just below the "two and a half" and started multiplying by the dangling numbers. It only took a few steps to know that the numbers were people. The ledger was from the Office of Race

Purity. The people were Jews. The amounts were the prices paid for each betrayal. Between the two entries he could see that what was only worth the price of a packet of cigarettes had risen to a weekly salary. The less Jews there were to turn in, the higher their price. Forty guilders per person showed how rare this merchandise had become. He was afraid to look any further.

He knew he should stop at the end of July. He knew what waited for him on the next page, coiled to strike. He knew there would be relief, but he was not willing to pay the price. He should close the book and throw it away with all the other rubbish. That was all he was good for. Van de Vegan had said he was just a garbage man.

Ignorance could be bliss, but he did not really believe that. He grasped the cover and and pressed the book closed, but his hand would not release the grimy gray cloth. He wrestled with his own fist, but his weakness was not equal to this trial of strength. Even if he burned it, the book would still smolder in his mind. The uncertainty would be like waiting for the last firework that would never lighten the clouds. He surrendered, and his fingers rolled back the pages to "August - 1944."

It was on the fifth line. He read it aloud, "236 Prinsengracht - 8 - Ahlers - 320 guilders." It was the place. It was them. There were eight loaded into the truck. The smiling girl was worth forty guilders. The entry scorched his eyes, and he could smell the truck's exhaust. Doubt was impossible. The memory flooded his face and he tried to rub relief into his eyes. Tears would help, but there were none. Just the pain.

He sat solitary in his impotence and his shame. "Ahlers" jumped from the page and laughed at him. He could not tell if Ahlers was a man or a woman, but Ahlers was cackling in Jan's face and fanning it with three hundred and twenty guilders. The laughter pounded at his skull, rhythmic in its mockery of his own part in the girl's betrayal. He appealed to her smile and the pain collapsed to a dull throb. He begged the face for forgiveness. Her eyes still beamed at him. There was just a friendly sadness to her expression, and he found relief in what he thought was her sympathy. She knew he was sorry, but her smile posed the hidden question, "What will you do, Dutchman? What will you do?"

The challenge smothered him in soothing calm. The pain had crawled back into his eyes, but he could keep it imprisoned in those blue orbs until he found the strength to stand up. He grasped the pencil and forced his fingers to write "Ahlers" on his notepad. It was a fitting title to "8" and "320," and was all that he needed. There was no use writing down the address, for he could never forget it.

He slowly pushed back the chair and the legs shrieked on marble to echo the squeals of the slaughterhouse through the room and into the foyer. He rose, grabbed the ledger in his left fist and swung his coat around his shoulders like a bull fighter. He would find Joop. Joop would know what to do.

He thrust his left arm into his coat sleeve, walked around the table, and strode to the foyer. The scent halted him at the entrance. He looked up the stairs and saw Kootje walking down. She hovered in a perfumed cloud, sweet, moist as ripe fruit. He watched her place one foot on the next step, but something strange was happening to her. As she moved from step to step, her body stayed on all the steps behind her. She was moving down, but all the other Kootjes were standing still, each frozen on the step she had already left. Jan looked at each of them, and the vision was like the bellows of an accordion pulling a parade of Kootjes past him. At each step, one Kootje would merge into the next Kootje until they all gathered together in the foyer before him. Jan stood enchanted by the procession of women. Her perfume was the last of Kootje to leave. The open door blew a morning gust into the foyer and her scent quietly left the building.

Jan thought he had seen some bizarre reflection as between two mirrors facing each other, repeating the same image into infinity. The stairs had neither mirrors nor windows. The walls were too dull to cast such a magical image of the woman.

He stood in the afterglow of his hallucination, feeling a little ridiculous with only one arm in his coat. Out of the crimson mist in the corner of his eye, he sensed van de Vegen standing before him. The man was annoying and intruding on Jan's business. He vaguely heard the demand, "And just where do you think you're…" Van der Vegan spun once. His face smeared a bloody trail down the wall as he slumped unconscious to the floor.

Jan stepped gratefully into the morning, pulling on his coat, and wondering why his right hand was clenched in a painful fist.

Chapter 28

Memory Lane

Bobo had made his peace with the infernal bell. When the Liberation had allowed him to return to the shop, the booming demon was tamed into an annoying interruption. No longer would its knell herald doom. Now that the shop was fit for customers and had something to offer them, its playful tinkling was an invitation. He dropped his broom in the dark room, obeyed its brassy summons, and stepped through the door to the counter.

Two Canadian soldiers stood relaxed before him. "Ban oo bake oor pishers?" one of them asked. Bobo strained to comprehend their accents and with shrugged shoulders and a hand pressing his ear forward, like a drunken bat, politely mimed, "I can not understand." The taller soldier's eyebrows appealed to the shorter soldier, who dug his forefingers into his mouth, spread wide his lips, and revealed toothless pink gums. The tall man nodded enthusiastically and opened his empty mouth. The short man mimed clicking a shutter, and Bobo exclaimed, "Ah!" The soldiers raised supplicating hands into the universal sign for "What now?" and Bobo responded with open arms inviting them to the back room.

He placed his new clients before the camera and waited as they finished combing their hair. The soldiers crossed their arms and struck a pose that reminded Bobo of wanted posters in the Old West. It was not his business if his customers wanted to look like Jesse James. When the camera was charged with film and they were ready, Bobo commanded them to say "Cheese." Their mouths spread wide, they slurred "shleeze," the camera flashed, and their moment was now immortalized in silver nitrate. Bobo could not resist a smile and was happy to enter their rough bonhomie. He was curious as to whether they had fallen victims to gum disease, a rifle butt, or a friendly brawl, but it was more important that these two friends wanted a memorial of their missing teeth.

They put on their caps, and Bobo noticed they both used two fingers to measure the distance between their right eyebrows and the edges of their cap bands. Apparently there was some uniform code which they automatically obeyed when getting dressed. Bobo enjoyed the rest of their dumb show. For the next half hour, three pairs of hands and a comical repertoire of eager grimaces and sloppy smiles revealed that Bobo was a real photographer, pliers in the hands of a dentist had removed their teeth, they were planning to get very drunk, and Dutch women were very pretty.

The rubbing of fingers and thumbs accompanied by inquiring shrugs told Bobo they wanted to know "How much?" The fingers were fluent in numbers, but it was impossible to translate the gestures into guilders, dollars, and cents. The tall soldier cut through the misunderstanding when he pulled a fistful of coins from his pocket and rattled them on the counter. Bobo pointed to a large silver coin, and his hunched question solicited, "Thlifty slents." Bobo calculated that this was half of one Canadian dollar. He pulled the coin aside and raised two fingers. The soldier pushed a second coin to join the first and mimed "Really?" Bobo enthusiastically nodded and watched the pair of them slurp through a discussion that had to be about the money. Bobo wondered how they would be able to haggle the price with no teeth.

The soldiers reached some sort of agreement. They beamed at Bobo, and cut out two more coins from the silver and copper herd. The tall soldier swept the remaining coins off the counter and into his pocket. Bobo understood that they wanted to pay two Canadian dollars for two prints of their portrait. Bobo showed them his pocket watch. Their eyes narrowed to follow his finger circling the glass face twice. The finger then pointed to the floor. After a moment's soggy consultation, they nodded agreement that they would be back in twenty-four hours to collect their "pisher," waved their farewells, and clanged out of the shop. Bobo returned to his labors, for although the back room was cluttered, it was now clean.

Liese had brought Sarah to the shop for an adventure. She had taken one look at the filth, and soundly berated Bobo to declare war on the squalor. When she saw where he had been sleeping, she let out a yowl and shamed him into handing over his bedding. She could not tell where the sheet ended and the cobwebs started. The solitary blanket filled her with as much revulsion for the room as she was flooded with sympathy for the man who had been sleeping under its dirty mantle. She had stormed out of the shop casting commands to "sweep up the garbage" behind her, and Bobo was overjoyed to obey.

The next day she returned with the sheet laundered and butchered into cuts of useful rags. He sheepishly grinned his embarrassment, when she offered him the folded blanket, "It looks so much better now that it is no longer brown." He accepted her loving scolds and felt he was worthy of a good nagging. Her visitations were enough to make the shop into his home, no matter how temporary he imagined his residence would be.

The garbage consisted of mountains of old photographs. He knew they were precious to somebody and started to sort them into piles. The floor soon held files of prints organized by category and date. As with every good photographer, Bobo had written the date and the sitter's name on the back of the print. He organized the cards according to when the image was captured. He could sit for an hour at a time tossing the cards as if he were a bored croupier, until he had a little stock for each month in a year. Once the month was filled, he sorted each picture according to subjects and dates, so that "January - 1936" was divided into "Portraits," "Celebrations," "Weddings/Funerals," "Sports," and "Holidays." He soon realized that this was not merely making order out of chaos. There was money in all these memories.

Willie's portrait in the window had attracted people to the shop, not because they were interested in Willie, but because the picture reminded them that their lives extended back beyond their most recent catastrophes.

The first man had stepped to the counter with his hands clutched in anxiety and asked, "I wonder if you have any photographs of the van der Leiden family?" Bobo had no idea who they were, but enquired if the man had any recollection of when the photographs had been taken. The reply of "sometime about ten years ago" brought out the box labeled "1936." Bobo offered the carton of jumbled cards and left the man to search in peace.

Bobo busied himself with one of Liese's immaculate rags and evicted the dust from a drawer. He sneaked glances at the man quietly fingering each one of the photos. The man's face tightened in recognition. Bobo did not wish to intrude upon the silent search, but when he glanced up, one photo rested on the counter. The shuffling in the box resumed until the man pushed it away. Bobo was as politely attentive as a funeral mute. "How much for these?" the man asked gruffly. Bobo looked at two photos of a small boy about seven years old. The face was framed between two candles on a cake and a white armband circled the boy's right sleeve. Clearly it was a portrait of a First Communion. "Ten cents, each," Bobo said, cheerily.

The man selected coins out of a small purse, and shook his head, "This new money confuses me." Bobo lightened the man's embarrassment. "The new silver is very bright." The man took refuge in small talk. "I hear these are minted in America." Bobo nodded agreement. "American silver is so much better than German zinc." That coaxed a wry smile from the man and he put on his glasses to read "Ten" on the coin. He placed the two coins on the table and Bobo offered him the yellowing prints. The man summoned up the most courteous "Danke" and was gone.

Bobo leaned with his palms on the counter, peering at the coins. The currency had indeed been minted in America. The Dutch had quickly accepted the new money but kept the old names. The denominations of five, ten, and twenty cents, quickly became stuivers, dubbeltjes, and kwartjes. Bobo picked up the ten cent piece and reflected how the dour Dutch could so quickly turn most things into a ridiculous joke.

Hitler had made his personal lackey, Arthur Seyss-Inquart, into the Governor of the Netherlands. The German master was jovially hated, but his growing brutality made laughter dangerous. The people armed themselves with simple humor and nicknamed Seyss-Inquart, zes-en-een-kwart, because he was only worth six and a quarter cents. Bobo remembered that Willie had welded some coins onto an old cigarette lighter. The little sculpture intrigued Bobo, but he could find no meaning to it. Willie told Bobo to "count up the coins." The total added up to six and a quarter cents. Willie had reduced their overlord to small change. He had flicked the lighter's wheel and whispered, "We'll burn that bastard for half the price." Jokes could be very costly. Bobo placed the two coins beside the golden guilder the old woman had paid for Willie's photo.

When he returned to the piles of photos, he decided to try and match the prints with as many of the negatives as he could find. It would take weeks to join the positives with the negatives, but by then, he would have the prints gathered in chronological order. He had almost convinced himself that the job wouldn't be so bad, when the bell and the footstep said that Joop had arrived. This was odd for a morning. Joop usually visited in the afternoons.

Joop's concentrated frown greeted Bobo's salute. "So, having a break from the world of high art?" he asked. Joop shot back a wry smile. "Got tired of learning about a maulstick." Bobo chuckled and assured him, "I'd like to take that stick to his back."

"He has his women, for that," Joop said.

"They showed up again?"

"They were very calm," Joop said questioningly. "The young one was very helpful."

"That means she wants something," Bobo huffed.

Joop sat on the edge of the display window's platform, and Bobo waited for Joop's frustration to percolate into words.

"I just can't understand them," Joop burst out.

"That's to be expected," Bobo replied. "They don't understand themselves."

"He seems to have wives and girlfriends all over the place."

"Probably does. But you have made one mistake."

"Just one?" Joop asked.

"You think he is married."

Bobo smirked around Joop's confusion. Joop laced his fingers around one knee and rocked back and forth through his thoughts. "And that's my mistake?" Joop demanded

"Such people don't have marriages, at least not the way you think about a marriage."

"So what is it?" Joop asked

"It's just a set up."

"He has a harem?"

"In a manner of speaking," Bobo conceded. "It doesn't matter to him or to the women. Everything is just temporary."

"So, he thinks he has an endless supply of such women?" Joop asked.

"Oh yes," Bobo said.

"Just lining up to join his little set-up?"

Bobo could feel the contempt oozing from Joop. He watched Joop clutch his knee tighter. That was always the sign that he hated admitting that he could not understand something. He never knew if Joop was afraid of the unknown or ashamed of his own ignorance. He cast a thought to relieve Joop's mounting aggression. "For such women, a good marriage is looking forward to a better divorce," he confided.

"So, it's just money."

"Just money."

Bobo looked at Joop as if he had just explained the principle of gravity, and then bit his tongue. There was no reason Joop would know any of this. He was young and his experience was limited to managing a small textile factory and fighting against the greatest evil that had ever befallen them. Bobo had often marveled that Joop was one of the small people who did very big things. He solved problems immediately, looking for the quickest route to the solution. Dirk had been a complicated genius, but all his brilliance was useless without Joop making his hare-brained schemes a reality. Dirk had admitted this when they were smuggling the British survivors out of Arnhem. Bobo had reminded Dirk that Joop's greatest triumph was keeping them all alive. But now Joop faced a reality that was beyond his understanding. Bobo knew he had to give Joop the knowledge that his life had withheld. There were limits, but they would go beyond them together.

"It's almost as if nothing really matters to them," Joop speculated.

"Oh there is a lot that matters to them. It's just not the same things which matter to us," Bobo said.

Joop shook his head, as if casting a fly out of his ear. "I have something to show you," Bobo confided. From under the counter he pulled a thin magazine. Its few pages were bound by simple staples, as if it had been starved of news. Bobo pointed his finger to the picture of the Queen filling the front page. He read out the headline, "The Mother of the Nation." Joop was careful to follow Bobo's lead.

Wilhelmina's return from exile had been cheered as the rebirth of the country. She had actually set her first steps on Dutch soil before her whole domain had been liberated. She was protected behind the British and Canadian armies. As more territory was freed, she was able to return to her palaces. She brought her son, Prince Bernard, who was making sure that the Dutch liberated themselves as much as they could. When he returned to his own house and saw the squalor the Germans had hurriedly left behind them, he wanted to burn the palace. The Queen talked him out of torching Het Loo and informed him that she would be living in a simple cottage, so she could share the trials of her people.

It was no publicity stunt, for she really wanted to live the life of a simple Dutch woman. So the magazine displayed her cooking the royal family's dinner over a wood stove. She could have been taken for an aging plump peasant woman going about her household chores.

Bobo pointed to the picture of the Queen holding the frying pan. "This is what they hate more than anything," he explained.

"You mean van Meegeren is no monarchist?" Joop asked.

"I mean that the very worst thing for any of these people is their Queen in a housedress."

Joop studied the photo, and Bobo's idea burrowed through his ignorance. "So they are loyal to the Queen," Joop said. "As long as she is their queen," Bobo finished.

Bobo turned over the front page and the next two pages were filled with photographs of government ministers. There were all wearing striped trousers and cut-away morning coats. Some raised their top hats to the photographers, and others just cast a haughty scowl at the lens. Joop immediately saw the contrast between the Queen and the gentlemen of her cabinet. Joop grasped the front page between his thumb and forefinger and swung it back and forth. At each swish of the paper, the Queen grew bigger in Joop's imagination. "She doesn't look like she would fit in with this lot," he mused.

"That is the whole point," Bobo said. "She doesn't."

Joop studied his thoughts, and his eyes begged Bobo for more. "They need her more than she needs them," Bobo said.

"And van Meegeren's stable of ladies?" Joop asked.

"They want something from him, and he is holding it back." He waited for the recognition to flash in Joop's eyes and then pointed to the pictures of the ministers. "They want something from her, and she is holding it back."

"What do they want from a Queen?"

"Their places. After all, they are Her Majesty's Ministers. Without her, they are just storefront mannequins in rather loose pants."

"So she is their problem," Joop said.

"Just imagine what an insult it is for such finely tailored gentlemen to have to bow to a housewife. I can almost hear them cursing their royal 'huis vrouw'."

Bobo picked up the five and the ten cent coins from the drawer and pressed them with his thumb onto the counter. His finger circled Wilhelmina's face on the ten cent coin. "Loyal to the Crown," he whispered. He picked up the five cent piece, and Joop stared at Her Majesty's profile. "And to the Half-Crown," Bobo said.

"So, it's all about the money," Joop said.

"Yes," Bobo assured him. "They want the money."

Bobo tried to fathom Joop's thoughts from his worried face. "The same money we don't have," Joop confessed.

Bobo's opinions led Joop to his own problems. He could no longer ignore them. They both knew they were trapped between the Flight Control Office and the van Meegeren's studio. They were paid in ration cards, but they all knew that such pasteboard currency was as unreliable as trading cigarettes for food. Joop had been evading the reality of their situation, but he could hide nothing from Bobo. Their government salaries were quicksand. They would have to find an income that wasn't tied to the men in the striped trousers.

Joop remembered Dirk telling him about civil servants spreading a rumor that Queen Wilhelmina was a secret agent of the Communists. They had laughed at the thought of the Royal Dumpling passing state secrets to Moscow, when there was no such thing as a secret in all of Holland. Now he thought there might be something behind the joke.

Malicious gossip was one of the best ways to hide a plan. They themselves had spread lies to guard a greater truth. Maybe these gentlemen of the government were doing the same thing, only this time, they were trying to control the throne. He well knew that the loyalties of the most patriotic could be bought, but he had never thought they would poison the Queen's reputation. Bobo was right; look to the money.

The bell clanged, and a young boy entered the shop with a confident step. Joop slid away from the counter with the magazine and resumed his seat on the window ledge. He calmly pretended to read, in case the bell announced trouble. Joop looked at the smart blue jacket that gave the lad an official air. The boy marched up to the counter and demanded, "Are you Mr. Lermolieff?" Bobo's eyes narrowed over the greasy blond hair, "That depends on who wishes to speak with Mr. Lermolieff." Bobo's tone befuddled the boy, who stood a little less certainly before the counter. He pulled an envelope from his jacket pocket. "I have a letter for Mr. Lermolieff." Bobo offered his hand. "I'll see that it is delivered." The boy hesitated long enough for Bobo to snatch it.

Even though his errand was complete, the boy dawdled in a way familiar to Bobo. "Do you sell pictures?" the boy asked. Bobo caught the nervousness in the voice. "Yes. I have pictures on a variety of subjects." The boy's eyes glinted in anticipation, until Bobo asked him, "Would you like to see a picture of a naked lady?" The sudden knowledge that the old man knew exactly what he wanted made the boy hide his embarrassment behind his indignation. "Certainly not," he protested and spun on his heel to make a hasty exit. Bobo yelled after him, "They're of your mother."

Joop's laughter drowned out the jolly bell. He dropped the magazine on the counter and asked, "What did the delivery boy leave?" Bobo held up the envelop and ran his finger over the embossed crest. "It's from the court." Joop smirked. "What do they want now?" Bobo's finger slit open the envelop and he unfolded the letter. "What they want is five thousand pages of stationery," he answered. He passed the page to Joop, who immediately saw it was an order from the Central Criminal Court of Amsterdam. "They need new letterheads for their paper," Bobo added. Joop read aloud, "The name and address of the court on the left of the crest. To the right of the crest in bold, 'Case Number and Date.'"

Bobo rubbed his chin and said, "We have plenty of foolscap paper. Now we just need the right ink." Joop knew exactly where to find it. Now was the time to call in a favor or two from Spierdijk's newspaper friends. "Can you do it?" Joop asked. "Of course. We still have the hand press. I can design the letterhead and cut out the die. In a week, they'll have their ten boxes of their brand-new stationary, for their brand-new court."

They stood pondering this strange commission. Neither of them wanted to thank a benevolent providence, until they had proof that this was actually a good thing. Joop pulled up his collar and turned to the door, "I'll get the ink."

Bobo smoothed out the creases of the court order and laid it on the counter beside the magazine. His eyes darted between the new commission and the photograph of the Queen. "I suppose they both have their courts," he mused to himself, "but hers is in the kitchen."

He put the order into the drawer to lie beside the coins and returned to studying the magazine photo. His eyes studied the Queen's dress. It was so simple, that it could be found on any woman in Holland. He followed the lines of her hips, wider than the square of her starched apron. The sleeves were gathered over her matronly elbows and held in place by two buttons. She looked very comfortable in the ample skirt. He felt the old thrill of a new idea bubbling behind his eyes.

Chapter 29

Lazarus

The bell clattered softly, and Bobo leaned back to peer from the dark room into the shop. He straightened quickly when he saw the customer standing rigid at the counter. He waited for the man to become impatient and stepped into the shop.

"Good afternoon, Judge," he greeted with and attentive air.

"Ah, yes," Judge Voss said with friendly superiority.

"Have you come about the stationary for the court?"

"As a matter of fact, I have," Voss answered.

Voss pulled a page of blank paper from his coat pocket and unfolded it on the counter. He pointed to the crest, and Bobo examined the letterhead with professional concentration.

"I am so glad to see the lion restored to its rightful place," Voss confessed.

Bobo had placed the Dutch lion in the center of the letterhead. The animal's rampant right paw raised a sword, and the other grasped a clutch of seven arrows in its claws. He had crowned the tawny head with Wilhelmina's diadem. Bobo stood calmly waiting.

"The previous emblem seemed inappropriate for the times," Bobo assured him. The Judge took a moment before releasing his compliments. "Yes, excellent work." He evaded Bobo's stare. 'We can hardly dispense justice under a swastika."

The Judge stood still, but his eyes darted around the shop. Bobo sensed indecision in his hesitation. "I have some questions about paper," Voss said casually.

"I would be happy to discuss the material with you."

"Unfortunately, I have left them at the court."

The Judge made a great display of restrained friendliness, fanning Bobo's suspicion. "Why don't you come to my chambers?" Voss offered. He was angling for something, and Bobo imagined that he was both Voss's bait and the fish.

"When would be convenient for Your Honor?" he asked.

"About eight this evening?" Voss suggested.

Bobo nodded and kept his mouth shut. Voss folded the paper back into this pocket. "Until this evening." He turned and carefully opened the door. The wind gusted from the street, and Voss gently closed the door behind him. The bell bowed to his departure, but barely tinkled.

Bobo's gaze followed Voss' back across the street, until he disappeared into the crowd. The Judge had given him an invitation he couldn't refuse.

The Judge's chambers smelled of wax. Bobo watched Voss' shadow waltz over the gleaming wood panelling and thought that the servants must have vanquished decades of dust to make the room shine with such brilliance. He sat upright in the high-backed armchair, smiling at Voss's tales of the Occupation. The Judge was enjoying his anecdotes and swayed to the rhythms of his tales. Bobo thought Voss's arms were as articulate as a drunken Frenchman, but he was mindful to play the part of the old comrade. Bobo caught himself being charmed by Voss's stories of Dutch courtiers and German generals. "Of course they all had their pictures, so van Meegeren's little business is entirely plausible," Voss concluded. Bobo heartily agreed that counterfeiting was a very profitable business in both peace and war, and guarded his every word.

"You were interested in paper," Bobo suggested, trying to bring the banter back to Voss' stated purpose for this friendly chat. "Actually, I have an interest in many papers," the Judge confided after glancing to the door. Bobo stiffened at Voss' intimation that he was sharing a guilty secret with one who understands both secrets and guilt.

"I asked the Immigration Service to search their records for the name Lermolieff." Bobo's eyes narrowed at the casual admission of his discovery. "They gave me an entrance visa from some Belgium border crossing."

Voss paused to judge the reaction, but Bobo's face revealed only boredom. Voss added, "There was also an application for permission to reside, dated 1936."

Voss was supremely confident that he was playing his cards in the right order. "The address listed was a hospital in Switzerland."

Bobo wriggled his nose and sighed, as if this bit of gossip was the most tedious of the Judge's anecdotes. A faint smirk wriggled over Voss's lips. "How long were you a patient at the Dymphna Institute, Mr. Roberto Giovanni Morelli?"

Bobo clenched his teeth, hoping this was all that Voss knew. For ten years he had battled the horror of Dymphna. He kept it shored behind stout walls of forgetfulness, but the nightmare always threatened to surge over the banks. When it became too much to bear, Bobo thought he was the little boy with his finger in the dyke, screaming for help. Voss's words ambushed him, and Madeleine's smiling face floated on the deluge of his memory.

They had assigned Madeleine to him, with the calm assurance of his failure. She was about nine years old, stood four feet high, and weighed eighty pounds. The space in her patient record for parents and/or next of kin was blank. She was a prime example of microcephaly, but the attendants dubbed her the happiest of the pinheads. Her every waking moment was a dance. She would hop and whirl through the hospital's corridors, until she crawled exhausted into Bobo's lap. She was christened The Mad Dancer, but when Bobo stroked her distended skull, she was simply Little Maddy.

Bobo guided her through the cycle of experts, but she laughingly defied their increasingly exasperated attempts to discover a cure. Her first therapist gave up, when she would not sit still long enough to reveal her incestuous obsession to murder her father. Bobo pointed out that she was mute, only to be dismissed from the consulting room. The next specialist concluded that Maddy's dance was her natural, but mentally limited, attempt to connect with the world soul. Her laughter and her dervish contortions were signs of her desperation to break the bonds of her inhibitions and release her mind. Bobo rejected the prognosis with the obvious fact that Maddy was the clinic's most unrestrained patient. Then a new therapy crept into the institute.

The faculty and staff were offered a series of lectures by Europe's most eminent psychologist. His intellectual authority was unassailable. He sadly informed them that the most rigorous research in Germany had discovered the obvious and very regrettable truth that nature makes mistakes. This stark fact was unavoidable, and they must have the courage to face the truth. Incurable cases were useless eaters and would always be a burden to themselves and to others. The medical profession had a sacred duty to show mercy to such unfortunates. Maddy was scheduled for mercy.

Bobo first attempted to reason with the director, and when that failed, resorted to shouting rage. He was warned of the consequences of his unprofessional behavior. Bobo ignored the threat and continued his tirade. He did not see the attendant walk into Maddy's room clutching the syringe.

Bobo collapsed when he had no more strength to fight. The mercy was swift, but its suddenness broke Bobo. When he regained consciousness, Maddy's smile still hovered over the autopsy table. They had sought her soul at the point of a scalpel.

The next morning he left Dymphna. The rucksack slung over his shoulder held his clothes, some money, and the few documents that recorded his life. He started to walk downhill, and the decline made his legs fly from the horror. He stopped running when the North Sea swirled around his knees.

Voss saw the red tide rise behind Bobo's eyes, and hoped he had not gone too far.

"Doctor Morelli," Bobo said.

"I was under the impression that you were a patient in this mental hospital with the strange name."

"I was on the medical faculty of the St. Dymphna Institute for Incurables."

Voss was not pleased to have his conclusions so completely disproved. His presuppositions were rarely challenged, but this man was destroying his conjectures with provable facts. Bobo's eyes bored into Voss. "I am sure that the Swiss authorities will attest to my medical certification, if you care to enquire. I will give you the address. It's in Lausanne."

"Is that why you speak with a French accent?" Voss observed.

"I can hardly speak Dutch with a Swiss accent."

"Why did you make your home in Holland?"

"The shared culture."

Voss looked at Bobo as if he were crazy, for he could find nothing in common with the southern mountain people.

"The Swiss and the Dutch love cheese and chocolate," Bobo affirmed. "I just left the cuckoo-clocks behind."

Bobo's wry humor told Voss he was losing this game. Months of interrogations would be useless on this man. When he thought he had some control over his guest, Voss could always use a more circuitous route to whatever Morelli was so successfully hiding.

Bobo pulled his pipe from his pocket, and Voss watched him delicately pull pinches of tobacco from a small pouch. Bobo carefully selected the brown shreds and his thumb gently pressed them into the bowl. Priming his pipe bought some time, for Voss' questions were like ropes thrown through raging and indifferent waves.

They stared over the chasm of their experiences.

Bobo blocked Voss at every turn. Voss felt trapped by Morelli's nonchalant disinterest. He decided that only trust would work. He picked up a paper from his desk and offered it to Bobo. "This is the paper which so intrigues me," he said.

Bobo did not have to read it. Voss could not escape Bobo's glare. Voss read aloud the bold type in German and Dutch, "The following criminals have been executed by order of the Chief Commandateur of Deventer." Voss paused before intoning, "Included in this list of the condemned are the names of Joseph Piller and Jan Flushing."

Bobo flushed with pride to hear such official confirmation of his success.

"How did you do it?" Voss asked.

Bobo smelled the question's sincerity. "It was as easy as child's play," he confessed.

"Please tell me." Bobo heard the need in the Judge's voice.

"I printed the execution warrants," he simply stated. "We gave them to the newspapers, and they published the full list of names."

"It was that simple?"

"The newspapers reported the deaths of Piller and Flushing, among others."

Bobo's thumbnail struck a match-head and the flame fluttered before Voss' eyes. He watched Bobo tease the fire over the bowl and the smoke engulfed them in sulphur and spices. Bobo blew the smoke away from Voss. "When we returned the warrants to the Gestapo, I simply included the fakes."

"So everybody thought they were already dead."

"As I said. It was child's play."

"Clearly, it worked," Voss said with evident admiration.

"There were twelve of us," Bobo continued. "Four remain alive. I suppose that is not a bad average."

Bobo judged that Voss was genuine in his desire for the truth. He would not have kept such souvenirs, if he had any other reason than to quench his curiosity. He decided to join Voss' quest. "How did you know?"

"The paper," Voss said. "You must have supplied the paper."

"It was all that I had."

Voss felt a trust he thought had died long ago. Morelli was drawing more out of him than he expected. He started to enjoy their confessions. "The Germans always used cheap paper for their execution warrants. This one stood out because of its quality."

"So, only the paper made you suspicious of the document?" Bobo enquired.

"I have known since July of 1943. The paper itself screamed that you were alive."

"Next time, I will use newsprint," Bobo joked.

Voss could not restrain himself. He longed to enlighten Morelli about his own survival. "Like all criminals," he explained, "the German are sticklers for the law. They must have everything nice and legal. So, they shoot the people first and then find their victims guilty. It is their version of pleasure before business, but they are very businesslike in their crimes."

Bobo felt Voss' need and quietly puffed his pipe. The cloud rising around Morelli's head was like the incense burning when Voss proclaimed his lawyer's vows.

"They sent me so many such pieces of paper," Voss sighed. "All for people who were already dead. I had to sign their fictions under a seal stating that the court authorized the punishment."

Bobo could taste the hatred in Voss' words. They were far more bitter than his pipe stem. "So, you kept this one warrant out of thousands."

"Yes," Voss said. "But you remained dead."

"But why did you keep this one?" Bobo pressed.

"There had to be some memorial to such imaginative courage."

Voss leaned back in his chair, and Bobo knew the man experienced some relief, but could not tell what it was. He felt long abandoned emotions when Voss said, "You faked your own deaths. Hid your lives in a mountain of corpses. I truly admire what you have done."

Bobo understood that Voss' signature had filled graves. Thousands of murders had flowed from the nib of his pen. Bobo could not refuse the man what little comfort he had left to offer. "Judge Voss. I understand your pain."

"And what is your diagnosis, Doctor Morelli?"

"I don't think you want to know."

"Let me be the judge of that."

Bobo felt his pipe grow cold in his palm. Voss' eyes begged, and Bobo summoned all his capabilities to answer this silent appeal.

"I see a boy filled with a love for justice. The boy devours the books of law and is welcomed into the fellowship of advocacy. The boy is now complete, and the man revels in his profession. But then, the laws change. They gang together and pull out knives. The lawyer watches the laws flay justice and is terrified that such beautiful things have become monstrous. The laws turn on the lawyer, and he hides under a judge's robe. But he knows the law, and fears the law's thirst for blood."

Voss slumped before Bobo's words. The old pity stirred in Bobo, but pity was cheap. Voss' tormented face demanded more. The compassion welled within Bobo, and he greeted it as a friend he thought was long gone. He leaned forward, until his eyes raised Voss's face to his own. "I know you can not say the thing that so hurts you. But I know you have the courage to hear my words. Medicine can not heal. The law can not protect the innocent. But we can still hope."

"But where will we find the cure for our souls, Doctor?"

Bobo could not answer. He understood the limits, but he also knew that Voss must go beyond them. "You wondered at the name of the institute," he said.

Voss raised his troubled brows, and Bobo knew it was time to confess and to absolve. "Dymphna was a woman about a thousand years ago. People would come to her for the miracle of healing."

Voss nodded his agreement. There was more that Morelli could tell him, and he waited until Bobo revealed, "Dymphna is the patron saint of the insane." He felt an edgy comfort in the knowledge that Morelli had struggled with some shame forever sealed in a restless grave.

Bobo roused the courage to tell his patient, "Our science and philosophy can not understand a miracle, but we can still hope."

And so they sat, two men aged beyond their years, accepting they had not the time to grow a mellowed friendship, each hoping for the mercies of Saint Dymphna.

Chapter 30

Fishing Behind the Net

Jan's need wore down Joop's opposition. His pleas to find somebody named "Ahlers" were as constant as they were insistent. Joop knew this was important to his friend, so he stepped into the maze of Jan's troubled mind.

"This could be just another crazy goose chase," Joop objected.

"But it's the only thing that fits," Jan almost screamed.

"So, who the Hell is this Ahlers?" Joop demanded.

Jan exploded in a torrent of incomprehensible details. Joop's ears scrambled to catch "the eight they took that morning." He was almost thrown off balance with Jan's shouts of "only three hundred and twenty." The more Jan fluttered the pieces of paper before him, the more worried Joop became. He felt the force of Jan's hate in his cry of, "That's all they were worth." Now, Joop remembered that rotten mess.

Joop had received the warning about the razzia. They were always getting such warnings, and so many of them turned out to be false alarms. All they had been given was "tomorrow" and an address somewhere on the Prinsengracht Canal. The danger signal vanished as quickly as it was sounded, just like the people who were ducking and diving all over Holland. They were probably hiding in a back-house. He had entrusted Jan with the job of getting them out before the fatal knocking on their doors. Joop knew such divers. They believed they were safe in their holes, but never thought of an escape route. Even a mouse knows the nest needs both an entrance and an exit. So many of the disappeared found out too late that their refuge was also their trap. Joop had learned that the hunted must escape well before they could hear the hounds. That was why Jan was supposed to get them out the night before the dawn raid. Tomorrow was always too late.

Jan was sprouting all sorts of nonsense about finding this Ahlers. He wanted to go to Scheveningen because "they have a big prison there." Joop said it was a great idea, but pointed out that Scheveningen was sixty kilometers away, past the Hague, and they had no way of getting there. "Besides, it's on the sea coast and you don't have a good coat." Jan saw the sense in Joop's objections, so he immediately suggested that "Ahlers might be in Camp Vught." Joop gently pointed out that there were so many Germans at the camp that it would take forever to separate the Dutch collaborators from their old masters. Joop decided to take Jan where he could do no more harm to himself. "Come on. Let's go," Joop ordered, and Jan paced in step beside him.

"Where are we going?"

"Levantkade," Joop answered.

Jan banged his palm into his forehead in exaggerated self-mockery. "Why didn't I think of that?"

"Because you're supposed to be the stupid one," Joop assured him.

They laughed their way eastwards along the river, and the gulls wheeled above them in a rowdy cloud. Joop felt a strange calm in their screeching serenade and wondered to himself how such simple things now gave him so much pleasure.

It was a short march to the Levantkade. Jan had once worked those docks as a longshoreman, and Joop hoped the place's familiarity would help him.

After the Liberation, all the male collaborators of Amsterdam were herded into the Levantkade wharfs. The makeshift prison had blossomed until it spilled over into the Sumatrakade to form its own little town within the city. A chain-link fence surrounded the two docks, and the only way out was to scale the wire walls and swim to shore. It was a very short distance over the water, but a bullet could fly faster than anybody could swim. Dutch police and soldiers paced the perimeter with rifles slung over hunched shoulders. The prisoners called it the Amsterdam Alcatraz, but it was more of a relief than a complaint. If they couldn't get out, nobody could get in.

They approached the footbridge over the canal, and Jan remained silent as Joop led them to the guard post. Joop smiled to see a simple black velvet rope baring their way. He laughed at the absurdity of a prison using the same barrier as a movie theater. Behind the rope loomed a huge man whose scowl wiped the smile from Joop's face. Joop gazed at the bars of blue and white stripes running over the jersey hugging the bulging chest and deduced that the guard was a sailor. "What do you want?" the sailor demanded. The tone could wither any challenge to his authority.

"We're looking for information about a collaborator," Joop said.

"So is everybody else. Who are you?"

"Captain Piller from the Flight control Bureau of the Ministry of Finance," Joop proclaimed quickly.

Joop looked at a youth in a dirty soldier's uniform sitting on the concrete embankment with a rifle resting across his thighs.

"Right," the sailor said, as if he'd heard this ten times that day. He jerked his chin to Jan. "And this streak of shit?"

"Lieutenant Flushing," Jan proudly admitted.

The sailor's face rearranged itself into a faint smirk at Jan's answer, and Joop was pleased to hear a kindlier note when he asked, "How about some proof, Captain and Lieutenant?"

Joop fished out his wallet and extracted his Canadian ID card from the Irene Brigade. The sailor's eyes lingered over the crown above the logo 'Princes Irene' as if remembering a painful love and asked with mocking accusation, "Why didn't you say so?"

He cast his grin around Joop and Jan and enquired in a conspiratorial whisper between sidelong glances, "Who are you looking for?"

Joop's voice filled with camaraderie and he offered his most relieved smile. "Somebody called Ahlers."

The sailor stroked his chin, and Joop wondered if their paths had ever crossed. "You'll need to talk to the Administration," he told them. He unhooked the velvet chord from the railing and instructed the soldier to, "take them to Petersen." The soldier stood without a word, slung his rifle over his shoulder, and walked across the footbridge. The sailor pointed the velvet chord snaking through his fist at the soldier. "Follow him," he commanded. Joop offered thanks and the sailor nodded in appreciation. Joop and Jan stepped onto the bridge's rickety boards. The guard slouched ahead of them, the only sign that they should follow. "Pleasant fishing," the sailor shouted over the water in a cloud of laughter.

They could smell the cages before they saw them. The old loading bays had been turned into a make-shift prison with chicken-wire walls and scatterings of straw. Now Joop knew why Amsterdammers called the recently released the Straw Men because their clothes would be peppered with the trampled husks they slept in. The deeper they penetrated into the camp, the greater the noise. They were surrounded by shouts and cries, snarls and whines, all coated in forced merriment. The men had nothing to do but wait either for release or condemnation and filled their time with chatter as endless as it was futile. The laughter ranged from defiant sarcasm to whimpering self-pity.

Jan thought the place sounded like a field of grumpy chickens, all frantically scratching the earth and attacking each other for any morsel their beaks could grab or steal. The mayhem was frightening, but the air was worse. The combined stench of thousands of unwashed bodies scratched at their throats. They stepped over the runnels flowing from neglected latrines to the sleeping quarters and avoided the puddles of spillage. Jan pointed to the seagulls heading out to sea and said, "There's nothing worth shitting on here."

Their guide trundled around the old warehouses that had been pressed into service as barracks. He led them to a large concrete building, and Jan remembered it was the transfer depot where he used to work. When he was last here, they processed shipments of crates, not people. The guide opened a door and they walked into pandemonium

Hundreds of men were lined up, waiting their turn to speak with officials sitting behind tables. Each man consulted a sheaf of papers, and Joop thought they were all practicing their lines for their appearances before their judges. The guide leaned over one of the tables and shouted at an official in a rumpled suit. The man looked over Joop and Jan and demanded, "What do you want?"

"We're looking for a man," Joop bellowed back.

"So are half the women of Amsterdam."

Joop wanted to escape, but his loyalty to Jan kept a tight rein on his impatience. The official consulted some papers, and with another jerk of his head, told the guide, "Take them to Mr. Petersen." The guide nodded and led them to an office door. Joop thought that the whole place was run on a nod, a wink, a jerk of the head, the swivel of a chin, and the point of the finger. "It's probably useless to actually talk to each other in this place," he thought. The guide opened a door and his shout introduced them as, "Officers from the Irene." The man sitting at the desk rose to their titles and the soldier sauntered back to his slouching guard post.

Petersen closed the door, and Joop and Jan were deafened by the silence. He offered them chairs, and Joop welcomed the man's friendly grin. "A mere formality, but may I see some identification?" They offered up their tattered cards to Petersen's practiced glance and accepted his comradely assurance. "I'll be happy to help you."

"Have we met before?" Joop asked.

"In a manner of speaking. Dirk Kragt told me about your activities. He spoke highly of your work after Arnhem."

"Dirk's a fine fellow," Joop said.

"I knew him before the war, but I have also read the newspaper accounts of your present investigation."

"We are here on a very different matter," Joop added.

"No doubt," Petersen grinned. "This forgery affair is very unique. But to details. Whom do you seek?"

"We have only a last name. Ahlers," Jan said.

"That's more than I usually get here," Petersen confessed "You have probably already gathered that we do not cater to the elite criminals, such as your office."

"The camp looks packed," Jan said.

'This is just the tip of the pile," Petersen admitted.

"How many?" Joop asked.

"In the last six months, we have had to deal with over one hundred and twenty thousand members of the Dutch Nazi Party."

"I had no idea," Joop exclaimed.

Petersen cast his sardonic smile over Joop and Jan and seemed to appreciate their shock. "And that's not counting those who have been released or shipped to the prisons."

"So," Jan complained. "We're looking for a needle in a haystack."

"You should be so lucky," Petersen responded. "You can find a needle with a magnet. You're looking for a turd in a dunghill."

Joop was thankful for the office's isolation from the processing shed. This information needed a quiet place to fathom. Petersen sensed their sincerity and was gratified that they understood his task and appreciated the challenge. It was a relief to share his terrible knowledge with someone looking for the truth. His day was always crowded with the lies the accused thought he would believe. "You have the big criminals at Flight Control," he sighed. "Here we have the informers, the thieves, the petty pimps. I sometimes feel sorry for them, until I remember what they have done."

Joop nodded his commiseration. "It would be best if Lieutenant Flushing explained."

Jan felt happy that Joop was encouraging him and followed the silent warning to be brief. In as few points as he could offer, Jan explained the payments and the number of Jews arrested on the date. He put forth the name and waited.

Petersen sat back and assured Jan. "You are completely correct. This is the pattern we have discovered. First there is the report to the Office of Race Purity, then the arrest, and the payment. Their fee is the proof of the crime."

"Which crime?" Joop asked.

"Both," Petersen blurted. "The crime of paying for your victims and the crime of receiving payment for supplying the victims."

It was all so simple, and they were glad that Petersen was such a complete authority on something they only vaguely understood.

Jan swelled with relief when Peterson stood and told them, "I'll look for what we have on this Ahlers, who enriched himself by three hundred and twenty guilders for the price of eight Jews." He disappeared into the noisy storm and shut the door behind him. Joop and Jan didn't know what to do in his little office, so they just waited.

"Reminds you of the old factory, doesn't it?" Jan said.

Joop nodded slowly. "Smells different."

They were at a loss for words, but each held tight to his fears and hopes. Joop wanted Jan to get some relief from this visit. Jan dreaded the knowledge he so desired.

Petersen returned with two cards. "You're in luck. Double Sixes." and offered them the cards. They read the names and raised their heads in a simultaneous and silent question. Peterson chortled. "We had two Ahlers here. Both were named Tonni. You'd think their parents could be more creative."

"That was very quick Mr. Petersen," Jan said.

"Both are Antony Ahlers, so they were together in the index under 'A-A'," he said.

"Can we talk to both of them?" Joop asked.

"First you have to find them."

"Can't we interrogate them here?" Jan almost pleaded.

Petersen sighed into his confession. "Both of them were arrested for confiscating radios. Pretty minor criminals. But we couldn't figure out just who they were, so we had to release both of them on insufficient evidence."

"We have the evidence," Jan protested.

"But we do not have the accused," Petersen said with regret.

"So both Ahlers are free." Joop stated.

"Don't know about that," Petersen added. "Check the prisons, but if their wives find them first, I would enquire at the morgues."

Petersen read the dejection in Jan's face. "I am so sorry that this is all I can do for you, young man." He turned to Joop and the face was crimson indignation. "Captain Piller, you have to deal with the big fish. Here were get only the small fry. Unfortunately, you have been fishing behind the net."

"In any case, Mr. Petersen, we want to thank you for your help," Jan said.

"Take down their addresses. They're on the cards."

Joop scribbled quickly into his notebook and stood to take his leave. Joop noticed the first Anthony Ahlers resided in Groningen. Ahlers Number Two had an Amsterdam address. The next step was clear. Peterson extended his hand to both of them, and his grip held wishes for their success. "Can you find your way back to the guard post?" he asked. He laughed heartily when Jan answered, "We'll follow our noses."

They left Petersen to his desk work, and Joop was slow to wend his way through the maze of the desperate, the

-265-

resigned, the hopeful, and the indifferent. Jan had a determined spring in his stride, and Joop was wondering if a new demon was floating around in his head. They must be Legion.

Jan marched up to the guard post at the bridge. The sailor smiled and was friendlier at their leaving than at their arrival. "Could Petersen help you?" he asked.

"Seems our quarry slipped through the net," Joop said.

"We have all we need," Jan exclaimed.

Jan trundled across the bridge; it's wooden lathes bouncing in time to his steps. Joop had to lengthen his stride to keep pace with Jan's determined march. He grabbed Jan's arm to stop him and asked, "Where are we going?"

Jan breathed heavily but slowed to keep Joop by his side. Joop looked at the address Petersen had given him and saw nothing special in 253 Prinsengracht. Jan immediately knew where Ahlers lived. He could see the row of houses facing the canal. He could feel the warmth of the whimpering street lamps. But he also could count the ten steps between Ahlers' address and the house of the smiling girl.

Chapter 31

Vernissage

Joop handed the note to Bobo and threw his arms in the air. "Now what does he want?" Bobo flipped open the little folded page and immediately knew what van Meegeren was up to. "It seems he wants the pleasure of the company of Mr. and Mrs. Joseph Piller at his vernissage."

"What the Hell is a vernissage?" Joop demanded. "And where are we supposed to get it? Whatever it is."

Bobo smiled to cool Joop's temper. "A vernissage is a soiree."

"What? Another party?"

"This one is special," Bobo said. "It is a party. An artist invites only the most important guests when he unveils a new painting."

"So why doesn't he just say 'Come to my party'?"

"Ah," Bobo explained, "Then it would not be special."

He understood the word was new to Joop. "It's called a 'vernissage' because the painter puts the final varnish on his painting. It's a big deal."

Joop was content to follow Bobo's lead, and his submission scuttled his bad temper.

"So what are we supposed to do?" he asked

"You show up at 8:00 in the evening dressed in your finery," Bobo explained. "Then you swallow some terrible wine and compliment van Meegeren on his great triumph."

"Another bullshit session." Joop added.

"Yes."

"Doesn't he get enough of that?"

"Apparently not."

Bobo appreciated that a vernissage was a new experience for Joop. He lessened Joop's apprehension and assured him, "But this time, it will be a catered affair."

Joop sighed as if he had been told to do over-time after an exhausting day.

"There will be all sorts of important people there," Joop said.

"Yes," Bobo casually agreed.

Bobo pulled the same invitation from his coat pocket and admired van Meegeren's neat handwriting. "I got one too."

When Joop brought the invitation home, Liese was more concerned about their clothing than the other guests. Joop had his suit. Her Herculean efforts had kept it clean and fresh. She had a woolen skirt, one good blouse, and a pair of shoes that were more accustomed to cracked streets than smooth carpets. Joop told her that the floors at the office were marble. "Your shoes won't make any noise."

They had laughed about turning up to the ball in Cinderella's house clothes. "They will think I'm the cleaning lady." They decided they would not look for better clothes but would wear what they had. Liese cackled at Joop's brazen defiance when he said, "If clean and neat are not good enough for such people, they are not good enough for us."

Jan was happy to take care of Sarah for the few hours they would be van Meegeren's guests, and they enjoyed the fresh air as they walked to the old Goudstikker Gallery. The building cast its welcoming light upon the street and halfway over the canal. Liese thought the house was happy to see them, for it must have been many years since its halls had hosted a happy occasion.

They mounted the steps to the front door, and one of the guards held it open for them. "Good Evening, Captain and Mrs. Piller," the guard greeted them. Joop smiled his bemused "Thank you, Sergeant ver Dinken," and escorted Liese into the foyer by her arm. They heard the music of the Glenn Miller Band swinging down the stairs. "Quite a gala evening," she said.

They walked up the stairs, expecting another salute from the guard, but were greeted by a woman's smile, as broad as her hips. "I am so delighted that you could come," she effused over Joop. Joop took a step back and replied in his commanding tone, "May I have the honor to present my wife, Mrs. Elizabeth Piller." Liese did not know what to do, so she extended her hand and told the woman, "Please, my name is Liese," The woman howled and held her sides. "Then you can call me Kootje."

Liese would not submit to the woman's amusement at her very common name and turned to her husband. "Joop has told me all about you. It is so nice to see you in the flesh." Joop strangled his grin. The common joke around Amsterdam was to politely compliment a new acquaintance with, "You're looking very fleshy tonight," to be followed by the question, "Who have you been eating?" Kootje was oblivious to the implication and led them into the studio.

Van Meegeren was busy pointing to the painting and lecturing Sergeant and Mrs. de Groot. Liese saw that the picture was taller than van Meegeren and dominated the room. "What do we do now?" she asked. Joop shrugged. "I suppose we wait for him to finish with de Groot." They walked over to the work table, where Bobo was thumbing through a stack of records. He was operating an old windup

Victrola. Liese read "String of Pearls" on a record label and saw a woman wearing just such a necklace approaching them.

The woman offered them glasses of sparkling wine from a silver tray and mumbled, "So glad you are here." Joop introduced Liese, but the woman just turned and walked away with her tray thrust before her. "The Old One," Joop said. "That explains the bad mood," Liese answered. "At least tonight she's wearing more than pearls and shoes." Liese remembered how Joop had recounted van Meegeren's anecdote about his ex-wife's abilities as a naked hostess and gurgled into her glass.

Bobo abandoned the stack of worn records and offered Liese his hand on a limp wrist. "So glad you are here," he mimicked through fluttering eye lashes. He saw his little joke relieved some of her tension.

Joop's eyes circled the sparseness of the room, and he asked Bobo, "Are we early or late?" Bobo nodded through his half turn, "I think we may be the whole guest list," he surmised. "What about his rich friends?" Liese asked. "Looks like they had something better to do this evening," Bobo observed.

Joop felt a pang of sympathy for van Meegeren. This evening was important for him. That so few people had bothered to accept his invitation must be a great disappointment.

The Old One shuffled over the cold floor, and her tray tempted Sergeant and Mrs. de Groot away from van Meegeren. They followed her to another table where there was something to eat. Van Meegeren sported a charming smile to greet Joop and Liese. "Well, you must be the infamous Liese. Joop never stops talking about you." He clasped her hand and patted her fingers. "Thank you so much for inviting us," she said. Van Meegeren bathed her with an appreciative smile. "Not as thankful as I am that you are here." She caught his enthusiasm, but his face confirmed everything Joop had told her. She could not help feeling a bit sorry for him.

Van Meegeren tapped his wine glass with his ring. His hand gently patted the glass, until its tinkling spread rippling silence through the studio, and all turned to their host.

"Ladies, gentlemen, distinguished guests. It is with a profound pleasure that I present to you, *Christ Discovered in the Temple*. He stepped to the side and spread his arms wide, offering them the finished canvas.

Liese looked at van Meegeren's hand held high. He seemed not to notice that the wine was spilling over the rim and dripping from his fingers. Mrs. de Groot gasped in approval and her husband shouted "Bravo," and started to applaud. The others awkwardly balanced wine glasses in clapping hands. The Old One looked like she was trying to keep down her bile. Nobody knew what was expected of them, so they all just shifted from foot to foot and waited. Van Meegeren stepped forward and soothed their unease.

His voice seemed to speak to each individually. "The court has graciously offered me the chance for my talent to prove my innocence. I am eternally grateful for such consideration." He raised his glass to Joop's blushing face.

"You are all aware that I was charged with creating a painting which would be similar in style and execution to *The Woman Taken In Adultery*. There is no need to tell you how I sold that painting to Goering." He waited for the twittering to spend itself, carefully reading their faces, before he continued. "My Friends, I share with you my sincere thanks for your magnificent support throughout my trial." He paused to let their admiration sink in. "I must admit to you that it is a terrible thing to place one's talent on the altar of the law. Because of you, Dear Friends, I have trusted to my brush to prove my innocence and have survived this terrible ordeal."

He threw his arm in an wide arc before the painting and proclaimed, "This, is my last piece." Bobo's head jerked towards Kootje, but when he felt Joop's elbow jab his arm, he returned his attention to the painting.

Van Meegeren used his wine glass as if it were a teacher swinging a pointer and explained, "The theme is 'The Christ Child Discovered in the Temple.'" He gave them all an entertaining account of the frantic parents searching the streets of Jerusalem for their lost child and only finding him when they went back to the temple. "They were astonished to see their son expounding the law to the leaders of their religion."

Liese had heard the story, but she had never believed the part about the child being so precocious. The worried parents always struck her as more lifelike. The relief at finding the boy would be enough for her. Jesus sounded like a spoiled brat, when he told his mother that he was going about his father's business. If Sarah ever did such a thing, she would receive a well-deserved spanking.

Bobo heard a shuffling behind him and turned to see the guard squad milling around the table and sniffing after plates of pickled herring and trays piled with bread and cheese. Bobo raised his chin at the aroma and saw Judge Voss framed in the doorway. Van Meegeren was too engrossed in his own words to notice, so Bobo nodded a silent greeting. The Judge stood behind Bobo.

Van Meegeren explained that the six figures surrounding the Christ Child were the most learned men of their time. "It is one of the wonders of the Scripture that such wisdom comes from the mouth of a child." He told them, "We find the truth in the most unexpected places." When de Groot grunted his approval, van Meegeren developed his theme. "Nobody expected the young boy to be so knowledgable, but we know better." Mrs. de Groot led the other guards in an appreciative and gentle clapping that warmed van Meegeren to his subject. "My Dearest Friends, you see before you the incontrovertible evidence that I am the creator of *The Woman Taken in Adultery*. This painting before you is proof that I sold a fake to our enemies to save our national heritage. Who knows what else the thieves would have taken. If I had not offered my hostage to their German greed, so many more of our Dutch treasures would have been looted from our beloved country."

Joop stood rigid, waiting for the final twist. Van Meegeren lowered his voice, and they all strained forward to hear his words. "I was charged with treason, but the painting before you is the testament to my patriotism." He whispered to them, "Seeing is believing."

They did not know what to do. This confession left them looking at each other. Van Meegeren jumped into the silence. He raised his glass and shouted, "God Save the Queen." They raised their glasses to follow his loyal salute and responded as enthusiastically as they could. Voss kept peering around the swaying bodies at the painting. Something was tickling his memory, as if a flea were circling his ear.

Van Meegeren called to Bobo, "Please, take a picture," and moved aside for the guests to form a line. Bobo pulled the Kardon from his pocket and waited for the giggling to stop. With a few waves of his hand, he compressed the line into his viewfinder. Van Meegeren stood in the center, his face a study in triumph. Kootje took her place beside him and pressed her red flecked hair into a wave. Mrs. van Meegeren stood away from her former husband, but her face beamed in the pleasure of their company. She could have been a hostess at any society gathering, from ten years ago. Joop and Liese looked very out of place. The de Groots resembled lottery winners in shock. The squad of guards struck poses that reminded Bobo of the Keystone Cops.

Bobo angled his body behind the camera and commanded them all to say "Caviar." The flash caught their laughter, and he knew the print would capture their joy.

Van Meegeren informed them, "It is a good thing that we do have some caviar," and led them to the plates of hors d-oeuvres at the work table.

Bobo walked up to the painting as if responding to a challenge and the seven figures squinted their indifference to his presence. The Boy Jesus sat in the center of the painting with a book opened on his lap. He was expounding something from the white pages to the six doctors of the Temple surrounding him. Bobo stepped back to take in the whole scene, and Joop and Liese soon joined him.

Liese's eyes searched the picture. She knew it took a lot of work to make such a big picture, but it all seemed like so much nonsense over nothing. She could not connect the images to her own experience. She gazed at the Christ Child and there was something strange about him. She looked deeply into the face, as if trying to get the attention of a stranger who was ignoring her. There was something peculiar about the hair. It was parted in the middle of his head and reminded her of dried strawberries in milky chocolate. Her eyes followed the trail of brown strands to the shoulders. When she looked closer, she saw that the hair was limp and had split-ends. Why would his mother not take better care of his hair? Joop gently clasped her hand. She could feel his unease flowing out of the painting.

Liese looked at the boy's lips, and they made her blink. The lips were very red, redder than any man she knew. She heard a laugh and turned to watch Kootje cackling at something de Groot had said. Streaks of wet lipstick stained Kootje's teeth. Liese saw that Kootje wore the same shade of red as Jesus in the picture. Then she knew. It was Kootje's mouth. She turned to Joop and Bobo, nodded at Kootje and said. "Look." Kootje shook her head, and the laughter shivered her hair. Bobo turned back to the painting. Liese pointed to the boy Jesus and whispered. "It's her."

Bobo knew that van Meegeren was a copyist. He could imitate more than he could create, so he needed to work from models. That was why he had used Joop's and Jan's eyes for his Christ Child. Liese had caught the connection between the Young One and the boy in the picture. There was no mistaking her observation. The face of the very girl-like Jesus was Kootje. Bobo sensed there was more, but would not name the thing he saw.

Judge Voss joined them. "This is a very sparse audience for such an artistic event," he said. Bobo and Joop greeted him with a smile, but Liese was busy looking for more clues in the painting. "It seems there are more guests than we see," Bobo said. Voss was confused by the cryptic remark but followed Bobo's command. "Look at the painting."

Voss's eyes scanned over the figures. The Christ looked like someone he would have sentenced for public solicitation. He was not interested in paintings. They were little more than expensive wallpaper to him. He would much rather spend an evening at a concert than walk across the street to see some scrapings on cloth. "I don't really have an eye for pictures," Voss said, and blinked away his boredom. Bobo's hands went up in supplication, so Voss looked closer.

The faces of the men surrounding Jesus were like people he had met but could not remember. He felt the same irritation as when he saw people in a crowd he only half recognized. They annoyed him because he could not quite place them.

His eyes fell on the doctor sitting to the right of Jesus, and it all came back. He pointed to the face and exclaimed. "That's Bredius." Bobo raised his palm to his head in sudden recognition. "Ah. So it is." Joop asked about the name. "Bredius is a renowned art connoisseur," Bobo said. When this did not pierce Joop's confusion, he added. "Bredius is the world's expert on Vermeer," he added. In his mind, Joop juggled the knowledge of this expert with the picture of the Jewish lawyer. Voss turned to Bobo. "Bredius also had the good sense to say that van Meegeren was a very good painter of society portraits." Joop asked, "So this Bredius is one of his friends." Bobo could not tear his eyes away from the portrait of Bredius clothed in Jewish robes. "Van Meegeren hates Bredius because Bredius laughed at van Meegeren's very meagre talent."

Voss's finger quivered to another figure in the background. "I know him." Bobo and Joop almost shook waiting for Voss' next revelation. "He was the Director of the Rijksmuseum over twenty years ago." Joop had never seen this person, but accepted Voss' identification because he would have known such important people.

Voss' finger trembled again to the figure on the right. "That is Baron van Heeckeren." Joop asked if he was another friend of van Meegeren. "Maybe," said the Judge, "But van Heeckeren is no friend of van Meegeren." Voss informed them that van Meegeren had painted the Baron's portrait, but then the Baron refused to have anything to do with the artist. "They had a falling out?" Joop asked. "It's more like the Baron would not let him in," Voss said.

Liese turned back to the men and listened intently to the Judge. "I have known the Heeckeren family since I was a child. Such people would have nothing to do with the likes of Henricus Antonius van Meegeren." Joop understood. The men in the picture were the people van Meegeren most hated.

The Judge's words bathed the canvas in a light more lurid than they could have otherwise seen. Now they all knew that the painting was an act of revenge. It was a composite of the people Van Meegeren most detested, with the lips and hair of someone he was supposed to love.

The painting made Liese feel very uneasy. The boy who was a girl sat among old men who were leering at him. The respected doctors of the law became six old perverts lusting after this child who was neither man nor woman. She thought that she was making too much out of the picture, but then she saw the glint in van Meegeren's eye. He was looking at Kootje and his face silently proclaimed, "I own this." The men in the picture could be planning to do something very bad. She did not want to look any more at the picture.

Voss' eyes turned to Bobo. "I am sure you have more insights than I am prepared to venture," he said.

"The noses," Bobo answered.

"What about the noses?" Voss demanded.

"You've also seen them before."

Bobo knew exactly what they were. Each of the doctors sported the hook nose that had glared from a thousand Nazi posters warning the people of the dangers of The Eternal Jew. The profiles were straight out of the propaganda posters that had splattered the walls of their lives for five years. Bobo wondered if van Meegeren had cut the outlines from Nazi comic books.

Voss saw that Van Meegeren had put his mistress into the middle of the painting and surrounded her with all the men who rejected his friendship and ridiculed his talent. He had transformed all those men into caricatures of Jews.

They stood before the painting sharing their discoveries. Voss put their thoughts into words. "He's laughing at us all."

Van Meegeren invited his guests to the table. "Try this caviar," he suggested. Liese watched him pop a pungent corner of toasted bread into his mouth. He declared the morsel delightful, and Liese scowled at the stray eggs dripping from his mouth.

Bobo's attention was captured when van Meegeren strained to open the lid of a very large jar. It was an old pickle jar, but when the lid was pried off, it released the acrid stench of varnish mixed with linseed oil. The studio quickly stank of greasy fish.

Joop saw van Meegeren step up to the painting, swirling a broad brush in the jar. Van Meegeren waved his arm quickly over the canvas, and a brilliant sheen followed every arc of his hand. They watched van Meegeren shellac his final work of art, sealing the figures forever under a hard, transparent shell. The gleam dripped from the brush, flooding the canvas. Liese saw her own face emerge from the lustrous flashes and felt relief. There was a finality to this vernissage, and she welcomed the knowledge that, when he was finished applying the lacquer, she would be finished with all the works of Han van Meegeren.

Joop clenched his jaws and tightened his fingers around Liese's hand. Everything about van Meegeren was perfectly clear. He would not evade the plain truth. The painting was the most vile thing he had ever seen.

Chapter 32

Bouquet

Voss slowly polished his desk. The cleaners had restored the panelling lining his chambers, but they never touched his desk. It seemed to Voss that they were afraid of disturbing his work. Maybe the massive bureau intimidated them. Each morning he would buff the surface with a towel until his palms felt the waxy warmth from the wood. He enjoyed this little morning ritual, and if he were honest with himself, it gave him an excuse to delay dealing with his increasingly depressing cases. When he saw his own reflection, he could procrastinate no longer, so he folded the towel and sorted the mail.

The envelopes formed a little hill, but he did not have to open them to read them. Since the news reports, the demands for compensation had assaulted his office. He joked to himself, "Après van Meegeren le déluge." He grasped his letter opener and attacked the first envelope with the all the resignation of utter boredom. He slit the cover and the writer informed Voss of "the considerable financial embarrassment" he was suffering at the hands of a fraud. He tossed away the missive and stabbed at the next envelope conveying the usual complaints how van Meegeren had "violated my trust" and suggesting that "torture was too good for this detestable miscreant." Their accusations were almost identical and Voss grunted, "Two fools share one hat."

The next complainant detailed van Meegeren's methods of "employing a third party to rob the trusting." They were all the same and all came from some of the wealthiest men in the land. Voss shook his head at the folly of all these sophisticated men who had invested their fortunes in fake paintings. He knew their outrage was not only for the money they had lost to van Meegeren's trickery, but also because they had all been so willingly fooled. They bellowed for the blood of the monster who had cuckolded them. Voss judged that the letters would not be quite so vicious, if van Meegeren had only seduced their wives or daughters. His crime was that he had screwed them out of their money. Safely held under the custody of the court, they demanded justice. The justice was to be restitution of the money they had paid him in such good faith. Voss laughed at the familiar refrains of "the necessity for absolute confidentiality," and "relying on your discretion," in order to "avoid any further embarrassment." All ended with a demand for van Meegeren's head on a plate. Voss sighed to himself, "I should have commissioned him to paint John the Baptist and Salomé." Their only real argument was that their cupidity was exceeded only by their gullibility. Each claim for compensation proved Goering was not his only dupe. If half the letters were true, van Meegeren had been robbing the rich for at least twenty years, and nothing had been going to the poor. There had to be an extensive ring involved. One man alone could never have done so much damage for so long. Van Meegeren's legal circus had been an amusement, but now it revolted him.

Voss had not yet developed an old man's cynicism. It was the boredom that sapped his zeal. Everything was so normal. Normal thefts were followed by normal drunken beatings, and in their turn, were replaced by normal murders. His daily duties had become a parade of mediocrity punctuated by low intrigue in high places.

He turned for relief to his list of appointments. Routine would be better than this bleating of the fleeced, but with his first caller came disappointment. The list informed him that "Prosecutor van den Broek begs the court's indulgence at 9:30 a.m., if it please Your Honor." He grimaced at the prospect of another interview and grumbled to himself, "So, the vultures are circling and they have sent their most trusted scout." The eminent prosecutor would plead their cases, but it was more like pulling the pelt from a rancid corpse.

He ignored the light tapping at his door. A little waiting made his visitors more attentive. When he heard just the right combination of apprehension and annoyance in the knocking, he commanded, "Enter." Van den Broek appeared, but dared not step further into the room without permission. Voss mustered his most kindly and disarming greeting. "Good Morning, Councillor." Van den Broek stepped towards the desk, and Voss spread an inviting arm to the high-backed chair. "Please. Do sit down."

Van den Broek sat himself on the edge of the seat and placed a file on his knees. "Thank you for seeing me on such short notice," he said.

"Is there any urgency to your matter which I can facilitate?" Voss asked.

Van den Broek offered the file. "May we discuss the van Meegeren affair?"

"Which one?" Voss asked. "He seems to have had great success with the ladies."

"I am more concerned with the business of the state than with his personal adventures."

"Ah, yes." Voss recalled. "I must congratulate you on your recent promotion."

"The Minister is of the opinion that I require a rank commensurate with my present duties."

"And it is these duties which bring you here this morning?"

"Yes, Sir."

Voss threaded his fingers together and sat relaxed, waiting for van den Broek to get to the point, whatever it was. He remained silent and enjoyed his guest's growing discomfort. "I have had a word with the Minister," van den Broek commenced, but Voss cut off his preamble. "Which one?" he demanded.

Van den Broek expected that the mention of the Minister would command Voss' full attention, but the man seemed oblivious to protocol.

"Why, the Minister of Justice, of course," van den Broek added uncertainty.

"Ah, yes," Voss seemed to remember. "Justice."

He stopped talking and looked into the distance over van den Broek's shoulder. "It is rather confusing these days."

"What is confusing?"

"All these comings and goings in the government. Seems that as soon as I get used to one minister, he is replaced by another. I think they should install revolving doors in the Palace of Justice, just like they have in department stores. It would be so much more convenient."

Van den Broek tried to follow Voss' ramblings and lead them back to his immediate concerns. "There have been many changes now that the Government has returned from exile."

"No doubt, no doubt," Voss agreed. "In the good old days, you know, before the war, we could rely on a cabinet lasting longer than a few weeks."

"There is much reorganizing to be done."

"And you are just the man for the job. I was under the impression that you worked for the Minister of Finance."

"My present responsibilities involve liaison between both ministries."

"That's quite bit of toing and froing," Voss commented. "You must get very tired."

Voss had also buffed the seat of the wooden chair, so his visitors always felt they were about to slide onto the floor. He could feel van den Broek's unease and watched him fidget with his file. When van den Broek could no longer suffer the Judge's silence, he took a deep breath and told him, "The Ministers of Justice and Finance have come to a decision concerning van Meegeren."

"Really?" Voss said with exaggerated surprise. "He has yet to be convicted of anything."

"We all know that the man is as guilty as sin. This trial is a formality."

Voss bit his lip to curb his laughter. He hoped van den Broek would think he had indigestion. "And just what have the Ministers decided?"

"We think that it is in the best interests of the country that this matter be brought to a speedy conclusion," van den Broek pronounced.

"Have you any suggestions as to that happy ending."

"Personally, I would have him hanged immediately. As an example."

"I am sure you would," Voss grinned. "But I can't imagine how his execution would be much of a deterrent to others equally determined to make a killing in the art market."

"Justice must be swift and sure."

"And the swiftness will ensure that he does not become a bigger problem."

"I think you get my drift."

"Ah," he sighed. "The Brabant Maid."

Voss leaned back in his chair and steepled his fingers and thumbs under his nose. He savored the bemused memory of the old tale of the Maid of Brabant. It must have been two centuries in the past, when that girl was so generous with her favors and so indiscriminate in her lovers. The outraged townspeople of Brabant dragged her before the court and charged with indecent fornication. She was sentenced to three days of public shame in the stocks. Voss smiled to think that the Good Christians of Brabant had believed that the pillory was a cure for nymphomania. The court had pronounced that while restrained and displayed, the people were given liberty to abuse her person. The result was that the judge, the jury, the witnesses, all the lawyers, and half the men of the town came down with the pox. Voss wondered which the Maid of Brabant enjoyed more, the three days of continuous coupling or the revenge she served them all in a piping hot dish.

"Forgive me," van den Broek begged, "Who is this Brabant Maid?"

"Nobody," Voss said.

Van den Broek wondered if Voss were going senile and speculated that there soon might be a vacant bench requiring a new judge.

"I could put him in the public pillory," Voss suggested, "But he seems to enjoy the attention."

Voss would not share his knowledge that van Meegeren was the perfect example of the gallows orator or the fiddler in the stocks. Van den Broek could not restrain his annoyance. "There are grave economic consequences to his crimes."

"I think your grammar is faulty when you use the plural," Voss corrected. "He is charged with only one crime, treason."

"It is evident that he had major financial dealings with the enemy. That is economic treason."

"My word," Voss blurted. "I am astounded by your adjective, which I do not find in any of our statutes."

"New times call for new laws."

"Especially when the crime has such grave economic consequences."

Van den Broek was on the edge of losing his temper and wondered if the Minister could have Voss replaced. "We have been robbed of all of our industry. Our currency reserves have been looted. We have nothing left of any value."

"Ah, yes," Voss agreed, as if it were a completely new thought. "Our works of art are now highly profitable commodities."

Van den Broek offered Voss the file, and Voss accepted it as if it were a tasty morsel for his lunch. "Thank you so much for your excellent work in this matter, Councillor." Voss tossed the file onto his desk. "I will add this to my own records of the investigation."

Van den Broek rose and excused himself. "Thank you for your indulgence, Your Honor." Voss did not rise, but only turned his eyes to the door. "Please inform the Minister that I am confident that the punishment will fit the crime." Voss ignored the proffered hand and watched van den Broek shuffle to the door.

The Judge mused to himself. "Of course, all of this has grave economic consequences. When van Meegeren is through with them, their paintings will be worthless." Voss grimaced at the thought of van den Broek, "If his neighbor's house were on fire, he'd warm his own ass." The Prosecutor was just the first crow at the carcass. He recalled how one counterfeiter had ruined the stock exchange five years before the war. Nobody knew if the money in their pockets was worth the very high quality paper it was printed on. The man had been sentenced to ten years in prison, and the sentence was lighter than anything the bankers wanted to do with him. "He really pissed in their soup," Voss chuckled aloud as he opened his own file.

He spread the papers before him in chronological order. Piller's report was a mere three succinct pages, detailing how the painting *The Woman Taken in Adultery* was recovered from Goering's horde and repatriated to Holland by the Monuments, Fine Art and Archives Division of the American Army. He reread his own order that van Meegeren was to paint a picture in the same style as the recovered painting, to prove that he was the actual creator of Goering's treasured Vermeer. He picked up a bundle of photographs and flipped through them. Morelli had been most careful to capture van Meegeren at each stage of the new painting's composition.

The first photograph showed van Meegeren standing before the empty canvas. He looked well-fed, expensively dressed, and very haughty. The subsequent photos revealed the painting in each stage of its execution. As he flipped through the pictures, the figures filled the canvas. People appeared as if they were a growing crowd, until the six Learned Doctors of the Law surrounded the Christ Child. The painting seemed to grow bigger in each photograph.

Something in the wad of images was tickling his imagination. The photographs posed a problem he could not understand and promised an answer he could not yet see. He enjoyed riddles, but only when they offered a clear solution. There was something here and he was determined to know what it was.

He imagined the photos as an arrangement of cut flowers standing in a vase. Each photo was as distinct as the individual blooms, but what did the whole bouquet offer him?

He placed the photographs on his desk in the order in which Morelli had taken them. He chuckled to think that there was only one rogue in this little gallery. He surveyed the line of images, but this time, he concentrated on the artist rather than the painting.

Voss could see van Meegeren age from photo to photo. Morelli had taken pains to capture images of van Meegeren at work on the canvas. Voss presumed he had done this to comply with the order of the court that a record be kept to prove van Meegeren had actually painted the canvas.

The jaunty dandy of the first image, gradually became more hunched over. In the middle of the series, Morelli had snapped van Meegeren with a cigarette in one hand and a glass in the other, contemplating an empty portion of the canvas. This photo was a watershed. After it, van Meegeren seemed to grow smaller, until in the last photo, he sprawled exhausted in a chair beside the completed painting.

Voss repeated his examination and contemplated each of the photographs in turn. The crisp suit of the first few photos gave way to dirty smocks. Near the end of the sequence, van Meegeren appeared in a moth eaten sweater. Sometimes he was full of energy and brandished his brush as if it were a rapier. Midway through the collection, there were more pictures of van Meegeren fortifying himself with a glass. Eventually, the raised glasses replaced the brushes. He could see in one picture that van Meegeren held one cigarette between his stained claws while another burned in the ashtray on the table. The man was living on alcohol and nicotine. Near the end of the line, van Meegeren was clearly exhausted. Voss could not tell from the photo if van Meegeren was dead drunk or dead.

Voss leaned back in his chair confident that he had solved the riddle and his mind clutched the confirmation of a suspicion that had bothered him from the beginning. Now he knew he was right. The more van Meegeren approached the end of his composition, the more he became depleted of life. If this album were a bouquet, the flowers wilted, withered, and died with each click of Morelli's camera.

He looked over the rows of images parading across his desk until they pushed up beside the clutch of letters. Agreeing to their demands for a judicial murder would be casting roses before swine.

Voss picked up the last photograph and gazed long at van Meegeren's body slumped in the chair. The painting was finished, and so was van Meegeren. This was the last stroke of his life as an artist, and he knew it. Voss understood what he had to do. The most fitting punishment for such an accomplished libertine would be to set him at liberty.

Chapter 33

Release

De Groot packed van Meegeren's few things into a little valise. Kootje had brought him a clean shirt, underwear, and socks, so the box held only a few bottles of cologne and cigarette tins. "That's all there is?" Joop asked. De Groot's sigh threatened to become a chuckle, but he only said, "His needs are simple." Joop jerked his head, and de Groot carried the rattling case into the studio.

Van Meegeren stood with his back to the painting, adjusting his tie. "She should be here shortly," Joop exclaimed, and van Meegeren nodded his approval. He looked through the door to the staircase. "I must say," he confessed, "the Judge has been true to his word."

Joop had read the command of the court with much relief and a tinge of regret. Voss had pronounced that "since the defendant has fulfilled all the requirements of his commission, he is now given liberty to return to his residence and await trial." Joop had asked about any special procedures, and Voss had assured him that "no further restrictions are necessary." Voss was confident that van Meegeren would not abscond. If anything, the promise of the trial was a guarantee of his good behavior. The release papers did not require a bond to be posted. Voss confided to Joop, "He has nowhere left to go."

Van Meegeren stepped up to De Groot, who stood waiting with the valise. He patted de Groot's shoulder, offered his hand, and whispered, "Well done. True and faithful guard." De Groot was touched by the gesture, and when he shook hands, felt the roll of money nestle in his palm. He whispered his sincerest appreciation for such consideration. He slipped his hand into his coat pocket and walked down the stairs, leaving van Meegeren and Joop to finish the rituals of judicial release.

Joop walked to the work table, cluttered with the discarded tools of the painter's trade. "I'll have these sent to your house," he said. Van Meegeren rummaged in his pockets for his cigarette case and barely glanced at the litter of brushes and paints. He extracted one fresh tube from the silver rectangle and hunched over his lighter. "Don't bother," he coughed, sucking the flame.

Joop looked over the glass jars stained with dirty turpentine. The brushes lay where they were last dropped and the paint had dried in their hairs. Pigments dripped from lidless tubes onto the palettes encrusted with the residues of forgotten hues. Joop felt a sadness rise with the acrid fumes. The materials had served their purpose, so they were to be abandoned. That they could be so easily dismissed with a whiff of a cigarette made Joop pity them as he would orphans.

Van Meegeren picked up the jar of lapus lazuli. "Take this," he commanded. Van Meegeren thrust out his chin, and his lips curled into a smirk around his cigarette. Joop shook the jar and something more than stray grains of stone rattled around the glass. "Open it," van Meegeren whispered. Joop's fingers were moist around the jar, but his fist twisted off the lid. Inside he saw a key and heard van Meegeren quietly order. "Take it out."

With the key between his thumb and forefinger, Joop looked at a tag dangling from its head. "Read it," van Meegeren demanded. Joop saw an address neatly printed on the cardboard tag. The bold printing left no doubt that van Meegeren had inscribed the numbers and letters himself. Van Meegeren stood close and breathed his final temptation. "Go to that house. On the second floor, there is a bedroom to the left. Under the floorboards, you will find a metal box." Joop's eyes flashed in wonder and fear. Van Meegeren grinned, and his breath assured Joop, "You will never have to work again." Joop turned his gaze from the rotted stumps of van Meegeren's teeth. He wanted to throw the key into a canal and take the last of the lapus lazuli to its distant home and cast the azure grains to the winds.

They heard her feet clatter up the stairs and turned to the open door. "That must be Kootje," van Meegeren said.

She filled the doorway for the moment it took to enter the studio. Van Meegeren extended his arms, and Kootje threw her hands around his neck. Joop withdrew, so as not to intrude upon their very public intimacy. "Come, come, My Dear," she said, and van Meegeren followed her out of the studio as if she were taking him home from school. "I'll make the special soup you like so much," she told him.

Van Meegeren held onto her arm as she guided him down the stairs. Joop followed his tread and saw van Meegeren wince painfully from step to step. He had remained in his studio for the last few months, and so his legs had grown unaccustomed to walking down stairs. Joop thought it was very strange that someone would forget how to use stairs, but then he remembered all the alcohol that had gone through his body. Joop was amazed by just how much he could drink. Van Meegeren was never really drunk, but he was also never completely sober. He seemed to be maintaining the alcohol level in his system, so Joop decided that the gin must be like the water in a steam engine, always having to be topped up and very dangerous if the boiler ever ran dry.

Joop wondered what would become of him now that he had finished the painting. The old wife hadn't bothered to take him home, so van Meegeren was now the duty of the young girl.

When they got to the bottom of the staircase, van Meegeren stopped to catch his breath. Kootje stood holding him as he gasped the air, but his coughs echoed through the building. Joop recalled that they had what Bobo called a set-up, so Kootje was his new mistress, but this was more of a title than an occupation. She would care for the old man, but van Meegeren had not the health for such a woman. Joop easily imagined that such an encounter could be fatal. She might just kill him, if he weren't doing a good enough job of that on his own.

The experts ceased their squabbling when they heard Kootje's heels tap down the stairs. They emerged from both salons and crammed themselves under the archways. Joop saw Jan's face in the crowd to the left, but there was not the usual smile. Jan looked very serious and his face betrayed his curiosity.

Van Meegeren breathed deeply and pulled his spine to its limit. He held himself close to Kootje, raised his hat, and cast pleasantries to his left and right. "Good Morning, Gentlemen," he hailed the faces staring at his exit. "So nice to see you today," he admitted to a complete stranger to his right. De Groot stood with the door open and the audience started to clap. Joop looked down from the top of the stairs and van Meegeren grew an inch taller amidst the applause. Kootje led him out of the building and they disappeared into the morning fog.

Bobo dangled the key before his eyes. It swung between him and Joop and sprayed tiny dazzles over the counter. Joop looked around the shop, as if to check for prying ears. "So what do we do with it?" Bobo tossed the key onto the counter and stroked his chin. "It could be another one of his tricks," he said.

"He was very precise," Joop said.

"Second floor. Room on the left," Bobo repeated.

The thing lay between them, beckoning and repelling at the same time. Whatever they decided, they would do together. Van Meegeren's gifts had a way of always coming back to van Meegeren and robbing whomever accepted his generosity.

"It must be money," Bobo exclaimed.

"He said, 'You'll never have to work again'," Joop recalled.

"Well you won't ever work again, if this thing blows up in your face," Bobo warned.

"You don't really mean that he's hidden some booby trap for us under the floorboards?" Joop protested.

"Whatever it is, we won't find out standing here with our thumbs up our asses."

They looked into each other's eyes full of curiosity wrapped in greed. The key was a promise and a temptation. Van Meegeren claimed he had hidden a metal box. He had suggested that it was full of money. But he had implanted the key in Joop's mind. Bobo could feel the frustration when Joop threw up his arms. "Ach. Treasure hunts are for children's tales."

"I have to admit. He has an extraordinary talent," Bobo sighed.

"How so?" Joop asked.

"He finds people's needs and plays on their their greed. He can sell a fake for millions because he is as avaricious as his victims. But with you it's different."

"Different? You mean I too can be bought?"

"Not bought. Call it a downpayment on the rest of your life."

Bobo wanted very much to discover what was behind all this chicanery. No matter how deeply they concealed their own thoughts, van Meegeren had an almost magical ability to see through people. He could smell vulnerability. "He knows full well that you're in need of money," Bobo told Joop. "He knows you have a wife and a daughter depending on you. If he can remove all of your fears for the future, he will be the hero to the end of your days, and all the days of Sarah as well."

Joop saw the sense in Bobo's reconstruction of something that would happen in the future and which would also never be. Now Joop appreciated the enormity of the offer. Yes, he would not have to work for the rest of his life, but that life would be a memorial to his benefactor. There would be no getting rid of van Meegeren, when even the food they put in their mouthes depended upon his one act of kindness.

"Throw it in the canal and walk away," Joop decided.

"Then we will never know. The question will remain forever unanswered and unknowable. Then he wins as well," Bobo explained.

Joop was back to the horns of the dilemma and could feel himself squirming on each prong. Either way, he had to know.

"What would you do?" he almost begged.

Bobo felt the same power drawing him back to the key. The thing was accursed, and that was only part of its beauty. "I would go," he confessed.

"Why? Just to get more trouble?"

"Just to get a clear idea of what he's up to."

Bobo started to put on his coat, and it was the sign that they would follow van Meegeren's golden trail. Joop stretched his back and waited for Bobo to shut up the shop. Bobo turned a half malicious face to Joop and asked, "You know the address?"

"It's one of his houses."

"How do you know that?" Bobo asked in genuine surprise.

"We got a list of his properties when we grilled van Stuyvesande, months ago."

"How many properties?"

"There were over a hundred," Joop recalled.

Bobo closed the door behind him and followed Joop's lead to the river. "So you know where this place is?"

"Oh, yes."

The late afternoon was glooming into evening, and the air was moist with the promise of rain. They wended their way through the crowds and slowed through the throng in Dam Square. Joop stopped and Bobo wondered about their interruption but was glad that Joop had slackened their pace to a rest. Joop looked up at the statue of Atlas squatting atop the old palace. Joop turned to weave through the street behind the building and then turned to stare over the river. "I know exactly where we're going."

Bobo fell into determined silence as they marched through a maze of alleys to the bridge. Joop sensed Bobo's gentle wheezing. "It's very close." Bobo was glad that they would soon be at the journey's end. But this was no time to fall back. Even if he keeled over, he would keep pace.

Joop turned them into a small street and stopped before a three story building. It was clearly a residential house, and Bobo wondered what the people would think when they invaded their privacy. Joop pulled the key from his raincoat pocket and read the address on the tag as a final confirmation. "You really want to do this?" he demanded of Bobo. Bobo knew they had to get into the house to retrieve the box. There was no other way of knowing. He merely nodded once, and they climbed the stairs to the front door.

Joop knew about this house and what he knew made him fearful of what he would find behind the door. He had first encountered this address on Spierdijk's map, but then it was black with deadly dots.

His fist was clenched, but his knock was soft with fearful restraint. Bobo heard the distant echo. He wanted to run away. Joop stood waiting for the door to open and be confronted by the astonished residents. It was a full minute before he turned to Bobo and whispered, "Maybe they didn't hear." Bobo nodded and Joop rattled the door handle. They waited. At the next loud and empty knock, Bobo speculated, "Maybe they're out."

Joop leaned back to look up at the windows and they glared a dim sheen back at him. He thrust the key into the lock up to the hilt. He wiggled his fingers until he heard a faint crack and realized that the door was held fast with only one turn of the lock. He pushed with his hand and the door exposed a slit of the darkened interior. Bobo grabbed Joop's left arm by the sleeve and commanded, "Don't." Joop turned to whisper, "We've come this far." Bobo was adamant, "No further. Look through the door."

Joop's foot pushed the door, and the hinges screeched in protest. He stared into skeletal emptiness. Bobo stood beside Joop and they saw only the painted rectangles on the walls where rooms used to be. There were no floors, and below them the basement was a shimmering flood of stagnant river water. The beams crossed from one wall to the next, but everything else had been stripped long ago.

"Termites," Bobo said.

Joop burst into relieved laughter. They had been given directions to this house, but it had been stripped bare. People had taken everything that could burn from the floors to the roof to keep warm during the winter. They had not frozen to death because, little by little, they had fed the whole house into their hearths. Only the bricks remained. They could burn in an air raid, but not in a Miracle Stove. Bobo looked up to see a new moon shining through the barren rafters.

The was no second floor. There was no bedroom. The floorboards had been ripped and if there had ever been a metal box, it was long gone. Joop turned to Bobo and a sardonic leer scarred his mouth. "Well, if anybody is never going to work again, it's not going to be us."

Joop felt the joy of disaster averted. It was as glorious as escaping a razzia or talking their way through a checkpoint. Joop gave silent thanks that he would never be in van Meegeren's debt. He owed nothing to the man who had promised him everything. Now he was forever relieved of any debt to his prisoner. It was good to awake from a nightmare, but it was even better to rouse from tempting visions. Bobo was right. It was better to know than to be forever accusing himself with "If only" and "We could have been so rich." Joop laughed to know that he would never be lashed by unrequited greed.

Bobo tilted his head to the crescent moon and bellowed, "It's the thought that counts."

Chapter 34

Souvenir

Spierdijk could barely contain his rage and his jubilation. He was ranting so violently that Bobo was concerned that he would break something. "If he smashed the window, I'll never find enough glass to fix it," Bobo thought with growing trepidation. Spierdijk threw the big book at the counter and the dust spiraled around his hot head. Joop was ready to grab him but decided that talking would cool his mind more than tackling would restrain his body. "How could they have such a thing? And in Berlin of all places," Joop asked.

"You can get anything in Berlin, if you have the money," Spierdijk sneered.

"So how much did it cost?" Joop asked.

"One American dollar. Can you believe it? Just one dollar."

"I can certainly believe it," Bobo chuckled. "Too bad there isn't more to sell."

The absurdity calmed Spierdijk just enough to listen to Bobo's sardonic suggestion. "We could pile up the books in the window and set up a little booth for him." Spierdijk shook his head and shared in the fantasy of Bobo's sarcasm. "Let's put up a big sign saying *Teekeningen No.1.* People would come just to see their hero sign his Collected Works.'"

Spierdijk laughed at the imaginary line forming outside the shop to buy their inscribed copy of van Meegeren's book of drawings and reproductions. His anger had not subsided enough to get Bobo's drift when Bobo turned to Joop, winked and said, "We'd never have to work again."

Bobo turned his attention to the volume that had inflamed his anger, but he also sensed Spierdijk's joy in finding such incontrovertible   proof. He examined the book's cover and was not impressed with the artwork. It was a large folio bound in black covers. From the center of the cover sprouted a large red ball with the number '1' inscribed in black. Gold lettering emblazoned van Meegeren's name at the top of the cover, but the title was at the bottom. Bobo puffed to Spierdijk and Joop, "He always has to get top billing." Bobo jumped into the pause between Spierdijk's laughter and his next shouting fit. "Why does it look so beat up?" he asked.

"It looks like where it was found, in the ruins of the Reichschancellery."

Bobo could smell the dirt, dust, and carbon rising from the book. Even the tattered edges told a story and he wanted to hear it again.

Spierdijk had dutifully travelled to Berlin on assignment from his newspaper. It was only supposed to be a two week trip, but there were so many accounts to report and so much bureaucracy tying up the reporting that he had stayed three months in the ruined capital. There was little to do, other than file stories of the misery of the Berliners and join their treks into the countryside searching for anything to eat. Spierdijk thought that this hunt for anything edible was just like the Dutch during the Hunger Winter, except that the German farmers drove a harder bargain. He'd seen the family jewels exchanged for a bucket of potatoes and made a note that if he ever wanted to sell expensive sparklers, he would start collecting his stock at the farms ringing Berlin.

There were also the sight-seeing tours. Berliners were happy to take a dollar from anybody in an Allied uniform or a clean coat and guide them through the center of the city pointing out, "That used to be the Headquarters of the Gestapo," or "Hitler's first mistress is under that pile of bricks." The Russians guarding the ruins of the Chancellery were the best organized. They offered everything for sale in fluent English, French, and German. An American from California had difficulty understanding a Russian's heavy Brooklyn accent. Spierdijk was not shocked when a flatfooted giant with an open pistol holster asked him in perfect Dutch, "Would you be interested in acquiring a souvenir of victory?" Spierdijk was so intrigued and so grateful to converse in Dutch that he would have followed the Russian anywhere.

The American planes had redecorated Hitler's headquarters with about one hundred tons of high explosives and put on a final coat of incendiaries. The gutted shell resembled any building in Rotterdam the Germans had bombed five years ago. As he placed his feet carefully in the Russian's footsteps, he felt like he was walking in the hills. The place exuded a smoldering stench, and since the fires had long since burned themselves out, Spierdijk guessed that the smoke was rising brick dust or possibly the souls of those forever entombed.

The Russian led him into a maze of tunnels and every room was crowded with people from all the Allied nations eagerly examining the wares the Russians offered. Spierdijk noticed that each room was piled with articles from different countries, so that one could purchase furniture from France and haggle in French. Another hole was a stall for German cameras. Watches were so common that only the petty traders offered their captured timepieces on trays suspended from strings around their necks. Spierdijk half expected to turn a corner and be offered spaghetti and Chianti in Italian from a Cossack waiter. Clearly, the Comrades were much more efficient capitalists than he had expected. The whole place was like an Arab bazaar and he smiled to himself to think of his guide suggesting, "Let me take you to the Casbah."

Instead, the Russian stopped before a shattered doorway and whispered, "I think you will find many things of interest here. You look like a man of refined taste." When he stepped over the crumbling threshold, Spierdijk saw tables full of Dutch books. Paintings rested against the walls and it seemed that for a price, the Russians could also supply him with a genuine Dutch painter. Spierdijk remembered a story about a florist in Chicago who catered for the funerals of gangsters. It was rumored that the florist would not only supply the flowers, but also the corpse, for a price.

The Russian let Spierdijk's curiosity draw him further into the cave. When he started shuffling through the books, the Russian complimented, "I knew you were cultured. You would rather read and gain knowledge than lie drunken in a pool of your own vomit." Spierdijk found himself drawn to this strange man, who was so careful in his use of Spierdijk's own language. There must be a wonderful story behind this man and his dictionary, and Spierdijk was about to ask him how he had learned Dutch so well, when the cover assaulted him. He picked up the book and blew off the dust to reveal van Meegeren's name. Amazed that this would seek him out in such a place, he turned the pages to some drawings of Delft. The Russian quickly responded to

Spierdijk's interest. "Possibly this author is one of your friends?" he prodded. "I know him," Spierdijk admitted. "He is certainly not a friend." The Russian nodded in sympathetic understanding and knew there was some anger between the Dutchman and the book. He speculated that the book was somehow connected with an old wrong, but would not delve further into something that was so obviously painful to his customer. "Where did you get this?" Spierdijk asked. "From Hitler's library," the Russian said. Astounded by the chances of this book coming directly from Hitler's personal collection, Spierdijk doubted the Russian's word. Still, there were so many strange coincidences that they had become the new normal in this new world that was like a scorched phoenix. He had fallen down the rabbit hole, so he should not be shocked if the Mad Hatter carried a machine gun and Alice was a whore. "How much?" Spierdijk demanded with surprising rudeness.

"One dollar," the Russian said.

"Does everything in Berlin cost one dollar American?"

"Everything and everybody," the Russian responded with a regretful sigh.

Spierdijk fished two one dollar bills from his wallet and presented them to the Russian. "Some things are worth more." The Russian sensed the urgency in Spierdijk's offer and noted that the man did not haggle like the rest of them. There was something fine, something gentle in the offer of double money and the Russian wished to acknowledge his appreciation. "And some things are priceless," he said.

Spierdijk was getting lost in the book, when the Russian pointed to the cover and asked, "Please help me. I do not know what this word means." Spierdijk followed the man's finger to the title. "Oh, Teekeningen" he pronounced carefully. "It means 'Works.'" He saw the confusion settle on his pupil's face. "That is 'Works' like an artist would call his collection of pictures his 'Works.'" The man's face brightened with understanding. "Ah. Proeezvedeneeya eezkoostva." Now it was Spierdijk's turn to be confused. "Works of artistic work. A collection of such works." They beamed to one another in mutual comprehension, and Spierdijk thought the man would value the meaning of the word more than the money.

The Russian quietly led Spierdijk back through the underground market and into the wan sun. He turned and offered a sincere 'Danke' and the Russian responded, "Nichevo" and translated, "It's nothing." Spierdijk walked away and mumbled to himself, "And everything."

Bobo's finger turned the pages filled with cheesy drawings of churches. They could have graced the counters of tourist kiosks. There was a drawing of the tomb of William the Silent and Bobo said to Joop and Spierdijk, "This would make an excellent postcard." On other pages Joop saw a strange scene of sailors dancing with completely naked women. The women looked bored and Joop wondered if their feet smelled.

Spierdijk shot out his forefinger and spun the book towards him by the spine. He threw open the cover. "Here's the real story." Joop and Bobo gazed into the inscription on the title page and Bobo translated from German, "To my beloved Führer in grateful tribute, from H. van Meegeren, Laren, North Holland, 1942."

The words filled the shop and silenced their anger. A cold fury replaced any residue of sympathy. Each thought of what he was doing in 1942. While van Meegeren was inscribing this volume, they were huddling from the terrors of the arrests. Their friends were being murdered by the friends of the man who had signed his name "in grateful tribute." Joop tried to swallow his shame that he had ever believed in this swindler. Even if it had only been for a while, he had allowed himself to be charmed. In their different ways, each had all said to wait for proof before final judgement. Their basic decency had given him the benefit of the doubt. That was what he had betrayed, and they had helped him to pilfer their own good natures. Even when they most suspected his duplicity, they had wanted to believe that there was some good in him, if they could only find it. Now, there was no doubt.

"So much for our patriot," Spierdijk spat.

Their eyes bored into the signature. They all agreed with Spierdijk's pronouncement, "He is condemned by his own works, in his own words, under his own hand."

Chapter 35

Sentry

Jan counted the steps between 253 and 263 Prinsengracht. Only twenty paces separated Ahler's address from the house of the smiling girl. Ever since Petersen had given them their meagre clues, every inquiry had proved empty. Ahlers no longer lived at his address. The woman who answered their knock was clearly telling the truth, for she had lived there only three months and spent most of her time looking for her husband, the husband who had been abducted to Germany to do volunteer work. All her papers showed her to be nothing more than a simple and distraught housewife, but they also proved she had no connection with the slippery Ahlers. They had followed Petersen's suggestion and visited the prisons and the morgues. The jails were fuller than the dead houses, so Joop quipped, "Life is getting better."

They had heard a vague rumor about an Ahlers, "a sneak of a real bastard" who "deserved to rot," but all they got from the officials was another Ministry of Justice document releasing him from the internment camp at Westerbork. The signature was a blurred smudge and the stamp looked like it had been applied with the inky bottom of a beer bottle. During a completely unrelated interrogation, Jan had asked about Ahlers and been informed, "He fucked off to the Indies." From the prisoner's reaction, Joop judged that Ahler's was very lucky to escape his friends. All roads led to nowhere or Sumatra, and all points in between. Joop said it would be best to let it go for now, hoping that Jan would just give up the futile search and relinquish this obsession. Jan had agreed, but Joop knew he was lying.

Jan had taken to visiting the street in the late evenings. The Ahler's house was now full of boarders. After their trip to Westerbork, he watched the new landlady pulling two young boys into the house by the their ears and threatening them with "a damn good beating when you father comes home."

When the street was empty, he would start his walk. He no longer had to count. There was something soothing in just trying to figure out what went on behind those closed doors and blinking windows.

The girl's house was some sort of business. There was a sign proclaiming that the Pectacon Company dealt in herbs, spices, and seasonings. It was an import business and explained why he always smelled something exotic when he made his rounds. After a while, he could distinguish between cinnamon and nutmeg, but the aromas kept changing, so he figured Pectacon was still in business. Whatever they were doing, the house did not exude decay.

He paced down the street, past four houses, and stopped before Ahler's former residence. The building smelled of sweat and unwashed feet. The boarders seemed to be sharing everything, except soap. Jan looked back down the row of buildings to the girl's house, trying to imagine what had happened in both dwellings. He toyed with the idea that Ahlers had escaped to the East Indies on the same boat that brought the spices to Pectacon, and he could not contain his laughter at the notion.

His head jerked back to the girl's house when a light came on. It shone out of a window on the third floor. It was late, and the spice workers had left for home hours ago. In all his visits, the house had been as silent as it was dark. This one light told him someone was living there.

Ten days ago, he had decided to watch the house every evening at eleven o'clock. The first night, he hid in the shadows away from the street lamp. After that, he would lean against the canal railing to get a glimpse of who was in the room. He could never make out a person, but he could see shadows walking across the ceiling. Someone had to be in that room. He quietly turned and walked back to the Westerkerk.

His own room was a only a short walk through the market, but he wanted to avoid the moonlight and linger in the shade of the church wall. He looked down the canal but could see only the bare pavement. Whoever was in that upper room was staying there. The stones behind him were warming his back, and he wondered if anybody was watching him as he was watching the house. The streets were so silent he could hear the water gurgling through the city. A slight breeze keened in his ears and for a moment he fancied the graves in the church yawning. Maybe Rembrandt was stretching himself awake and wondering where he had dropped his brushes. When he was sure nobody was watching, Jan stepped onto the cobble stones leading back to the house. He had to know that the light was not a hallucination.

His curiosity quickened his pace until he saw an acute angle of light play across the street, mount the embankment, and dive into the canal. He had not been seeing things. The apex of the triangle glowed and shimmered on the water. It was as real as the soles of his shoes bending over the stones. He studied the reflection and the confirmation of its reality grew with his concentration. The light started to slowly shrink. The right side of the angle reduced the quivering patch by half. He heard a rusty squeak above his head, but dared not step further into the street to look up. Someone was closing a shutter. He waited through the heartbeats for the left side of the light to fade, and when it disappeared, the groaning shutter became the final thump of a window closing.

He waited, counting his breaths until there was a longer pause between the numbers. When he heard 'forty seven' in his mind, he turned and retraced his steps to the church. There could no longer be doubt. He was not imagining. The light and the sound were all the proof he needed that someone was living in that building.

Jan paused his visiting for three nights, but resumed his determination to stand his guard below the window. He walked through cloud dappled moonlight to the canal and stopped to search the water for the light. Three times on three separate nights, it greeted him, and each night he strayed closer to its reassuring warmth. He had grown accustomed to its glow and hoped it was inviting him to a greater intimacy than he could dare. The electricity had been restored throughout the city, so an evening lamp was now normal and taken for granted. The days of parcelling out the watts like rationed bread were over. On this night, he could lean against the canal wall and bathe in the light's wan brilliance.

The light exploded into darkness and it frightened him into an apprehensive stillness. The rusty shutter hinges had given him no warning. Before he could escape, the door opened across the street and a man's tall and hatted silhouette framed the doorway. The man shut the door behind him and walked down the steps. He stood in front of the house facing Jan. The man looked directly at him. The broad brim of his fedora hid the man's face.

The man stepped into the middle of the street and stood with his feet apart and his hands in his pockets. Jan felt he had been shot when the voice hit his ears. "Good evening." Now that his fantasies stood before him in a crisp raincoat, he clenched his fists and returned a cheery, "Good evening."

The man took two steps closer, and even though Jan stood on the pavement, he had to look up to the face and the kindly voice. "I have seen you gazing into the canal on a few occasions. The water is very beautiful, this time of night." The voice relaxed Jan's fingers. "Yes. I like the reflections." The man nodded his agreement. "I have some difficulties sleeping and when I saw you the other night, I imagined that we share the same wakefulness."

Jan caught the invitation lurking below the diagnosis of insomnia and whispered, "Yes." The man stepped closer. "I sometimes find it is helpful to walk once around the market. Would you care to join me?"

Jan returned a relieved "Thanks" and got into step with his new acquaintance. Jan slowed his pace so as not to tire the man. His slow but determined shuffling said that he was suffering from some illness.

Jan stood beside him when the man stopped by the side of the Westerkerk. "They say there are many famous people buried in that church," the man exclaimed, his voice sliding into a rising question. Jan looked at the man's left arm swinging to embrace the wall. The sinews stretched proud on the back of his hand and fanned out his fingers. The wedding ring slid down to the white distended knuckle and its looseness told Jan that the man was recovering from starvation. "Yes," Jan affirmed. "Rembrandt is buried in that wall." The man was eager for more and Jan told him as much of his father's tale as he could remember. The man was very pleased with the story of the wife controlling her husband's finances. "That was very smart of her," the man chuckled. "My experience is that we should have the women take care of the money. They are more responsible than us when it comes to finances."

Jan snorted his assent and they continued their journey down the side of the market square. "A cool night is good for the breathing," the man said. Jan made up some nonsense about how the cold expands the lungs, but managed to sound very scientific. They spoke of the weather and the healing chill, and Jan assured him that "next winter will be better than the last." The man smiled to say, "It could hardly be worse." When he spoke, Jan noticed his words seemed to squeeze through the gaps in the man's teeth. There was the barest hint of a smile, but there was no mistaking that it was hers. The man was somehow related to the smiling girl, but Jan did not want to speculate he was her father. He did not recognize this face from the razzia. There were too many people and the operation had been too quick for him to register all of their faces. The girl was the last, so her face was the first in his memory.

The church's windows soared above them almost from the ground to the roof and each pane shivered in the moonlight. Jan and the man looked up when they heard the wind moan through the top of the tower. The man turned to Jan and asked, "Do you think it is insane if I thought the church was talking to us?" Jan accepted the admission as a compliment and assured him, "Not at all. Things talk in all sorts of strange ways." The man laughed, exposing more teeth, and Jan was certain.

They came to the end of the street, turned towards the tramlines bounding the square, and walked back to the canal. Jan stopped and said, "I live down this street." The man nodded his farewells. "I hope we can have another pleasant walk sometime." Jan greeted the invitation with shy silence that was only broken when the man said, "Mine name is Otto." Jan's face broadened. "I am called Jan." The man tipped his hat and offered, "Until next meeting, Jan." and walked slowly back through the islands of lamplight to his home.

Chapter 36

Trial

Joop pushed open the door and led his little procession into the courtroom. He stopped as soon as he saw the chattering crowd, and Jan, Bobo, and Spierdijk compressed together into a curious knot. The room was packed, but Joop heard his name called over the noise. He looked up to see van Meegeren's arm beckoning him from the dock. He pushed his way through the throng until he could hear van Meegeren say, "I'm so glad you came. I've saved you the best seat in the house." Joop shrugged his thanks and turned to the bench guarded by de Groot. They filed past the sergeant until Jan was able to sit beside Joop and Bobo could just squeeze between Spierdijk and Jan. Joop turned to warn the coterie, "Settle in for an ass-numbing morning." They all squirmed until they pushed a lady further along the bench and liberated enough space to be comfortable.

Joop surveyed the room and saw dozens of paintings lining the court. *The Christ Child and the Doctors* stood on Bobo's easel and took pride of place beside the dock. Joop was a bit surprised that van Meegeren was already at his post in the dock, but noted that the room provided a full house for the performance.

Van Meegeren resumed his seat in the dock, rested his elbow on the railings, and cupped his chin in his palm. Bobo watched him strike a pose of indulgent boredom. Bobo sat in his own thoughts wondering what the spectacle would reveal that he didn't already know. He pulled his attention away from the dock and concentrated on the ranks of paintings surrounding them. The courtroom was a gallery and it looked like they had raided the Dutch Masters rooms of the Rijksmuseum. The public benches were ranked between the two rows of paintings and Bobo thought this could be a lesson in the wonders of Dutch painting. All the greats were there. He saw Frans Halls' *The Witch of Haarlem,* but she held her pewter stein in the wrong hand. He peered into her face and knew she was just a little too drunk to raise her brimming tankard. Beside her Christ was having his feet washed, but Bobo thought it was such an awful parody that it should be entitled *Pedicure at the Rubens Foot Salon.* From fame to frame the parade of van Meegeren's travesties surrounded them.

Bobo was overcome by how each of the paintings drew in the viewer. They were like small children clamoring for attention. En masse, the whole ensemble was a riot of selfishness. He knew there was something behind all the noise of these images, but it eluded his grasp. He examined a Rembrandt *Self-Portrait,* but the figure wore modern clothes. It was an excellent study in Rembrandt's highlighting, but the face was cock-eyed and was actually van Meegeren's mug-shot in oils. It was his attempt to put himself back in time. Bobo stopped at the portrait of a girl smiling directly at the viewer. It purported to be from the brush of Vermeer, but that man would never have painted anything so frightening. Bobo wondered why he felt fear and became lost in the expanse of the girl's upper teeth. Nobody would have exposed so much enamel three hundred years ago. The teeth that remained would be black. Even the famous *Girl With a Pearl Earring* only showed the two front teeth because she was bucktoothed. But it was the girl's eyes that scared him. In forcing that terrible smile, van Meegeren had pulled her skin to the sides of her face and the eyes were islands of insanity. The only Vermeer painting Bobo could remember with such eyes were those of the *Girl With a Wine Glass* and she was clearly drunk. Van Meegeren's copy had similar eyes, but they were sober and crazy. The last time he saw such eyes, Bobo had to run away.

The noise evaporated around Bobo in a rumble of rising bodies. He stood with the rest to watch Judge Voss enter the court. He strained his head around the expectant crowd and watched Voss take his place behind a curved desk whose wings opened to the courtroom. One either side of him clerks and other lawyers took their places and carefully laid out their documents. Spierdijk saw the regulation photograph of Queen Wilhelmina hanging behind the judge, but she was flanked on either side by van Meegeren's copies of *The Supper at Emmaus* and *The Witch of Haarlem*. He whispered to Joop, "Her Majesty has fallen into bad company."

Van Meegeren rose and looked over the courtroom. Voss took his time seating himself. The room shuffled into their seats, and van Meegeren was the last to sit. Joop watched Voss discuss something with the clerks and lawyers who sat on either side of him. He wondered what they were saying, but slowly he found that he didn't care. He slumped into his seat and let a welcome lethargy encompass him. When he looked at van Meegeren's profile, he saw the intensity of the man's interest. He was smothered in the proceedings, but to Joop all this activity meant precisely nothing. The months of caring for van Meegeren had taken their toll, and Joop was as detached from the courtroom as if he were dutifully waiting for the climax of a boring performance. Everybody knew how it would end.

Voss consulted with the clerk, who was a bit confused that the judge was so carefully instructing him on his duties. They both knew what he was supposed to do because he had been recording the judge's cases for three years. But if the Judge wanted a meticulous record kept, that would be what he would get. Voss was going through the motions of his instructions and giving the room time to settle. He wanted everybody to hear every word. He bellowed in his most authoritative voice, "Is the defendant present?"

Van Meegeren answered as loudly, "Present, Your Honor," and waited as if for applause. The courtroom stiffened in expectant attention as Voss called for "the State Prosecutor to present his case." Van den Broek rose and informed the court that he would be calling for the testimony of experts. Voss nodded and the machinery of the formal accusation ground into motion. Voss barely glanced at the calling of some professor of Chemistry and ignored the swearing in as he grumbled to himself, "There are liars, damned liars, and then there are expert witnesses." He speculated on how much the professor was being paid for his performance.

Bobo grimaced at the testimony of the chemical composition of van Meegeren's paint. Van den Broek took pains to explain, "The accused devised some new combination of chemicals to give his paint an aged appearance." Bobo suspected this already, for this problem had kindled his professional curiosity. He suspected some drying agent that could not be detected with the usual alcohol test. Aged paint would not leave a residue when the canvas was wiped with an alcohol soaked swab. New paint stained the cloth.

Van den Broek's long explanation of the chemical process was putting the court to sleep and Voss noticed that even the witness was bored. Van den Broek asked if the chemist had found any unexpected results. The witness was quick to say that there was some sort of plastic mixed in with the paint and that this substance hastened the drying process of oil based pigments.

Bobo watched van den Broek approach the dock and engage van Meegeren in some cat and mouse game about chemistry.

"You purposely added this material in your attempts to imitate Vermeer's paint," van den Broek accused.

"Of course, I did."

"And why was that?"

"Because I am an extremely professional forger."

"And just what did you use in your professional work?"

"Bakelite."

Bobo snapped his fingers in admiration. Bakelite was not only plastic, it was ubiquitous. It was first fabricated only fifty years ago, but now it was in everything from telephone handles to car parts. Every small radio receiver was housed in a Bakelite cabinet. All van Meegeren had to do was melt an old radio and he could mix it with pigment. When it dried in a few hours, the paint would be as hard as if it had cured for centuries.

"And how did you stumble upon this technical solution to your problem of aging the paint?" van den Broek prodded.

"There was no stumbling," van Meegeren sneered. "It was the result of exhaustive experimentation."

"How long did your experiments last?"

"Three years," van Meegeren proudly proclaimed. "I tried various types of oil, but the results were uniformly gooey."

"Gooey?" van den Broek wailed.

"I use the word because I doubt you would know of the viscosity of semi-soluble substances. The paint had to be perfectly dry with no moisture remaining. In the end, I used Bakelite because it hardened very quickly. As a result, my painting technique had to speed up to the point where I could compose while the medium was in a soluble state."

The audience laughed at van den Broek's indignation, but Bobo seemed to be staring into a distant past. He remembered an ancient lecture in chemistry and how the university was excited about this new wonder material. The Professor of Chemistry wrote out the formula for a new plastic which an Englishman had invented. He then demonstrated how it could be molded into any shape and he defied the students to find some object which could not be quickly fabricated from Bakelite. He stumped all their objections and showed them his fountain pen and they were amazed that this new substance could be found in such a common object. Bobo had written down the formula and remembered that he had seen it before. After the lecture, he had searched through his notes and raided the science library until his curiosity was fully satiated. He stared at the page of chemical combinations for practical application and read the formula to himself. He closed the book and knew that Bakelite was almost chemically identical to formaldehyde.

Bobo stared at van Meegeren's back and shook his head in wonder that he had used the same substance to fake his paintings as an embalmer used to preserve his corpses. He wondered if there was so much difference between the two uses of the so closely related formulae. Now he knew why he so hated the smell in van Meegeren's studio. It was really a mortuary for art.

"With this Bakelite substance, you were able to fool the experts?" van den Broek accused.

"With the Bakelite, I was able to create a seventeenth century painting in the twentieth century," van Meegeren explained as if to a slightly dull child. "I did not have to fool the experts. They were doing a good enough job on their own."

Voss looked through the titters to the prideful smirk spreading over van Meegeren's face. He was impressed by how quickly van Meegeren could twist anything. Expert liars had appeared in his court, but this was the first time that such an accomplished liar had presented himself as a mere accomplice to those who lied to themselves. The victims of his schemes were actually the perpetrators of their own delusions. Van Meegeren was an adept at casting his own guilt onto his victims. It was quite a feat.

Voss heard the voice rise in frustration. "You people don't understand," van Meegeren berated. "This is no mere copy. When I painted these pictures I resurrected the artist. How many times have you heard it said, 'if only Rembrandt had painted a nocturne'. How often have we lamented that Vermeer painted so few masterpieces. In the executions of these paintings, Vermeer lived again through me. Our souls became one and I was Vermeer."

Voss froze in astonishment. He looked over to Bobo, his eyes pleading for understanding. He knew van Meegeren was guilty and this trial a formality, but the man would have his day in court, no matter what the accusation. Van Meegeren would be sentenced to a year in prison, but this last revelation made Voss wonder if the convicted should be incarcerated not in a prison, but in a mental asylum. He would have to discuss this with Morelli.

Jan sat with his face flowing into sleepy boredom. He had long ago lost any interest in such gentlemen. He had seen enough of them in the files he had been chained to for months. So many names were in those documents that he had been raised to revere because they were rich, or they were leaders, or because they represented a church or a school. Those files had drained him of all respect.

Van Meegeren was just another gentleman who happened to be very rich because he was very smart and his wealthy friends were very stupid. That was about it, as far as he was concerned. He could only think of the people who were not the friends of gentlemen, the deported, the skeletal children scraping garbage cans, and Otto.

Their walks had continued until they became a nightly parade. Otto had been slow to take their talks beyond the weather and to ask about Jan's experiences. He had valued Jan as "a brave fighter in the Resistance," and Jan never denied the praise. He told Otto the truth of their adventures, but wondered if it was really lying when he did not tell him the whole truth. Slowly Otto told him of his time in Germany, of the camps and the diseases and the constant brutality. One night Otto confessed, "The very worst thing was that I was nobody." Jan found just enough courage to ask for an explanation, and Otto was relieved to tell him. "When you are reduced to something that is fed, even just enough to keep alive, and your only purpose is to do what they tell you, you are worse than an animal. You are nothing to them and to those around you. The longer it goes on, the more you become convinced that they are right and that you really are nothing."

Jan stood silent and let Otto talk through his ordeal. He would not try to match his sorrows, for then he would have to admit to Otto that he was responsible for Otto's pain. He would help Otto to heal and to vanquish the terrible nothingness inside him, but the price was that Jan had to keep his own hurt to himself. Otto spent most of his day going from office to office looking for his wife and his daughters. Every helper said that they were checking lists of prisoners taken and prisoners released and that when they had a match, they would be able to tell him more about his family. Jan knew there would be no match. He and Joop had been some of the first to have documentary evidence of the death camps. Jan knew what had happened to the smiling girl, but dared not share this with Otto. While there was uncertainty, there was some hope, and Jan refused to strip his friend of this last comfort. He continued to assure Otto that one day the names would match and all would be well again.

Voss slouched in his chair. He leaned over to the recorder and asked, "Are you getting every word of this?" He was assured that the trial record would be as complete as it was accurate, but he was glad that he had taken the precaution of hiring a second stenographer. The twists in van Meegeren's words were tangled enough, but Voss knew that when he came to read the final transcripts, more secrets would be revealed. He sat back to enjoy this little comic opera, confident that he could read the libretto at his leisure.

"But you did have problems with the cracking of the paint," van den Broek said.

"The only problem was to have the paint crack in the same way as it would, if it had hung on a wall for three hundred years."

"But you could not wait for the cracking because you had to sell your paintings under the name Vermeer."

"Oh, not just Vermeer," van Meegeren yawned. He swept his arm around the courtroom in a slow and confident arch. "There were also Rembrandts, Frans Hals, Rubens, and all the other glories of our land."

His bragging was no longer met with amused laughter. Joop sat in his own private confessional accusing himself of being a fool, but there would be no absolution. He chuckled to himself that Catholics had a good deal. They could lie, and cheat, and steal, and then go into their big box, tell their priest what a terrible person they were, and be forgiven with the payment of a few prayers and the lighting of an expensive candle. He wondered if there was a church big enough for all the candles van Meegeren would have to light.

But Joop asked himself, "What of my own candle?" He could see only one tiny flame flickering in the gloom. His confession would be that he wanted to get ahead by breaking the van Meegeren treason case. To do that, he had to believe his ambition was a good thing, with even better results. He was an officer of the court. Lieutenant Piller had been promoted to Captain Piller, and he liked the rank, even though he did not have a uniform to display his badges. His star case had given him a position and a function in the government that would have been impossible in the old factory. There, he was just plain Piller, the man who kept the workers at their looms. It was good work and paid enough for them to have nice furniture. It would all have been so normal, if it were not for the Occupation. He and Liese had been honest with each other when they first started working with the Resistance. They were patriots to one another, but their loyalty was helping to liberate their country. They knew they would probably not survive and had made provision for some relatives to raise Sarah. Joop laughed to himself that they had survived by taking such huge risks. It was so ironic. If they had stayed in their little nest, they would have starved. But they had thrived because they had jumped into the fight just one step ahead of the hounds.

All through the investigation, Joop had wavered between loving and hating the man. He had to admire how van Meegeren was such a fox that he could disguise himself as one of the hounds and run with them. Were they so very different? He had used his guile to keep alive. Van Meegeren had done the same. The only difference was the number of zeros he put on the price of his phony paintings. Joop had done something similar, to keep himself, Liese, and Sarah from the fate the monsters planned for every Jew. Van Meegeren got out of the war with millions. Joop escaped it with his life. There was the difference. There was no price on a life. His very existence was priceless, and that was its worth. Joop imagined that one candle in his mind and told himself, "It's just money." He thought of Liese and Sarah and knew he had the greater prize.

"The experts have testified that you would have had problems in the heating of your canvases. Would you care to explain how you solved this dilemma?" van den Broek inquired.

"With great pleasure," van Meegeren almost crowed. "Now that you understand the actions of a semi-soluble mixture, you will have to understand the drying process has to be carefully administered." He paused to gauge the effect, but Voss politely demanded, "Would you please continue."

"We were vacationing on the Riviera and I was working on the drying problem. You see, some of the canvases were too big for the stove."

"The stove?"

"Yes, I baked the canvases in the kitchen stove."

"So what was the problem?"

"The size of the painting was determined by the opening in the stove. I could never create a painting that was more than fifteen inches wide."

"Why was this such a problem?"

"People pay more for big ones."

"And you eventually supplied the larger paintings?"

"Yes. You will notice that paintings are rather flat," van Meegeren observed and waited for the room to cease laughing at his condescending tone. "I had to find an oven that was very shallow but also very deep and wide. This would make it possible to increase the sizes of the canvases."

"And you found such a device?"

"My wife and I became bored with the casinos, so we decided to take a trip into the north of Italy. To look at museums."

"You found an oven in a museum?"

"Beside the museum. When we stopped for lunch, we chose to dine on the local cuisine. The Italian common people eat a type of round bread with various condiments, such as meat and cheese. Sometimes they add vegetables, but I do not recommend them. To cook this bread, they have a special oven where they can bake three or even four of these flatbreads at once. I think they call it pizza."

Voss was not interested in the diets of the Italians, but the mention of baking three or four of these pies in the oven at the same time made him calculate the extent of the fraud.

Van Meegeren was a one-man factory of fakes. There was not only the quality of his salesmanship to consider, but also the quantity of his goods. If he had faked only one painting, he would not have needed an oven which could bake four pies. Clearly van Meegeren was working at a much higher rate and volume of production than anybody suspected. He looked over to see Spierdijk's eyes flash and his face scowl.

"Pizza," Spierdijk spat to Jan. Spierdijk didn't vent his anger because it was useless, and Jan looked like he was asleep. He thought his newspaper report on the finding of *Teekeningen No. 1* would be the moment of truth for van Meegeren, but the readers had disappointed him. He had taken the book to his editor, who immediately saw the evidence of van Meegeren's treason. What could be better proof than his own signature on his gift to Hitler? The editor decided that the best way to deal with the knowledge was for Spierdijk to write his article and then wait to publish it. The editor convinced Spierdijk that "it will have greater impact closer to the trial." They had geared up for a record sales edition, and one week ago, Spierdijk's report, complete with photographs, had appeared in the newspaper. They sat back waiting for the telephone to ring off its handle. People would be so enraged that they would have to publish follow up pieces, and Spierdijk had enough for at least ten more articles. The phone remained maddeningly silent. Eventually, Spierdijk and the editor went looking for subscribers who had read the news, but their only interest was in the winning numbers of the lottery.

They tried quizzing other journalists, who all complemented Spierdijk on his journalistic investigation and waited to be offered another drink. After a few bottles, they revealed that people were tired of such depressing stories. They showed Spierdijk a survey one of their papers conducted asking who were the people's choices for the most famous Dutchmen. The Queen was naturally at the top of the list. Van Meegeren was second. Prince Bernard came in at third. Spierdijk laughed to think that such a fraud was ahead of the Prince who commanded the Dutch Forces of Liberation.

The trial approached and revealed the enormity of van Meegeren's popularity. Spierdijk arrived early at the court, but the entrance was blocked by a film crew. They were setting up their tripods and cameras in the street ready for the arrival of their celebrity. Van Meegeren had walked casually towards the court and stopped to smile for the cameras. He answered a few questions with a vagueness that was thrilling to the reporters, tipped his hat, and sprang up the steps to his trial.

Spierdijk sat in his bench listening to more of the legend being spun every time van Meegeren opened his mouth. He asked himself repeatedly if his profession was a complete waste of time. Why should he report the news when the only real news was the false hope of getting rich with a piece of pasteboard costing a few cents? The people had completely ignored Spierdijk's reporting because they wanted a hero and this charming rogue suited them. He wondered if he could emigrate, but decided this would only be changing cages. He was caught in a land for which he had fought to tell the truth, and peace had just liberated the people's appetite for fantasies. He did not want to think that this was the way it had to be. After so much suffering, everybody was just too exhausted to deal with anything more serious than a comic book. Van den Broek's grating voice jerked Spierdijk out of his reverie.

"You claim that you alone are responsible for these paintings, but your wife must have been your most faithful accomplice," he shouted.

"My wife knew nothing about the forgeries," van Meegeren shouted back and started to rant about Joanna's innocence. When van den Broek pressed the point of the wife's involvement, van Meegeren defended her most chivalrously by explaining that "she is actually very stupid."

Voss wondered why this was the first time in the proceedings that van Meegeren became agitated. He clearly was insulted by van den Broek's line of argument and fought back at any suggestion that his wife was involved. "Well," he thought, "at least he has the decency to protect his wife."

But as soon as the thought surfaced, Voss wondered why he had used the word "protect" instead of "love." There was no tradition of marital fidelity in the van Meegeren menage. That was evident by all the well-proven gossip of alcoholic orgies of excess. The former Mrs. van Meegeren didn't seem the type of woman to stay home mending socks. It was the "protect" that stuck in Voss mind, so he looked carefully at the figure gesturing in the dock. The only thing he ever protected was his money. So why this heat in defending his ex-wife's good name? There was precious little of that. Then Voss remembered the divorce. He had read the final settlement between them and was struck by van Meegeren's generosity. He had signed over the titles and deeds of all his properties to his wife. Her lawyers had filed the papers and all was in order. Voss now had to ask himself why van Meegeren had done this. He could have kept half the properties and still given his wife a tidy sum. Voss almost shouted, "My God" when his mind found the answer. The divorce was all part of his plan. Van Meegeren knew he was finished the moment Piller knocked on his door. He divorced his wife, transferred all his property to her, knowing that he would be caught. Once convicted, all his property would be confiscated by the state. He would be destitute. If his wife were innocent of any crime, her property would remain hers forever. He could then serve his time in prison, and upon release, get the money from her. If she refused, he could make another confession and she would be ruined. The divorce was insurance. His future silence was his threat. He could blackmail her with one word.

Voss sat back and saw just how diabolical were van Meegeren's methods. This trial was his triumph. All the paintings in the court had been sold for very high figures. The moment he confessed to being a forger, the value of those painting plummeted. This trial was his revenge on all the people who had rejected him and laughed at his paintings in his own name. He proved he was a great artist by forging the masterpieces of the great and then selling them to the most wealthy men in the land. As long as he kept his mouth shut, he was rich. To extract the last full measure of his revenge, he had to confess that he was a fraud. This was why he was so eager to answer in open court. He was destroying the market in expensive paintings. Voss finally understood that van Meegeren was throwing a bomb into every art collection in Holland. His confession today was sinking all their ships, and all he had to do was speak. His divorce settlement was his lifeboat, and all he had to do was keep his mouth shut.

Voss had to admit just how accomplished was this crime. The evidence van den Broek was presenting was being confirmed by van Meegeren himself. Van den Broek thought he was impressing the court with his skill, but all the time he never realized that he was trapped with every question he so vainly fired at the accused.

The Judge relaxed into his understanding of what was before his eyes. He looked into the court and concentrated on Joop and his comrades. Voss knew they had survived by faking their own deaths. What a quirk of fate that they had been brought here by a complete scoundrel who had faked Holland's artistic glories. He saw that Spierdijk had joined them. He had read the exposé of van Meegeren's gift with its obsequious inscription. That proved the depths of his greed and his treason. But he was on trial for fraud and his book was not admissible as evidence. It just condemned him more than anything van den Broek could offer.

Piller's little Resistance cell was finished. Van den Broek was now in charge of some Committee of Reconciliation. There would be no need to hound collaborators when the committee was charged with reconciliation. Soon the Bureau of Flight Control would be disbanded and they would be cast aside. Voss sincerely hoped that they would continue their activities in the peace as they did in the war. The country needed people who would stand for something greater than the most immediate gratification. Spierdijk would be essential in telling the truth, but he would have to wait for a time when people were ready to hear it.

Van Meegeren's voice faded from Voss' ears for he had already decided that the man was guilty and that the sentence would be only one year in prison. He sincerely hoped that after today he would never again hear of Henricus Antonius van Meegeren.

Chapter 37

Belling the Cat

Joop sat cross-legged in the garden. He listened to the thrum of the sewing machine sailing from the kitchen window. Liese was explaining to Sarah how the stitching had to be doubled because the dress was a working dress and not a frock for parties. Liese had been right all along. Emst was their real home.

The village had been forgotten at the intersection of two roads and didn't even warrant a name in tiny letters on the larger maps. They could escape along one road, as the police trundled down the other, and there were just enough huts and sheds and forgotten mines to hide from a razzia. The little house had been their haven, for the owners would never return from the raid that robbed their lives. But the very seclusion that had spared them was now a hinderance. Emst had no rail link to Amsterdam, so Joop had begged the use of a car from the government. Judge Voss had visited Bobo, and a few days later, a chauffeur appeared with some documents and a car and left without the beat up jalopy

Liese and Sarah would soon be finished with another dress and they would have a trip to the Big Town to see Bobo and Uncle Jan. The saucer of milk that nestled on the grass beside his knee would be the last dish to be washed before they set off. He hoped the treat could entice Princess before Liese came looking for the saucer.

The cat had posed a problem he had never anticipated. In Amsterdam, there was nothing to hunt. They had cared for Princess so that her flesh hid her ribs, and her coat gleamed beneath their thin fingers. But since they returned to Emst, the cat had discovered a wonderland of mice, birds, and rabbits. The sudden appearance of such easy prey had brought out the wild joy within their pampered Princess. Joop had seen her jump from the window after a squirrel, but the streak of brownish gray was too quick for her more urban experience. That was when Joop realized he had to do something about the cat.

For all her short life, Liese and Joop had protected Sarah from the war's horrors. She was just learning to talk when the Germans infested their country, but now she was learning to question. There was a "why" for everything, and Joop was sometimes exhausted trying to explain everything that was new to his daughter and very old to him. They had kept her in the house in Emst, and Joop thought it a type of miracle that they had been able to shelter her from the murderous insanity that stormed around them. The Amsterdam children had become used to death. Liese had seen that the city boys were indifferent to misery. She was frightened for Sarah when the eyes of old men stared vacantly through the shrunken cheeks of a child. Liese and Joop had seen boys and girls casually walk over corpses without breaking step. Joop had never thought that Princess would be the herald of mortality for Sarah.

Joop had pondered the possibilities. He could forestall the hunt by feeding the cat, but Princess was also a bit of a glutton. It was in her nature to hunt, and there was nothing Joop could do to change that. He knew with absolute certainty that there would come a day when Princess would bring home a trophy. Sarah would cry for the dead bird, and Joop would have to explain that everything living would some day die. It was something he could not evade, but he was desperate to leave that awful lesson for some time in

Sarah's future. There was just too much joy for terrible realities to end her days of innocence. Something inside him pleaded to keep such knowledge away from her, for just a little while longer. He shuddered to think that Princess would drag home a mauled baby rabbit, and he would have to explain to Sarah why her best friend had killed the Easter Bunny.

He looked over the grass, but there was no sign of the cat. He glanced to his left, where the red ribbon lay coiled beside his leg. This had to be done, and he steeled himself to remain calm, for the cat would scamper away at the first whiff of his anxiety.

If he could not keep the cat away from the hunt, he could keep the hunted away from the cat. It was then he remembered the bell. When they had found the old sewing machine, the farmer had left a little box in one of its drawers. Liese had opened it to see old bobbins, stray spools of thread, blunt needles, and a tiny bell. They had laughed to imagine that the machine was so old it had fabricated a cap of bells for a court jester. Joop had retrieved the box, and the bell was no bigger than the end of his thumb. The sewing machine also held a castoff length of deep velvet ribbon, too short to trim a dress, but just long enough to circle the cat's neck. He would have to bell the cat.

It had been an old joke that "belling the cat" was the country way of saying, "you have to accomplish a difficult task." After five years of risking as many fatal tasks as they had survived, Joop laughed at the absurdity catching Princess and trying a bell around her neck. But there was also a fear which he did not understand. It was like a guest he could not tell to leave. He wished this fear was as simple as expelling a drunk from a tavern, but the thing lingered, slumped in its own stupor. It was only a cat. Others would have quietly strangled the animal and claimed that Princess had wondered off. That would have been cowardly and left Sarah grieving in her abandonment.

Joop whispered "Mcgrowl," to the wind, but there was no answering mew. He tried to puzzle through his fear and hoped that Princess would have pity on his vigil and appear out of nowhere. Bobo had told him that the ancient Egyptians prayed to cats to find lost things, because cats could vanish into thin air and that was probably where the lost thing was hiding. Strange. A hidden cat could tell you where to find whatever you had lost. No cat could retrieve what they had lost.

Their only work was gone with dissolution of the Bureau of Flight Control. This was like the days when the Germans closed the factory. The quiet life they had expected had been ripped from them, and those years would never come back. The guns had shattered their dreams and malicious hunger ate their hopes. Joop felt himself wanting the comfort of the hopelessness they had lived through. "At least then we had nothing left to lose," he chuckled to himself.

That was when the fear jerked itself awake. Now there was hope, so he was afraid of disappointment. The prospect of their own deaths had been strangely normal. Peace had brought with it the uneasy certainty of a future. Now the certainty and security evaporated with the Bureau. This indefinite tomorrow was his fear, and Joop could not hide from it.

He gazed at his open hand and counted their few blessings on his fingers. He pulled at his little finger and told himself they were alive. That could not be doubted. He snapped the joint in his ring finger, and the crack reminded him that he was married to a woman who could fill him with more courage than than he had on his own. He pulled his middle finger forward until it crackled Sarah's name. Three fingers added up to his life. A life, a wife, a child. So many others had none of these.

He smiled to think that greedy people would complain about their poverty, but these fingers held riches beyond his avarice. He raised his index finger to his nose, and for a moment, saw Bobo and Jan dancing on its tip. He would never have met such people, if he had stayed in the factory. Jan was a troubled child, but his need offered Joop the satisfaction of leading him into a deeper manhood. He would never abandon Jan, and Liese had quietly volunteered to be the boy's big sister. Bobo was so smart. He knew things Jan could barely perceive, but there was a wonderful playfulness to all his learning. He could explain things to Joop, without making Joop feel the shame of his own ignorance. There was fun to this learning, and Joop wanted such pleasures to continue.

The thumb remained, standing crooked as a question mark, defying Joop to retreat into cynical despair. He waggled his thumb before his nose and asked it what it was. He was not offended by the thumb's silence, but the image of Bobo's shop was as familiar and as shocking as a Jack-in-the Box. Together, they would build whatever they could and they would keep walking through the temptations of despair. Joop curled his fingers to his palm and the thumb pulled his fist to greet the future.

The grass sang a swishing whisper, and he turned to see Princess stalking his raised hand. He dropped his arm to rest beside the saucer and opened his palm to welcome the bundle of curious fur. She stopped just out of reach and sat blinking defiantly. He breathed slowly and studied her eyes as she turned to the dish's temptation. One raised nose and a familiar nod of her head, and Joop dipped his finger into the milk. He splashed the pearly pool, drawing Princess closer to his trap. She thrust herself forward, eager for the treat.

Princess knew the man was not the young girl, so he would have to be tamed by her wary shuffle to the little plate. The aroma pulled her forward, but she kept the plate between her and the man. With a few deft licks, she started a white stream thrusting into her mouth, and slowly closed her eyes in delight. This man had never hurt her, and she remembered the first time she licked his fingers clean of that meaty paste. He had disappeared and left her with that woman. The house was as empty as her stomach, but when the man came back, he brought her to the girl and the new woman, and they were very comfortable. Now the man was petting her head as she drank the milk, so she crouched in comfort and let the man stroke her fur.

Joop felt the calmness of the animal seep up his fingers. He kept stroking her back until he could feel the little pulses of her purring mix with her drinking. The animal was happy. It would not run and hide, so Joop continued to caress her coat and let her enjoy the drink.

Princess licked the saucer clean, and Joop joked to her, "You'll pull the paint from that dish." She seemed to know that this was not the last of the man's kindness and decided to tell him they were friends. Joop felt her back press into his leg, as she raised her paw to wash her face. She looked up once to him and slowly closed her eyes. He wondered if this was a cat's way of saying "I love you," or if it were the prelude to a satisfied burp, the way Sarah had told them she was full when she was a baby. He returned to stroking Princess with his right hand, as his left felt for the ribbon.

He was careful to grasp the bell tightly, so it would not tinkle and frighten the cat. Princess turned her attention from her ablutions to the little red tail escaping from between the man's fingers. Joop dangled the ribbon before Princess's nose and let her claw catch its frayed end. The man teased her with the red tail, but she was enjoying the chase, so she sat waiting for his next move. Joop pulled the end of the ribbon over Princess's neck and she strained to catch the new toy. He waited for her to feel the accomplishment of winning this little game and when he heard her growl in pleasure, he gently pulled the ribbon ends together and tied them in a neat bow on the scruff of her neck.

Princess pounced back, and the bell rang under her chin. Joop was satisfied that the material would hold firm. When she became more accustomed to her collar, he would rearrange the ribbon and tie more knots to secure the red circle. He watched Princess shuffle away from him towards the kitchen door and whispered to himself, "Better to be a live mouse than a dead cat." She stopped once and looked back at him to cast an accusing scowl and then slunk into the house to find Sarah.

Joop sat on the grass listening to Sarah explain to Princess that her new collar was very pretty and that the bell was just to scare away the birds. He raised his fist to his lips and surrendered to the certainty that nothing within his grasp was fake.

Acknowledgments

So many people contributed to the writing of *Fake* that it is impossible to thank them all.

I first became aware of Joop Piller while reading *The man Who Made Vermeers* by Jonathan Lopez. This is the best treatment of the van Meegeren frauds and is a masterpiece of research. When I followed Lopez's notes, I discovered that very little is known about Joop Pillers. It seemed that Joop's story could be a composite of all the activities of the Dutch Resistance, and so his character was the creation of those historical experiences.

Fake could not have been written without the help of Bede Mitchell, Dean of the Henderson Library at Georgia Southern University. Bede procured the books which were beyond my grasp and made the writing possible.

Barbara Moore and the staff of the Franklin Memorial Library, Swainsboro, Virginia Bolton, Ann Buxton, Gladys Collins, Karen Hidlebaugh, Windy Ward, and Willene Williams deserve special mention for their invaluable help in acquiring books through the Georgia Pines Interlibrary Loan System.

No book can be birthed without the keen insights of Beta Readers. Very special mention must be made of the excellent Beta Readers: David Graham-Clarke, Bede Mitchell, Stephen Preston, Karen Taylor-Lambie, Karen Sollars, Donald Straub, and Brooks de Wetter-Smith. Their perceptive minds and applied imaginations are to be valued and celebrated.

The greatest acknowledgement must be to my wife, Anna, who has made all of this possible.

Thomas Thibeault

Born in Canada, raised in
Ireland, Thomas Thibeault
now lives in the United
States with his wife, Anna,
and their twelve cats.

He has retired from a
thirty-year teaching career,
which has taken him to
Russia, England, the Middle
East, and the Far East.

Those travels also involved
working as a deck hand,
soldier, truck driver in
Africa, art model in Ireland, train brakeman in
Canada, and a tour guide at the Pyramids.

Thomas brings a wealth of experience to writing
which expresses our primal experiences.

Half a century of wide reading, wider traveling,
and concentrated thinking have provoked
Thomas into writing.

Printed in Great Britain
by Amazon

71171590R00193